STAR WARS

THE
OLD REPUBLIC™

REVAN

BY DREW KARPYSHYN

STAR WARS

MASS EFFECT

TEMPLE HILL

THE CHAOS BORN

STAR WARS

THE OLD REPUBLIC

REVAN

DREW KARPYSHYN

DEL REY • NEW YORK

Star Wars: The Old Republic: Revan is a work of fiction. Names, places, and incidents either are products of the author's imagination or are used fictitiously.

2012 Del Rey Mass Market Edition
Copyright © 2011 by Lucasfilm Ltd. & ® or ™ where indicated. All Rights Reserved. Used Under Authorization.

Excerpt from *Star Wars: The Old Republic: Annihilation* by Drew Karpyshyn copyright © 2012 by Lucasfilm Ltd. & ® or ™ where indicated. All Rights Reserved. Used Under Authorization.

Published in the United States by Del Rey, an imprint of Random House, a division of Penguin Random House LLC, New York.

DEL REY and the HOUSE colophon are registered trademarks of Penguin Random House LLC.

Originally published in hardcover in the United States by Del Rey, an imprint of Random House, a division of Penguin Random House LLC, in 2011.

This book contains an excerpt from *Star Wars: The Old Republic: Annihilation* by Drew Karpyshyn. This excerpt has been set for this edition only and may not reflect the final content of the forthcoming edition.

ISBN 978-0-345-51135-5
eBook ISBN 978-0-345-53282-4

Printed in the United States of America

www.starwars.com

www.delreybooks.com

20

Del Rey mass market edition: October 2012

ACKNOWLEDGMENTS

Revan's story stretches all the way back to the original *Star Wars:* Knights of the Old Republic, and I want to thank everyone at BioWare who contributed to that fantastic game. Similarly, I owe a debt of gratitude to everyone at Obsidian who worked on KOTOR 2, and everyone at BioWare Austin who helped create the *Star Wars:* The Old Republic MMO. But most of all I want to thank all the *Star Wars* and Revan fans who have waited so many years for a conclusion to this tale: without your undying support this novel would never have happened.

THE STAR WARS LEGENDS NOVELS TIMELINE

BEFORE THE REPUBLIC
37,000-25,000 YEARS BEFORE
STAR WARS: A New Hope

c. 25,793 YEARS BEFORE *STAR WARS: A New Hope*

Dawn of the Jedi: Into the Void

OLD REPUBLIC
5000-67 YEARS BEFORE
STAR WARS: A New Hope

Lost Tribe of the Sith: The Collected Stories

3954 YEARS BEFORE *STAR WARS: A New Hope*

The Old Republic: Revan

3650 YEARS BEFORE *STAR WARS: A New Hope*

The Old Republic: Deceived
Red Harvest
The Old Republic: Fatal Alliance
The Old Republic: Annihilation

1032 YEARS BEFORE *STAR WARS: A New Hope*

Knight Errant
Darth Bane: Path of Destruction
Darth Bane: Rule of Two
Darth Bane: Dynasty of Evil

RISE OF THE EMPIRE
67-0 YEARS BEFORE
STAR WARS: A New Hope

67 YEARS BEFORE *STAR WARS: A New Hope*

Darth Plagueis

33 YEARS BEFORE *STAR WARS: A New Hope*

Cloak of Deception
Darth Maul: Shadow Hunter
Maul: Lockdown

32 YEARS BEFORE *STAR WARS: A New Hope*

STAR WARS: EPISODE I
THE PHANTOM MENACE

Rogue Planet
Outbound Flight
The Approaching Storm

22 YEARS BEFORE *STAR WARS: A New Hope*

STAR WARS: EPISODE II
ATTACK OF THE CLONES

22-19 YEARS BEFORE *STAR WARS: A New Hope*

STAR WARS: THE CLONE WARS

The Clone Wars: Wild Space
The Clone Wars: No Prisoners

Clone Wars Gambit
Stealth
Siege

Republic Commando
Hard Contact
Triple Zero
True Colors
Order 66

Shatterpoint
The Cestus Deception
MedStar I: Battle Surgeons
MedStar II: Jedi Healer
Jedi Trial
Yoda: Dark Rendezvous
Labyrinth of Evil

19 YEARS BEFORE *STAR WARS: A New Hope*

STAR WARS: EPISODE III
REVENGE OF THE SITH

Kenobi
Dark Lord: The Rise of Darth Vader
Imperial Commando 501st

Coruscant Nights
Jedi Twilight
Street of Shadows
Patterns of Force

The Last Jedi

10 YEARS BEFORE *STAR WARS: A New Hope*

The Han Solo Trilogy
The Paradise Snare
The Hutt Gambit
Rebel Dawn

The Adventures of Lando Calrissian
The Force Unleashed
The Han Solo Adventures
Death Troopers
The Force Unleashed II

REBELLION
0–5 YEARS AFTER
STAR WARS: A New Hope

NEW REPUBLIC
5–25 YEARS AFTER
STAR WARS: A New Hope

THE STAR WARS LEGENDS NOVELS TIMELINE

 NEW JEDI ORDER
25–40 YEARS AFTER
STAR WARS: A New Hope

The New Jedi Order
Vector Prime
Dark Tide I: Onslaught
Dark Tide II: Ruin
Agents of Chaos I: Hero's Trial
Agents of Chaos II: Jedi Eclipse
Balance Point
Edge of Victory I: Conquest
Edge of Victory II: Rebirth
Star by Star
Dark Journey
Enemy Lines I: Rebel Dream
Enemy Lines II: Rebel Stand
Traitor
Destiny's Way
Force Heretic I: Remnant
Force Heretic II: Refugee
Force Heretic III: Reunion
The Final Prophecy
The Unifying Force

35 YEARS AFTER STAR WARS: A New Hope

The Dark Nest Trilogy
The Joiner King
The Unseen Queen
The Swarm War

 LEGACY
40+ YEARS AFTER
STAR WARS: A New Hope

Legacy of the Force
Betrayal
Bloodlines
Tempest
Exile
Sacrifice
Inferno
Fury
Revelation
Invincible

Crosscurrent
Riptide
Millennium Falcon

43 YEARS AFTER STAR WARS: A New Hope

Fate of the Jedi
Outcast
Omen
Abyss
Backlash
Allies
Vortex
Conviction
Ascension
Apocalypse

X-Wing: Mercy Kill

45 YEARS AFTER STAR WARS: A New Hope

Crucible

DRAMATIS PERSONAE

Bastila Shan; Jedi Knight (human female)
Canderous Ordo; Mandalorian mercenary (human male)
Darth Nyriss; Dark Councilor (Sith female)
Darth Xedrix; Dark Councilor (human male)
Meetra Surik; Jedi Knight (human female)
Murtog; security chief (human male)
Revan; Jedi Master (human male)
Lord Scourge; Sith Lord (Sith male)
Sechel; adviser (Sith male)
T3-M4; astromech (droid)

A long time ago in a galaxy
far, far away. . . .

PROLOGUE

HERE THE DARKNESS REIGNS ETERNAL. There is no sun, no dawn; just the perpetual gloom of night. The only illumination comes from jagged forks of lightning, carving a wicked path through angry clouds. In their savage wake thunder shreds the sky, unleashing a torrent of hard, cold rain.

The storm is coming, and there is no escape.

Revan's eyes snapped open, the primal fury of his nightmare wrenching him awake for the third night in a row.

He lay still and quiet, turning his focus inward to ease the pounding of his heart as he silently recited the opening line of the Jedi mantra.

There is no emotion; there is peace.

A sense of calm settled over him, washing away the irrational terror of his dream. Yet he knew better than to merely dismiss it. The storm that haunted him each time he closed his eyes was more than just a nightmare. Conjured up from the deepest corners of his mind, the storm had meaning. But try as he might, Revan couldn't figure out what his subconscious was trying to tell him.

Was it a warning? A long-forgotten memory? A vision of the future? All three?

Careful not to wake his wife, he rolled out of bed and went into the refresher to splash some cool water on his face. Catching a glimpse of himself in the mirror, he stopped to study his reflection.

Even now, two standard years after rediscovering his true identity, he still had trouble reconciling the face in the mirror with the man he had been before the Jedi Council had turned him back to the light.

Revan: Jedi; hero; traitor; conqueror; villain; savior. He was all these things and more. He was a living legend; the embodiment of myth and folklore; a figure that transcended history. Yet all he saw staring back at him was an ordinary man who hadn't slept in three nights.

Fatigue was taking its toll. His angular features had become thin and drawn. His pale skin accentuated the dark circles under eyes that stared back at him from deep hollows.

Bracing a hand on either side of the sink, he slumped his head and let out a long, low sigh, his black, shoulder-length hair falling forward to cover his face like a dark curtain. After several seconds he stood up straight, using the fingers of both hands to sweep his hair back into place.

Moving quietly, he made his way from the refresher and across the small living room of his apartment. He proceeded out onto the balcony, where he stopped and stared out across Coruscant's endless cityscape.

Traffic in the galactic capital never stopped, and he found the constant buzz and blur of shuttles speeding by soothing. He leaned out over the railing of the balcony as far as he could, his eyes unable to pierce the darkness to make out the planet's surface hundreds of stories below.

"Don't jump. I don't want to have to clean up the mess."

He turned his head at the sound of Bastila's voice behind him.

She stood at the threshold of the balcony door, the bedsheet draped around her shoulders to ward off the night's chill. Her long brown hair—normally pulled back up from her forehead into a bun on top and a short ponytail below—hung loose and sleep-tousled. Her face was only partially illuminated by the glow of the city below, yet he could see her lips pressed into a wry smile. Despite her joking words, he could see real concern etched on her features.

"Sorry," he said, stepping away from the rail and turning toward her. "Didn't mean to wake you. Just needed to clear my head."

"Maybe you should speak to the Jedi Council," Bastila suggested. "They might be able to help."

"You want me to ask the Council for help?" he echoed. "You must have had too much of that Corellian wine at dinner."

"They owe you," Bastila insisted. "If it weren't for you, Darth Malak would have destroyed the Republic, eliminated the Council, and all but wiped out the Jedi. They owe you everything!"

Revan didn't answer right away. What she said was true—he had stopped Darth Malak and destroyed the Star Forge. But it wasn't that simple. Malak had been Revan's apprentice. Against the wishes of the Council, the two had led an army of Jedi and Republic soldiers against Mandalorian raiders threatening colonies in the Outer Rim . . . only to return not as heroes, but as conquerors.

Revan and Malak had both sought to destroy the Republic. But Malak had betrayed his Master, and Revan had been captured by the Jedi Council, barely alive, his body and mind shattered. The Council had saved his life, but they had also stripped his memories and rebuilt him as a weapon that could be unleashed against Darth Malak and his followers.

"The Council doesn't owe me anything," Revan whispered. "All the good I've done can't balance out the evil that came before."

Bastila brought her hand up and put it gently but firmly over Revan's lips.

"Don't talk like that. They can't blame you for what happened. Not anymore. You're not the same man you were. The Revan I know is a hero. A champion of the light. You redeemed me after Malak turned me to the dark side."

Revan reached up and wrapped his fingers around the delicate hand resting on his lips, then softly pulled it down. "Like you and the Council redeemed me."

Bastila turned away, and Revan instantly regretted his words. He knew she was ashamed of her involvement in his capture and her role in erasing his memory.

"What we did was wrong. At the time I thought we had no other choice, but if I had to do it over again—"

"No," Revan said, cutting her off. "I wouldn't want you to change anything. If none of this had happened, I might never have found you."

She turned back to face him, and he could see the hurt and bitterness lingering in her eyes.

"What the Council did to you wasn't right," she insisted. "They took away your memories! They stole your identity!"

"It came back," Revan assured her, pulling her close and wrapping his arms around her. "You have to let go of your anger."

She didn't fight his embrace, though she stood rigid at first. Then he felt the tension melting away from her body as she lowered her head onto his shoulder.

"There is no emotion, there is peace," she whispered,

reciting aloud the same words Revan had sought solace in only a few minutes earlier.

They stood there in silence, holding each other until Revan felt her shiver.

"It's cold out here," he said.."We should go back inside."

Twenty minutes later Bastila was fast asleep, but Revan lay on the bed with his eyes open, staring at the ceiling.

He was thinking about what Bastila had said about the Council taking his identity. As his mind had healed, many of his memories had returned, along with his sense of self. But he knew parts were still missing, possibly gone forever.

As a Jedi he knew the importance of letting go of bitterness and anger, but that didn't mean he couldn't still wonder about what he had lost.

Something had happened to him and Malak beyond the Outer Rim. They had gone to defeat the Mandalorians, but they had returned as disciples of the dark side. The official story was that they had been corrupted by the ancient power of the Star Forge, but Revan suspected there was more to it. And he knew it had something to do with his nightmares.

A terrible world of thunder and lightning, shrouded in perpetual night.

He and Malak had found something. He couldn't remember what it was, or where it was, but he feared it on a deep, primal level. Somehow he knew that whatever the terrible secret might be, it was a threat far greater than the Mandalorians or the Star Forge. And Revan was convinced it was still out there.

The storm is coming, and there is no escape.

PART ONE

CHAPTER ONE

LORD SCOURGE RAISED the hood of his cloak as he stepped off the shuttle, a shield against the wind and pelting rain. Storms were common here on Dromund Kaas; dark clouds perpetually blocked out the sun, rendering terms like *day* and *night* meaningless. The only natural illumination came from the frequent bursts of lightning arcing across the sky, but the glow from the spaceport and nearby Kaas City provided more than enough light to see where he was going.

The powerful electrical storms were a physical manifestation of the dark side power that engulfed the entire planet—a power that had brought the Sith back here a millennium before, when their very survival had been in doubt.

After a crushing defeat in the Great Hyperspace War, the Emperor had risen up from the tattered ranks of the remaining Sith Lords to lead his followers on a desperate exodus to the farthest reaches of the galaxy. Fleeing the Republic armies and the relentless revenge of the Jedi, they eventually resettled far beyond the borders of Republic-charted space on their long-lost ancestral homeworld.

There, safely hidden from their enemies, the Sith

began to rebuild their Empire. Under the guidance of the Emperor—the immortal and all-powerful savior who still reigned over them even after a thousand years—they abandoned the hedonistic lifestyles of their barbaric ancestors.

Instead they created a near-perfect society in which the Imperial military operated and controlled virtually every aspect of daily life. Farmers, mechanics, teachers, cooks, janitors—all were part of the great martial machine, each individual a cog trained to perform his or her duties with maximum discipline and efficiency. As a result, the Sith had been able to conquer and enslave world after world in the unexplored regions of the galaxy, until their power and influence rivaled those of their glorious past.

Another burst of lightning split the sky, momentarily illuminating the massive citadel that loomed over Kaas City. Built by slaves and devoted followers, the citadel served as both palace and fortress, an unassailable meeting place for the Emperor and the twelve handpicked Sith Lords who made up his Dark Council.

A decade earlier, when Scourge had first arrived on Dromund Kaas as a young apprentice, he had vowed to one day set foot inside the citadel's exclusive halls. Yet in all his years of training at the Sith Academy on Kaas City's borders, he had never been granted the privilege. He had been one of the top students, marked by his superiors for his strength in the Force and his fanatic devotion to the ways of the Sith. But acolytes were not permitted inside the citadel; its secrets were reserved for those in direct service to the Emperor and the Dark Council.

The dark side power emanating from within the building was undeniable; he had felt the raw, crackling energy every day during his years as an acolyte. He had drawn on it, focusing his mind and spirit to channel the power through his own body to sustain him during the brutal training sessions.

Now, after almost two years away, he was back on Dromund Kaas. Standing on the landing pad, he could once again feel the dark side deep inside his bones, the sizzling heat more than compensating for the minor discomfort of the wind and rain. But he was no longer a mere apprentice. Scourge had returned to the seat of Imperial power as a full-fledged Sith Lord.

He had known this day would come eventually. After graduating from the Sith Academy he had hoped for a posting on Dromund Kaas. Instead he had been sent to the fringes of the Empire to help quell a series of minor rebellions on recently conquered worlds. Scourge suspected the posting had been a punishment of some type. One of his instructors, jealous of the star pupil's potential, had probably recommended that he be stationed as far from the seat of Imperial power as possible to slow his ascent to the upper ranks of Sith society.

Unfortunately, Scourge had no proof to back his theory. Yet even exiled to the uncivilized sectors on the farthest borders of the Empire, he had still managed to forge his reputation. His martial skills and ruthless pursuit of the rebel leaders caught the notice of several prominent military leaders. Now, two years after leaving the Academy, he had returned to Dromund Kaas as a newly anointed Lord of the Sith. More important, he was here at the personal request of Darth Nyriss, one of the most senior members of the Emperor's Dark Council.

"Lord Scourge," a figure called out over the wind, running up to greet him. "I am Sechel. Welcome to Dromund Kaas."

"Welcome *back*," Scourge corrected as the man dropped to one knee and bowed his head in a gesture of respect. "This is not my first time on this world."

Sechel's hood was pulled up against the rain, covering his features, but during his approach Scourge had noticed the red skin and dangling cheek tendrils that marked him as a pureblood Sith, just like Lord Scourge himself. But while Scourge was an imposing figure, tall and broad-shouldered, this man was small and slight. Reaching out, Scourge sensed only the faintest hint of the Force in the other, and his features twisted into a sneer of revulsion.

Unlike the humans that made up the bulk of the Empire's population, the Sith species were all blessed with the power of the Force to varying degrees. It marked them as the elite; it elevated them above the lower ranks of Imperial society. And it was a legacy that was fervently protected.

A pureblood born without any connection to the Force was an abomination; by custom such a creature could not be suffered to live. During his time at the Academy, Lord Scourge had encountered a handful of Sith whose power in the Force was noticeably weak. Hampered by their failing, they relied on the influence of their high-ranking families to find them postings as low-level aids or administrative officials at the Academy, where their handicap would be least noticed. Spared from the lower castes only by their pureblood heritage, in Scourge's eyes they were barely better than slaves, though he did have to admit that the more competent ones could have their uses.

But never before had he encountered one of his own kind with as feeble an attunement to the Force as the man huddled at his feet. The fact that Darth Nyriss had sent someone so vile and unworthy to greet him was unsettling. He'd expected a more substantial and impressive welcome.

"Get up," he snarled, making no effort to conceal his disgust.

Sechel quickly scrambled to his feet. "Darth Nyriss sends her apologies for not coming to meet you personally," he said quickly. "There have been several attempts on her life recently, and she only leaves her palace under the rarest of circumstances."

"I'm well aware of her situation," Scourge replied.

"Y-yes, my lord," Sechel stammered. "Of course. That's why you're here. Excuse my stupidity."

A crash of thunder nearly drowned out Sechel's apology, heralding an increase in the storm's intensity. The driving rain started to come down in stinging sheets.

"Were your Master's instructions to leave me standing here in this downpour until I drowned?" Scourge demanded.

"F-forgive me, my lord. Please, follow me. We have a speeder waiting to take you to the domicile."

A short distance from the spaceport was a small landing pad. A constant stream of hovercabs was landing and taking off—the preferred way for those of the lower ranks who couldn't afford their own speeder to traverse the city. As was typical at a busy spaceport, a thick crowd surrounded the base of the landing pad. Those just arriving quickly fell into the queues waiting to hire a driver, moving with the disciplined precision that was the hallmark of Imperial society.

Of course, Lord Scourge had no need to step into the line. While some in the crowd cast sharp glances at Sechel as he tried to force a path through, the throng quickly parted upon catching sight of the towering figure behind him. Even with his hood drawn against the rain, Scourge's black cape, his spiked armor, his dark red complexion, and the lightsaber prominently displayed at his side clearly marked him as a Sith Lord.

The individuals in the crowd showed a wide variety of reactions to his presence. Many were slaves or indentured servants out running errands for their masters;

they wisely kept their eyes fixed on the ground, careful not to make eye contact. The Enlisted—the ranks of ordinary individuals conscripted into mandatory military service—snapped smartly to attention, as if waiting for Scourge to inspect them as he passed by.

The Subjugates—the caste of offworld merchants, traders, dignitaries, and visitors from planets not yet granted full status in the Empire—stared with a mixture of wonder and fear as they stepped quickly aside. Many of them bowed as a sign of respect. On their homeworlds they might be rich and powerful, but here on Dromund Kaas they were well aware that they ranked only slightly above the servants and slaves.

The only exception to the rule was a pair of humans, one male, the other female. Scourge noticed them standing at the foot of the stairs leading up to the landing pad, stubbornly holding their ground.

They were wearing expensive clothes—matching red pants and tops trimmed with white—and both clearly wore light armor beneath their outfits. Dangling from the man's shoulder was a large assault rifle, and the woman had a blaster pistol strapped across each hip. However, the two humans were clearly not part of the military, as neither displayed the official Imperial insignia or any indication of rank on their garb.

It wasn't unusual for Subjugate mercenaries from other worlds to visit Dromund Kaas. Some came seeking profit, hiring their services out to the highest bidder; others came to prove their value to the Empire in the hope of one day being granted the rare privilege of full Imperial citizenship. But mercenaries typically reacted with deference and humility when confronted with someone of Scourge's rank.

By law, Scourge could have them imprisoned or executed for even a trifling offense. Judging by their confrontational behavior, they were blissfully unaware of this fact.

As the rest of the crowd parted, the mercenaries remained in place, staring defiantly at Scourge as he approached. The Sith Lord bristled at the continued lack of respect. Sechel must have felt it as well, because he quickly rushed ahead to confront the pair.

Scourge didn't slow his pace, but neither did he make a move to catch up with the scurrying servant. At this distance, he couldn't hear what was being said over the wind and rain. But Sechel was speaking frantically, gesturing and waving his arms while the humans stared at him with cold contempt. Finally, the woman nodded, and the pair slowly moved out of the way. Satisfied, Sechel turned and waited for Scourge to arrive.

"A thousand apologies, my lord," he said as they mounted the steps. "Some Subjugates lack a proper understanding of our customs."

"Perhaps they need me to remind them of their place," Scourge growled.

"If that is your wish, my lord," Sechel said. "However, I must remind you that Darth Nyriss is expecting you."

Scourge decided to let the matter drop. They climbed into the waiting speeder; Sechel at the controls. Scourge settled into the luxurious seat, pleased to note that the vehicle had a roof—many of the hovercabs were open to the elements. The engines engaged, and they rose to a height of ten meters before the speeder accelerated, leaving the spaceport behind.

They rode in silence, drawing ever closer to the massive citadel that stood at the heart of Kaas City. But Scourge knew this was not their destination today. Like every member of the Dark Council, Darth Nyriss was allowed access to the Emperor's citadel. In the wake of two recent assassination attempts, however, Scourge fully expected her to stay within the walls of the personal stronghold she maintained on the outskirts of Kaas City, surrounded by her most trusted staff and servants.

This didn't strike Scourge as cowardly in any way; Nyriss was simply being practical. Like any high-ranking Sith, she had many enemies. Until she discovered who was behind the assassination attempts, exposing herself unnecessarily was a foolish and unwarranted risk.

Yet her practicality had to be balanced against the understanding that her rank was based solely on strength. If Nyriss appeared weak or ineffective—if she was unable to take firm and decisive action against whoever was plotting her death—others would sense it. Rivals both off and on the Dark Council would prey on her situation, leveraging her vulnerable position to their own advantage. Darth Nyriss would not be the first of the Emperor's inner circle to lose her life.

That was why Scourge was here. To root out the secret masterminds behind the assassinations, and destroy them.

Given the importance of his mission, he couldn't understand why Nyriss hadn't sent a full honor guard to escort him through the city. She should want everyone to know of his arrival. He was proof that steps were being taken to solve her problem; a warning to any other rivals who might be emboldened by the recent attempts on her life. Keeping his arrival almost secret served no purpose . . . at least none Scourge could see.

They passed by the Emperor's citadel and made their way to the western edge of the city. After several more minutes, Scourge felt the speeder begin to slow as Sechel brought it in for a landing.

"We're here, my lord," Sechel said as the vehicle touched down.

They were in a large courtyard. High stone walls stood to the north and south. The east end was open to the street; the west was bordered by what Scourge assumed was Darth Nyriss's stronghold. In many ways the building resembled the Emperor's citadel, though on a significantly smaller scale. The architectural similarities were more than just an homage to the Emperor. Like his citadel, this building would serve both as Nyriss's dwelling and as a fortress she could fall back to in times of trouble, and it had been designed to be simultaneously ornate, imposing, and easily defensible.

The courtyard itself was populated by half a dozen large statues, each several meters wide at the base and easily twice as tall as Scourge. The two largest depicted humanoids in Sith robes—a male and a female. They stood with their arms raised slightly forward, their hands palms up. The man's face was hidden by a hood—the common depiction of the Emperor. The woman had her hood thrown back to reveal fierce Sith features; if the sculptor's work was accurate, Scourge knew this was his first glimpse of what Darth Nyriss actually looked like.

The other statues were abstract pieces, though each incorporated Nyriss's household emblem—a four-pointed star inside a wide circle. The ground was covered with fine white pebbles. A rare type of lichen that thrived in the gloom of Dromund Kaas had been planted in decorative patterns throughout the stone, the faint purple glow providing a ghostly illumination. A smooth path of finished stone led from the massive double doors that marked the entrance to the stronghold, through the center of the courtyard, and out to the small landing pad where their speeder had touched down.

Sechel scrambled out of the vehicle and raced around to open the exit hatch on the other side for his passenger. Scourge stepped out of the speeder and into the rain, which had lessened only slightly during their journey.

"This way, my lord," Sechel said, heading down the path.

Scourge followed him, fully expecting the doors to swing wide at their approach. To his surprise, the entrance remained sealed. Sechel didn't seem taken aback, however. Instead, he turned to the small holoscreen on the side and pressed the call button.

A flickering image materialized on the holoscreen—a human male of about forty. He appeared to be wearing the standard uniform of an Imperial security officer, and Scourge surmised he was the head of Nyriss's personal guard.

"Our guest has arrived, Murtog," Sechel explained, nodding in Scourge's direction.

"Did you verify his identity?" Murtog asked.

"W-what are you talking about?" Sechel stammered.

"How do we know this is the real Lord Scourge? How do we know this isn't another assassin?"

The questions seemed to catch Sechel completely off guard.

"I don't . . . I mean, he seems to be . . . uh, that is . . ."

"I'm not letting him in until I have proof," Murtog declared.

Sechel glanced back over his shoulder at Lord Scourge, his expression a mix of humiliation and fear. Then he leaned in close to the holocomm and, in a low voice, said, "This is completely inappropriate. You've overstepped your authority!"

"I'm the security chief," Murtog reminded him. "This is completely within my authority. Just give me five minutes to confirm everything's on the up-and-up."

Scourge stepped forward, grabbing Sechel by the shoulder and yanking him aside.

"You dare insult me by making me wait out in the rain like some beggar?" he spat at the screen. "I am a guest! Darth Nyriss herself invited me!"

Murtog barked out a sharp laugh. "You might want to check your facts on that."

The holoscreen clicked off abruptly. Scourge turned around to find Sechel cowering against the wall.

"I'm sorry, my lord," he said. "Murtog has become somewhat paranoid since—"

Scourge cut him off. "What did he mean when he told me to check my facts? Was I invited by Darth Nyriss, or not?"

"You were. Of course you were. Sort of."

Scourge raised his hand toward Sechel and reached out to the Force. The servant began to gasp and clutch at his throat as his body was lifted slowly up into the air by an invisible hand.

"You will tell me what is going on," Scourge said, his voice devoid of all emotion. "You will tell me everything, or you will die. Do you understand?"

Sechel tried to speak but could only cough and sputter. Instead he nodded frantically. Satisfied, Scourge released his hold. Abruptly Sechel dropped the full meter to the ground, where he landed in a heap, grunting in pain before scrambling to his knees.

"It wasn't Darth Nyriss's idea to hire you," he explained, his voice still raw and rough from the choking. "After the second assassination attempt, the Emperor suggested that her own people could be involved. He suggested she bring someone in from the outside."

Suddenly it all made sense. The Emperor's will was absolute; a "suggestion" from him was a de facto order. Darth Nyriss had invited him here because she'd had no choice. Scourge had assumed he was an honored guest, but in actuality he was nothing but an interloper. His presence was an insult to her loyal followers, and a reminder that the Emperor doubted her ability to deal with the assassins herself. That was why he'd received such a meager reception, and why Nyriss's security chief had reacted to him with such hostility.

Scourge realized he was in a precarious situation.

His efforts to investigate the assassinations would be met with resistance and suspicion. Any mistakes—even those that were not his fault—would be blamed on him. A single misstep could spell the end of his career, or even his life.

He was still pondering this new information when he heard a speeder approaching through the storm. The sound was innocuous, but it instantly put his senses on high alert. His heart began beating rapidly and his breathing quickened. A rush of adrenaline caused his cheek tendrils to twitch and his muscles to tense.

He drew his lightsaber and glanced up at the sky. At his feet, Sechel cried out and covered his face, assuming the lightsaber was meant for him. Scourge ignored him.

In the darkness of the storm, he could just make out the speeder's silhouette heading straight for them. He reached out with the Force, probing the vehicle and its passengers. He felt a bolt of anger rip through him as his suspicions were confirmed: Whoever was in the speeder was coming to kill him.

All of this, from Scourge's first awareness of the speeder to confirmation of its hostile intent, took less than two seconds. Time enough for the speeder to close the distance and come bearing down on him.

Scourge leapt to the side as a barrage of blasterfire was unleashed from the vehicle. He hit the ground in a roll that brought him to his feet just in time to spring clear of a second series of bolts. Moving with the blinding speed of the Force, he raced across the courtyard, bolts ricocheting off the ground just behind him every step of the way. He dived behind the cover of the Emperor's statue, his mind assessing the situation.

The speeder had to be equipped with an autotargeting blaster cannon; there was no other way the shots could have tracked him so closely on his desperate run for cover. Even a Sith Lord couldn't evade that kind of fire-power forever. He had to disable the vehicle.

The speeder was heading away from him, circling around for another strafing run. Before it could complete its turn, Scourge stepped out from behind the statue and launched his lightsaber across the courtyard. The crimson blade went spiraling through the night, tracing a wide, looping arc. It clipped the back end of the speeder, sending up a shower of spark and flame, and continued on its trajectory to return to Scourge's outstretched hand.

The hum of the speeder's engine pitched into a screaming whine as it completed its turn. Black smoke, barely visible against the dark clouds, billowed out from the rear engine. The vehicle began to lurch and wobble, losing altitude rapidly even as it opened fire yet again.

Scourge ducked back behind the Emperor's statue, pressing his back firmly against it as a shower of bolts rained down on him. A second later the speeder flew overhead, its angle of attack dropping so steeply it actually decapitated the statue he was hiding behind.

The heavy stone head toppled down toward him, forcing Scourge to break cover to avoid being crushed. At the same time, he saw the speeder slam into the ground. Emergency repulsor fields absorbed the impact, saving the vehicle from being smashed to bits, but it still hit hard enough to send a piece of the damaged engine flying.

Holding his lightsaber high above his head with both hands, Scourge charged the downed speeder. Two passengers scrambled from the wreckage, shaken but unharmed. Scourge was only mildly surprised to recognize the two red-clothed mercenaries he'd encountered on the speeder pad back near the spaceport.

The male was on the far side of the speeder, struggling to get his blaster rifle out of the wreckage. The female was on the near side, her blaster pistols already drawn. Scourge was less than five meters away when she opened fire.

He didn't bother trying to block the bolts. Instead, he launched himself upward, his forward momentum carrying him in a high, somersaulting leap that arced over both the woman and the damaged speeder. The sudden move caught her off guard, and though she fired several hurried shots, none hit him.

Twisting 180 degrees as he flew through the air, he landed on the other side of the speeder, right beside the male mercenary just as the man was bringing his own weapon to bear. Before he could fire, Scourge slashed his lightsaber diagonally across his enemy's torso.

As the man's corpse toppled to the ground, Scourge turned his attention back to the first mercenary. By this time she had spun to face him, and as her partner went down she unloaded another series of shots, forcing Scourge to duck behind the speeder for cover.

This time several of her blasts found their mark. Scourge's armor absorbed the worst of the attack, but he felt a searing pain in his shoulder as a small amount of the particle beam energy found its way through a joint in his armor to scorch his flesh.

He focused on the pain, transforming it into anger to fuel the Force for a savage counterattack. At the same time, instinctively, he drew upon his opponent's fear, adding it to his own passion and further amplifying the power he was gathering.

Channeling his rage, he unleashed a concentrated wave of energy that struck the woman square in the chest. The impact lifted her off her feet and sent her flying backward through the air. Her journey was cut short when she slammed against the base of one of the abstract statues. The sudden stop jarred the pistols from her hands, leaving her momentarily defenseless.

Scourge placed one hand on the hood of the speeder and vaulted over it, rushing to close in on his prone foe before she could regain her footing. But the mercenary was quick: She scrambled to her feet and pulled out a short electrorod, its tip crackling with a charge potent enough to knock an opponent unconscious with even a grazing blow.

Scourge pulled up short. The mercenary dropped into a fighting crouch, and the two combatants circled each other warily.

Had he wanted to, Scourge could have ended the encounter right then and there. Without her pistols, electrorod or not, the mercenary had no chance against a Sith Lord with a lightsaber. But killing her wouldn't get him what he really wanted.

"Tell me who hired you and I'll let you live," he said.

"Do I look that stupid?" she countered, feinting and making a quick lunge that Scourge easily sidestepped.

"You're obviously skilled," he told her. "I can use someone like you. Tell me who hired you, and I'll let you work for me. That, or throw your life away."

She hesitated, and for an instant Scourge thought she might drop her weapon. And then the night was shattered by the sound of multiple blaster carbines. The bolts hammered the mercenary in the back, sending her stumbling toward Scourge. He saw a look of total bewilderment on her face as she sank to her knees. Her mouth moved, but no words came out. Then she fell facedown in the gravel, dead.

Turning, Scourge saw half a dozen guards standing in the courtyard near the door leading into the stronghold. Among them was a human wearing a commander's uniform. He was short, broad-shouldered, and barrel-chested, with close-cropped blond hair and a neatly trimmed blond beard that contrasted sharply with his dark brown skin. Scourge recognized him from the holo: Murtog, Darth Nyriss's head of security.

Before Scourge could say anything, Sechel exclaimed, "About time you got here."

He was still cowering against the wall, in nearly the exact same place Scourge had left him after the brief interrogation that had preceded the ambush.

"Get up," Murtog told him, and the Sith lackey did as ordered.

"Clean this mess up," Murtog snapped at his guards, who scrambled to obey.

Satisfied, the security chief slung his weapon over his shoulder and nodded in Scourge's direction. "Darth Nyriss will see you now."

CHAPTER TWO

AS MURTOG LED THE WAY through the halls of the stronghold, Lord Scourge did his best to ignore the pain radiating from his wounded shoulder. Instead he focused on his surroundings, hoping to learn more of Lord Nyriss before they came face-to-face.

The interior architecture was typical of Sith aristocracy: a series of long, wide corridors with thick stone walls, vaulted ceilings, and countless imposing steel doors, all closed to conceal the rooms behind them. The halls were lavishly decorated in bold colors: red, black, and purple. Expensive woven rugs covered the floors, and the walls were lined with a collection of pictures, sculptures, and holoprojections worthy of any museum.

Murtog set a quick pace, giving Scourge little time to study the works. However, Sechel—trailing a few steps behind—provided a running commentary on significant pieces as they marched past.

"This is a bust of the infamous warlord Ugroth. He swore fealty to Darth Nyriss a dozen years ago when she led an Imperial force into his sector to subdue a potential uprising.

"This holoprojection was a gift from Queen Ressa of Drezzi to thank Darth Nyriss for her merciful treatment of the royal family when the Empire conquered their world. Her husband was executed, but the queen and her children were spared.

"This portrait commemorates Darth Nyriss's victory during . . ."

Realizing he wasn't going to gain any real insight from Sechel's descriptions, Scourge tuned him out. Still, he understood and appreciated the overt display of opulence. Nyriss was a member of the Dark Council; she was one of the twelve most important and influential individuals in the Empire. The material treasures were a symbol of her own worth; a reminder to any visitors that she was a being of rank and power.

Numerous sentries stood guard throughout the halls. They nodded in acknowledgment as Murtog passed. Such a high number of guards stationed inside the stronghold was a bit atypical, but considering the recent assassination attempts it wasn't unexpected. Scourge wondered if Murtog would increase their numbers, given the most recent incident . . . though Scourge wasn't convinced it had actually been an assassination attempt.

The dark side fed on passion and raw emotion, but it was important to temper it with cold analysis and reason. Even as he marched to meet his new liege, Scourge's mind was trying to piece together the parts of a puzzle that didn't seem to fit.

The alleged assassins had struck in the courtyard, exposing their presence while still outside the secured walls and gates of the stronghold. Even if Scourge hadn't stopped them, there was no chance they could actually have gotten inside the building to strike at Nyriss. Which probably meant she wasn't their real target: He was.

But who had set him up, and why? Murtog seemed a likely candidate. Though only a human, he had risen to a prominent rank in Nyriss's service—a position almost on par with Scourge's own newly appointed status. The first lesson Scourge had learned during his time at the Academy was that your peers could be your most dangerous rivals, Force-users or not.

And Murtog had every reason to feel threatened. He had failed to find those behind the assassination attempts on his liege. Scourge's arrival was a direct challenge to his competence as security chief. What better way to eliminate a potential rival than to expose his incompetence by killing him in a staged assassination attempt? That could explain why Murtog refused to let Scourge in when they'd first arrived, and why Murtog's soldiers had killed the female mercenary just when she'd been on the verge of surrendering.

However, Murtog wasn't Scourge's only suspect. Sechel had similar self-preserving motives. If Scourge succeeded in his mission, he would likely be rewarded with a permanent position that would surely rank above the servile Sith adviser in Darth Nyriss's hierarchy. Sechel had managed to find himself a niche in Sith society by clinging to his role as an adviser to Nyriss. It made sense to assume he would do anything in his power to remove an individual he viewed as a threat to his own position of power.

Scourge had witnessed Sechel speaking to the mercenaries at the spaceport earlier. At the time it had seemed he was shooing them away out of respect for a high-ranking Sith Lord newly arrived on the planet. Now Scourge wondered if he had been giving them last-minute instructions. The fact that Sechel had survived the battle in the courtyard was also suspicious. It was possible he was just lucky or had the highly evolved survival skills of a true coward, but it was also possible the mercenaries had been careful not to fire anywhere near him.

Murtog rounded another corner. The pain in Scourge's shoulder was becoming more intense as his armor rubbed against the wounded flesh. Yet he kept pace with the stocky human, refusing to show any sign of weakness.

The hall came to a dead end against another imposing door. This one, closed like all the others, was flanked by Sith apprentices. He doubted Nyriss would have made the Sith answer directly to a human, so they were probably not under Murtog's direct command. But based on the fact that they made no move to challenge the security chief as he approached, it was clear to Scourge that Murtog enjoyed a privileged position in Nyriss's household.

Murtog stepped forward and rapped his knuckles gently on the door, then took a step back and stood at attention.

While they waited for an answer to the knock, Scourge realized there was a third possibility: Murtog and Sechel might have been working together to plan the attack in the courtyard. At the Academy, lesser students would sometimes conspire together to bring down a more talented individual. It wasn't hard to imagine the same kind of thing happening outside the facility's walls, as well.

For the moment it wasn't possible to know which of his theories—if any—was correct. But Scourge knew he'd have to watch his back.

The door opened to reveal a young Twi'lek. She was clad in black robes, with Nyriss's four-pointed star emblazoned in purple on both the chest and back, surrounded by a red circle. A shock collar was fastened securely around her neck, but even without it, her status would have been immediately obvious simply because of her species.

When the Sith had fallen into full retreat during the last days of the Great Hyperspace War, they had taken with them a number of prisoners captured during their early victories over Republic worlds. Those prisoners—mostly humans and Twi'leks—had been condemned to a life of slavery.

By the Emperor's order, no slave could ever be granted his or her freedom, and the status of the parent would be passed down to the child generation after generation. Because of this directive, there was never any doubt about the role of any Twi'lek in the Empire—they were and always would be slaves, descended from ancestors too weak to save themselves from the Sith invaders.

The slave bent to one knee and kept her eyes to the ground as Murtog, Scourge, and Sechel stepped through. Then she closed the door behind them and retreated into a corner.

The well-lit room appeared to be a study or private library. The walls were lined with shelves, their ancient wooden frames warped by the weight of the treasures they bore.

Scourge couldn't help but stare in wonder at the collection. During his days at the Academy he had seen only one physical manuscript—an ancient tome dating back more than ten thousand years to the arrival of the first Dark Jedi on Dromund Kaas. The book was considered a priceless artifact, one of the academy's greatest treasures.

Yet here dozens—if not hundreds—of volumes filled the shelves on the left wall. Most of the books were large and thick, their bound pages protected by covers of leather or some similarly cured hide . . . though Scourge guessed that not all of them were made from skin cured from mindless beasts. They had an antiquated look about them, though most appeared to be preserved in good condition, if somewhat worn from use. Obviously Nyriss had paged through them many times.

The shelves on the right wall contained reference material that looked even more ancient and delicate. Loose leaves of yellowed parchment were held in place with delicate wire clips; rolled scrolls were encased in clear protective tubes. A hinged glass cover sheltered several books that looked as if they might crumble into dust should a strong breeze pass through the room.

But not everything in the room was an archaic relic. On the rear wall was a large bank of holodisks and datacards, and in the center of the room was a computer workstation where a figure Scourge could only assume to be Darth Nyriss sat hunched, staring at the display monitor. The hood of her loose-fitting cowl—red, accented with purple and black—was pulled up over her head, and the long, loose sleeves even covered her hands and fingers as she worked at the terminal.

Neither Murtog nor Sechel made any sound to announce their presence, so Scourge took his cue from them and stood silently while Nyriss focused intently on the computer's display. Her cloaked form blocked any view of the screen, so it was impossible for him to see what she was studying. However, he thought he could hazard a guess: Darth Nyriss was well known for her proficiency in the ancient arts of Sith sorcery.

During his time at the Academy, Scourge had discovered that there were many ways to draw upon the power of the Force. His natural talents had led him down the path of the warrior: learning to channel his emotions into strength and raw outbursts of lethal energy. But other students had trained with the Inquisitors, studying a very different curriculum.

Millennia earlier, those who followed the dark side had learned to harness and shape the Force through complex rituals that could control the mind of an enemy and sometimes even warp reality itself. Much of this arcane knowledge had been lost, but those who managed to unlock even a few of the secrets of the past were often rewarded with a more subtle—though just as potent—form of power.

It was rumored that the perpetual storms of Dromund Kaas were the result of the Emperor performing one of these rituals. Scourge didn't know if that was true, but he knew that Nyriss had gained her place in the Dark Council through her knowledge and understanding of things he could never hope to fully grasp.

After several minutes Nyriss pushed herself away from the desk, rose from her chair, and turned to face them, pulling back the hood of her cloak as she did so.

Scourge was taken aback by her appearance, though he did his best to hide his reaction. Like him, she was a pure-blooded Sith. But her face was creased with deep wrinkles, and the tendrils dangling from her cheeks and chin were withered. Her skin was pale, more pink than red, and mottled with dark brown age spots.

He didn't know how old Darth Nyriss was, though he knew she had served on the Dark Council for nearly two decades; only two other members had longer tenures. Despite this, he had been expecting someone more akin to the fiercely beautiful woman depicted in the statues of the courtyard. Instead, he was confronted with a shriveled hag.

Unbidden, the words of one of the instructors at the Academy leapt to the forefront of his mind: *The Force can be bent to your will, but often there is a cost. The most powerful rituals of the dark side exact a toll few are willing to pay.*

Perhaps Nyriss was not really as old as she appeared. A lifetime spent delving into the ancient secrets of Sith sorcery had given her one of the highest positions in the Empire. Maybe it had also drained her of her youth and vitality.

"Not what you expected?" Nyriss said as if reading his mind, a sly smile on her cracked and flaking lips.

In contrast with her decrepit features, her voice was strong and vibrant, and she stood tall and straight. A sharp gleam in her eye further belied her venerability, leading Scourge to surmise that her appearance was intentional.

There were a number of ways to stay young and beautiful; Nyriss could easily have afforded them had she wished to. Instead, she had chosen to let herself age prematurely. Either she didn't care about the superficiality of physical attractiveness, or she chose to flaunt the ravishing effects of the dark side as a symbol of all she had learned and accomplished.

"Forgive me, my lord," he said with a slight bow, employing the gender-neutral honorific used to address Sith Lords of either sex. "There was an incident on my arrival that has left me a little off-balance."

"I'm well aware of what transpired in the courtyard," Nyriss said, tilting her wizened head in the direction of the monitor. A still image of Scourge in the first few seconds after the battle was frozen on the screen, captured by one of the stronghold's security cams. "You dealt with the assassins quite efficiently."

Scourge hesitated a split second before replying. He wanted to speak with Nyriss about his suspicions, but both Murtog and Sechel were in the room. Even if they hadn't been, it was dangerous to throw out unfounded accusations implicating two of her highest-ranking followers without proof; they wouldn't have been in their current positions if she didn't have some level of trust in them.

"I expect this will not be the last such incident," he said, choosing his words carefully.

"It appears you are wounded," Nyriss remarked, noticing the scorch marks on the shoulder plating of his armor. "Do you need medical attention?"

"It can wait. The injury is not serious, and the pain is irrelevant. I would rather finish our business here."

Nyriss nodded in approval. "I would like to hear your analysis of the attack," she continued. "Perhaps we can learn something of who was behind it."

"That would have been easier if Murtog's troops had not killed the second assassin just as she was about to surrender," he replied.

From the corner of his eye he saw Murtog bristle, but the security chief remained silent.

"You think Murtog made a mistake?" Nyriss pressed.

"He was somewhat overzealous in his efforts to eliminate an immediate threat," Scourge answered diplomatically.

Sechel stifled a high-pitched giggle, and Nyriss shot him a stern glare.

"Let's continue this conversation in private," she said, dismissing Murtog and Sechel with a wave of her hand.

The two quickly bowed and turned to the door, which had already been opened by the Twi'lek slave, who closed the door behind them before retreating to her corner.

"You have something you wish to tell me," Nyriss said once they were gone. "Discretion and subtlety have their place, but now when you speak to me I expect total candor."

Scourge nodded.

"Let me guess," she continued. "You suspect my own people are behind these recent attempts on my life."

"No one is above suspicion," Scourge admitted. "But I assume you have very thoroughly investigated everyone on your staff. If they were guilty, you probably would have discovered something by now."

"I'm glad to see you understand I am not completely incompetent."

"I do not believe the attack in the courtyard was another attempt on your life," Scourge said. "I think the mercenaries were hired to eliminate *me*."

"And since Murtog sees you as a rival and potential threat, you naturally suspect he was behind it."

"Possibly. Or it may have been Sechel. Or both working in concert."

"And what do you have to base this on?"

"Mostly circumstantial evidence. But my instincts feel there is enough to act on."

"You expect me to turn on two of my most trusted servants based on little more than your hunch?"

"My instincts are seldom wrong," Scourge said. "My reputation is well earned."

"So what is it you suggest I do? Dismissal? Execution?"

Suddenly the conversation felt like a test, as if Nyriss was trying to evaluate him based on his answers. If so, he was ready for the challenge.

"It would be foolish to throw away someone as valuable as either Murtog or Sechel without concrete proof," Scourge replied. "But I would like the chance to interrogate both of them."

"A good interrogator can make a subject admit to anything," Nyriss countered. "Even something that isn't true."

"Torturing a false confession out of them wouldn't serve any purpose," Scourge assured her. "I need the truth, and I would be careful not to do any permanent physical or mental damage. If one or both prove to be innocent, I'm sure you would want them to be just as capable when they return to their post as they were before my questioning."

A flicker of approval on Nyriss's face convinced Scourge he had given a satisfactory answer. However, the test was not over yet.

"If I did allow you to question them, whom would you speak with first?"

"Your security chief. Murtog."

"Why Murtog?"

"If he's guilty, he will be easier to break."

Nyriss raised an eyebrow in surprise. "You think Sechel could withstand interrogation longer than Murtog?"

Scourge knew it sounded unlikely: a trained soldier should easily outlast a cowardly sycophant. "Murtog is physically stronger," he said, "but tolerance for pain is useful only against the simplest and least effective interrogation methods. There are far more subtle and effective ways to get answers. Murtog, like most soldiers, will have had training in interrogation resistance. I know these techniques, and I know how to counter them. Sechel, on the other hand, is far less predictable. On the surface he seems weak and helpless. But he has risen to a position of rank by using cunning, creativity, and quick thinking. It will take me time to truly understand how his mind works. I will have to learn all his tricks before I can set my trap. His interrogation would be a much more involved and complicated process than Murtog's."

"Very impressive," Nyriss remarked. "However, the interrogations won't be necessary."

Scourge shook his head, puzzled.

"You were right about the mercenaries, but I already know who hired them to try to kill you."

"Who?"

"Me."

"You?" Scourge exclaimed. Her admission had caught him off guard.

"After the second assassination attempt, Murtog and Sechel found a lead. I hired those mercenaries to follow up on it. But before they could, the Emperor decided to interfere, forcing me to bring you in. Your arrival left me with an excess of outside agents, so I told Sechel to instruct the mercenaries to try to take you out of the picture. Consider it a test."

"Of course," Scourge muttered, silently cursing himself for being so shortsighted.

He had originally assumed Nyriss had brought him here because she had heard of his success in his earlier postings. If that had been true, she would have had no need to reassure herself of his potential.

But the truth was very different. As she herself had said, his presence here was only because of what she considered to be the Emperor's interference in her affairs. Given that, it was only logical she would want proof of his competence.

"If they managed to kill you, then you weren't worthy of serving me," Nyriss explained. "If you killed them, then you proved that they were a waste of resources. Either way, I would be left with the most suitable candidate for the job."

Scourge wasn't resentful over what Nyriss had done; in fact, he admired her for it. His only regret was that he had been blind to her machinations.

"I've spent too much time away from Dromund Kaas," he grumbled. "I've forgotten the ways of the Sith."

"That time away is what earned you this post," she reminded him. "It wasn't just your success at quashing the rebels and eliminating their leaders. The Emperor chose you because he knew you had been removed from the politics of Dromund Kaas and the Dark Council; you were untainted by any allegiance to a secret master who might be involved in the conspiracy against me. That made you a candidate I couldn't possibly object to."

There was almost something insulting in her tone, as

if Scourge's lack of political experience was a personal weakness. Perhaps it was.

Nyriss had held on to her position for the past twenty years; to do so required as much cunning and intelligence as raw power. Next to her, he was little more than a naïve child.

The realization excited him. Now that he had survived Darth Nyriss's unexpected initiation, he would have a chance to learn at the feet of a master manipulator . . . providing there wasn't another attempt on her life.

"You said you found a lead," he said, quickly moving on to the reason he had been sent here in the first place. "Something you wanted the mercenaries to follow up on."

Nyriss didn't reply right away. Instead she seemed to be studying him. "You are familiar with the details of the last attempt on my life?" she asked finally.

"One of your serving droids was replaced with a duplicate," Scourge said, recalling the details from the file. "The droid was equipped with a disruptor beam; it was programmed to fire once it had a clear shot at you, but the bolt missed and struck one of your servants instead."

"My best chef. I still haven't found a replacement for her," Nyriss said with what seemed like genuine remorse. "The droid wiped its memory core immediately after the attempt, but Sechel was able to slice the core and salvage some of the data."

"Was he able to identify who programmed the droid?"

"No, but he was able to determine where it was manufactured—a privately owned plant on Hallion."

Scourge recognized the name. Hallion was a recently conquered world; it had been brought into the Empire's fold only in the last decade. The difficult transition from private enterprise to an Imperial economy was still taking place. No doubt it would be easy to convince those who owned an asset like a droid manufacturing plant to

strike back at the Empire before it seized full control of
the facility.

"You want me to go check out the plant," Scourge
guessed.

"I want Sechel to check out the plant," she clarified.
"Once inside, he can slice into their computer network
to find out who arranged the purchase. I hired those
mercenaries you dispatched to get him past security.
That task now falls to you."

"When do we leave?"

"Not for a few days. I'll send a file to your quarters
to get you up to speed. And a med droid to fix up your
shoulder."

Scourge nodded, and Nyriss turned away and seated
herself back at the computer, dismissing him without a
word.

For a moment he simply stood there, gathering himself as he processed everything that had happened.
Sechel and Murtog hadn't been behind the attack at the
gates, but that didn't mean they weren't plotting against
him. He was still an interloper, still a potential rival for
the favor of their mistress. If they saw an opportunity to
eliminate him, they'd surely take it.

He felt a gentle tug on his elbow. Glancing down he
saw the young Twi'lek slave at his side. The door to the
hall was already open; she ushered him out of the room
in silence, then closed the door behind him.

Sechel was waiting for him in the corridor. "Lord
Scourge," he said with a bow, "I would be honored to
escort you to your room. I promise there won't be any
more ambushes on the way."

There was something almost mocking in his tone.
Scourge's initial impulse was to slap the insolent wretch
across the mouth with the back of his hand, but he
quickly realized that would be a mistake. Nyriss clearly
valued Sechel over him, at least for now. He would have

to prove himself to her before he could take the liberty of putting the fawning adviser in his proper place.

"Lead the way," he ordered. His tone was arrogant, yet inside he was feeling the first stirrings of self-doubt. His arrival on Dromund Kaas had not gone as planned. Things here were not as simple as they had been at the Academy or out on the border regions. Here, even a non-Force-sensitive Sith like Sechel was held in higher esteem than he was, which meant Scourge was both expendable and vulnerable. He'd have to be very careful if he hoped to survive long enough to win Nyriss's favor.

CHAPTER THREE

THE GALACTIC MARKET on Coruscant was as busy as ever, but nobody paid any attention to Revan as he made his way through the crowds. Almost two years had passed since he had been proclaimed the savior of the galaxy. Though the Senate had awarded him its highest honor, the Cross of Glory, in a ceremony broadcast across the HoloNet, and his name was well remembered, his ordinary and rather unremarkable features had faded from public memory. In the aftermath of the presentation he had become a reclusive hero, eschewing public appearances and declining interview requests from any and all media outlets. He had shaved off his beard, and he rarely wore his Jedi robes out in public, making it even less likely anyone would notice him.

He liked being anonymous; it was one of the reasons he had settled on Coruscant. With one trillion people it was easy to blend into the crowd. That was even truer here in the Galactic Market, the most cosmopolitan section of the Republic's capital world. Merchants and shoppers of virtually every known species gathered to conduct commerce in a kaleidoscope of colors, shapes, and sizes. Red-skinned Togrutas intermingled with blue-skinned Twi'leks; diminutive Sullustans haggled with massive Hutts; fish-like Mon Calamari shared the streets with feline Cathar. Among such a diverse and interesting group, nobody paid any attention to a lone human and his astromech droid.

Unfortunately, the lack of attention meant that many in the crowd accidentally kicked, bumped, or tripped over T3-M4 as he scooted along at Revan's heel. The droid expressed his displeasure with a steady stream of angry beeps and chirps.

"Now you know why I told HK-Forty-seven he couldn't come," Revan told T3. "He'd probably try to clear a path through all these 'meatbags' with a flame-thrower."

The astromech responded with a long, low whistle, and Revan laughed out loud before adding, "Let's not and say we did. Besides, we're almost there."

They reached their destination a few minutes later: the Dealer's Den, a small cantina in the far corner of the Galactic Market that offered drinks, dancers, and gambling. The Dealer's Den catered to the seedier elements of Coruscant society: black-market smugglers; thugs and bounty hunters; stim and spice dealers. As a result, the clientele was predominantly a mix of species with unsavory galactic reputations. Scattered among the Rodians, Chevin, and Kubaz were a handful of humans, including the man Revan had come looking for: Canderous Ordo.

The Mandalorian was sitting by himself at a small table in the far corner, his back to the wall as was his habit. He was wearing his familiar outfit of tan pants, a leatheris vest, and a sleeveless black shirt that left his heavily muscled arms bare in order to display the clan mark tattooed on his left shoulder. His hair was styled in a brush cut, accentuating his square jaw and rugged, no-nonsense features. He still looked every bit the part of a mercenary, though Revan knew he hadn't accepted a job since they'd teamed up to take down Darth Malak two years earlier.

A scantily clad Twi'lek dancer was giving Canderous a private performance as he sipped on a blue-tinged drink. Despite the distraction, he noticed Revan immediately. He raised a meaty hand in a wave and shooed away his entertainment.

The dancer shot Revan an angry glare as she stomped away, her head-tails twitching with irritation.

T3 beeped in surprise.

"I guess he's a good tipper," Revan answered with a shrug.

Nobody else paid them much attention as they crossed the cantina floor and took a seat at the Mandalorian's table.

"You look like death warmed over," Canderous said by way of greeting. "Is being married to Bastila really that bad?"

"I'm not getting much sleep lately," Revan admitted. "Bad dreams," he added as Canderous arched an eyebrow. "Besides, you're one to talk. Looks like you haven't shaved in three days."

The Mandalorian smiled and caressed the stubble across his cheeks and chin with an open palm. "The ladies around here like their men to have rough edges. You want something to drink?"

Revan shook his head. "Not from here. That concoction you've got looks like it could peel the enamel off my teeth."

Canderous shrugged and raised his glass to his lips. He took a long swig, closed his eyes, and shuddered.

"It's an acquired taste," he admitted. "So why are you here? I get the feeling this isn't just a social call."

"I've got some questions about the war."

Revan didn't need to clarify; for Canderous there was only one war that mattered. He and Revan had fought on opposite sides, mortal enemies who knew each other only by reputation long before they joined forces against Malak and became friends.

"Not much to say. We lost. You won," Canderous said with a shrug. "We thought we could conquer the Republic, but instead we ended up a broken people."

He spoke with a casual indifference, but Revan knew him well enough to sense the bitterness and regret behind his words. The Mandalorians had been a proud and noble culture, fighting battles to win honor and glory; now the clans were scattered across the galaxy, reduced to working as mercenaries and thugs for the highest bidder. Revan didn't like bringing up such a painful topic, but there was information he needed, and he felt this was the only way to get it.

"There's one thing I never understood about the Mandalorian Wars," he pressed. "What started them? Why, after all these centuries, did you suddenly decide to launch an all-out attack on the Republic?"

"It was Mandalore's idea."

Revan knew that Canderous wasn't referring to the original founder of his people. For centuries, each successive leader of the Mandalorian clans had symbolically taken up the name of Mandalore as a way to simultaneously honor his cultural heritage and reinforce his own authority. To distinguish among rulers, each chose an honorific to define his or her reign, such as Mandalore the Conqueror or Mandalore the Indomitable. The most recent ruler had called himself Mandalore the Ultimate.

"Mandalore felt the Republic was weak," Canderous continued. "Vulnerable. He summoned the warriors of the clans, and we followed him into what we thought would be our greatest conquest."

There was no need to ask if Canderous or any of his fellow warriors had hesitated. When Mandalore called, the clans answered. While there might be battles and disputes among those seeking to be Mandalore's successor when he fell, once the decision was made there was never any dissent or debate.

"Things were going fine until you came along," Canderous said with a grim smile. "You and your followers turned the entire tide of the war against us. Eventually you killed Mandalore, and everything changed."

Revan couldn't actually remember any of his battles against the Mandalorians; they were buried in the part of his mind that had been locked away when the Jedi Council turned him against Malak. But he had studied up on his own history enough to fill in the missing details from Canderous's narrative.

In battle after battle, Revan had led the Jedi and Republic forces to victory. Realizing defeat was inevitable, Mandalore the Ultimate had challenged Revan to single combat, and Revan had accepted.

Though the Mandalorian fought valiantly, in the end he was no match for the Jedi Order's most powerful champion. But it wasn't enough for Revan to simply defeat his enemy. In Mandalorian culture, the death of one leader was merely an opportunity for another warrior to seize control of the clans by claiming the fallen Mandalore's helmet. To prevent this, Revan had stripped the helmet from his vanquished foe's corpse and hidden it on an unknown world.

For a warrior culture defined and bound by tradition and honor codes, the loss of Mandalore's Mask was a crippling blow. Denied the sole item recognized as the symbol of leadership, the Mandalorians could not choose a new Mandalore. With no universally acclaimed ruler, the various clans began to fight among themselves for power. Their armies became fragmented and ineffective, and within weeks a series of decisive victories by Revan's troops forced the Mandalorians to accept an unconditional surrender.

The humiliating defeat and the loss of Mandalore's Mask destroyed the once proud culture. Canderous had spoken of this once during the time they'd spent together stopping Malak. Surprisingly, he didn't blame Revan for what had become of the Mandalorians. He blamed Mandalore for not being strong enough to win their battle; he blamed the brothers and sisters of his clan for being too weak to pick up the pieces so they could rebuild their society. But mostly, he just didn't talk about it.

Revan hated picking at the old wound, but he felt he had no choice.

"Is there anything else you can tell me? About what happened before Mandalore declared war on the Republic? Anything unusual that might have been a catalyst for the war?"

Canderous tilted his head to the side and squinted one eye. "This have anything to do with those bad dreams you mentioned?"

"It might."

The Mandalorian nodded. "You're getting more of your memories back, aren't you?"

"Only bits and pieces. I keep having visions of a world I don't recognize. The whole planet is covered in electrical storms, day and night."

"Doesn't sound familiar," Canderous said after a few moments of thought. "What do you think it means?"

"I wish I knew. But I've got a bad feeling about it."

"And you think it's connected to our war against the Republic?"

"Think about it," Revan explained. "Mandalore the Ultimate decides to do something none of his predecessors even considered: launch an all-out war on the Republic. Malak and I defeat you. But after that, we mysteriously take our troops and disappear into the Unknown Regions beyond Mandalorian space. When we return, we decide to launch a war against the Republic, too."

"It does seem like sort of a strange coincidence," Canderous agreed. "You think you ran across this storm-covered planet in the Unknown Regions?"

"I'm not sure. But something happened to us out there. Something made us turn against the Republic. Maybe it's connected to Mandalore's decision to attack the Republic in the first place."

"And you think whatever this thing is, it's still out there? And it's still dangerous?"

"I feel like visions are a warning. Like part of my old self is trying to tell me something I can't afford to ignore." Revan sighed. "Sounds a little crazy, doesn't it?"

Canderous barked out a laugh. "After everything we've been through, this just feels like old times." He looked at Revan. "So what is it you want me to do?"

"I want to know more about Mandalore the Ultimate. But nobody's going to talk to an outsider like me. I need someone who can talk to the clans and get answers."

There was a long silence while Revan waited for Canderous to reply. He noticed that the Mandalorian's fingers were gripping his glass so hard, they were turning white.

"I've spent most of the last five years trying to avoid other Mandalorians," he finally muttered.

"I wouldn't ask if I didn't think it was important."

Canderous took a deep breath and downed the rest of his drink, closing his eyes and shuddering just as he had with the previous gulp.

"You know why I've been hanging around this kriffing bar for two years, turning down everyone who came to offer me a job?" he asked. He didn't bother to wait for a reply. "I had a feeling you were going to get mixed up in something interesting, and I wanted to be around for the fun. Guess this is it."

"I knew I could count on you, Canderous."

"Let me reach out to some people," the Mandalorian said. "See what I can dig up. Can't promise I'll find anything, though."

"I'm kind of hoping you don't," Revan replied. "But neither one of us is that lucky."

CHAPTER FOUR

LOCATED IN A REMOTE SYSTEM far from any major hyperspace lanes, Hallion was a small and insignificant planet among the dozens of worlds dominated by the Sith Empire. Its only remarkable features were the seven small natural satellites that orbited the world, just barely large enough to be considered moons. On this evening four of them were waxing full, their combined glow illuminating the darkness enough for Scourge to clearly make out the details of the Uxiol Droid Manufacturing plant's exterior even without his night goggles.

"Your blueprints didn't show a security fence," he whispered.

He and Sechel were huddled in a small copse of trees on the edge of a field roughly twenty meters from the plant.

"Maybe it's new," Sechel replied, also speaking softly. "Shouldn't be a problem, though. Once you're on the other side you can just open the gate and let me in."

Scourge had noticed a remarkable change in Sechel during the mission. The sniveling boot-lick that had greeted him at the spaceport on Dromund Kaas was gone, replaced by someone who was intelligent and self-confident. Obviously, the personality he had displayed on their first meeting had been a ruse; a cover he used to hide his true nature from outsiders. He was still probably useless in an actual fight, but Scourge was beginning to understand how he had risen to such a prominent position in Nyriss's household. He had compensated for his lack of the Force by developing his mental skills; and apparently Sechel had enjoyed a very successful career with Imperial Intelligence before becoming Nyriss's chief adviser.

"If they've got autoguns on the roof, we'll be dead before we get anywhere near that maintenance door," Scourge growled.

"It's a manufacturing plant, not a fortress," Sechel assured him. "Most of their security is electronic. You know, stuff I can slice. The worst you'll have to deal with is a couple of roving security droids."

"Patrol drones or assault droids?"

"Patrol drones. UDM doesn't manufacture assault droids. Too expensive for a small company like this." After a short pause, Sechel added, "Are you always this skittish on a job?"

"Only fools charge ahead without knowing what lies in wait," Scourge answered through gritted teeth.

It was more than the other's insolence that grated on him; Sechel's question had struck a nerve. There was something about this job that made Scourge uneasy. Part of it was being forced to work with a partner; normally he worked alone. Yet there was more to his unease than the presence of the Sith crouched beside him. It wasn't anything he could put his finger on, but something felt *off*. It made him hesitant, more cautious than usual.

"You're sure the entrance code will work? It's not going to set off some kind of alarm?" he asked, trying to think of anything that could possibly go wrong. "I can handle a few patrol drones, but if a dozen of them come down on us all at once we're in trouble."

"The code will work," Sechel promised. "This is a simple job."

He was right. This was a simple job, and Scourge was forced to admit that maybe the problem wasn't the mission.

"Taking things for granted is a good way to get yourself killed," Scourge told him as he stood up, trying to justify his behavior even as he struggled to push away the self-doubt creeping through the corners of his mind.

He made a final check of his equipment and armor, then slid his night goggles into place. The world took on an eerie green glow as the illumination from the moons above was enhanced tenfold. He drew his lightsaber but didn't ignite it.

According to the blueprints they'd gone over, there weren't supposed to be any cams. But there wasn't supposed to be a fence, either.

"Meet me at the gate," Scourge said. Not bothering to wait for a reply, he broke from his cover, sprinting toward the three-meter-high security fence. Building speed with a dozen quick steps, he launched himself into the air, his cape billowing out behind him. He cleared the fence by only a few centimeters, close enough that he could feel a tingle in the soles of his boots from the lethal current coursing through it.

At the apex of his leap he hung suspended in the air for just an instant; then gravity reasserted its hold and he plummeted to the ground. He landed in a three-point stance, using his free hand to help absorb the impact.

He turned his head quickly from side to side, looking to see if there was any reaction to his sudden arrival. Fortunately, his entrance had gone unnoticed.

Crouched low to the ground, he ran along the perimeter of the fence, heading to the gate he and Sechel had spotted earlier. As he approached, he noticed a single droid posted as a guard.

It was conical in shape, a little more than a meter tall, and half a meter wide at its base. It hovered a meter off the ground, and three long, thin legs dangled below it, each ending in a trifingered claw. A ring of lights encircled the main body two-thirds of the way up, blinking in some indefinable pattern. Scourge's night-vision goggles distorted all colors to varying shades of green, but he could clearly make out a two-tone pattern on the droid's hull—probably gray and orange, Uxiol Droid Manufacturing's corporate colors.

It was clearly a patrol drone, just as Sechel had promised. Assault droids were much larger—at least twice the size—and were usually designed as two-legged walking units. They were covered in thick plate armor, and tended to have heavy blaster cannons mounted on their exterior—neither of which the floating sentry possessed.

The patrol drone's sensors were focused on the gate, not on the Sith warrior bearing down on it from behind. Once he closed to within ten meters, Scourge ignited his lightsaber and launched it with a quick flick of the wrist. The spinning blade easily sliced through the unreinforced plating of the droid's hull and into its control circuits, sending up a shower of sparks before returning to Scourge's hand.

The hovering drone dropped to the ground, its repulsors rendered nonfunctional. Two of its three legs were pinned beneath the conical body; the third jutted out at a strange angle, mangled by the fall. The row of blinking lights flashed erratically, internal sensors overwhelmed by the catastrophic damage. But still the droid managed an awkward spin that brought it face-to-face with the intruder. A panel on its hull slid open, and Scourge could just make out the circular tip of a small internal blaster taking aim as he closed in for the final blow.

The drone fired, but its targeting systems were no longer operational and the bolt flew high and wide. Scourge was on it before it had a chance to try again. His boot delivered a heavy kick, toppling the droid helplessly onto its side. Two quick chops from his lightsaber finished the job, and the row of flickering lights went dark.

Scourge was breathing hard from the exertion. Defeating a droid never gave him the same rush as killing a flesh-and-blood foe, but he could still feel the adrenaline pumping through his veins, washing away his earlier unease about the mission.

With the sentry dispatched, he was able to focus on the control panel beside the gate, though he kept his lightsaber drawn and ready just in case. Fortunately it was a standard layout, and he was able to cut the power to the fence and open the gate with a few simple button pushes. Sechel was already waiting for him on the other side.

He glanced down at the disabled patrol drone as he passed through the gate, and gave Scourge a look that seemed to say *I told you so*. Scourge ignored him and headed for the maintenance door. Sechel scrambled after him.

The small maintenance door was made of heavily reinforced durasteel. Scourge doubted even his lightsaber would be able to penetrate it. Hopefully, he wouldn't have to try.

Sechel stepped up to the security pad beside the door and entered a long series of numbers. Scourge stood watch, in case any more patrol drones appeared. After a few tense seconds there was a soft beep from the security pad, and the door slid open.

"See?" Sechel said. "No alarms. No assault droids. Nothing to worry about."

"We're not done yet," Scourge replied, shouldering past him and into the manufacturing plant.

They found themselves standing in a narrow, dimly lit corridor. If the blueprints they had were accurate, it should lead them into the plant from the rear. From there they would have to cross the production floor to the records office, where Sechel would slice into the plant's network to find out who had paid UDM to manufacture the custom-built droid that had tried—and failed—to kill Nyriss.

"Stay close," Scourge instructed Sechel as he removed his night-vision goggles with his free hand and clipped them to his belt. "If we run into trouble, hide in a corner and try not to get shot."

"That's what I do best," Sechel assured him.

Scourge set off down the hall, Sechel following a few steps behind. It continued straight for about thirty meters, then made a sharp left turn that terminated in a closed door.

Unlike the door that had given them access to the plant, this one didn't appear to be reinforced or locked. From the other side Scourge could clearly hear the deep, rhythmic thud of heavy machinery churning away.

He pressed the access panel on the wall, his muscles instinctively coiling as he dropped into a fighting crouch. The door slid open to reveal the plant's main production floor, and a wave of intense heat smacked him in the face, momentarily taking his breath away. But he relaxed a second later when he realized there was no ambush waiting for them on the other side.

The manufacturing floor was massive—at least a hundred meters across and easily twice as long. Numerous doors and passages lined each wall, dozens of exits all leading to different areas of the plant. A network of metal catwalks and stairwells crisscrossed the room. In the center was the source of the intense heat: four enormous vats of molten metal, each ten meters tall and twenty meters in diameter.

Half a dozen long conveyor belts extended from the vats to run the entire length of the manufacturing floor, each covered with thousands of individual parts and pieces waiting to be assembled into functional droids. The giant engines powering the belts crashed and churned, drowning out all other sound.

Hundreds of bipedal assembly droids lined the conveyor belts, but Scourge knew they didn't present any type of threat. Assembly droids were severely limited in their programming, incapable of performing anything other than the simplest jobs. Unlike the patrol drone he'd dispatched earlier, these would ignore his presence and continue working at their assigned tasks. Apart from the assembly droids, there didn't appear to be anyone around. The plant's flesh-and-blood supervisors would have left for the night long before. Reaching out with the Force, he could sense no other living beings in the vicinity.

"Well?" Sechel asked, trying to peer past Scourge's massive frame to get a better view of what lay beyond the door.

Even though Sechel was right behind him, it was almost impossible to hear his voice over the conveyor belt's pounding engines. Scourge signaled *all clear* and stepped through.

The records office was located in the southwest corner of the plant, adjacent to the manufacturing floor. They'd have to cross nearly the entire length of the room to get there, and Scourge was perspiring heavily under his armor after only a few seconds. The heat was oppressive; the air almost seemed to stick in his throat. The deafening clang of the engines was relentless.

He cast a glance back at his companion. Even though Sechel wasn't wearing armor, he was lagging well behind. Clearly, a life of upper-class luxury had left him thoroughly unprepared for the physical demands of the manufacturing floor's unexpectedly harsh environment.

But he struggled gamely onward, wheezing with every labored step.

The entrance to the records office turned out to be locked.

"Hurry up and get us inside," Scourge shouted. He wanted to get the information and get out. More important at the moment, he knew the office would probably be climate-controlled.

Too weary to nod, Sechel leaned against the wall and punched in the security code.

The door didn't open.

"Try again," Scourge pressed, thinking that in his weakened state Sechel might have hit a wrong key. "Be careful this time."

With painstaking precision, Sechel tapped out the code a second time. The roar of the engines drowned out any sound, but Scourge could see the control panel turn red. The words ACCESS DENIED flashed on the display.

Sechel's mouth moved in an inaudible curse and he tried for a third time, but Scourge already knew it was hopeless. The door required a different code than the one they had used to get past the exterior entrance.

Scourge raised his lightsaber and yanked Sechel out of the way. He heard the man shouting, but couldn't make out the words. Gripping the hilt of his lightsaber with both hands, he brought the blade crashing down on the panel, splitting it in two and carving a long, deep furrow in the wall behind it.

The door sprang open—and suddenly Scourge's eardrums were nearly shattered by a long, whooping siren. He grabbed Sechel by the collar and tossed him into the room, silently cursing himself for making such a foolish mistake.

"Slice into the network and get what you need. I'll hold off security."

Sechel didn't waste time with an answer: He began frantically typing at one of the terminals.

Scourge could feel the cool air spilling out of the records office and washing over him. He allowed himself a few seconds to bask in its luxury, then turned to face the inevitable enemy onslaught, determined not to make any more missteps.

Two hovering patrol drones similar to the one he had dispatched earlier were the first to arrive on the scene, swooping down to floor level from one of the catwalks near the eastern wall. Scourge charged, moving with the supernatural speed of the Force.

The drones opened fire, but Scourge never changed course, relying on his armor to absorb their blaster bolts. One of the bolts narrowly missed his ear; two more slammed into his chest. He felt the impact, but it wasn't enough even to knock him off-stride.

He dropped into a forward somersault as the droids unleashed a second volley, knowing they would be targeting his exposed face and head. The bolts flew harmlessly over him as he tucked, rolled, and then came back up on his feet, finally close enough to retaliate.

The patrol drones were not made for close combat. A series of vicious cuts with his lightsaber put a quick end to the encounter. The droids fell to the ground in a shower of sparks, their spindly legs twitching for a few seconds before they shut down completely.

Scourge turned his attention to the next two patrol drones. He dispatched the first by hurling his lightsaber at it, knocking it from the air with a single well-placed throw before it even got close enough to use its internally mounted blaster.

The second took evasive action, dropping down behind the conveyor belt and a line of assembly droids. It skimmed along the ground, closing the gap until it popped up from behind its cover so it could fire at point-blank range. Scourge made sure it never got the chance.

Reaching out to grab the drone with the invisible hand of the Force, he slammed it back down to the ground. Its legs snapped off and went flying; its exterior hull cracked in multiple places; several of the welded plates tore loose. All the lights on its body went dim.

The alarm sirens were still howling; it wouldn't be long before security droids stationed in other sections of the plant showed up. If the droids kept arriving in small groups of two or even three, Scourge knew he could hold off several more waves at least. If they arrived in greater numbers, he was going to have a problem.

He was breathing heavily, the sweat so thick on his red skin he felt as if he had been swimming in the ocean. The Force had sustained him so far: protecting him from the worst of the heat and allowing him to move faster than his enemies could react. But he could draw on it for only so long before exhaustion set in. Already he could feel himself tiring. Sechel had to locate the information soon, or they'd have to retreat empty-handed.

He saw three patrol drones enter from one of the passages at the north end of the manufacturing plant. Two more were moving in from the east. Grimacing, Scourge tightened his grip on his lightsaber and prepared to do battle yet again. Instead of closing in on him, however, the droids kept their distance.

The reason for their puzzling behavior became clear a moment later when a massive assault droid lumbered into view. Like the patrol drones, it had the gray-and-orange finish common to all UDM models. But that was where the similarities ended.

Three meters tall and covered in thick armor plating, the security droid walked on a pair of hinged-metal legs, each as thick around as Scourge's waist. Its armless body was thick and wide, two meters on every side, topped by a pair of heavy blaster cannons instead of a head.

The droid broke into a run toward him, moving fast despite its bulk. At the same time, it opened fire with both cannons. Scourge leapt for cover behind the nearest conveyor belt, unwilling to trust his armor against such overwhelming firepower.

The security droid didn't let up; the bolts ripped into the conveyor belt and the hapless assembly droids lined up along it.

Crouched low, Scourge ran back toward a nearby stairwell leading up to the narrow catwalks that ran above the manufacturing floor. A shower of twisted, scorched metal rained down on his back—bits and pieces of those assembly droids unfortunate enough to get in the way of the cannon fire.

From the corner of his eye he saw the patrol drones swooping in to join the fray. Because of the engines and sirens, he couldn't hear the assault droid coming after him, but he could feel its heavy footsteps vibrating the floor.

Reaching the stairwell, he took the steps three at a time. The assault droid continued to fire, but it wasn't designed to take out aerial targets. Its bulky armor plating limited its vertical range of motion, and from the floor it couldn't get the proper angle for a clear shot toward the ceiling. Its bolts ricocheted off the reinforced metal of the catwalk's safety rails and floor, but none even came close to its intended target.

Scourge's elevated position on the catwalk didn't help against the patrol drones, however. Their repulsors allowed them to rise up to the level of the catwalks with ease.

With the five hovering patrol drones closing in on him, Scourge raced toward the vats of molten metal in the center of the room. The catwalk he was on passed right beside the nearest vat. As he drew closer, the heat became almost unbearable. He felt his skin blistering, but he ignored the pain and continued onward.

The drones were rapidly closing in. Two of them swooped in from the side, trying to cut him off. Their path took them directly over the vat, and Scourge seized the opportunity. Drawing on his rapidly dwindling reserves, he used the Force to knock one of the drones off-course, sending it careening sideways into its partner. The midair collision wasn't hard enough to inflict any direct damage, but it caused both to spin out of control. Unable to right themselves in time, they tumbled down into the vat, where the bubbling molten metal closed over them.

The three remaining patrol drones altered their course to steer clear of the vats, confirming Scourge's fear that the trick would only work once. They opened fire, but their target suddenly reversed his direction to race back along the catwalk toward the assault droid on the floor below. One of the bolts struck Scourge squarely between the shoulder blades, but luckily it didn't penetrate his armor.

The assault droid continued to fire ineffectually at Scourge from below as he charged at it. He closed the gap until he was directly above it, then grabbed the catwalk's safety rail and vaulted over the side. He landed directly on the square, flat top of the assault droid and chopped down with his lightsaber.

The blade bit deep into the droid's armor plating but failed to reach any of the internal circuitry. The droid shook angrily from side to side, and Scourge was thrown off. Rolling to absorb the landing, he scrambled to his feet and circled behind the droid. He knew his only chance was to stay on its blind side, so it wouldn't be able to bring its blaster cannons to bear.

He slashed at the armor-plated body twice more. The

first blow left a scorched furrow. The second—delivered in precisely the same location—went all the way through. The assault droid reacted with a shudder, momentarily listing to one side. But before Scourge could follow up with another attack, it kicked out with one of its massive legs, catching him in the chest and sending him crashing to the ground.

A sharp pain shot up from his side, and he knew at least one of his ribs had been cracked. The assault droid was slowly, jerkily, turning to face him. The three remaining patrol drones were once again bearing down on him, close enough to open fire.

Scourge scrambled forward on his hands and knees. The assault droid was tall enough for him to crawl under its legs and take shelter beneath its body. The blaster bolts from the patrol drones ricocheted ineffectually off the larger droid's armor plating. The assault droid returned fire, its programming instinctively identifying anyone firing at it as a hostile threat. Its blaster cannons tore through the patrol drones, reducing all three to scrap.

At the same time, Scourge drove his lightsaber up into the assault droid from below. To save costs and improve mobility, the underside of the droid wasn't equipped with the heavy armor plating that protected the rest of its exterior, and the blade went deep. Scourge stabbed the vulnerable underbelly twice more before rolling clear and springing back to his feet.

Staggering, the droid tried to turn to face him. It was leaking thick, black lubricant from where Scourge had sliced it open, the liquid forming a rapidly spreading pool beneath its feet. A muffled explosion came from somewhere inside the droid, and a wisp of smoke curled out. Its legs sagged, and it slowly toppled forward, then lay still.

Scourge didn't have time to savor his victory. A swarm

of patrol drones poured into the room, emerging alone or in pairs from passages on both the north and south walls. At the same time two more assault droids marched into view, and the Sith Lord's spirits sank.

There was no shame in fleeing a battle that couldn't be won; only a fool continued to fight against impossible odds. Yet even if he were willing to risk Nyriss's wrath by abandoning Sechel, Scourge doubted escape would be possible. There were too many droids, and he was nearing the point of total exhaustion.

With a grim smile he raised his lightsaber, prepared to inflict as much damage as possible before he died. And then suddenly everything went dark.

Scourge fumbled for his night goggles, knowing the illumination from his lightsaber wouldn't be enough to fight by. He yanked them from his belt and slid them into place, then stood stock-still, stunned by what he was seeing. None of the droids had taken the opportunity to advance on him. The assault droids hadn't moved; the patrol drones had all fallen to the ground.

Only then did he register the fact that it wasn't just dark—it was silent. The deafening engines had ground to a halt. The conveyor belts were quiet, and even the assembly droids seemed to be frozen in place.

He punched the comlink on his wrist. "Sechel? Are you there?"

"You're still alive?" Sechel asked. He sounded surprised, but before Scourge could ponder that, he swiftly added, "Good. I was afraid you wouldn't make it."

"What just happened?"

"I copied the files I needed from the records office. Then I sliced into the power grid and used the emergency override to shut everything down. Figured you could use the help."

"I could have handled it if it wasn't for the assault

droids," Scourge said, making no effort to hide the accusation.

"Assault droids? Really? Must be a new prototype UDM is working on."

"Where are you now?" Scourge asked.

"Still near the records office."

"Stay there—I'll come get you."

"I don't think we have time for that," Sechel said.

"What are you talking about?"

"You know those big vats? They use trivium generators to melt the metal. Shutting down the power grid destabilized the reactor cores."

"How long before they blow?"

"Not long enough to keep discussing it."

Scourge took the hint. Forcing his weary legs into a run, he raced across the pitch-black manufacturing floor. His broken ribs made it almost impossible to catch his breath, and his thighs and calves were on fire. He caught up to Sechel halfway down the maintenance corridor they had used to enter the building.

He didn't say anything as he ran, conserving what little breath he had for a final push to get clear of the blast radius. He burst through the maintenance door and into the cool night air, Sechel only a few steps behind him.

Jumping the security fence wasn't an option in his current state, so he headed for the gate he'd unlocked for Sechel at the start of the mission. He was slowing down, the weight of his armor sapping the last of his strength; he drew on the Force to give himself a last burst of speed. Sechel caught up with him a few steps before the gate. The blast wave caught them an instant later.

Fortunately, most of the explosion was contained within the plant, preventing them from being pulverized by the concussive force. As it was, they were swept off their feet and sent tumbling through the security gate by a wall of air, sound, and shards of glass. Scourge hit the ground, rolled onto his stomach, and instinctively covered the back of his head as debris rained down around them. He lay there for about thirty seconds, dazed, ears still ringing.

He forced himself to his feet, triggering a coughing fit. The broken ribs made it feel like his chest was being stabbed as he hacked up blood-flecked phlegm. The back of his head and neck were also bleeding: flying glass had cut him in at least a dozen places, though his armor had shielded most of his body.

Confident that none of his injuries was life threatening, he turned his attention to his companion. Sechel lay facedown on the ground beside him, not moving. He hadn't been wearing any armor, and his back was a bloody mess. Though the glass shards had shredded his clothes and the flesh beneath, all of the wounds looked superficial.

Scourge prodded him with his foot until he finally responded with a groan.

"Get up," Scourge wheezed. "I'm too weak to carry you."

Sechel did as ordered, and the pair of them limped back through the forest toward their waiting shuttle. Behind them, the UDM plant burned.

CHAPTER FIVE

REVAN RARELY VISITED the Jedi Temple on Coruscant anymore. Though technically still a member of the Order, he couldn't help but feel like an intruder as he mounted the steps and passed between the twin rows of statues that stood guard at the entrance.

Many Jedi, particularly the Padawans and younger Jedi Knights, considered him a hero, a living legend. But the more conservative Masters held a very different view. Some resented him for leading thousands of Jedi to their deaths in the war against the Mandalorians. Others could not forgive him for the millions of Republic soldiers and citizens killed when he and Malak returned from the Unknown Regions as conquerors. Officially, he had been redeemed and returned to the light, but there were those who still felt he bore the indelible corruption of the dark side.

To be fair, Revan had done little to try to convince them otherwise.

At the top of the stairs he passed through the Temple entrance, crossing the long, marble floor as he made his way to the interior courtyard.

The Council had offered to find a suitable Master to retrain him in the proper ways of the Jedi—an offer he had flatly refused. Revan had learned too much about the Force, both the light side and the dark, to take instruction like some common Padawan. His contrariness might have been overlooked had Bastila not chosen a similar path. At one time she had been the Order's bright young star. But Malak had temporarily turned her to the dark side, and the Council believed that she also needed to be retrained. When she refused, some of them saw a familiar pattern: Revan leading a promising young Jedi away from the accepted teachings of the Order.

Their marriage further exacerbated the situation. The Jedi Order opposed emotional attachments, believing they were a stepping-stone to destruction. They taught that love begat jealousy, which led to the dark side. But Revan had seen its redemptive powers firsthand. It was his love that had brought Bastila back to the light; their emotional bond had wrought salvation for both of them.

Denying or attempting to utterly control emotion, Revan felt, was a fool's game. Jealousy was actually the result of ill-prepared Jedi being overwhelmed by feelings they had never learned to face. Revan believed Jedi could be taught to use positive emotions like love and happiness to strengthen their connection to the Force in the same way that hatred and anger gave power to those who followed the dark side.

Emerging from the entrance hall, Revan was struck as always by the magnificent view. The Jedi Temple had been built atop a massive mountain, its rooftop converted into a huge open-air courtyard that overlooked Coruscant's endless cityscape a full kilometer below. A towering spire had been built on each of the courtyard's corners, and a fifth spire, larger than the others, rose up from the center.

Small clusters of robed figures, a mixture of Jedi Padawans, Knights, and Masters, filled the area. Some made their way quickly through the garden paths on business. Others lounged on benches or by fountains, taking a break from chores or training exercises.

Revan kept the brown hood of his traditional Jedi cloak up to avoid being recognized. He wanted to conduct his business and be on his way as quickly as possible. The sooner he left the Temple, the better.

He hadn't always felt this way. In the first few weeks after Malak's defeat, when he was still being honored and feted as the savior of the galaxy, he had approached the Council with an offer to share his new understanding of the Force with the other members of the Order. He had expected some resistance, of course. The Council was stuck in the old ways. They didn't understand that the Force was alive. They couldn't accept that it had evolved beyond their staid teachings. Yet he had been unprepared for the sheer hostility of the Council's reaction.

Not only did they reject his offer, but a handful of Councilors had wanted to banish him from the Order. Fortunately, cooler heads had prevailed. Revan was a hero. The tale of his redemption and return to the light had spread throughout the galaxy . . . though the sordid details of how the Jedi had stripped away his identity had been carefully excised. The wiser members of the Council understood that the legend of Revan was far too valuable to throw away simply because they no longer had any use for the man himself.

In the end a compromise was reached. The Jedi would not speak out against his marriage to Bastila. Officially, both would still be recognized as Jedi in good standing, with all corresponding rights and privileges. In exchange, Revan promised not to spread his heresy to other members of the Order.

At first, Bastila wanted to reject their terms. But Revan convinced her that an ideological war with the Jedi Council served no purpose. They had done their part; it was time for them to fade from history and live out the rest of their days in peace.

And so they had . . . until Revan started having those blasted dreams.

That was why he was there now. Canderous was out among his own people, seeing if he could find some connection between the war and a planet shrouded in the darkness of eternal storms. He'd been gone several weeks, and Revan had yet to hear back. But rather than sit around and do nothing, he'd decided to do a little investigation of his own.

Moving with long, quick strides he made his way to the spire on the northwest corner of the courtyard. This tower was home to the Council of First Knowledge, a collection of five Jedi Masters and their underlings who specialized in the history and lore of the entire Order. It was also home to the Temple Archives—by far the galaxy's largest assembled collection of documents, data disks, and holocrons. It was often said that if an item did not appear in the Archive records, then it did not exist.

Despite the bold claim, Revan doubted he'd find anything to explain his dreams lurking in the stacks. He'd actually come here in search of something else. *Someone* else. A name from his past.

Massive chunks of his memory were still missing. To fill in the gaps, he'd need to speak to someone who had been with him during that time. Someone who had served beside him in the war.

Malak had been his right hand during the campaign against the Mandalorians. But Malak was dead; Revan would get no answers there. Yet there had been another—a powerful Jedi named Meetra Surik. Meetra had been among the first to join Revan's cause, and she quickly proved herself to be a brilliant tactician and military leader.

Recognizing her potential, Revan had made her a general, giving her control over nearly half of the Republic and Jedi troops under his command. Meetra had been instrumental in defeating the Mandalorians, dealing them a devastating blow during the Battle of Malachor V . . . though at a cost nearly impossible to fathom.

He hesitated only briefly at the door leading into the spire, steeling himself for what he might find. Then he entered the building and mounted the long, spiral staircase leading up to the first floor of the Archives.

Revan had defeated Mandalore shortly after Meetra's victory at Malachor V, effectively ending the war. Then he and Malak had set off into the Unknown Regions, while Meetra had returned to face the judgment of the Jedi Council. She hadn't spoken to Revan since; he didn't even know where she was.

He knew some of the details of what had happened. On her return, the Jedi Council had declared her a traitor for following Revan. They had stripped her of her rank and banished her, branding her as the Exile. According to the rumors, she had left Republic space and simply disappeared. Yet Revan felt there was more to the story.

Meetra hadn't tried to contact him following Malak's defeat. Even if she had left Republic space, she surely would have heard of Revan's redemption by now. The fact that there had been no word from her was disturbing.

Once he had tried to reach out to her with the Force. Serving in battle with someone formed a special bond; even across the breadth of the galaxy he should have been able to get some vague sense of her presence. Yet he had felt nothing. The simplest explanation was that she had become one with the Force, but Revan couldn't allow himself to believe she was dead. After surviving the horrors of Malachor V, an anonymous death in the Outer Rim simply didn't seem fair.

He stepped from the spiral staircase and onto the fourth-story landing, then pushed open the door to the second floor of the Archives. He was relieved to see there was nobody else around; he wanted to do his research in private.

Passing through the tightly packed stacks of data disks, he took a seat at one of the holo-terminals. He wasn't sure exactly what he was looking for, so he simply entered Meetra's name into the index.

Several entries came up, including an official report on Malachor V compiled by one of the Jedi Archivists. He made a mental note of the reference number, retrieved the data disk from its shelf, and inserted it into the terminal.

He spent the next few minutes reviewing the report, but failed to come across anything he didn't already know. Malachor V had been a trap, a ploy to lure the Mandalorian fleet in close enough to the planet to unleash the mass-shadow generator—an experimental superweapon that would draw upon the gravitational anomalies unique to the Malachor system to instantaneously destroy every ship orbiting the planet.

Revan split his fleet in two, giving command of one half to Meetra. While he led his forces against Mandalore's flagship, he ordered his most trusted general to use her fleet as bait to lure the bulk of the Mandalorian ships within range of the mass-shadow generator.

The Mandalorians had taken the bait, and once they were in range Meetra gave the order to engage the mass-shadow generator. The atmosphere exploded in a flash of fire, leaving only ash behind. Everything on Malachor's surface—every plant and tree, every animal and insect—was instantly vaporized by the intense heat. The ground cracked and heaved, leaving deep scars across the blasted landscape.

At the same time hundreds of ships, Republic and Mandalorian alike, were yanked from orbit by the creation of an irresistible gravity vortex at the planet's core. They crashed into the surface of the world, striking with such velocity that their hulls actually penetrated several kilometers into the ground, burying the twisted wreckage and broken bodies. Tens of thousands of lives were snuffed out in a fraction of a second.

Revan's and Meetra's ships had both been safely beyond the range of the superweapon, though whether that was by luck or design Revan honestly couldn't say.

His memories of that time were gone, and looking back on his actions, he couldn't fully explain or justify them. Had he known what was going to happen, willingly sacrificing thousands of his own followers to achieve ultimate victory over the Mandalorians? Or had something in the plan gone horribly wrong?

The report wasn't so ambiguous: it claimed Revan and Meetra both knew what would happen. It declared them criminals of war and mass murderers. The author of the report speculated that Malachor V was proof that even then Revan had already embraced the ways of the dark side.

But Revan wasn't interested in the opinions of some anonymous Jedi Archivist; he only cared for the facts . . . particularly what happened to Meetra after the battle. And here the report was severely lacking.

All he could glean was that she had returned of her own free will to face the Council, which summarily banished her from the Jedi Order and Republic space.

"I should have guessed it was you."

The voice came from behind, sharp with indignation.

Revan rose from his chair and turned to face the speaker. She wore the traditional robes of a Jedi Archivist, though Revan knew she was in fact a Jedi Master. She was young for the position, about Bastila's age, but her hair was platinum white. She had cold blue eyes, and a pale complexion that spoke of a life spent inside the Archives, well sheltered from the rays of the sun.

"Atris," Revan said with a nod and a forced smile, silently cursing.

Once a close friend of Meetra's, Atris had refused to join those who had gone to battle the Mandalorians. A staunch traditionalist, she had shared the unfavorable opinion of Revan common to the older, more conservative Masters. Of all the people who could have interrupted his search, he could think of few he wanted to encounter less.

"Still trying to recapture your lost memories?" she asked a little too smugly, and Revan understood that her arrival was no accident.

Atris must have tagged the report he'd been reading so it would alert her whenever it was referenced. There were no rules or regulations against this kind of security feature, but it was rarely done. As a rule, those who served the Council of First Knowledge respected the right to personal privacy of Jedi visiting the Temple Archives.

Yet even though Revan had sought to keep his investigations private, he had done nothing wrong. And he still needed answers.

"This report seems to skim over some of the relevant details," he said. "Shoddy work," he added on a sudden hunch.

He saw Atris bristle and he knew he'd guessed right: not only had she tagged the report, she'd also prepared it.

"Maybe you just can't see the obvious truth in front of you," she snapped.

Revan smiled. Despite all the Jedi teachings about

peace and serenity, he'd always had a knack for riling up overly sanctimonious members of the Order like Atris.

"Guess I just need your great wisdom to help me understand what I'm missing."

"What makes you think I would do anything to help you?"

"I'm still a Jedi, and Meetra's sentence is a matter of record," he reminded her, suddenly serious. "I have a right to know the truth of what happened. All of it."

"What more is there to tell? She made the mistake of following you. You led her down the path to the dark side. She committed an unforgivable act, and for this the Council banished her."

"It was a desperate act during a desperate time," Revan said. "And the mass-shadow generator was an experimental prototype. How could the Council be sure Meetra even knew what would happen? What if it was all a mistake? A terrible accident?"

"The mass-shadow generator was a weapon of war," Atris replied with a cool, rational calm. "Its sole purpose was death and destruction, and she gave the order to activate it. How is that an accident?"

"But she obviously regretted her actions, and she surrendered voluntarily to the Council. Why wouldn't they show her mercy?"

"They needed to make an example of her." Atris made no effort to hide the bitterness in her voice. "She became a symbol for all those who had defied the will of the Council. Mercy was not an option."

"It can't be that simple," Revan pressed. "My crimes were far worse, yet the Council gave me a second chance."

"You could still be of use to us."

Revan sensed there was something she wasn't saying. "What does that mean? Meetra was a powerful Jedi. Why didn't the Council try to redeem her?"

The archivist shook her head in disbelief. "You really have no idea what you did to her, do you?"

"No, I don't," Revan snapped, allowing his frustration to bubble over. "My memory has more holes in it than a Kaminoan sponge. So why don't you just tell me?"

Atris bit her lower lip and glared at him. Then, perhaps realizing that answering his questions was the quickest way to get him to leave, she began to speak.

"Meetra was much closer to the mass-shadow generator than you were. She felt the shock wave; it nearly killed her. Left her vulnerable. At the same time, she felt the deaths of the Mandalorians and her fellow soldiers through the Force. It was all too much to bear in her weakened state. It would have killed her." She paused for emphasis, before continuing. "Instinctively, she protected herself the only way she knew how. She cut herself off from the Force . . . permanently."

"I'm sorry," Revan said sincerely. "I had no idea."

"Really?" Atris replied angrily. "Then why did you and Malak leave her behind when you went into the Unknown Regions? You realized she was of no further use to you, and you abandoned her. That's why she came back to the Order to face judgment."

"I didn't see that in your report. Is that fact, or just speculation?"

Her refusal to speak was reply enough.

"Even if what you say is true," Revan continued, "I'm not the same man anymore. Is it right to still hold me accountable for those crimes?"

"A chalarax can't change its spots," she muttered under her breath.

Revan was too busy trying to process all he had learned to react to her comment. If Meetra was cut off from the Force, that would explain why he hadn't been able to sense her presence. That meant she could still be alive somewhere; she might still know something that could help him understand the meaning of his vision.

"Do you know where she went?" he asked. "I need to speak with her."

"Haven't you done enough already?" Atris demanded. "It's your fault she defied the Council and betrayed the Order. It's your fault she fell to the dark side and was branded the Exile. It's your fault she cut herself off from the Force. For a Jedi, that's a fate worse than death!"

"I've come closer to death than most," Revan countered, "and I can assure you that's not true."

Atris snorted in contempt. "That is the difference between us. I live for the Force. You live for yourself."

Revan shrugged, knowing a philosophical argument wasn't going to get him any closer to finding Meetra. "Whatever you think of me," he said, "I did not compel Meetra into any of this. She made her own choices. And it should be her decision now if she wants to speak to me again, not yours. If you know where she is, you have to tell me."

"I haven't spoken to her since her trial," Atris answered through gritted teeth, and Revan knew she was telling the truth. "I do not know where she went, and I hope I never see her again. The Exile betrayed the Order, as did you.

"You're not welcome here. Go back home to your *wife*." Atris spoke the last word with such venom, she nearly choked on it.

"Uh, uh, uh," Revan said, wagging his finger at her. "There is no emotion; there is peace."

Her lip curled up in a snarl and she spun on her heel and stormed out of the room. Revan waited until the sound of her feet on the stairs faded, then sat slowly back down in the chair.

With Atris gone, he could let his sarcastic mask slip. Despite what he'd said to her, he couldn't help but feel responsible for Meetra. He'd refused to give Atris the satisfaction of seeing his guilt and grief, but now that he was alone, the emotions came flooding to the surface. Most of his specific memories of Meetra were gone; he could recall only disjointed bits and pieces. But she had once been one of his closest friends, and he still felt a powerful emotional connection to her.

Slumping forward, he buried his face in his hands. He expected tears to follow, but that didn't happen. Instead, he just felt a hollow, numbing sorrow. After several minutes, he took a deep breath to collect himself and rose to his feet. Then he headed out the Archives door and down the stairs.

He'd come to the Temple in search of an old friend and confidante, hoping she could help him understand the dreams that plagued his nights. Instead he'd found a dead end and learned the grim truth about the one they called the Exile.

"No wonder I never come here anymore," he grumbled under his breath as he made his way across the courtyard and headed for the exit.

CHAPTER SIX

A WEEK HAD PASSED since the mission on Hallion. Daily doses of kolto had healed Scourge's wounds; even his cracked ribs were fully mended. But his pride and confidence were still wounded. The mission had been a success, but things had gone a lot less smoothly than he would have liked. No doubt Sechel's report to Nyriss would paint each of his mistakes in the most garish tone.

He was desperate to find some way to vent his frustrations, and today he had finally felt well enough to visit the stronghold's exercise yard for a much-needed workout. He rarely went more than two or three days without practicing his drills, knowing that his continued survival would often depend on his martial expertise.

Though there were others in the yard, none was a worthy sparring partner. He would gain little from testing himself against any of Murtog's soldiers. Even the guard captain himself wouldn't present any real challenge to a fully trained Sith Lord.

Instead he performed a complex routine of drills designed to hone his reflexes, all while wearing his heavy armor. His crimson blade hummed as he cycled through the aggressive thrusts and cuts of Juyo, the seventh form of lightsaber combat. The weapon moved so fast that it was nothing but a blur, but each strike was precise and controlled.

In the middle of his routine he noticed that Nyriss's young Twi'lek slave had entered the yard. She stood patiently off to one side, her head bowed respectfully.

Scourge put an abrupt end to the session, knowing she would be here only if Nyriss had sent her. He flicked his lightsaber off and clipped it to his belt before crossing the yard to her.

"Darth Nyriss wishes to speak to you," the Twi'lek said softly, keeping her eyes focused on the ground.

"Will Sechel be there?" he demanded.

"I do not know, my lord," she replied.

Scourge frowned. He had not seen or spoken with Sechel since their return.

"Take me to Nyriss."

The slave nodded, then turned and set off. Scourge fell into step behind her.

He'd sought Sechel out several times over the past week, but the aide always seemed to be off on some task or assignment. It could have been coincidence, but it was also possible Sechel was avoiding him.

If that was the case, Scourge might know why. During his recovery, he'd had plenty of time to think back on the mission. Rehashing it in his head had brought several inconsistencies to light—things Sechel might not want to discuss with Scourge face-to-face.

The slave was leading him through the east wing of the stronghold. She was moving quickly ahead of him, but with his long legs Scourge had little trouble keeping up. As he walked, he continued to mull over the issue of Sechel.

At the time he'd credited the aide with saving his life by shutting down the manufacturing plant's power grid and disabling the security droids. Now he wondered if that had been an accident. The more he thought about it, the more the evidence seemed to indicate that Sechel hadn't wanted him to survive the mission.

Sechel had obviously needed Scourge's help to get past the drones and the fence outside the plant. And he'd needed Scourge to hold off security long enough for him to slice into UDM's computer network. But after that, Scourge became expendable. Once the droids were deactivated, Sechel no longer needed the Sith Lord to protect him.

What at first sounded like a paranoid fantasy became more and more plausible as Scourge recalled specific details of the mission. He had no way of knowing how long it had taken Sechel to slice into the network, but he'd likely found the files he was looking for in the first few minutes. Looking back, it seemed as if he could have shut down the power grid much sooner than he had.

What if Sechel had waited as long as possible before deactivating the droids, hoping they would have enough time to kill Scourge? From the records room, Sechel couldn't have seen what was happening out on the manufacturing floor. He'd probably assumed Scourge was already dead by the time he shut everything down.

That would also explain why Sechel hadn't bothered to contact him with a warning that the plant was about to explode. He'd only mentioned the reactors because Scourge called him on the holocomm after everything went dark. If Scourge hadn't initiated the holocall, Sechel might have slipped away in the darkness alone.

Sechel's early assurances that UDM didn't have assault droids were also suspect. The units Scourge had encountered could have been experimental prototypes, as Sechel had claimed, but it was also possible he'd known about them all along and hadn't said anything, hoping Scourge would be caught off guard by their arrival.

Three pieces of circumstantial evidence—a possible delay in shutting down the droids, Sechel not contacting him to warn about the impending explosion, and the unexpected presence of the assault droids—weren't enough for Scourge to be certain of anything. Yet the fact that Sechel now seemed to be avoiding him further strengthened the Sith Lord's desire to question him in a very long, very private session. Unfortunately, that talk would have to wait. Sechel still enjoyed Nyriss's protection, and Scourge wasn't willing to risk the Dark Councilor's wrath by interrogating him. Not yet, at least.

They had reached the door to Nyriss's private chamber. Scourge briefly considered whether he should say something about his suspicions to her, then decided against it. Sechel was an expert at political maneuvering; if he was guilty, involving Nyriss would only work in the adviser's favor. Better to confront him directly when the time was right.

The Twi'lek slave knocked lightly on the door, and Nyriss's voice called out, "Enter!" from the other side.

Once again, Nyriss sat at the computer console in the center of the room. As she rose from her chair and turned to face Scourge, the slave closed the door, sealing the three of them alone in the room.

"I was given word you have recovered from your injuries," Nyriss said.

"Nothing serious, my lord," Scourge replied.

"You seem to have a habit of getting wounded in my service."

"I was surprised by the assault droids."

"And I'm surprised they gave you so much trouble."

Scourge remained silent.

Nyriss stretched her dry, cracked lips into an unsettling grin that seemed to fill the entire lower half of her wrinkled face. Scourge endured the rictus without comment until it mercifully faded.

"I find it odd that someone with your reputation would be hard-pressed to defeat a single assault droid and a few patrol drones, yet you dispatched my mercenaries with ease."

It was obvious she was getting at something, but Scourge had no idea what it might be. "I . . . I don't understand," he finally admitted.

"No, you don't," she agreed, briefly flashing another disconcerting smile. "Recite the Sith Code for me," she instructed, sounding like one of the trainers at the Academy.

"Peace is a lie; there is only passion. Through passion, I gain strength." The words came easily to Scourge; the mantra had been drilled into his brain during his training until it was second nature. "Through strength, I gain power. Through power, I gain victory. Through victory my chains are broken."

"You know the words, but you do not truly understand them," Nyriss admonished. "The dark side draws on the most powerful emotions: anger, hatred, fear. We are taught to use our emotions to unlock our true potential and unleash the Force against our enemies."

Scourge pushed down the impatience threatening to rise within him. She was saying nothing he hadn't heard countless times during his apprenticeship, but she must have a reason he wasn't yet seeing.

"The Force runs through every living being," she went on. "When we fight an opponent of flesh and blood, we draw on *their* emotions, as well. All who follow the dark side instinctively do this on some level—it is so instinctive that most instructors feel it does not need to be taught." She paused, and again he wondered where she was going with all this.

"I have studied your records from the Academy and observed your battle with the mercenaries in my courtyard," she said at last. "You have a special gift. You do not just feed on the raw emotions of your foe; you gorge yourself on them. You feast on their primal fear. It amplifies your hate and anger. It fuels the power of the Force. It transforms you into an instrument of death and destruction."

Scourge nodded. Battling a living foe was intoxicating; with each attack and counter he felt a rush of heat coursing through his veins, energizing and empowering him. Yet he had felt almost none of that at the UDM plant. "When I fought the security droid, there was nothing to grab on to. It was cold. Empty."

"Precisely. You tried to feed off its nonexistent emotions, and in doing so only made yourself weaker. I wonder that this wasn't observed in you; even the most powerful gift needs guiding to be used effectively." She shook her head. "You are so used to using your gift that you neglect the most basic source of power: yourself. The next time you find yourself in a similar situation, you must turn your focus inward. Draw on your own emotions, and you will destroy your mechanical enemies as readily as you slaughter your organic ones."

Scourge nodded. He did not like being lectured, but her observation was a good one: he realized that he had, indeed, learned to rely on the emotions of his enemies to feed his power, and he had not seen that such a gift could also be a weakness. But one that, with time and practice, could be overcome.

"A valuable lesson, my lord. One I will take to heart."

"I have enough sycophants working for me," she answered, brushing off his gratitude.

"But none can do what I do," Scourge reminded her.

Nyriss spread her lips into another gruesome smile, and Scourge resisted the urge to shudder as a chill crawled down his spine.

"I hope your restored confidence will serve you well on your next mission," she said. "The files Sechel recovered from UDM proved quite fruitful. He traced the payment for the custom droid sent to assassinate me back to a group of radical human separatists from Bosthirda dedicated to freeing their world from the tyranny of the Emperor and the Dark Council."

Heavy sarcasm dripped from her voice, and Scourge shared her contempt. There were some enemies he could respect; there were some causes he could understand even if he fought against them. This was not one of them.

There were recently conquered worlds that suffered under the Empire's yoke—planets like Hallion, where rebellion was to be expected. But Bosthirda had been part of the Empire for hundreds of years. Its people were full citizens, with all the rights and privileges of those on Dromund Kaas.

Human separatist propaganda might cry out against unfair treatment of their species, but Scourge knew their claims were unfounded. The original Dark Jedi who had taught the Sith tribes the ways of the Force millennia ago had been human. And though their bloodlines had been absorbed into the Sith aristocracy long ago, humans still made up the vast majority of the Imperial population.

There were human slaves, of course, but these were individuals born into the lower ranks of society, or those who had fallen through their own failures and weakness. Unlike other lesser species, they were not persecuted or discriminated against in any real way. There were no laws limiting their movements, no restrictions on what rank or position they could hold.

Humans could rise to the highest ranks of the Imperial military; a number of worlds were even ruled by wealthy and powerful human families; and the Emperor had appointed many humans to serve on the Dark Council. Of the twelve current members, five were human, including Darth Xedrix—the Councilor with the longest active service.

Humans had no right or reason to complain about

their status in the Empire. The separatists were nothing but ungrateful scum and traitors.

"Why did they target you?" Scourge wondered aloud. "Why not strike at the Emperor himself?"

"The Emperor is too well protected," Nyriss said. "Since they cannot get to him, one of the longest-serving members of the Dark Council is the next best thing.

"And they would never strike at Darth Xedrix," she added. "He is human; they probably consider him one of their own."

"What about Darth Igrol?" Scourge asked. "He is Sith, and he has served longer than anyone except Darth Xedrix."

"Igrol resides on Dromund Fels. Killing one of the Dark Council on Dromund Kaas—the Imperial capital—makes more of a statement." She paused. "They may also have chosen me because of my history with Darth Xedrix. Ever since I joined the Dark Council there has been animosity between us. At the time he was one of the most powerful members, yet even from the start he sensed my potential and feared it. For decades he has schemed against me, but I have outmaneuvered him every time, slowly building up my allies and influence while his have dwindled away."

Nyriss wasn't telling Scourge anything new. It was common knowledge that members of the Dark Council typically viewed one another as dangerous rivals, and there were always rumors of shadowy feuds being fought behind the scenes. Scourge believed the Emperor actually encouraged the infighting, since it dissuaded the various members from uniting their resources against him.

Despite what Nyriss claimed, however, her rivalry with Darth Xedrix had been anything but one-sided. Both had seen their fortunes rise and fall and rise again, with neither able to gain enough of an upper hand to eliminate the other.

Somehow Scourge didn't think it would be prudent to mention this.

"The separatists probably see my rivalry with Darth Xedrix as proof I dislike all humans. Untrue, of course, but a well-crafted lie will often serve where truth will not."

Her logic was sound, but the reasons hardly mattered. The separatists had tried to kill a member of the Dark Council. There had to be retribution.

"I will find these traitors and eviscerate them," he declared.

"They've already been found. Sechel was able to use the information he acquired at UDM to locate their base in the mountains of Bosthirda. If they heard about the destruction of the UDM plant, they may be suspicious. We must strike quickly, before they can move to a new location. My people are leaving for Bosthirda tonight; you will accompany them."

"You're sending Sechel with me again?"

Nyriss nodded. "They may have connections to other terrorist groups. Sechel will be able to slice their records and find out who they are working with. I'm also sending Murtog and his soldiers with you. Sechel will be your precision instrument; the soldiers will be your blunt tool."

Scourge would have preferred to leave Sechel behind, at least until he'd had a chance to confirm his suspicions. He briefly considered sharing his concerns with Nyriss, then decided to stick with his original plan of keeping them to himself. He'd just have to keep a close eye on Sechel during the mission, and be wary of walking into any traps. There would be plenty of time to deal with him once the separatists were eliminated and he had proven himself worthy in Darth Nyriss's eyes.

"The human filth will die, my lord," Scourge promised, bowing low. "I will not fail."

CHAPTER SEVEN

FOR THE SECOND TIME in the space of a single month, Revan found himself at a table in the back of the Dealer's Den, surrounded by the dregs of Coruscant.

"You couldn't have just contacted me via holocomm?" he asked Canderous as he took a seat.

T3 obediently rolled underneath the table to sit patiently at their feet, safely away from where the waitresses might trip over him.

"I need to talk to you face-to-face about this," the Mandalorian replied.

"Sounds ominous."

T3 chirped his agreement.

"You still having those nightmares?" Canderous asked.

"Sometimes. I'm dealing with it."

The dreams were coming only two or three times a week now, instead of every night. Revan didn't know if this was because his subconscious was gaining more control over the repressed memory, or if it had something to do with the fact that he was taking steps to investigate his vision. Whatever the explanation, over the past week he had finally been able to grab a few nights of fitful rest. It wasn't enough to get rid of the dark circles under his eyes, but he no longer felt utterly exhausted.

"Tell me what you found," he said.

"I didn't learn anything about a planet covered in storms and eternal night. But I did dig up something you might be interested in."

The astromech droid at Revan's feet beeped twice. It was obvious even to him that Canderous was hesitant to speak.

"I hope you're not waiting for me to try to buy this information from you," Revan joked. "I left most of my credits at home."

Canderous shifted uncomfortably, then leaned forward to speak in a low whisper. "I probably shouldn't be telling you this, you being a Jedi and all, but I think you have a right to know."

"If you're worried I'll go running to the Council with your secret, don't be."

"It's not just them. You can't tell the Galactic Senate, either."

"Whatever you've got to say must be pretty bad," Revan remarked.

"Depends on your point of view."

The big man leaned back in his chair and took a deep breath. Revan stayed silent, giving his friend time to gather himself.

"I got in contact with some of my people, just like you asked," Canderous said finally. "I found out that dozens of the strongest chiefs are gathering their clans at Rekkiad."

Revan recognized the name. Located in the Outer Rim system of the same name, Rekkiad was a virtually uninhabited world of ice and snow.

"They're planning another invasion," he guessed, assuming that was why Canderous was worried about the Jedi or the Republic finding out.

"No, they're not," Canderous assured him. "Not yet, at least. They're searching for Mandalore's Mask. They think you hid it somewhere on Rekkiad."

An image flickered through Revan's mind: he and Malak standing on the top of a glacier, surrounded by a swirling blizzard. It vanished before he could grasp it, retreating into the dark corners of his subconscious. Yet the brief flash of the resurfacing memory was enough to confirm what Canderous had said.

"I think they may be right," Revan muttered.

Canderous was silent, obviously expecting him to say more. But there wasn't anything he could add. The memory was gone.

"You know what the Mask means to my people," Canderous said. "Without it we are lost, vagabonds wandering the galaxy without a purpose. Recovering the Mask could be the key to restoring Mandalorian honor—and power."

Revan knew all this. That was why he had hidden the Mask after slaying Mandalore the Ultimate—a final act to demoralize a defeated foe. He'd hoped it would take the Mandalorians generations to recover from the loss of their most revered cultural symbol. Without it, the war-like clans would be too busy fighting among themselves for power to even think about conquering Republic worlds. But if the Mask were to be found again . . .

"Whoever finds it will be hailed as the new leader of the clans," Canderous continued. "Mandalore will rise again, and the Mandalorians will follow."

Revan knew that Canderous was sharing this knowledge with him out of loyalty. They had been through too many battles together for him to keep this secret. Yet he also understood why Canderous had been reluctant to speak. He was still a Mandalorian, and he feared for the future of his people.

The wounds of the Mandalorian Wars were still fresh

in the minds of the Jedi and the Republic. The looming specter of a Mandalorian army unified by a single war-like leader would not be ignored. Even if the Jedi Council refused to take action again, the Senate would send its fleets to crush the potential threat before it could begin.

In their disorganized and depleted state, it was unlikely the Mandalorians would be able to resist. After the inevitable defeat, the Senate would likely impose martial law over the surviving clans, forcing them to disarm and abandon the customs and practices of their warrior culture. If the Republic found out about this, the Mandalorians as Canderous knew them would cease to exist forever.

"Do you believe the Mandalorians will attack the Republic again if the Mask is found?" Revan asked.

"Depends who finds it," Canderous answered candidly. "Some of the clan leaders want nothing more than to avenge our defeat. Others would rather try to rebuild our society. We were great warriors before we started conquering Republic worlds; it's possible we can restore our honor without violating the treaty terms we agreed to."

The terms I forced you to accept, Revan thought.

It was ironic that Canderous was sharing all this with the architect of the Mandalorians' greatest defeat. Almost a decade earlier, Revan had been one of the few willing to take action against the invading clans. But he was not the same person he was back then. He no longer clung to the simplistic ideals of right and wrong or good and evil. He understood better than anyone that dark and light were intertwined in strange and complex ways. And on some primal level, he knew this was all somehow connected to his visions of a dark, storm-swept world.

The Mandalorians had the potential to be a very real

threat, but his visions had convinced him there was something far more dangerous lurking beyond the borders of known space. The fate of the entire galaxy might rest on the repressed memories trying to break free from the prison of his own mind, and sending a hostile Republic fleet to scatter the clans wouldn't get him any closer to unlocking the truth.

"I'm not going to say anything about this to the Senate or the Council," Revan assured his friend. "But whoever finds the Mandalore's Mask will shape the destiny of your people for the next thousand years. I think it might be a good idea for us to be there when that happens."

A broad grin spread across Canderous's scarred, square jaw, and he reached across the table and slapped the Jedi on the shoulder. "I knew I could count on you."

"Time to get the old gang back together for one last adventure."

"Not everyone," Revan countered. "Juhani and Jolee are Jedi; they still answer to the Council. They might feel obligated to say something about this."

"I got no problem with leaving the cat girl and the old man behind."

"I don't want to get Mission and Zaalbar mixed up in this, either," Revan continued. "They've worked hard to build up a nice import–export business over the past year. I don't want them to throw it all away."

"They would if you asked them to," Canderous noted. "Wouldn't even think twice about it."

"That's why I'm not going to ask. Mission's had it rough her whole life. Now that she's finally got it back on track, I'm not going to mess things up for her."

"Okay, scratch the Twi'lek kid. But what about Zaalbar? That Wookiee knows how to handle himself when things get rough."

"Mission and Big Z are a team. We can't break them up."

Canderous rolled his eyes. "We're getting a little short on bodies here."

T3 whistled loudly, and Revan reached down to give him a reassuring pat on the head. "Don't worry, little fella. You're too useful to leave behind."

The astromech droid whistled again.

"Good point," Revan replied. "HK's a little too trigger-happy to bring on this mission. Things tend to get bloody when he's around."

"You realize we're going to a planet overrun with Mandalorians?" Canderous reminded him. "Bloody is probably unavoidable."

"I'm hoping at least some of the clans can be reasoned with," Revan explained. "If we bring a homicidal assassin droid with us, I don't think they're going to give us much of a chance to explain why we're there."

"We're a little short on bodies," Canderous repeated. "What about that other Jedi who helped you during the war? Not Malak. The one they call the Exile."

"Meetra," Revan said.

"I heard she and the Council had a falling-out."

"I don't know where she is."

"Might be worth tracking her down," Canderous pressed. "She proved herself during the war."

Revan wasn't sure how much Canderous knew about Malachor V and the mass-shadow generator. The mission report was sealed away in the Jedi Archives; he might have no idea that she had lured thousands of his fellow soldiers into a trap. It was also possible he was fully aware of Meetra's actions, and respected her even more for making the ruthless but tactically brilliant decision to sacrifice thousands of her own people to achieve victory. In either case, Revan didn't want to get into the tragic tale of Meetra's banishment and her severance from the Force.

"She may have had a falling-out with the Council, but she's still a Jedi," he lied, doing his best to ignore the twinge of guilt he felt for his role in her ultimate fate.

"So who's that leave, then? You, me, and this half-sized bucket of bolts?"

Canderous gave T3 a playful kick with one of his heavy boots. The droid beeped angrily in response.

"Don't forget Bastila," Revan added.

"I thought you wanted to leave the Jedi out of this."

"She's my wife," Revan answered. "I'm not going to abandon her."

"Hey, it's your call," Canderous said, holding his hands up defensively. "She's welcome to come along. I mean, if you really think you can convince her that heading to the Outer Rim to explore Rekkiad's frozen wastelands is a good idea."

"Well," Revan said with a shrug, "we never did go on a honeymoon."

BASTILA WAS SITTING in the living room when he got home, watching holovids while she waited for him to return. Revan wondered if she'd been waiting long.

He hadn't told her where he was going, and he hadn't told her about sending Canderous off to investigate the Mandalorians—he just hadn't seen any point in worrying her if there was nothing she could do to help. Now that they had a plan, however, he was eager to share it with her. He just had to be careful how he explained it all.

"Sorry," he said as he crossed the room and bent down to give her a kiss. "I didn't know I'd be so late. You shouldn't have waited up."

"That's okay," she said, taking his hand and pulling him down onto the couch beside her. "I couldn't sleep."

Still holding his hand, she turned to face him. "I've got something to tell you," she said.

"Me, too. Big news."

"I bet mine is bigger," she said with a faint smile.

"That's a bet you'd lose," he warned her.

"I'm pregnant."

Revan was stunned into silence for several long seconds. When he finally managed to speak, all he could say was, "Okay, you win."

REVAN COULDN'T BELIEVE he hadn't noticed Bastila's pregnancy earlier. Though there were no visible physical signs of her condition, it should have been obvious. The instant she'd told him, he'd clearly sensed the life growing inside her through the Force.

"I must be getting senile in my old age," he said, caressing her still-flat belly.

"You've had a lot on your mind," Bastila reminded him. "And you haven't been sleeping much."

It was still too early to tell if it was a boy or a girl, but it didn't matter to Revan either way. He and Bastila were going to have a child; it was the happiest day of his life. There was just one small problem.

"Talk about bad timing," Bastila murmured, echoing his own sentiments.

Once he'd gotten over the joyful shock of her news, he'd told her about his meeting with Canderous.

"I have to do this," he said softly. "It's the only way I'm ever going to find out what that vision actually means."

"What if you don't find out?" Bastila countered. "Your nightmares are fading. Maybe in a few months they'll stop."

"Maybe," he agreed, though he didn't believe it. "But I think these are more than just old memories bubbling up. They're a warning. Even if the visions stop, the threat they represent would still be out there."

"Haven't you done enough already?" Bastila asked, her voice rising slightly. "You saved the Republic from the Mandalorians. You saved the Republic from Malak. And in return, you had your identity destroyed and were ostracized by the Council."

She pulled away from him, her anger building. "You don't owe them anything anymore," she insisted. "You've paid for your mistakes. You've sacrificed enough. You've earned the right to live out your days in peace!"

"If I don't do something, nobody else will," he said, shaking his head.

"So what? So nobody does anything. Whatever evil's lurking in the Unknown Regions might not show itself for decades! We could both be old and gray by then. We have a chance to live out our entire lives in perfect happiness. Are you willing to risk throwing all that away?"

It was tempting to give in. It would be easy to pretend nothing was wrong and just live in blissful ignorance like trillions of other beings in the galaxy. There was only one problem with her argument.

"I'm not doing this for the Republic," he explained. "I'm not doing it for you. I'm not even doing it for me. I'm doing it for our child. And our child's children. We might never live to see the horrors that are coming, but they will." He tightened his arm around her. "We have to protect the Republic for them. We have to risk our chance at happiness so they can have a life we might never know."

Bastila didn't answer. Instead she leaned against him, resting her head on his shoulder, and he knew she felt the same way.

"When do we leave?" she asked after a long moment of silence.

"You can't come with me," Revan objected gently. "What if I find something on Rekkiad? Some clue connected to my past? What if it leads me farther into the Outer Rim? Or even the Unknown Regions? We could be gone for months. Maybe longer. Do you really want to give birth on some uninhabited world on the edges of the galaxy? And then what will we do? How are we going to care for an infant under those conditions? I won't risk the life of our child like that. And I know you won't, either."

Bastila reached two fingers up and pressed them gently against Revan's lips. "If I say you're right," she whispered, "will you please shut up?"

He nodded silently.

"Because I can think of better things to do on the last night before you leave than talking."

Revan couldn't have agreed with her more.

BASTILA ACCOMPANIED REVAN and T3 to the spaceport. Canderous was already there, loading supplies onto the *Ebon Hawk*.

The *Ebon Hawk* had served Revan well during his hunt for Darth Malak. Owned by a succession of smugglers and pirates, it was one of the fastest ships in the galaxy. It had enough room to comfortably accommodate a crew of eight—with cargo and supplies—yet a single individual could pilot it when necessary.

Technically speaking, the *Ebon Hawk* still belonged to Davik Kang, a Tarisian crime lord. But Davik wouldn't be coming to reclaim it: he was long dead, his body buried beneath the ruins of Taris when Malak bombed the city-world from orbit.

"Be careful out there," Bastila said.

"I always am," he answered with a smile, wiping a single tear from the corner of her eye.

They didn't need to say anything else; they'd said their

true good-byes in private the previous night. Bastila's years of Jedi training had left her uncomfortable with public displays of emotion, but she stood up on her toes and planted a long, hard kiss on Revan's lips. Then she turned away and quickly left the spaceport.

Canderous raised a curious eyebrow but showed enough restraint not to ask why she wasn't coming.

They finished loading the ship in silence. Twenty minutes later the *Ebon Hawk* took flight.

CHAPTER EIGHT

BOSTHIRDA'S ORANGE SUN WAS SETTING QUICKLY.

Scourge, crouched in the shadows of a cramped alley in the warehouse district on the outskirts of Jerunga, the planetary capital, watched it disappear. As darkness fell, the photosensitive streetlamps kicked in, casting the entire district in a pale yellow glow.

The dim artificial illumination was enough to give Scourge a clear view of the two-story building across the street. From the outside, there was no way to tell that the structure was the separatists' base. There were no autoguns on the roof; no guards patrolled the perimeter. The loading bay doors were ordinary durasteel, rather than the reinforced kind used to construct blast doors. The windows were blacked out, and several security cams panned back and forth, surveying the street, but neither was unusual for buildings in this district.

Instead of military fortifications that might draw unwanted attention, the separatists relied on anonymity and secrecy to protect them. They would be unprepared for the wrath about to rain down upon them.

His comlink beeped softly, followed by Murtog's whispered voice. "Team is in position."

"Hold until my signal," Scourge replied. "Give me time to take out those cams."

"Could be droids in there," Sechel chimed in. "You sure you don't want Murtog's team to go in first and clear the way?"

Scourge gritted his teeth. Did Sechel know about Scourge's difficulties in taking down the droids at the UDM plant? Were his words a way of saying, *I know your secrets; I know your weaknesses*?

On the other hand, if Sechel was just making a joke based on what had happened on their last mission, then Scourge's paranoid overanalysis meant that the slimy little sycophant had gotten to him.

Neither option sat well with the Sith Lord, particularly since he still wasn't sure whether Sechel was trying to get him killed.

"Remember the plan," Scourge snapped. "The two of you stay back until I give the all-clear. We can't risk a stray blaster bolt taking out our Lord's favorite adviser; leave the dirty work to me and your team."

"Understood," Murtog agreed.

Keeping Murtog out of the battle wasn't the best tactical choice, but it was worth it to keep Sechel away from the action. Scourge didn't need to be looking over his shoulder while he was fighting the separatists. Plus, Murtog would be at a safe distance, as well—just in case he turned out to be a co-conspirator.

"I'll send the signal once I poke out their eyes," Scourge said, rising to his feet.

Careful to stay in the shadows, Scourge crossed the street to the building adjacent to the base and crept around the back. There he located the utility ladder running up the side of the building and climbed to the rooftop, from which he could look down on the roof of the separatist base. The gap between the buildings was substantial: nearly ten meters. Scourge measured the distance, took a dozen steps back, then ran to the edge and leapt over the precipice.

He pulled his knees up and tucked into a forward roll as he landed, then sprang to his feet, lightsaber drawn and ready. There were four cams on the roof, mounted on poles at each corner. In rapid succession he reached out with the Force and snapped them off one by one, sending them tumbling from their perches to shatter on the street below.

"Target is blind. Move in," he said into his comlink.

In the street below, small squads of Murtog's soldiers were approaching the building. Scourge waited while they launched their first volley of flash and stun grenades, followed by a round of suppressing fire as the soldiers took cover positions near the door. From inside came the sound of blaster carbines as the separatists returned fire.

Moving quickly but calmly, Scourge crossed the rooftop to the hatch built into the center. A few seconds later it swung open and a pair of separatists emerged—snipers coming to the roof to take a position on the attackers below.

Scourge hacked down the first with his lightsaber, then grabbed the second by the scruff of his collar and yanked him off his feet. The young human looked at him with abject horror, his panic so great that he never even thought to raise his weapon.

The Sith Lord fed on the man's fear, savoring it as the heat of the dark side rushed through him. Effortlessly toting the sniper along, he took three quick steps toward the rooftop's edge, then hurled the man over. The sniper's terrified scream was cut short a second later by his fatal impact with the ground below.

Scourge turned and raced back to the open hatch. He could hear frenzied shouts and blasterfire. An instant later an explosion rocked the entire building, followed by several seconds of silence. Another round of blaster-fire and shouting confirmed that Murtog's team had breached the entrance.

Scourge leapt through the hatch leading into the warehouse's upper floor. There were no interior walls; it consisted of a single massive room. In the far corner a staircase led down to the lower level. A row of mattresses ran along one wall, but the primary purpose of the space seemed to be storage. Crates and footlockers were scattered about, along with a haphazard collection of armor, weapons, and other military equipment. A computer terminal had been set up near the mattresses, along with four blank monitors that would once have shown the images from the security cams on the roof.

Scourge registered all this without conscious thought; his primary focus was on the twenty-odd humans struggling into their combat gear to join the battle downstairs. Unfortunately for them, that was never going to happen.

Like a red wind, Scourge swept through their ranks, slashing left and right, hewing off limbs and decapitating bodies. Violent bursts of the Force picked his victims up and tossed them around like rag dolls, breaking bones and shattering skulls.

The separatists offered virtually no resistance. They had been caught off guard; they hadn't expected an ambush from the roof. These were not soldiers. They were ordinary men and women who had received only the most basic training when they'd joined the cause. Scourge's savage and sudden assault, and the bloody carnage he left in his wake, sent them into a panic. He fed on their primal fears. Some he killed, others he left mortally wounded and writhing on the floor, their lives enduring for thirty or forty agonizing seconds while their high-pitched cries of pain fueled his bloodlust.

Had the separatists coordinated their efforts into a

focused and organized counterattack they might have been able to challenge him. But they just scattered, running for their lives. Scourge drank in their terror and confusion, and felt the growing power of the dark side. He channeled that power and refocused it, sending it out in waves that rippled across the room, further inciting the panicked retreat of his enemies.

When two women managed to resist the onslaught of fear and fight back, he was on them in an instant, cutting them down with a few quick slashes of his lightsaber. Everyone else was running. Some fled downstairs. Scourge let them go; they wouldn't get past Murtog's team. Others tried to hide, cowering behind crates and footlockers. But Scourge didn't need to see them to hunt them down. He could sense them through the Force, trembling and sobbing silently, their minds numb with shock, and he stalked them one by one, breathing hard not with exertion but excitement.

It was over in minutes. Only then, standing alone amid the bodies, did Scourge notice that the sounds of battle from below had ended.

Moving quickly, he crossed the room and descended the staircase. The floor below was similar to the one above: except for a row of offices built along the east side of the building, there were no interior walls; the floor was stacked with crates and piled with supplies. Bodies were scattered everywhere. Most were separatists, but Scourge noticed three or four wearing Nyriss's colors. The rest of Murtog's team were methodically searching the dead, looking for survivors to interrogate.

Scourge shook his head, knowing it was a waste of time. The greatest fear of any separatist organization was betrayal from within. Only the two or three top people would know anything useful, and they would never have allowed themselves to be taken alive.

Confident that the building was secure, he deactivated

his lightsaber and clipped it onto his belt. Then he activated the comlink on his wrist.

"All clear, Murtog. Get Sechel in here."

"We're already inside," Murtog's voice came back to him. "Found their control center in some offices at the back."

Scourge had to clench his teeth to keep from screaming with rage. He had given specific orders, and Murtog and Sechel had willfully disobeyed them.

He made his way toward the offices with long, purposeful strides. As he approached, his anger gave way to suspicion. There had to be a reason they had defied him. Were they simply undercutting his authority, or was it something more sinister. Were they setting some kind of trap?

As he drew near the offices, he saw both Sechel and Murtog huddled at a comm terminal. Surprisingly, there were no other members of Murtog's team nearby. Scourge approached cautiously, probing with the Force to see if he could detect any immediate threat.

Neither turned as he approached; their attention was focused entirely on the comm.

"Are there any others?" Murtog was asking.

"Not that I can find," Sechel replied. "But I might be able to—"

"I gave you two an order!" Scourge barked as he came up behind them.

They both turned to face him. Murtog's lips were pressed tightly together, and he seemed to have gone pale. But Sechel seemed more amused than scared.

"After you were gone I realized a flaw in your plan," he said with an ingratiating smile. "If the separatists had anything incriminating here in the base, they'd probably try to destroy it before we could get our hands on it. I told Murtog I might be able to salvage something if he could get me inside. But the longer we waited, the less chance we'd have to recover anything useful."

Scourge didn't say anything, his eyes fixed on Sechel with a piercing glare.

"We would have tried to contact you, but you'd already started the mission. We didn't want to distract you."

"Do you take me for a fool?" Scourge asked softly, his hand casually falling to the hilt of his lightsaber.

Sechel's smile faded, and Scourge caught a hint of fear in his eyes.

"I don't normally disobey orders," Murtog said, jumping in to try to defuse the situation. "But in this case Sechel was right. Once the separatists knew the battle was lost, they ran a cleaner program on their computers to erase all their datafiles. If we'd waited for your signal, everything would have been lost."

Scourge let the hand drop from his weapon. Now was not the time to settle this. But it was one more thing Sechel would answer for once he finally got a chance to speak with him alone.

"What did you find?"

"A recording of a recent communication," Sechel answered, pressing a button on the terminal.

A ghostly blue, three-dimensional image crackled into being, hovering a few centimeters above the holocomm. The frozen image was slightly under a meter in height, a perfect miniature of the speaker.

"Darth Xedrix," Scourge gasped.

"Most of the call was already erased by the cleaner program," Sechel explained. "But I was able to save this."

He hit another button and the recording began to play. It was obviously damaged; the image flickered in and out of focus, and the audio was plagued by bursts of static that cut off much of what was said.

". . . latest failed attempt . . ." Xedrix said, his voice thin and crackling. "Nyriss is dangerous, and must not be . . . keep allegiances hidden . . . stop the Emperor . . . madness must end . . ."

"Can you get anything more?" Scourge asked.

"Not here," Sechel answered. "Give me enough time and the proper equipment and I should be able to come up with plenty."

"Tell your team to load up every terminal and datafile they find," Scourge instructed Murtog. "Nyriss won't be pleased if we leave something important behind."

Sechel didn't say anything, but the grin on his face spoke volumes.

NYRISS'S PERSONAL SLAVE GREETED them at the front door as the three arrived back at the palace.

"My mistress received your message," she said to Scourge. "She wishes to speak to you at once."

"Get started on those datafiles as soon as Murtog's team finishes unloading them," he said to Sechel.

"Forgive me, my lord," the young Twi'lek said, her voice trembling slightly. "Darth Nyriss wants to speak to all three of you."

Scourge glanced from the slave to Sechel and Murtog, wondering if they knew anything more than he did. They only shrugged.

"Let's go," Scourge said with a brisk nod.

The Twi'lek turned and led them down the now-familiar corridors to Darth Nyriss's personal chamber. As she always did, the slave knocked once on the door and waited for acknowledgment from within.

"Enter," Nyriss called.

The slave opened the door and slipped to the side to allow Scourge, Murtog, and Sechel to crowd into the small room where Nyriss sat at her computer terminal, looking as if she hadn't moved since the last time

Scourge had seen her there. She flicked off the terminal, spun in her chair, and stood up.

"Is it true?" she asked, not even bothering to greet them. "Is Darth Xedrix a traitor to the Empire?"

"We found a recording of a call from him at the separatist base," Sechel said. "They were obviously working with him."

Despite the compelling evidence, Scourge wasn't fully convinced. Xedrix was human, which didn't sit well with some of the Sith pureblood families in the nobility of the Empire. Yet whatever petty prejudices he had endured in his life were insignificant compared with all he had achieved.

Darth Xedrix was the longest-serving member of the Dark Council, having joined a full decade before Nyriss. He had risen to the penultimate position in the Empire, and while Scourge could understand his desire to eliminate Nyriss or other potential rivals, it was hard to imagine that he would be bold enough to challenge the immortal, all-powerful Emperor.

"Xedrix's betrayal makes no sense," he said, feeling confident enough in his analysis of the situation to voice his opinion.

"It makes perfect sense if you know the man as I do," Nyriss assured him. "Xedrix is old and desperate. He knows his position has become vulnerable. Soon the Emperor will have no further use for him. In his arrogance, he thinks he can usurp the Emperor's position and save himself. That is why he plotted with the separatists to assassinate me. He knows those of us currently on the Dark Council would oppose him in his bid for power. He seeks to replace us with new members who are weak and inexperienced. He thinks he will be able to manipulate them and seize control of the entire Council, so that they will follow him when he finally moves against the Emperor."

Her explanation made sense. He had seen firsthand how those in power became desperate when they sensed their positions were threatened.

"It won't be long before Darth Xedrix learns of the attack on Bosthirda," Nyriss continued. "We must act quickly."

"I'm surprised the Emperor instructed you to deal with this," Scourge remarked. "I'd have expected him to order the Imperial Guard to arrest Xedrix."

"The Emperor doesn't know," Nyriss said.

"Darth Xedrix has allied himself with separatists," Scourge insisted. "He's a traitor to the Empire! It is our duty to report him."

"I don't think that would be the best plan," Sechel cautioned, ignoring Scourge and addressing Nyriss directly. "We have little evidence, and your rivalry with Xedrix is well known. If we come forward with these accusations, he will simply deny them. The Emperor is unlikely to act without first gathering more proof. This will give Xedrix a chance to cover up his involvement, or go into hiding."

"Sechel is right," Nyriss said. "The element of surprise is our greatest advantage. Xedrix doesn't know we have exposed his treachery. If we strike now, we can catch him unprepared."

It was obvious her mind was made up, and Scourge could follow the logic of her arguments. Yet he still felt uncomfortable not reporting Xedrix to the Emperor.

"An assault on his stronghold will be difficult," Murtog warned. "We don't have the numbers to overwhelm his defenses, and I don't like hiring mercenaries for a job like this. Too much chance one of them will sell us out to Xedrix."

"Perhaps assassination is the way to go," Sechel suggested. "Do to him what he tried to do to you."

"We would need a particularly skilled and accomplished

assassin," Nyriss said. She looked at Scourge. "Do you think you can get close enough to Xedrix?"

Scourge carefully considered all the variables before he replied. His first instinct was to propose an undercover operation, with him seeking a position on Xedrix's personal staff. Over several weeks he could study the routines of his intended victim and all his servants, patiently waiting for a chance to catch him alone, unarmed and unprepared. But there were no Sith among Xedrix's followers. Many Sith were prejudiced against humans. No doubt the Dark Councilor would never allow Sith too close to him, fearing they might one day turn on him.

Scourge might be able to find some other way to infiltrate Xedrix's inner circle, but as Nyriss had pointed out they needed to act quickly. There wasn't time for a prolonged undercover mission.

"Inside his stronghold he is untouchable," he declared finally.

"There may be a way to lure him out," Sechel said. "The separatists seem to use coded communications whenever they contact Xedrix. If I can replicate the code, I can send a message requesting an urgent meeting at some remote location."

"An ambush might work," Murtog agreed. "Xedrix won't want to draw attention to his treachery. At most, he'll have two or three of his most trusted followers with him. With enough troops we should be able to take him down."

"No," Nyriss said, shaking her wizened head. "Xedrix would sense it coming. Whoever we send will have to hide his presence through the Force until Xedrix walks into the trap."

It was obvious whom she was referring to, but Scourge was still reluctant. "Asking me to kill a member of the Dark Council is not as simple as you make it sound."

"I did not expect you to balk at this task," Nyriss

said. "He has committed treason. He brought this on himself."

"You misunderstand," Scourge said, choosing his words carefully. "The human traitor deserves to die. But he is a Dark Lord of the Sith. Alone, what chance will I have against him?"

"I should have known," Sechel said, grinning. "You're afraid."

"Fighting a battle I can't win isn't brave," Scourge shot back. "It's stupid."

"At least you have the courage to speak your mind," Nyriss said.

"You already have enough sycophants," Scourge replied, glaring at Sechel.

Nyriss flashed one of her ghastly grins, sending a chill down Scourge's spine. Somehow he kept himself from shuddering.

"I think the two of us should continue this conversation privately," she said.

Sechel and Murtog bowed and left without a word. Scourge was pleased to see they were chastened by their sudden exclusion. Nyriss didn't speak until the Twi'lek servant had closed the door behind them.

"You are right to be cautious," she said. "But you underestimate your own abilities."

Scourge's thoughts jumped back to the slaughter at the separatist warehouse; he remembered the energy and exhilaration he'd felt. He could sense his power was growing. His connection to the dark side had never been stronger. But butchering poorly prepared soldiers was not the same as facing highly trained Sith. "Xedrix won't come alone. He'll have me outnumbered."

"Xedrix surrounds himself with acolytes of the dark side. Your talent will let you feed on their power and turn it against them. The greater your opponent's connection to the Force, the stronger you become."

"Strong enough to kill a member of the Dark Council?"

"Against me, you would stand no chance," Nyriss replied. "But Xedrix is old and infirm. And he is human—they are a lesser species. Over the decades, the dark side has exacted too great a toll on his body. He is a hollow shell of what he once was. He holds on to his current position only because of his cunning. His followers obey him without question, too frightened of his reputation to see how age has ravaged his flesh and left him weak."

Nyriss paused, waiting for Scourge's response. He wasn't eager to offer one without carefully considering everything he had learned.

He believed what Nyriss had told him about his own abilities: He had felt the truth of it in his most recent battles. But he wasn't ready to trust her. If Xedrix was really as weak as she claimed, she wouldn't need Scourge's help to eliminate him.

The truth was, Scourge wanted to kill Xedrix. It wasn't just his loyalty to the Emperor, though he firmly believed the only fit punishment for treason was death. He wanted to test himself against a member of the Dark Council; he wanted to prove to himself and to Nyriss that he was worthy of this task. If Darth Xedrix fell to his hand, his name would be hailed and feared throughout the Empire. Nyriss would be indebted to him for eliminating her rival, and the Emperor would reward him for executing a traitor.

It was unlikely he would be chosen to replace Xedrix on the Dark Council. Scourge was still too young, too unknown. He hadn't forged the necessary political alliances or built up a cadre of servants and followers. Yet this would be a bold first step; it would make his name known in the halls of power. And when another vacancy opened on the Council down the road—in five years, or maybe ten—he would be the leading candidate.

"Tell Sechel to set up the meeting," he said.

Nyriss smiled again, but this time Scourge didn't find it so unnerving. Instead, he found himself wondering if it would be her he replaced when he finally ascended to his rightful position.

CHAPTER NINE

REVAN STARED AT the flickering topographic map of Rekkiad on the *Ebon Hawk*'s navigation screens. The glacier-covered world had never been settled; no cities or villages dotted his screen. The scans revealed nothing but a frozen wasteland of ice and snow, stretching off for hundreds of kilometers in every direction.

According to Canderous, the Mandalorians had set up a temporary landing field somewhere on the planet's surface. The clans that had gathered on Rekkiad worked together to maintain and protect the vessels there; it was effectively neutral ground. Outside the landing field, however, each clan laid claim to its own territory—a claim they were willing to fight to defend.

Neither Revan nor Canderous thought it was wise to take the *Ebon Hawk* to the communal landing strip. Outsiders weren't welcome among the Mandalorians. Canderous figured they'd have better luck dealing directly with Clan Ordo, his own people.

The original plan was to land within walking distance of Clan Ordo's base camp and approach on foot. Using spaceports was rarely a preferred option for the kind of smugglers and miscreants who had owned the *Ebon Hawk* throughout its history, and many had installed customized upgrades to allow the ship to land in less-than-ideal conditions. But Revan doubted they had ever intended to visit a world as inhospitable as Rekkiad, and he was starting to have second thoughts.

Gale-force winds hammered the ship's hull, causing it to buck and lurch, and a blizzard of swirling snow and ice limited the range of the *Hawk*'s sensors. To get close enough for the topographic scan, Revan had to bring them in only a few hundred meters above the surface of the world—close enough that one wrong move could send them crashing into the surface.

T3 beeped anxiously at Revan's side, crowding the pi-lot's chair as Revan fought to keep the ship level.

"Get Canderous up here," Revan barked. "Tell him to check those grid coordinates again."

The little astromech droid spun around and sped off in search of the third member of their crew.

A gust of wind caused the ship to veer down and to the left. The safety restraints bit into Revan's flesh as he jammed the throttle forward and yanked back on the stick, pulling the ship up out of a steep dive moments before it hit the ground.

The ship veered off course, and suddenly a massive glacier jutting up from the planet's frozen surface mate-rialized on the nav display.

Revan banked hard to avoid plowing into the wall of ice, but even the lightning-fast reactions of a Jedi couldn't entirely overcome the *Hawk*'s momentum. The ship was spared a direct hit, but its underside clipped a sharp outcropping of ice.

The impact sent the *Hawk* into a spiraling, twisting roll. Revan wrenched the stick from side to side, fighting for control. Using the Force, he was able to anticipate and react to the erratic flight with instantaneous preci-sion adjustments, keeping the ship aloft until it regained its equilibrium.

The immediate crisis averted, Revan took the *Hawk* up to a safer altitude and set the autopilot. Then he slumped in his chair and let out a long, low sigh. After a few seconds he straightened up, readjusted his restraint belts, and checked the instrument panel.

A blinking red warning light confirmed his fears: the impact with the glacier had damaged the landing gear.

Revan muttered a curse under his breath, just as a much louder string of profanity came from Canderous staggering into the cockpit. T3 rolled in after him, beeping indignantly.

"You trying to smash us into gree pulp back there?" Canderous grumbled, plopping down into the copilot's seat. "I thought you knew how to fly this rusted slagheap."

"I thought you said Clan Ordo had set up a camp somewhere on this frozen rock," Revan shot back. "Couldn't see a blasted thing on those grid coordinates you gave me."

"Maybe they moved to another location," Canderous said with a shrug. "Can't have gone too far, though. Not in these conditions. Do a ground scan of the area and they'll probably turn up."

"That's what I was doing," Revan replied through gritted teeth. "Turns out it's a good way to get up close and personal with a glacier."

Canderous glanced over at the warning light. "That why that red light's blinking?"

"The landing gear got smashed up when we clipped the glacier."

"You couldn't just fly around it?"

Revan rolled his eyes.

"Go down for another look," Canderous advised after a few moments of strained silence. "Clan Ordo's gotta be close by."

"Even if we find them, then what? You really expect me to bring the ship in on busted landing gear?"

"You're a smart guy," Canderous answered, shifting to get comfortable in his seat. "You'll think of something."

There wasn't much point in continuing the argument, so Revan let it drop. Yet he couldn't help but wonder at the recent change he'd noticed in Canderous.

As long as he'd known the Mandalorian, he'd sensed an underlying tension in him. Like a soldier in enemy territory, he was always ready for a fight. As a Mandalorian, he was never fully accepted by those in the Republic, and he knew it.

Now, however, he seemed different. He was still gruff and taciturn. But ever since they'd left Coruscant, he'd been less grim, more relaxed. He was eager to be back among his own people, and he wasn't about to let a few minor setbacks like a missing camp or damaged landing gear stop him.

To be fair, Revan had no intention of abandoning their quest, either. There was too much at stake to turn back. Which meant Canderous was right: the only real option was to keep looking for Clan Ordo's camp and hope they got lucky.

Revan brought the *Hawk* in low again, but this time he throttled it back to half speed. The swirling winds still made for a rough ride, but at least he'd have more time to react if something went wrong.

"See if you can do something to give our sensors a boost," he said to T3.

The little astromech chirped with pleasure and extended a small probe from a panel in his side to interface directly with the *Hawk*'s systems.

While T3 worked, Revan began a standard search pattern with the original coordinates for the camp at the center. Taking the *Hawk* around in ever-widening circles, he spiraled outward, letting the sensors scan the ground for signs of life. Suddenly T3 began beeping excitedly. Canderous leaned forward to look at the scanner's display.

"I think your droid's got some rust on the brain," he said. "I don't see anything."

Revan knew better than to doubt the little astromech. "Can you enhance the image?" he asked T3.

T3 responded with a low whistle, and a second later a static-filled thermal image appeared on the screen. The details were difficult to make out, but it appeared to be a small collection of tents and temporary shelters built against the leeward side of a small mountain of ice and snow.

"Could be them," Canderous admitted, reaching out one of his massive hands to give T3 a friendly pat on the head. The droid squawked an indignant protest, and he quickly pulled his hand back.

"Doesn't look like there's a landing strip at the camp," Revan noted. "See any place for us to touch down?"

The display zoomed out as T3 adjusted the *Hawk*'s scanners to pan rapidly back and forth across the snow. A few seconds later they zoomed in again.

"Perfect," Revan said with a smile. "Nice work, Tee-Three."

"Uh . . . that's not a landing strip," Canderous cautioned. "It's a giant snowdrift."

"With the landing gear shot, we're going to need something to cushion the blow when we hit the ground."

"You really think this'll work?"

"Sure," Revan replied. "But you'd better strap yourself in, just in case."

Canderous scrambled to lock in his safety belt as Revan sent the *Hawk* into its descent. T3 scooted across the cockpit to the metal braces anchored to the floor and locked his wheels in with a metallic *thunk*.

Fighting wind and gravity, Revan struggled to keep the damaged ship level as he took it down. Seconds before they touched ground, a blast of wind grabbed the *Ebon Hawk* and pitched it hard to starboard. Revan jammed the stick to port, desperately trying to keep the ship from flipping over. It slammed into the snowbank at a forty-five-degree angle, carving a fifty-meter-long trench in the powder before finally coming to rest.

Looking through the small cockpit window, Revan could see nothing but blue-white flakes; the entire front half of the ship was buried in the drift. But the sensors indicated that, apart from the already damaged landing gear, the *Hawk* had survived relatively unscathed. More important, so had its passengers.

Revan carefully unbuckled his safety belt, knowing he would have bruises where the straps had dug into him during the collision. Beside him, Canderous was doing the same. T3 simply unlocked his wheels from the braces and rolled free.

"I guess sometimes it's not so bad being a droid," Canderous groaned as he stood up, rubbing his right shoulder with his left hand.

"You mean like when you're marching through a blizzard?" Revan asked. "This snowdrift's at least five kilometers from the campsite."

Canderous only grunted in reply.

While the big Mandalorian gathered the gear and supplies for their trek from the cargo hold, Revan and T3 ran diagnostics on the *Hawk* to determine the full extent of the damage.

"Doesn't look too bad," Revan commented when they were done. "Think you can fix it up while we head off to the camp?"

T3 beeped twice.

"It's going to be hard for you to keep up out there in

the snow," Revan reminded him. "Besides, someone has to stay and guard the ship."

The astromech reluctantly whistled his consent.

"You get started on repairs; I'll go give Canderous a hand."

It took them almost an hour before they were ready to venture out into the frigid wasteland. They were bundled up head-to-toe in thick winter garb: snow pants, hooded jackets, scarves, goggles, heavy boots, and fur-lined gloves—all of it white to provide camouflage in case they ran into trouble.

Canderous had armed himself with a heavy repeating blaster carbine. He offered a similar weapon to Revan, but the Jedi shook his head.

"You don't want to be swinging that lightsaber around when we get to the camp," Canderous said. "Jedi aren't too popular out here."

Revan frowned, then nodded. He knew Canderous had a point, but he didn't relish the idea of lugging the massive gun along. He picked up a pair of blaster pistols. "I'll get by with these," he said, sliding them into the straps on either hip.

"Suit yourself," Canderous said with a shrug. Then he added, "When we get to the camp, let me do the talking. Remember: these are my people."

"I can live with that," Revan said, hitting the switch to lower the cargo hold's loading ramp. "But if we're going to get there before dark, we'd better get moving."

They maneuvered the hoversled they had loaded up with supplies down the ramp and out into the raging blizzard. The howling wind threatened to knock them off their feet and made conversation almost impossible. The swirling snow almost blinded them, but Revan had entered the camp's coordinates on a portable locater to keep them on track, and he used hand gestures to communicate their route to Canderous. The heavy layers of clothing made the subzero conditions bearable; the hard labor of trudging through the snow over uneven terrain helped warm them up, too.

After almost two hours of slow progress, Revan saw the dim outline of a small mountain ahead of them. He signaled to Canderous, indicating that the camp was on the other side. The Mandalorian nodded, and signaled back that they needed to step up the pace. Revan nodded his agreement. The light around them was fading as Rekkiad's sun—invisible through the storm—slowly set. The last thing they needed was to have to press on in total darkness.

As they skirted the base of the mountain and reached the leeward side, the wind died to almost nothing. It wasn't long before they could see the soft glow of lights from the camp.

Gradually more details of the camp came into view. There were roughly a dozen small tents set up only a few meters away from a sheer wall of ice at the mountain's base. Set away from the tents was a roughly constructed shack; Revan noticed a pair of generators hooked up to it, no doubt to provide power and heat, and he guessed it doubled as a meeting room and a supply center for any stores that would suffer if left out in the cold.

Several sleds were scattered among the tents, some laden with supplies, others empty.

On the far side of the camp were four large, tarp-covered mounds. Revan's heart sank.

As part of the terms of the surrender, he'd ordered the Mandalorians to disassemble their infamous Basilisk war droids—great metal beasts the Mandalorians often rode into combat. Judging by the size of the covered objects, and by whatever hints of shape weren't obscured by the tarps, some of the defeated had chosen to ignore his decree.

"One more step and we paint the snow with your brains!" a voice shouted out.

Four sentries rose up into view from behind the drifts, two on either side of Revan and Canderous. Dressed in heavy cold-weather clothes of mostly blues, golds, and browns, they were armed with blaster rifles, which they had carefully trained on the interlopers.

"Lay your weapons down and identify yourselves!" The speaker—a male—was the sentry closest to Revan on his left.

Out of the corner of his eye, the Jedi could see that Canderous was holding his ground, careful to avoid any sudden movement but not making any effort to obey the order. Revan decided the smart thing to do would be to follow his lead.

"My name is Canderous of Clan Ordo," the big man shouted. "And I don't lay down my weapons for anyone!"

From the stunned silence it was clear his name had gotten their attention.

"How do we know you're really Canderous?" one of the other sentries demanded. This was also a man's voice, deeper than the first.

"Well, Edric," Canderous replied, "I could punch you in the face until I straightened out that crooked beak of yours, but we'd probably all freeze to death before I finished."

The sentry barked out a laugh, slung his gun over his shoulder, threw his arms wide, and ran to enclose Canderous in a fierce hug. "It's good to see you again, brother!" he shouted.

Revan was relieved to see that the other sentries had also lowered their weapons. They came forward to form a tight circle around Canderous as they clasped his hands, slapped him on the back, and offered loud traditional greetings in Mando'a.

After a few minutes the one Canderous had called Edric spoke up again.

"Let's get you and your friend out of the cold," he said in Basic. "Leave your sled; we'll have someone else come get it."

The other three sentries stayed at their post as Edric led Revan and Canderous through the camp toward the supply shack in the center. As they passed the tents, heads poked out to see what was happening; shortly a small crowd had grown in the newcomers' wake. Revan could hear a buzz of excitement building, but his Mando'a was too rusty, and he couldn't pick out what was being said.

At the door of the building, Edric stamped his boots clear of snow before going inside; his guests did the same.

The first thing Revan noticed was the warmth. His goggles fogged up, and he was only too happy to remove them to get a better view of the surroundings.

As he had suspected, the shack served as both supply hut and meeting room. There were seven or eight Mandalorians already inside the building, lounging among the crates and packages, using them as makeshift furniture. In one corner was a massive pile of coats, scarves, and gloves. Edric was already stripping off his cold-weather gear and tossing it on the pile. Revan quickly and gratefully followed suit.

Canderous didn't have a chance to do the same. The instant he removed his goggles and unzipped his hood to expose his face, he was swarmed. Another round of traditional Mando'a greetings rose up from the well-wishers, and Revan couldn't help but notice the pure joy on his friend's face as he was reunited with the other members of his clan.

One of the things Revan had always admired about the Mandalorians even as he'd fought them was their loyalty. The ties that held a clan together went beyond friendship and even family; it was an essential part of the culture, ingrained in children from the day they were born or adopted into the clan.

Not wanting to detract from the moment, he stood a respectful distance away. He was just beginning to wonder how much longer the celebratory reception would continue when the door swung open and a tall, broad-shouldered figure forced its way into the room.

The door slammed shut, and everything went silent. Nobody spoke as the figure peeled away the layers of clothing, revealing the face of an attractive woman. She had olive skin, and her straight, shoulder-length black hair was streaked with purple and red highlights. Her high, sharp cheekbones were tattooed with intricate blue swirls. Her eyes were also blue, but so pale they looked like shards of ice.

Unlike everyone else they had come across, she didn't rush over to greet Canderous. Instead, she glared at him without saying a word.

"*Su cuy'gar*, Canderous," she finally said.

It was a common Mandalorian greeting, but something about the way she said it made Revan think the literal translation of the words—So you're still alive—was closer to her true intent.

"*Su cuy'gar*, Veela," he replied softly.

She took a step toward him, then snapped her head to the side to stare at Revan. She was tall enough to look him in the eye.

Without looking back at Canderous, she asked him in Mando'a, "Do you want me to speak Basic so the Outsider can understand us?"

"I understand well enough," Revan replied in her native tongue.

Veela arched her eyebrow in mild surprise, then turned

her attention back to Canderous. "What are you doing here?"

"Is that any way to greet a clan-brother?" Canderous asked.

"Are you still my clan-brother? You left us after the war. You deserted Clan Ordo to become a mercenary."

"There was no Clan Ordo after the war," Canderous snapped back at her. "Tegris was dead. We had no leader. We were scattered. Broken. Defeated. I wasn't the only one who left."

"We heard you were working for the Jedi," Veela said, her voice low and hateful.

In the silence that followed, the sentry called Edric spoke up. "*Cin vhetin*," he said, and there was a general murmur of agreement from the others in the room.

The literal translation of the phrase was "driven snow"—appropriate given the conditions outside. But Revan knew that the true meaning of the phrase was closer to "The past is in the past." The Mandalorians believed that once you took up the arms and armor of the clan, your past was irrelevant. Edric was saying that whatever Canderous had done over the past few years was irrelevant now that he had returned.

From Veela's expression, it was difficult to tell if she agreed with him. But she let the matter of Canderous's past drop.

"I'm the leader of this clan now," she insisted. "I still have a right to know why you're here."

"To help Clan Ordo find Mandalore's Mask."

Veela tilted her head to the side, as if getting a different angle might help her see whether Canderous was being completely honest with her.

"And what about this Outsider?" she asked, pointing to Revan.

"He is my friend. My brother. He will help us in our search."

"Do you have a name, Outsider?" Veela asked.

"His name is Avner," Canderous said, cutting Revan off. "He's a mercenary. We met while I was working for Davik Kang."

"You can't speak for yourself?" she asked, still focused on Revan. "I thought you understood Mando'a. Am I going too fast for you?"

"I understand," Revan answered. "You speak well."

There was a gasp from the crowd, followed by the sound of stifled, nervous laughter.

Revan knew full well the insult he had given. The Mandalorians were warriors; they had nothing but contempt for diplomats and politicians. They valued actions over words, and he'd just implied that Veela was all talk.

"Brother Canderous vouched for you, so you can stay," Veela said through clenched teeth. "But if you betray us, I'll kill you. If your weakness causes one of my people to get hurt, I'll kill you. If you slow us down, I'll kill you. Is that clear?"

"Wait . . . what was that second one again? Maybe I should write this down."

There was another round of stifled laughter. Veela pretended not to hear it as she turned back to Canderous. "Welcome home, brother," she said flatly.

She grabbed her winter gear, quickly threw it back on, and left without saying another word. Once she was gone, the others in the room seemed to relax.

Revan motioned to Canderous, calling him over to join him in the corner before he was swallowed up in a crowd of old friends.

"*Avner?*" he whispered in Basic. "That's the best name you could come up with?"

"What's wrong with *Avner?*"

"You just rearranged the letters in *Revan.*"

"Relax. Nobody out here's going to—" Canderous

stopped abruptly as he noticed Edric ambling toward them.

"Don't judge Veela too harshly," the sentry said, misinterpreting their hushed dialogue. "She's a good leader, but she has a temper." He looked at Revan. "You should remember that the next time you provoke her."

"I just got caught in the middle," Revan protested. "Canderous is the one she's really mad at. I get the sense you two have a history."

"You could say that," the big man admitted. "She's my wife."

CHAPTER TEN

SCOURGE HAD BEEN WAITING inside the cave on Bosthirda for nearly an hour when he finally heard the faint sound of a speeder landing outside. A few minutes later he heard footsteps coming down the passage. He smiled. Unlike his previous missions for Nyriss, this time he was not plagued with doubts and uncertainties. The anticipation of the coming kill kept him well focused on the task at hand.

As expected, Darth Xedrix hadn't come alone. A pair of Sith acolytes—humans, one male, one female—preceded him, striding into the cave, lightsabers drawn. They wore light armor under robes of blue and gold, the colors of their liege.

The circular cavern was only ten meters in diameter and dark. The only illumination came from their blades and the glowing fungus that clung to the rough rock walls. Scourge crouched in the shadows, wrapped in a cloak of the dark side that both made him invisible to the Force and helped to ward off the chill of the subterranean air. He remained motionless as the pair passed within a few meters of his hiding place, patiently waiting.

Darth Xedrix trailed his escort by several paces. Unlike his acolytes, he had not drawn his weapon, and he wore no visible armor beneath his robes. He was several centimeters taller than Scourge, but much thinner. He had thick, shoulder-length white hair, but no beard. His face was lined, though not as extensively or deeply as Nyriss's, and there was a hint of a stoop to his shoulders and a cautious frailty about the way he moved.

His appearance recalled Nyriss's words: *He is human—they are a lesser species. Over the decades, the dark side has exacted too great a toll on his body. He is a hollow shell of what he once was.*

Yet Scourge could sense the Councilor's enormous power. Darth Xedrix was still a member of the Dark Council, and underestimating him would be a fatal mistake.

The moment the tall human passed Scourge's hiding place, Scourge leapt, igniting his lightsaber as he flew through the air. For a moment he thought his first strike would find its mark, and he was almost disappointed at the thought of ending Xedrix's life so easily. But at the last instant the human's own blade materialized seemingly out of nowhere to intercept the blow.

They exchanged a quick flurry of thrusts and parries. Scourge tried and failed to draw on his foe's fear and anger—Xedrix was too controlled, and it felt more like fighting a droid. Scourge forcibly thrust his own fears away and reached deep inside himself to find the fury he needed.

He had maneuvered himself so that he was behind Xedrix, blocking the passage that was the only route into and out of the cave. The two acolytes had already spun around and rushed in to join the fray, and he prepared himself to deal with them, too.

But suddenly he had only those two to deal with as Xedrix backed away. He seemed to be more obsessed with preserving his own life than killing his enemy—a weakness that left him content to let his two underlings face this unknown foe while he stayed at a safe distance.

The two apprentices launched themselves at Scourge, unleashing their rage as they drew on the power of the dark side, unaware that their anger was feeding their opponent, as well.

The female came in high, her lightsaber slashing at Scourge's head. At the same time the human male came in low, looking to chop at his enemy's legs.

Scourge ducked under the woman's blows, spinning to the side as he parried the lightsaber at his knees. The pair came at him again, once more coordinating their attacks, this time trying to flank him on either side. Scourge lunged forward, splitting the attack by diving into a forward roll that took him between his two opponents.

For an instant he was vulnerable; one quick cut from either foe could have ended his life. But they were inexperienced, and they hadn't expected him to move *toward* them. By the time the woman reacted with a backhand swipe of her weapon, the moment had been lost. The lightsaber hummed by his cheek as he tumbled between them, but he emerged unscathed.

The man was slower to react. By the time Scourge was back on his feet, the acolyte was only just starting to turn around. The Sith Lord delivered a quick kick to the back of the man's knee; the man pinwheeled his arms as he fought to regain his balance.

Scourge saw the opening and delivered what would have been a lethal blow had the woman not thrown herself between them and parried the blow. Her move was reckless and foolhardy, but Scourge hadn't been expecting it, and her impulsive reaction saved her companion. It also exposed her weakness.

The female was the more dangerous opponent, but she obviously cared for her partner. She was willing to put herself in harm's way to defend him—a flaw Scourge could easily exploit.

He abruptly changed tactics, shifting from the conventional defensive positions of the Soresu form to the acrobatic attack sequences of Ataru. Taking two quick steps to gain speed, Scourge leapt at the nearby cavern wall, planted both feet on its vertical surface, then pushed off hard to launch himself in a spinning flip over the man's head.

His opponent tried to turn and pivot to keep Scourge in front of him, but the furious burst of action was too fast for his lightsaber to track. He was late bringing his blade up to protect his head, once again exposing himself to a lethal strike.

This time when the woman moved in to protect her partner, Scourge was ready. He had purposefully directed his leap so that he came in at a sharper angle than necessary, leaving barely enough room for the female to come between him and his supposed target. When Scourge suddenly redirected his blade mid-leap to strike at her instead, she instinctively stepped back to absorb the impact with her own weapon. But with her partner crowded directly behind her, there was no room. Their bodies collided and their feet tangled together, sending both of them crashing awkwardly to the ground.

Scourge landed beside their prone forms. He brought his heavy boot crashing down on his fallen foe's face, relishing the wet crunch of cartilage and bone beneath his heel. Her body spasmed, the muscles locked in the seizures of her death throes.

The man had scrambled to his feet, but instead of throwing himself at Scourge, he only stared at the woman's twitching corpse. Scourge could taste his horror and fear; they gave him a fresh burst of energy. He lashed out with the Force, striking the man in the chest hard enough to send him stumbling back several steps into the cavern wall.

The man struck the rough-hewn rock hard enough to knock the lightsaber from his hand, leaving him unarmed. With a casual flick of his wrist, Scourge sent his own lightsaber spiraling toward his defenseless foe. At the last second, the man threw up his hands in a vain effort to protect himself, but the glowing blade easily sliced through his palms and throat before ricocheting back to Scourge's waiting grasp.

As the human's corpse crumpled to the ground, Scourge was already turning to face his last remaining foe. Darth Xedrix was standing motionless in the center of the cavern, watching the action with a cool, detached reserve. His lightsaber was still drawn, but he held it casually at his side, the blade pointed toward the floor.

"I know you," he said, his voice echoing off the chamber's stone walls. "Nyriss's new pet. Lord Scourge." He wrinkled his features in distaste. "Why do you purebloods always choose such ludicrous names for yourselves? Do you think it's intimidating?"

Scourge didn't reply. Instead he raised his blade and began a slow, cautious advance.

Xedrix laughed. "Are you really that stupid, Scourge? Has Nyriss actually convinced you that you have the strength to stand against a member of the Dark Council? Has she promised you riches and power if you defeat me?"

"She didn't need to promise me anything," Scourge answered. "You are a traitor to the Empire. It is my honor and duty to kill you."

"Ah, now I understand," Xedrix said with a smile, twirling his lightsaber at his side. "She played on your loyalty to our glorious Emperor. How quaint."

Scourge stopped, suddenly aware that he didn't feel any fear emanating from his foe. There was no anger, either. He didn't get any sense of emotion coming from Darth Xedrix at all, and he realized the old man was consciously shielding himself from Scourge's awareness.

Scourge concentrated his focus, reaching out with the Force to pierce the veil Xedrix had wrapped around himself, only to find nothing but a swirling maelstrom of dark side energy.

Scourge broke into a run, charging at his enemy the instant he understood the nature of the trap. Xedrix had kept him talking while he gathered his power for a single, lethal attack.

Xedrix raised his left hand and unleashed his power in a storm of purple lightning. Scourge instinctively used the Force to throw up an invisible barrier to shield himself. The bolts arced through the air, ripping through the shield to engulf Scourge in electric agony.

He screamed, his voice rising above the hiss and crackle of the fiery energy coursing through his veins. Every nerve in his body exploded in excruciating pain as the lightning seared his flesh, cooking him in his own armor. He fell to the floor, curled into himself, his skin blistered and burned. The whole thing had taken only a few seconds.

"You didn't realize Nyriss sent you here to die, did you?" Xedrix mocked. "She never expected you to kill me. You were nothing but a message, a warning."

Ignoring the terrible pain, Scourge somehow forced himself to his feet. Xedrix raised an eyebrow in mild surprise.

"Is that what you call the attempts on her life?" Scourge gasped. "A warning?"

Xedrix laughed again. "You think I'm the one who hired those inept assassins? Nyriss has you twisted in knots. She's using you for a game far beyond anything you can imagine."

Scourge shook his head, trying as much to shake off

the residual effects of the lightning as to deny Xedrix's words.

"You feel your strength returning, do you?" Xedrix observed. "Think carefully before you challenge me again. I might not let you live next time."

"Why *did* you let me live?" Scourge wanted to know.

"You have potential," Xedrix said. "And thanks to you, I have need of some new apprentices. I could find a use for someone with your talents."

"You want me to betray Nyriss?"

"What do you owe her?" Xedrix demanded. "She used you. She sent you here to die just to make a point."

Scourge didn't answer. Instead, he was thinking back on everything that had happened since he'd first entered Nyriss's service. Nyriss had admitted to hiring the mercenaries to test him, but even after that, he'd still suspected Sechel of plotting to kill him. Had the conniving adviser merely been following Nyriss's orders all along?

"Nyriss betrayed you. Swear loyalty to me and I promise you the chance for revenge."

Everything Xedrix said made perfect sense, but on some deep, primal level Scourge felt he was being twisted and manipulated. The old human's words seemed to slither into the cracks and crevices of Scourge's mind, burrowing into his thoughts.

No! his mind screamed in silent protest. *It's a trick!*

But was it? Nyriss had convinced him he could kill Darth Xedrix, but a single burst of dark side lightning had nearly killed him instead. The only reason he was still alive was because Darth Xedrix was toying with him.

What if he's not toying with me? Scourge suddenly wondered. *What if he tried to kill me but failed?*

Nyriss had said that Xedrix was old and frail. She'd claimed the Force had ravaged his body; she'd said he only held on to his power through reputation and cunning. What if he was relying on those same tools right now?

Scourge reached out with the Force again, trying once more to catch a glimpse beneath Xedrix's veil. To his surprise he sensed something this time. Fear. Desperation. And almost no trace of the dark side burning inside his enemy.

All the pieces clicked into place. Nyriss was right: Xedrix was a shell of what he had once been. The entire time Scourge had been battling the two apprentices, Xedrix had been gathering his strength for a single surprise attack. When his apprentices fell, he'd stalled for even more time by taunting Scourge. And he still hadn't been able to gather enough power to kill his enemy.

The blast of lightning had taken everything the old man had in reserve. In Xedrix the flame of the dark side had become the faintest flicker. When he saw that Scourge had survived, he'd realized his only chance of survival was to trick him into switching sides. He'd tried to use the faint echo of the Force to dominate Scourge's mind, augmenting it with persuasive words in a form of temporary hypnosis. But he lacked the strength even for that desperate gambit.

The brilliant bluff had almost worked.

"Your words are hollow, Xedrix. Just like your power."

Scourge marched forward with grim determination. Xedrix brought his lightsaber up, but Scourge used his own blade to slap it aside with ease. The strength of the blow sent the weapon tumbling from the old man's frail grasp, the blade extinguishing as the hilt clattered onto the stone at their feet.

Xedrix staggered backward. He no longer pretended power: he looked desperate and afraid. "Please, Lord Scourge, I'll give you anything you want. Slaves. Wealth. Power."

"Power?" Scourge snorted in contempt. "You can't give what isn't yours."

He slashed his blade diagonally across Xedrix's chest, slicing him from shoulder to hip.

The old man gasped once before falling over backward, his eyes frozen wide in horror, seeming to stare up at the stalactites growing from the cavern ceiling.

Knowing that Nyriss would want proof of his death, Scourge reached down and grasped a fistful of the old man's hair with his free hand. Then he slowly drew his lightsaber across the Dark Councilor's throat, the glowing blade cauterizing the wound as he neatly severed the head.

He left the rest of the body—along with the corpses of the two apprentices—in the cave as he trudged back up the passage leading to the surface. As he walked, he couldn't help dwelling on Xedrix's warnings about Nyriss.

Much of what the old man had said to him had been lies, but the best lies were always built on layers of truth. It was entirely possible that she was using him. At the very least, he could assume she was keeping secrets from him.

Confronting her directly would be a waste of time. Fortunately, there were other ways to get information.

Despite the possible consequences, Scourge decided it was finally time for his private talk with Sechel.

CHAPTER ELEVEN

REVAN SHIVERED IN THE COLD. *Beside him, Malak said something, but the fierce wind whipping across the plateau devoured his words.*

"What?" Revan shouted.

"Are you sure it's here?" Malak called back.

"It's here," Revan said with a nod. "I can feel it."

"Maybe it's on the other side."

Revan glanced over at the other peak rising up beside them, barely visible through the swirling snow. It was nearly identical to the one they were on—a tall, narrow column of wind-carved ice and snow rising up several kilometers from Rekkiad's surface, its peak worn to a smooth, flat plain of ice.

"It's this one," Revan answered confidently. "The entrance is around here somewhere."

The two figures moved slowly back and forth across the exposed plateau, searching with the Force as much as with their eyes.

"Here!" Malak shouted. "I found it!"

Revan woke from the dream with a start, his mind groggy as he tried to get his bearings.

It was cool in the thermal tent he and Canderous

shared. The insulated lining kept out the worst of the weather, but the nighttime temperatures were still low enough that Revan felt a chill through two layers of clothes and his sleeping bag.

As his eyes adjusted to the soft glow of the small heater in the center of the tent, he was able to make out more details of his surroundings. Canderous was still asleep beside him, wrapped tightly in his sleeping bag and snoring loudly.

Revan's mind began to reassemble the bits and pieces from the previous night.

He'd hoped Canderous would offer more details about his marriage to Veela after she'd stormed out of the supply shack, but he'd stayed silent on the subject. Despite his curiosity, Revan hadn't pressed him.

Instead they'd spent the rest of the night celebrating the big man's return to his people. Edric and the others offered up countless tales of Canderous's youth. His many battles and victories against overwhelming odds were the stuff of legend among Clan Ordo.

They'd also offered up plenty of *kri'gee*, a bitter Mandalorian ale. Not wanting to be resented as an outsider, Revan had matched the other revelers drink for drink. The vile beverage packed plenty of kick; he hadn't had a hangover this bad since his wedding night. His head was spinning, his eyes were blurred, and his mouth tasted like he'd been chewing on bantha fur. He'd still be sleeping it off if not for the dream.

No, not a dream. Another memory bubbling to the surface.

He and Malak had been searching for something here on Rekkiad. Something that was somehow connected to Mandalore's Mask. He didn't know what it was, but with a little help he might be able to use the details of his dream to figure out where they had been looking.

He peeled back the sleeping bag and immediately

felt goose bumps prickling up on the flesh beneath his long-sleeved shirt. Ignoring the cold, he picked his way through the semi-darkness until he found his personal holocomm lying under a pile of clothes in one corner of the tent.

Scooting back into the warmth of his sleeping bag, Revan activated the device. "Tee-Three, can you read me?"

A tiny holographic image of the droid materialized in front of him, beeping with concern.

"Everything's fine," Revan reassured in a whisper. "Just try to keep it down. Canderous is still asleep."

The astromech's response was an excited whistle, though the volume was slightly lower than before.

"See? I knew you'd be able to put the *Hawk* back together without my help."

T3 beeped indignantly.

"Yeah, that snow gets everywhere. But it'll melt. Besides, you can worry about that later. I need you to do something for me. Start scanning the topography maps for two massive columns of ice standing close together. Two or three kilometers high, at least. When you find them, send me the coordinates."

There were roughly thirty seconds of silence on the other end before T3 chirped a reply.

"Great work, Tee-Three. Remember, keep an eye on the ship. I'll call you if we need anything else."

Revan turned off the holocomm, knowing the easy part was over. T3 might have been slightly annoyed with him, but dealing with the droid was going to be a whole lot easier than getting the snoring giant beside him up and moving.

"Wake up," he said, reaching across the heater to shake Canderous out of his slumber. "We need to talk."

Canderous grumbled something profane in Mando'a at him and rolled over onto his other side.

"It's important," Revan said, shaking him even harder. "You have to get Veela to move the camp."

"Huh? What? What about Veela?" Canderous mumbled, opening one eye.

"You have to get her to move the camp."

The eye closed again. "That's her call, not mine. She's the clan chief."

"I think they're looking for Mandalore's Mask in the wrong place."

Both eyes snapped open, and Canderous levered himself up to a sitting position. "Well, why didn't you say so?"

"EVERYBODY'S HERE," Veela declared. "Say what you have to say."

Revan's head was still pounding from the *kri'gee,* and in the close quarters of the supply shed her voice was loud enough to make him wince.

Including Canderous and Revan, a total of eight had gathered for the impromptu council. Veela had called them together at Canderous's insistence—three men and two women. Edric was there, and Revan recognized most of the others from the night before, though he couldn't recall their names.

"We have to move the camp," Canderous told them.

As when they first arrived, Revan and Canderous had decided to let Canderous do most of the talking. It would be easier to convince the Mandalorians if they heard the idea from one of their own—provided Veela was willing to listen to anything her husband had to say.

"Move the camp?" she asked incredulously. "You think it's so easy to just pick up and go?"

"It took our scouts weeks to find this location," one of the other women chimed in.

"This is a good spot," Edric agreed. "We're sheltered from the worst of the wind and snow. The mountain protects us from getting flanked, and the only way in is right past our sentries."

"Give me one good reason we should move," Veela demanded.

"Because we'll never find Mandalore's Mask if we stay here," Canderous answered.

There was a long moment of silence, his words hanging in the air.

"Nobody knows where Revan hid the Mask," Veela said quietly. "The clans have each staked out their territory, hoping it's in their destiny to find that which we all seek."

"Seems like a poor way to choose a leader," Revan offered.

Veela glared at him, but it was one of the other women who replied.

"Fate will make the choice for us. Whichever clan is destined to find the Mask, will."

"Is that how all the clans ended up here on Rekkiad?" Revan countered. "Fate? Chance? Blind luck?"

"You show your ignorance when you speak of things you don't understand," Veela said. "Fate and destiny are not the same as luck. It was not chance that brought us here. It was persistence. Perseverance. We are here because we are *strong*." She paused a moment, then continued a little more calmly. "When Revan hid Mandalore's Mask, most of our people scattered in disgrace. But some of us refused to give up. We stayed behind to look for what was lost instead of running off to become mercenaries and hired thugs."

As she spoke, her eyes flicked toward Canderous. Revan followed her gaze to see his friend staring at the floor in shame.

"For years we have kept up our search," she continued. "We know Revan disappeared for three days after the massacre at Malachor Five. There are only a handful of stable hyperspace lanes in that sector, only a few dozen habitable planets he would have been able to journey to in that time. So we have been searching each world in turn, scouring the surface meter by meter. On the first world there were less than fifty of us; it took us two years to explore the entire planet. But with each world our numbers grew. More clans joined in the search, and each clan's numbers increased. Our quest gave us purpose; it united us as a people once more."

She looked back at Canderous. "Slowly those who turned their backs on the Mandalorian ways have come trickling back. Now we number in the thousands. Over a hundred clans have gathered on Rekkiad. If we fail to find the Mask here, we will move on to the next world. And our numbers will continue to grow. Eventually we will find what we seek. And when one of our own finally reclaims Mandalore's Mask, our numbers will be legion. On that day the new Mandalore will call upon the armies of our people, and we will answer!"

She turned and glared at Revan once more. "That is what we mean when we speak of fate," she concluded. "We will find what we seek. It is inevitable. It is the destiny of our people."

The end of her speech was marked by a solemn silence. Looking around the room, Revan could see the power her words had on the other Mandalorians. Even Canderous had been moved.

"I can help you achieve your destiny," Revan promised. "I know where Revan hid the Mask. Listen to me, and I will help you find it."

"Impossible," Veela said with a shake of her head. "Nobody knows where he hid Mandalore's Mask."

"I have access to resources you don't," Revan insisted, choosing his words carefully. "Republic records. Military transcripts. Battle plans. Flight paths and navigation charts. You say you aren't even sure if the Mask is on

Rekkiad. But I am. The Mask is here, on this world. And with my help, Clan Ordo will be the ones who find it."

Veela didn't say anything at first. Instead she turned and fixed her gaze on Canderous. "Avner is your friend," she said, her words almost an accusation. "Can we trust him?"

"I wouldn't have told him of our search if I didn't trust him with my life," Canderous answered without hesitation. "And I wouldn't have brought him if I didn't believe he could help us."

All eyes focused on Veela as she considered all she had heard.

"Where do you suggest we move our camp to?" she finally asked.

"About fifty kilometers from here two columns of ice rise straight up, towering several kilometers above Rekkiad's surface."

"The Twin Spears," Edric blurted out excitedly. "Are you saying the Mask is there?"

"There is an entrance to a tunnel in the plateau on top of one of the pillars. The tunnel leads deep into the heart of the ice. I believe that is where Revan hid Mandalore's Mask."

"The Twin Spears are in Clan Jendri's territory," Veela warned. "If they catch us moving in on their turf, there will be blood."

"Did you really expect to find the Mask without having to fight for it?" Canderous asked.

Veela shook her head. Then she turned her attention to the rest of her advisers, scanning their faces, reading their emotions.

"Pack up the camp!" she shouted at last, thrusting her fist into the air. "We're marching on the Twin Spears!"

REVAN WAS AMAZED by the efficiency of the Mandalorians. Veela's order spread quickly through the camp, prompting everyone into a flurry of activity. Each individual had a specific job, which they carried out with military precision. Some took down the tents, wrapping them into tightly rolled bundles and packing them away into footlockers along with small personal items. Others emptied the supply hut, loading the crates of food, generators, heaters, and fuel onto the heavy cargo sleds.

Within an hour they were under way, all trace of their old camp left behind as three dozen men and women headed out in a long, well-spaced column.

A team of six led by Edric scouted up ahead to find the best path and to make sure the way was clear. Another half dozen fell farther back to guard the column's flank. The rest marched in pairs between the two patrols; while one pulled the cargo sled, the other marched alongside with weapons drawn, wary for an ambush. Every hour the partners would switch positions.

In the middle of the column, the six Basilisk war droids trudged along, each towing a massive cargo sled loaded with hundreds of kilos of gear. To Revan, they looked like five-meter-tall, two-legged dragons. They walked with heavy, lumbering strides, their wings folded beneath their long metallic bodies. High-powered laser cannons were mounted on their flexible, armored necks, allowing the droids to fire in all directions. Each was controlled by a single pilot seated atop the curved spine.

Not surprisingly, Veela was one of the pilots; commanding a Basilisk war droid was an honor reserved for only the most revered warriors of the clan. Revan couldn't help but notice Canderous casting wistful glances at the great metal beasts, recalling his own days of glory now that he was forced to walk beside them.

Veela set a grueling pace, which offered plenty of distraction from both idle thoughts and the biting cold. When they stopped for a one-hour break at midday, Revan felt as if he might collapse into the nearest snowbank. All he wanted to do was eat his food and rest up for the next leg of the journey, but that was not to be.

Like the night before, a steady stream of visitors came by to speak with Canderous. The older members of Clan Ordo came to recount stories of past adventures they had shared with him. Some of the younger ones who had been raised on tales of his exploits came to see the living legend with their own eyes.

Even as an outsider, it was obvious to Revan that his friend had been fully accepted back into the clan. But there was more to it than the mere joy of a prodigal son's return. The Mandalorians were energized, excited. Gossip had spread through the camp, and everyone seemed to know that Mandalore's Mask might soon be in their grasp. And though Veela had technically been the one to give the order to move out, everyone also seemed to understand that Canderous's arrival had been the true catalyst for this call to action.

The break ended far too soon for Revan's liking, but by calling on the Force to revitalize his tired limbs, he managed to stand up and get his feet moving when they set out again.

Darkness came well before they reached their destination. Edric and his scouts had discovered a small valley carved into the ice where they could take shelter for the night, and Veela called a halt to their march. The camp was set up as quickly and proficiently as it had been struck earlier that morning, and Revan soon found himself in a tent with Canderous, curled up in his sleeping bag on the verge of dozing off.

He estimated that they had covered thirty kilometers on their trek. The realization that they had gone well over half the distance already came as a welcome relief, allowing him to drift off into much-needed sleep.

There were no dreams to plague him that night,

though he did wake up once when he heard someone fumbling at the entrance to the tent.

"Someone's outside," he whispered to Canderous before realizing he was alone in the tent.

A few seconds later the exterior flap was pulled aside, letting in a blast of cold air. Canderous followed in its wake. He sealed the flap, quietly crept back over to his sleeping bag, and wrapped himself inside.

"Where've you been?" Revan whispered.

"Sorry. Tried not to wake you," Canderous replied.

"You didn't answer my question."

"Veela and I had some catching up to do," the big man said, and even in the darkness Revan could tell he was grinning from ear to ear.

They didn't speak again, but Revan couldn't help noticing the irony. When he'd left his wife behind to come here, he'd never imagined that Canderous would be reuniting with his own. He didn't begrudge Canderous his happiness, but it made him miss Bastila all the more.

They broke camp early the next morning, and by the time they stopped for lunch they could clearly see the distant outline of the Twin Spears through Rekkiad's perpetual ice fog and swirling snow.

"We're well inside Clan Jendri's territory," Veela said, coming over to sit beside Revan and Canderous as they tore into their rations. "Gotta stay sharp."

"Do you think they know we're here?" Revan asked.

"Hard to say. If they're anywhere near the Twin Spears, the scouts would have seen us by now. But it's a big territory. They could be a hundred kilometers away in any direction."

"Maybe we'll get lucky and they'll never know we're here," Revan said optimistically.

Veela glanced over at Canderous and shook her head.

"We Mandalorians have a saying," Canderous explained. "A warrior who doesn't hope for battle has no hope during battle."

"That's a good one," Revan admitted. "But here's one I like: You can't lose a battle you never fight."

"You can't win it, either," Veela said.

They finished their food in silence. Once they were done, the group set out again. Two hours later they reached their final destination, a small, low-lying patch of ground nestled between the Spears.

"Sleep well," Veela announced to her followers as they set up camp. "Tomorrow Clan Ordo will claim its destiny!"

THE ATTACK CAME just before dawn. Subconsciously, Revan felt the danger through the Force, causing his eyes to snap open a split second before the sentries sounded the alarm.

He was alone in his tent again. Obviously Canderous had decided to spend another night with Veela.

Knowing his friend would meet him on the battlefield, Revan kicked free of his sleeping bag and struggled quickly into his layers of clothing. Remembering his promise to Canderous, he tucked his lightsaber out of sight beneath his belt, arming himself instead with the twin blasters he had been carrying since they'd left the *Ebon Hawk*.

The sounds of battle could already be heard outside, and Revan charged from the tent to join the fray. All around him he saw the men and women of Clan Ordo, most clad only in underclothes and a few scraps of plated armor, battling the forces of Clan Jendri that were swarming in from all sides. Clan Jendri outnumbered Clan Ordo by almost two to one, though Revan noticed they had only four Basilisks.

The Basilisks swooped back and forth above the battle, raining blasterfire down from the sky. Immediately

Revan recognized the Jendri strategy: they had concentrated their attack near the Ordo Basilisks, hoping to keep Veela and her fellow pilots from reaching the deadly machines.

Revan opened fire with his blasters, drawing on the Force to augment his accuracy. His first volley dropped an enemy soldier charging toward him; his second took out a sniper half hidden on a ridge over twenty meters away. But he knew the battle wouldn't be won by blasters alone.

He sprinted across the center of the camp, heading toward the rear where the Ordo Basilisks were parked. Enemy blasterfire poured down, forcing him to duck, dodge, and weave, but none of the bolts found a mark.

Canderous and Veela had managed to get there ahead of him. Basilisk fire had them pinned down behind an outcropping of jagged, snow-tipped rocks, along with the rest of the Ordo Basilisk pilots.

Revan skidded to a stop, dropping to his knees and sliding the last few meters across the icy surface to join them. Canderous flashed him a fierce grin.

Moving in unison, Canderous and Veela popped up from behind the rocks to fire at the enemy war droids. The blasterfire ricocheted harmlessly off the armor plating, and they were forced to duck again when the Basilisk's rider veered it around to return fire.

"Welcome to the party!" Canderous shouted to Revan. "Got any bright ideas?"

"Have you tried shooting the pilots?" Revan asked.

"Easier said than done," Veela answered.

It was true; the Mandalorians riding on the back of the war droids were held in place by heavily armored saddles that protected most of their bodies. A few key spots near their heads and shoulders were vulnerable, but hitting a moving target that size would require a small miracle, even for Revan.

"All we need is to buy a few seconds," Veela said. "Just enough time for us to get into our Basilisks and fire them up."

Revan nudged Canderous with his elbow, drawing the big man's attention as he dropped the blaster from his hand and moved his open palm to cover the lightsaber hilt under his belt. Canderous responded with a faint nod.

"I can create a distraction," Revan said. "But you'll have to move fast."

"Whatever you're thinking, do it," Veela said. "If we don't get to our Basilisks, we don't stand a chance."

Discarding one of his blasters, Revan leapt over the rock, drawing and igniting his lightsaber in a single motion. The glowing green blade instantly drew the attention of all four Jendri Basilisks, as the pilots swung their beasts around to target the hated Jedi who had suddenly appeared in their midst.

Revan had fought plenty of Basilisks during his campaign against the Mandalorians. The trick was to keep moving and get in close enough to limit the effectiveness of their blaster cannons. Though capable of achieving high speeds during a bombing run or charging enemy lines, the droids were slowed down by their heavy armor whenever they tried to turn or change course.

He charged the nearest rider, zigzagging to keep the Basilisk from getting a clear shot. Running directly beneath the belly of the low-flying beast, he leapt high in the air to slash his lightsaber across the droid's tail. The energy blade ricocheted off the armor plating, but not before slicing through one of the stabilizing fins at the tip.

The pilot tried to pull his Basilisk into a steep climb so he could loop around and come diving back down at Revan—a difficult maneuver even without a missing stabilizer fin. The damaged droid tried to respond to his command, but it veered wildly out of control, turning on its side and nearly dumping the rider to the ground.

Revan took the opportunity to leap on the Basilisk's back, grabbing hold of the back of the pilot's seat. The Mandalorian reached back over his shoulder to grab at the stowaway, but Revan easily avoided his grasp as he slid his lightsaber tip through the back of the seat and through the pilot's torso.

The Basilisk screamed as the semi-sentient droid felt the death of its rider through the symbiotic link the Mandalorians shared with their mechanical mounts. Left without guidance or direction, the simple artificial intelligence programs reverted to a primal attempt to rid the Basilisk of its new rider; the thrashing sent the Basilisk into a deadly dive.

Revan leapt clear just before it hit the ground. His fall cushioned by the snow, he rolled, sprang back to his feet, and turned his attention to the three remaining Basilisks.

He wasn't surprised to see them circling high above him, well out of the reach of even a Jedi's leap. Just as he had learned how to fight Basilisks during the Mandalorian Wars, their riders had also learned the best strategies to use when facing a member of the Jedi Order. If they stayed at a distance and coordinated their fire, it was only a matter of time until they brought Revan down.

Fortunately, he wasn't fighting alone. His distraction had given Veela and the other Clan Ordo riders the time they needed. As the Jendri pilots prepared to retaliate against Revan, six Ordo Basilisks took to the air in attack formation.

Now outnumbered two to one, the Jendri pilots banked their war droids away from the enemy squadron and fled. Instead of pursuing, the Ordo riders turned their attention to the enemy forces on the ground.

The battle quickly turned into a rout. Even with superior numbers, the Jendri troops couldn't match the awesome firepower of half a dozen Basilisks. The carnage lasted less than five minutes before the Jendri ranks broke.

Revan didn't bother to participate in the final stages of the slaughter. He'd known the battle was over the instant Veela and the others took to the sky.

He looked around for Canderous and found him perched atop one of the Basilisks, screaming out a Mandalorian war cry as he arced back and forth across the field, butchering his enemies. Such vicious savagery was typical of Mandalorian warfare, and yet Revan knew that once the battle was over, Clan Jendri would hold no grudge against the victors. If Mandalore ever rose again and called them to fight alongside Clan Ordo, they would answer without hesitation.

His thoughts were interrupted when a great shadow passed over him, followed a second later by the heavy thud as Canderous brought his Basilisk in for a landing a few meters away.

"Better put that thing away," he said, leaping to the ground and nodding at Revan's lightsaber.

"Why, you think Veela's going to forget I have it?" Revan asked. But he extinguished the blade as he spoke.

"I doubt anyone other than the pilots saw what happened. No point advertising what you really are any more than we have to."

Revan changed the subject. "You think they'll try another attack?"

"No," Canderous said.

"You sure? I get the feeling they don't like us being in their territory."

"They fled the battle." Canderous grinned. "It's our territory now." His grin grew wider. "Felt good to fly into battle again."

"Where'd you get the mount?" Revan asked.

"Belongs to a young man named Grizzer. He still hasn't been tested in battle, so Veela told me I could use it if we ran into any trouble."

"When'd she tell you that?"

"The other night."

"You mean when you were sharing her tent?"

Canderous shrugged.

"What does Grizzer think about that?"

"Veela's the clan leader. He'll do what she says."

"And what's she going to say now that she knows I'm a Jedi?" Revan wondered.

"Guess we're going to find out," Canderous said as Veela's Basilisk swooped in to land beside them.

The Clan Ordo leader didn't say a word as she climbed down from her seat. She walked toward the two men, her expression unreadable.

"Go help with the wounded," she said to Revan. "You Jedi are good at that, right?"

He nodded.

"After that get some rest. Both of you. Tomorrow we climb the first Spear. Be ready to leave at daybreak." Her words were calm, almost casual, but there was a fierce intensity in her eyes that made Revan wonder if he'd made an enormous mistake.

CHAPTER TWELVE

"I WASN'T TOLD to expect you back yet, Lord Scourge," the guard at the gate said.

"Maybe Darth Nyriss didn't think you needed to know my schedule," Scourge replied, his tone dripping with acid.

The guard nodded and buzzed Scourge in.

Scourge moved quickly down the stronghold's halls, hoping his rebuke had shocked the guard into not reporting his arrival. The truth was, Nyriss didn't know he was back yet. He had been expected to contact her immediately after the mission to kill Darth Xedrix was over, but he'd stayed silent, hastening his return journey to Dromund Kaas so he could question Sechel before anyone else knew he had touched down on the planet. He'd arrived late at night, and if he was lucky, he'd catch Sechel asleep in his room.

In the servants' wing he paused at the large wooden door and tested the handle, expecting it to be locked. To his surprise, it turned silently in his hand. Was Sechel expecting someone? Or was he merely so confident in his position as Nyriss's favorite that he believed himself safe?

Scourge entered the room, silently locking the door

behind him, then crept through the darkness to the bed where Sechel lay sleeping beneath the covers. Reaching out, he placed his gloved hand firmly over Sechel's mouth.

Sechel woke with a start, thrashing and loosing muffled cries into Scourge's palm. The Sith Lord pressed down harder and leaned in close.

"Cry out for help and you're dead," he whispered in Sechel's ear. "Do you understand?"

Feeling the adviser nod, Scourge slowly drew his hand away.

"Lord Scourge?" Sechel asked softly. "Is that you? It's hard to see in the dark."

"No light," Scourge warned, knowing someone might see the glow from beneath the door and decide to investigate.

"I trust your mission went well," Sechel said. Scourge couldn't see the expression on the adviser's face, but he detected the faintest tremor in his voice.

"You're going to answer my questions," Scourge said.

"Of course, my lord," Sechel replied, reverting to the fawning, ingratiating tone he'd adopted at their first meeting.

"Meekness will not save you tonight," Scourge said. "The truth is your only hope of surviving this interrogation."

He pulled a short, sharp blade from his belt and pressed it against Sechel's cheek. "My first question is a simple one: Has Nyriss been using me?"

"My lord, why would you think—*mmph!*"

Scourge jammed his hand over Sechel's mouth, cutting off his words. Then he drew the edge of his blade slowly along the base of one of the fleshy tendrils dangling from Sechel's cheek.

The smaller man screamed in agony, but his cries were swallowed up in Scourge's glove. Scourge kept a steady pressure on the blade so that the fine edge sliced cleanly through the tendril, severing it. Blood began to weep from the wound.

Scourge waited until Sechel's spasms had stopped before he pulled his hand away. To his credit, Sechel was smart enough to limit further reaction to a soft whimper.

"When I ask a question, I want a direct and immediate answer," Scourge said. "So I will ask again: Is Nyriss using me?"

"Of course she is," Sechel mumbled. "She uses everybody."

"Was Darth Xedrix really working with the human separatists?"

"Yes."

Scourge analyzed the response, focusing on the tone, pitch, and inflection. Sechel was speaking the truth.

"Did Xedrix actually try to kill Nyriss?"

When Sechel hesitated, Scourge responded by slamming his hand over his mouth again. Ignoring the muffled pleas, he lowered his blade to the adviser's face and severed another tendril.

"Next time I take an eye," he said once Sechel had recovered from the pain. "Remember, direct and immediate answers."

Lying took thought and effort. It took time. Forcing a subject to answer quickly was a simple but effective tool.

He removed his hand again, ready to slash Sechel's throat if he cried out for help. Again, the adviser had the survival instinct to hold his tongue.

"Again: Did Xedrix actually try to kill Nyriss?"

"No."

The answer was spoken sullenly and resentfully, but Scourge could sense the truth behind the attitude.

"Who hired the assassins?"

"Nyriss did. She wanted to draw suspicion away from herself."

"Suspicion? Suspicion of what?"

"Ask her yourself!" Sechel spat.

Scourge sighed and clamped his hand over Sechel's mouth yet again. But before he could bring the blade to bear, the door swung open with such force it nearly broke free from its hinges.

Darth Nyriss stood on the other side, framed by the light of the hallway's glow lamps.

"I will answer all your questions," she said calmly, "but if you harm Sechel again, I will end you."

Scourge tossed the knife aside and slowly stood up from the bed. His heart was pounding, and he had to fight against the urge to go for his lightsaber. He'd known there were risks in coming after Sechel; now all he could do was hope his actions hadn't cost him his life.

"I assume this conversation will be in private?" he asked.

She nodded and turned away. Scourge didn't even look back at Sechel as he followed Nyriss out into the hall.

Darth Nyriss was silent until they reached her private chamber. Scourge was surprised to find that her Twi'lek slave was not present. It seemed that whatever was about to be said could not be trusted even to the Twi'lek's faithful ears.

"Are you loyal to the Empire?" Nyriss asked him.

"I thought I would get to ask the questions," Scourge replied.

"Remember your place," she warned. "Listen to what I have to say. When I am finished, you will have your chance to speak."

"I am loyal to the Emperor," Scourge declared.

"Loyal to the Emperor, or to the Empire?" she pressed. "They are two different things."

"What do you mean?"

"The Emperor is mad. Unchecked, he will destroy us all."

"For a thousand years the Empire has thrived under his rule," Scourge countered.

Her words were treason, but there was little he could do about it. If he tried to strike her down, he was fairly sure he would not be able to stand against her. Unlike Darth Xedrix, she was a Sith Council member in the prime of her powers. Now that she had told him her true feelings, she couldn't let him leave her room alive. Not if she felt he would report her to the Emperor. His only option—his only hope for survival—was to play along.

"The Emperor has expanded our borders," Nyriss admitted. "He has made us stronger. But he is only doing this for one purpose. He is planning an attack on the Republic. He intends to start another war with the Jedi."

"No," Scourge said, shaking his head. "Impossible."

The Great Hyperspace War had been one of the darkest times in the history of the Sith. Under the leadership of Naga Sadow, they had invaded the newly discovered Republic, seeking to conquer it as they had conquered every other civilization they had encountered. But despite their early victories, they had quickly lost ground. The Republic hadn't just defeated the Sith fleets; they had annihilated them. And then the Jedi had pursued the fleeing survivors across the galaxy, nearly hunting the Sith to extinction.

The decisive actions of the Emperor had saved them. He had led the remaining Sith into the unexplored regions of the galaxy, a decades-long flight that ended only when they rediscovered and reclaimed Dromund Kaas, their long-lost ancestral home. Fortunately, the Republic and the Jedi had never found them here—a small stroke of luck that had allowed the Empire to survive.

Over the next centuries, the Sith slowly rebuilt what

they had lost. They began to expand their Empire again. They conquered newly discovered worlds in sectors on the far fringes of the galaxy, far beyond the borders of Republic-explored space, safely hidden from the ever-vigilant Jedi Order.

Every Sith knew the story; it was taught to them at an early age. And while the official stance was that the Empire was slowly gathering its strength to one day strike back at their enemies, the truth was far different. Scourge and Nyriss both understood the folly of that path; they understood that the Empire could survive only as long as the Jedi remained unaware that the Sith still lived.

If the Emperor was really planning to attack the Republic again, he would be repeating the mistakes of Naga Sadow. He would start a war they couldn't possibly win, and this time the Jedi would not stop until they had wiped the Sith out completely.

"You're lying," Scourge insisted. "Attacking the Republic makes no sense. The Emperor is not a fool."

"No," Nyriss admitted. "He is no fool. He is arrogant. He is powerful. And he is mad." She looked directly at Scourge. "Some of us on the Dark Council learned of his plan. To save the Empire—to save our entire species—we formed an alliance, vowing to work together to bring the Emperor down."

"Was Darth Xedrix part of this alliance?"

"He was."

"Yet you betrayed him."

"He became a necessary sacrifice for the cause."

"If he was your ally, why did he have to die?"

"If the Emperor suspected the members of the Dark Council of allying against him, he would kill us all. We had to take steps to protect ourselves. To throw off suspicion, we had to distance ourselves from the separatists who openly oppose the Emperor."

"That's why you staged the fake assassinations against yourself," Scourge said. "If the separatists were targeting you, the Emperor would be less likely to suspect you were working with them."

Nyriss nodded.

"The plan was to have my own people 'investigate' the attempts on my life and place the blame accordingly. But then the Emperor sent you, and the plan had to change. Your arrival meant the Emperor suspected this was bigger than a simple separatist uprising. It wouldn't be enough to implicate a radical fringe group of terrorists."

"So you framed Xedrix."

"You can't frame someone who is guilty," Nyriss corrected. "I just exposed him. Xedrix really *was* working with the separatists. Every piece of evidence you uncovered on your missions was real. It had to be. I could not afford to be caught in a lie if you or the Emperor looked deeper into the matter. Allowing Xedrix to take the blame will confirm the Emperor's suspicion that the separatists were working with someone on the Dark Council. His death will keep my involvement—and that of my co-conspirators—secret."

"And you get to eliminate a longtime rival," Scourge added.

"A fortuitous bonus," Nyriss agreed, her face breaking into one of her hideous grins. "Xedrix will not be missed," she added. "He was a weak link in our chain. He was human, and his power was fading. If one of us had to be sacrificed, he was the most logical choice."

"Why tell all this to me?" Scourge asked.

"You already suspected something was wrong," Nyriss told him. "Why else would you have tried to interrogate Sechel? If I simply kill you, though, it might raise the Emperor's suspicions even farther. He sent you to investigate the assassinations; it would be better if you were the one to tell him Darth Xedrix was responsible."

She paused for a long moment before continuing. "During your service you have proven your worth to me. You are strong in the Force. Intelligent. Perceptive. You have incredible potential. My hope is that by revealing the truth I can convince you to join our cause. I would hate to discard such a valuable tool without good reason."

Scourge narrowed his eyes. This was too easy. Even if he swore allegiance to Nyriss, she couldn't just let him walk out of the room. The risk that he might report her to the Emperor was too great. She had to have some other way to protect herself, some angle he hadn't considered.

He realized he was in over his depth. Ever since he had come to work for Nyriss, she had been playing him. She'd twisted and manipulated him for her own purposes, and he had danced for her like a puppet on a string.

"What's the catch?" he finally asked. "How do you know I won't betray your confidence?"

"Very good," she said, smiling fiendishly in approval. "I would have been disappointed if you had simply accepted my offer. Short of killing you, there is no way I can completely eliminate the risk that you will try to expose me. But what proof do you have? Accuse me, and I will simply claim that you are the real traitor, trying to frame me after you killed Darth Xedrix.

"Remember: whatever actual evidence exists will implicate you, not me. He died by your blade. Are you certain you left no evidence behind that could implicate you in his murder? No drops of blood? No flecks of skin? No witnesses who can place you at the spaceport on Bosthirda the day Xedrix died?"

Scourge nodded in appreciation. He couldn't help but

admire how thoroughly Nyriss had entangled him in her web. "Let me guess—the files Sechel recovered from the UDM manufacturing plant and the separatist base will implicate me, as well?"

"Sechel is very good at what he does. Even the experts can't tell when he's doctored a datafile," she assured him. "Even with all the evidence pointing in your direction, it's possible the Emperor would still believe you over a member of the Dark Council, but honestly, he would probably kill us both just to be safe. That way the traitor is dead no matter which one of us is guilty. And I don't think you're the type to martyr yourself out of loyalty to the Emperor."

"So where do we go from here?" Scourge asked.

"Now I must persuade you to truly believe in our cause," Nyriss said. "It's not enough to secure your silence through threats and blackmail. When we finally move against the Emperor, I want you on our side."

"And how do you intend to convince me?"

"Have you ever heard tales of the Emperor's childhood?"

Scourge shook his head. "I don't even know what planet he's from."

"Few people do. He's hidden his past, because if the truth came to light none would follow him."

Scourge was interested despite himself.

"He was born almost a thousand years ago," she went on, "in the decades before the Great Hyperspace War with the Republic. He spent his childhood on Nathema, a lush and vibrant agricultural world on the far fringes of the Empire."

"Nathema? I've never heard of it."

"Once it went by another name, but that name has long been forgotten . . . just like the planet itself. The Emperor erased Nathema from the history books and the astrogation charts to hide all evidence of his crimes."

"Crimes?"

"Through the lost rituals of the ancients, he used the dark side to conquer death and make himself immortal. But his immortality came with a cost. Telling you what happened is not enough. You must see for yourself. Only then will you understand the price the Emperor was willing to pay. Only then will you understand why he must be stopped."

"And how am I to find this lost world?"

"I will take you there," Nyriss said. "Then you can witness the horror with your own eyes."

"How do I know this isn't a trap?" Scourge demanded. "Another elaborate trick to manipulate me into doing your bidding?"

"You don't," Nyriss admitted. "But what other choice do you have?"

She had a point. "When do we leave?" he asked.

"Patience, Lord Scourge," Nyriss said. "It will take several days before we are ready to leave. The journey is long, and we must be certain the Emperor never finds out. Traveling to Nathema is punishable by death."

"Will Sechel be joining us?"

"No. This is for your eyes alone."

Scourge nodded, silently wondering if the adviser would try to seek revenge for the brutal interrogation.

"You are part of the inner circle now," Nyriss assured him. "Sechel will not dare to harm you. See to your injuries," she instructed, noting the burns left behind by Darth Xedrix's lightning attack. "Then return to your room and get some rest."

As he turned to go, she gave him another of her unsettling smiles. "You might want to sleep with one eye open, though. Just in case."

CHAPTER THIRTEEN

CLAN ORDO'S VICTORY CELEBRATIONS continued late into the night. Six members of the clan, four men and two women, had died in the battle, a quarter of the casualties they had inflicted on Clan Jendri.

Veela had ordered all thirty bodies to be gathered together into a massive funeral pyre. Revan understood this mixing of friend and foe: they were all Mandalorians who had died in battle. By custom they were all due a warrior's funeral, regardless of which clan they had been fighting for. The pyre burned for hours, the flames lighting the night and warming the camp as the brothers and sisters of the fallen recounted tales of their bravery. They honored their memories through song and feast, simultaneously grieving their deaths and celebrating the resounding Ordo victory.

The ale flowed freely, but Revan had limited himself to a single mug. Because he had fought with Clan Ordo, he was entitled to join the revelry. But though he knew their customs, he wasn't Mandalorian. It was difficult for him to rejoice in the loss of comrades, no matter how honorable their deaths may have been. Revan was also wary of what Veela might do now that she knew he was a Jedi. Hopefully she just thought he was an anonymous rogue Master; if she knew who he really was there could be trouble.

Many Mandalorians despised the Jedi—and Revan in particular. Revan had been responsible for countless Mandalorian deaths, and he had stolen and hidden Mandalore's Mask, an act some considered a war crime. Considering Veela's fierce pride in her people and her culture, she probably wouldn't simply forgive and forget. Fortunately, it seemed like she wasn't aware of his true identity.

Over the course of the evening, Edric and several others came over to speak with him, making a point to include him in the clan festivities. Everyone seemed to know he had drawn the fire of the enemy Basilisks, allowing the pilots to reach their mounts. Interestingly, though, none of them knew any of the details of what had occurred out beyond the edges of the main battle. Obviously Veela had sworn the other pilots to secrecy.

He should have taken that as a good sign, but he kept catching glimpses of Veela and the other pilots watching him suspiciously. They might not know he was Revan, but they knew he was a Jedi and that clearly bothered them.

He wasn't sure if Veela had ordered them to stay silent out of respect for what he had done during the battle, or because she thought they still needed him to find Mandalore's Mask, or even because of her feelings for Canderous. But whatever the explanation, his secret seemed safe . . . for now.

When he finally climbed into bed late that night he was surprised to hear Canderous come stumbling into the tent a few minutes later.

"I thought you'd be with Veela."

"She's not too happy with me right now," Canderous explained. "I'll let her cool down for the night."

"Sorry about that."

"You did what you had to do," his friend answered as he settled into his sleeping bag. "Sooner or later it was going to come out anyway."

"How bad is this?"

"Veela doesn't like Jedi," Canderous admitted. "But she's hard to read. Hopefully she'll just hold a grudge for a few days." The big man rolled over onto his side. "Either that, or she'll try to kill us on tomorrow's climb."

Revan couldn't tell if he was joking.

THE WEATHER IN THE MORNING was the same as every other morning on Rekkiad—freezing cold, with fierce winds and swirling snow that limited visibility. Revan had been hoping for a calm, clear day so they could use the Basilisks to fly them up to the top. But even here at the base, unexpected gusts had enough strength to almost knock him off his feet. Higher up, the wind shear and lack of visibility would make an attempted landing on the summit suicidal, even for the most skilled pilots. Dangerous as it was, climbing to the top was the only real option.

"Bad conditions for an ascent," Canderous remarked as they stood at the base of the first Spear.

"This is as good as it gets," Veela said. "If you're scared, I'll get Edric to take your place and you can watch over the camp."

"The old man would probably have a heart attack halfway up," Canderous answered with a grin.

"He's only a year older than you," Veela pointed out.

"But I'm like a fine wine," he replied. "I get better with age."

The playful exchange eased some of Revan's concerns about the mission, though he still wasn't thrilled by the makeup of the climbing team. There were eight of them in total: Revan, Canderous, Veela, and the five other Basilisk riders, including Grizzer—the young man who'd given up his mount to Canderous.

Veela's picks made a certain amount of sense. Going after Mandalore's Mask was a great honor, and the Basilisk riders were among the most respected warriors in the clan. The only other person who might have been included was Edric, but he had been chosen to stay behind to lead Clan Ordo in case Veela and the others never came back.

Yet Revan couldn't help noticing that all of the climbers chosen knew he was a Jedi. And Edric, Canderous's oldest and most loyal friend, was being left behind. He wished he'd had a chance to talk to Canderous before they had left. Now all he could do was keep his guard up throughout the ascent, just in case.

They broke into two teams of four, the members of each team connected by a long length of climbing rope. Canderous, Revan, and two of the pilots made up the first group, Veela and the other three pilots the second. In addition to their winter clothing and gear, each climber had a twenty-kilo pack of supplies and rations strapped across his or her shoulders.

The two teams began their ascent simultaneously, moving along parallel paths up the sheer vertical surface of the wall of ice that made up the Spear's face. Each meter of progress was earned only by hacking into the ice, chipping away with a sharp-ended pick to create a small hold for a hand or foot, then hammering a braced pulley into the wall to secure the climbing rope. The pattern was repeated again and again.

Progress was slow and exhausting; a single misstep could send a climber plunging to a quick and gruesome death. Theoretically, the ropes and pulleys connecting each team should allow the other three members to bear the weight if one should fall, but none of them was inclined to test the theory.

* * *

AFTER ONLY FIFTY METERS, the roaring wind was already strong enough to rip away their voices, forcing them to communicate with simple hand gestures. Despite the cold, Revan was sweating heavily beneath his layers of clothing, his body warmed by the steady physical exertion as they battled their way meter by painful meter toward the top.

At least he was safe from Veela for the time being. The difficult climb required total focus and concentration from every climber as they worked in concert to reach the peak. Even if the Ordo pilots were plotting against him, they simply wouldn't be able to try anything until they reached the plateau at the top.

At the start of the climb the summit was invisible, lost in the swirl of snow and clouds. But by the fifth hour they had risen above the worst of the storm, giving them their first glimpse of the Spear's peak, illuminated by Rekkiad's pale orange sun.

They were well over halfway to their goal, but exhaustion and fatigue were beginning to impede their progress. As the altitude increased, the air became thinner, leaving all the climbers panting and gasping. The pack strapped to Revan's back seemed to have doubled in weight, and he could feel the straps digging into his shoulders even through his clothes. But there was little to do except ignore the pain and concentrate on the climb.

Veela's team was about fifty meters ahead. Suddenly one of their riders lost his footing and slipped. He dropped ten meters before the ropes abruptly stopped his fall, leaving him dangling helplessly at the end of the line. The abrupt stop had jerked his backpack partially around, twisting the shoulder straps so that his arms were partially pinned behind his back. Combined with the howling winds buffeting him back and forth, he was unable to reestablish a grip on the mountain.

Veela and the others began the slow and careful process of climbing back down to help him. It took about two minutes for Revan's team to draw level with Veela and her crew as they backtracked to rescue the wayward climber. Realizing the situation was under control, Revan's team pressed on toward the top.

Five minutes after the fall, Revan glanced back down to see that all four of Veela's team were once again safely in position. They were not trying to regain the lead, but moved more slowly and cautiously than before.

Two hours later Revan's team reached the top. Canderous was first; planting his feet firmly, he reached down to grab Revan's arm and haul him up. Revan did the same for the woman trailing behind him, and she did the same for the man behind her.

The top of the first Spear was a featureless plateau of slick ice covered by a thin dusting of snow. Looking across the gap between the two Spears, Revan could see that the other summit was as bare and featureless as this one.

"Now what?" Canderous shouted over the roar of the wind.

"If this is the right peak, there should be an entrance around here somewhere," Revan yelled back. A gust of wind shoved him sideways, and he almost stumbled.

"An entrance to what?"

Revan only shrugged. His vision hadn't shown him what he and Malak had discovered, and no more memories had bubbled to the surface during the climb.

They all set their backpacks on the ground and started a grid-pattern search over the plateau's surface. It didn't take them long to find what they were looking for.

Near the center of the plateau, under a dusting of snow, was a small durasteel hatch. Revan grabbed the handle and pulled hard, calling on the Force to give him strength when he felt his muscles beginning to strain. Slowly, reluctantly, the heavy cover swung open to reveal a ladder leading down into darkness.

"You stay here and wait for Veela," Canderous ordered the other two Mandalorians. "We'll go down and check it out."

He retrieved several glow sticks from his backpack on the ground, along with a blaster pistol. Revan didn't have a weapon in his pack. Everyone on the climb already knew he was a Jedi, and he was confident the lightsaber at his belt would be enough to deal with anything they ran into.

Not that he expected any trouble. It was hard to imagine a more remote, isolated, and inhospitable location. It was easy to see why he had decided to hide Mandalore's Mask here.

But where was *here*, exactly? Why was there a secret underground chamber built into the Spear, and how had he and Malak found it in the first place?

Canderous walked over to the hatch and dropped one of the glow sticks into it. It tumbled down, illuminating the length of the shaft as it fell. It stopped some thirty meters below, bouncing, rolling, and then settling on the ground.

"After you," Canderous said.

As Revan began the long descent, his mind started to spin. Brief flashes of dormant memories exploded into his consciousness, only to vanish before he could fully grasp them.

He had an overwhelming sense of déjà vu; he knew with certainty he and Malak had explored the dark chamber beneath the ice just as he and Canderous were exploring it now.

The sights and sounds of his previous visit blended with his current surroundings, the images overlapping one another, obscuring his vision and making him dizzy. It got so bad that Revan had to close his eyes, clinging to the rungs of the ladder with a tense grip.

"You okay?" Canderous asked from a few meters above. His voice echoed loudly off the rough-hewn rock walls.

"My past is catching up with me," Revan explained, shaking his head to dispel the vertigo.

He waited a few more seconds, and when he opened his eyes again everything had returned to normal. Taking a deep breath, he continued downward until he reached the bottom. The shaft ended in a tight, twisting tunnel that continued horizontally. Resisting the urge to draw his lightsaber, Revan pulled out another glow stick and started down the passage. Canderous followed close behind.

The tunnel was narrow, forcing them to walk single-file, but the ceiling was high enough that even Canderous didn't have to duck. It didn't take long for Revan to realize that they were walking on a slight decline, going ever deeper into the heart of the Spear. The air around them grew warmer, causing them to unbutton their jackets and lower their hoods.

As they continued on, Revan began to feel the unmistakable presence of the dark side. His hand dropped to the lightsaber at his belt, but he relaxed as he realized that the sensation was too faint to signify an immediate threat. Once the Force had been strong in this place, but over time—many decades, or even centuries—it had faded away to little more than a memory.

Eventually the passage brought them into a large circular chamber hewn from the rock. Easily thirty meters across, the chamber was empty save for a large stone crypt in the center.

"What is this place?" Canderous whispered.

"I think it's the burial chamber of an ancient Sith Lord," Revan answered. "Like the tombs on Korriban."

"Why would they bury him here in this frozen wasteland?"

To his own surprise, Revan knew the answer to that question. "He was an exile. He fled here with a handful of his fanatically loyal followers many centuries ago. When he died, they carved out this secret chamber to inter him so his enemies couldn't find and desecrate his remains."

"How do you know that?"

Revan shrugged. "I just know. Malak and I came here looking for this crypt. Someone must have told us about it."

"You mean someone like Mandalore?"

Another memory came crashing in on Revan, triggered by the words of his friend.

Mandalore the Ultimate lay dying at his feet. Coughing on the blood welling up in his lungs, he reached up and peeled off his Mask, the most sacred symbol of his people.

"It wasn't supposed to end like this," he said, his voice soft and low. "They promised me victory. Only now do I see how I was betrayed."

Revan tilted his head to the side, puzzled. "What are you talking about?"

"They tricked me. We were never meant to win this war. They used me and my people to test the Republic's strength."

"Who used you?"

"The Sith."

The recollection ended abruptly, slipping quickly back into Revan's subconscious. But in bubbling up to the surface, it had released a host of other trapped memories, and they crashed over Revan like a wave, staggering him.

"I remember," he muttered, placing his hand on the wall for support. "I remember."

"What?" Canderous asked anxiously. "What do you remember?"

Revan didn't answer. Instead he crossed the chamber to the sarcophagus in the center. Carved into the granite sides was an interweaving pattern of circles and diagonal lines, most likely a family crest or seal. The tomb's heavy stone lid was smooth and unadorned, but as Revan drew closer he could see marks and scratches along the edges, signs that it had been moved several times.

Reaching out to the Force, Revan focused on the lid. After a moment it began to move, the edge grating along the lip of the lower half of the sarcophagus as it slowly rose into the air.

Careful not to let the heavy lid drop, he moved it off to the side and gently lowered it to the floor. Then he stepped up to the sarcophagus and peered inside.

There were no remains to be seen. The enemies of the anonymous Sith Lord in the tomb must have found him after all, stealing his mummified corpse for some dark and twisted purpose. The missing body didn't come as a surprise to Revan, and he suddenly remembered that he and Malak had also found the sarcophagus empty.

But they hadn't left it that way. Inside was a datacron—a small cube similar to the holocrons used by the Jedi and Sith to record their teachings for future generations. However, unlike those powerful artifacts, the datacron was not created using the Force; it was simply a repository of information.

But Revan barely looked at the datacron. His attention was gripped by the object that lay beside it: Mandalore's Mask. And as he reached in and picked up the sacred relic, his mind flashed back to the moment he had left it there.

*   *   *

"So Mandalore was telling the truth," Malak said.

"Did you really think his last words would be a lie?" Revan asked.

"Now what?"

"We have our proof," Revan said. "The Sith are not extinct. They have to be stopped."

"What about the Mandalorians?"

"Without the Mask, they are nothing," Revan said, placing the Mask inside the empty sepulcher.

The memory ended, rudely snapping Revan back to the present. He lifted the Mask and held it aloft so Canderous could see.

The big man walked slowly toward him, as if in a daze. He didn't speak, but as he approached, his hands came up almost involuntarily, his fingers reaching out toward the lost symbol of his people.

Neither noticed Veela and the others enter the chamber.

"How dare you defile Mandalore's Mask with your filthy Jedi hands!" Veela shouted, breaking the spell that had momentarily enthralled the two men.

Revan looked up to see her standing at the cavern's entrance, flanked by the other climbers. All six Mandalorians were armed with blaster pistols, their muzzles aimed directly at the two men standing by the crypt.

"Veela!" Canderous demanded. "What do you think you're doing?"

"Put the Mask down and step away from the crypt," she commanded, ignoring him.

Moving slowly so as not to alarm anyone, Revan placed the Mask back in the crypt.

"Avner fought beside us," Canderous protested. "He led us to Mandalore's Mask. And you repay him with betrayal?"

Veela barked out a harsh laugh. "Who are you to talk

of betrayal? You turned your back on your people. And for what? To throw your lot in with Revan the Butcher?"

"When did you figure it out?" Canderous asked, not bothering to deny the truth.

"Once he revealed himself to be a Jedi, it was obvious," she said with a sneer. "Especially with that name. Did you really think rearranging *Revan* into *Avner* would fool us?"

"This isn't about him," Canderous said. "It's about me, isn't it?"

Veela bit down hard on her lip but didn't answer.

"I'm not here to claim the Mask for myself," Canderous assured her. "You're the rightful leader of Clan Ordo. I'm not here to challenge you."

"You still don't get it," Veela said, shaking her head. "*You* should be our leader, not me! *You* were our greatest warrior. *You* were our champion. Our hero. When Mandalore fell, you should have been the one to take his place!" She looked at him sadly. "Instead, you abandoned us. You abandoned me."

"I'm sorry," Canderous said softly. "When our clan fell apart, I was lost. I had to get away. I didn't know what else to do."

"You could have stayed and help piece it back together," Veela insisted, her voice cracking slightly as she lowered the blaster in her hand.

"*Cin vhetin,*" Canderous said. "I can't undo the past. But I'm here now."

"That's why I didn't tell the others in the camp," she admitted. "I didn't want to destroy your reputation by telling them you fell in with Revan."

"You didn't tell them because you're afraid they would agree with me," Canderous countered. "Revan is not our enemy. Not now. Without him, Clan Jendri would have slaughtered us. Without him, we would never have found Mandalore's Mask. Revan has proved himself to be our brother; and what you are doing brings dishonor on our clan!"

"No," Veela insisted. "You're wrong. Clan Ordo might accept a Jedi, but not him. Anyone but him."

"There's only one way to be sure. We let the whole clan decide."

"That's not an option," Veela replied, raising her blaster back up. "Revan cannot leave this chamber alive."

"You know Revan's reputation," Canderous warned. "And mine. There may be six of you, but do you really think you have a chance against us both?"

"We're not here to kill you," Veela told him. "Just him."

"And you expect me to stand by and do nothing?"

"I expect you to join us!" Veela shouted. "You are Mandalorian! Clan Ordo is your family, not Revan. You have to choose: him or us."

"It doesn't have to be this way," Canderous said evenly. "Lower your weapons. End this madness. We'll take Mandalore's Mask back down to the camp together."

"This is your last chance, Canderous," Veela said. "Choose!"

Her hand was trembling, making it difficult for her to aim. But the other five held their blasters steady and true.

"You can't win this battle," Revan said quietly, speaking more to the others than Veela.

"We killed dozens of Jedi during the war," Veela answered grimly.

"I'm no ordinary Jedi."

"Veela," Canderous pleaded, "please don't do this."

Her shoulders slumped and she let out a sigh of resignation. "Kill them both."

Revan was in motion, his lightsaber flashing to life,

before the words had finished spilling from her mouth. As Veela and two of the others—reacting slightly faster than the rest—fired their blasters, the green blade transformed into a spinning, twirling blur as he used it to deflect their bolts back in the direction of the shooters.

One of the deflected bolts struck its mark, taking down the woman on Veela's left. Canderous and Revan dived for cover behind the sarcophagus just as the other Mandalorians opened fire. Canderous popped up briefly to fire, sending the Mandalorians breaking for cover. There were precious few places to hide in the open chamber, however, and Canderous took two of them down before they made it to safety.

Veela and the other two survivors scrambled back into the passage near the chamber entrance, ducking out of sight around the corner to regroup. A second later a trio of grenades skittered across the floor, bouncing and rolling to a stop near the base of the sarcophagus.

The instant before they detonated, Revan reached out with the Force and hurled the heavy stone lid of the sarcophagus toward the grenades. It acted as a shield, absorbing the worst of the blast before exploding into pebbles and dust.

The explosion was deafening, though; the concussive force strong enough to knock both Canderous and Revan off their feet. As Revan struggled to stand up, the only sound he could hear was a high-pitched ringing in his ears.

Veela and her team seized the advantage and charged into the room, blaster pistols blazing. All three aimed at Revan, who just barely rolled clear in time.

From the corner of his eye he saw Canderous lying on his stomach, arms stretched out in front of him to brace his pistol on the floor as he took careful aim. An instant later, Veela went down from a clean kill shot through her heart.

Their attention drawn for just an instant by the body of their leader tumbling to the floor, the two remaining Mandalorians faltered. Revan used that moment to unleash a sidearm throw of his lightsaber. The blade went spinning out in a wide arcing path that ended both their lives before they could move.

Revan adeptly caught his lightsaber by its hilt as it returned to his hand, then slowly stood up straight, his ears still ringing. Nearby, Canderous still lay on the floor, frozen in the same position he had been in moments earlier. Slowly, Revan approached him, trying to see if he was injured.

The big man didn't move until Revan reached down and placed a hand on his shoulder. Then Canderous snapped his head around in surprise. He mouthed something, but Revan couldn't hear what he was saying, so he only shrugged in response.

Canderous pushed himself up off his stomach and onto his feet, leaving his pistol on the ground. He walked over to where Veela lay facedown on the floor and rolled her over.

Her eyes were wide, gazing unseeing up at the ceiling. Tenderly, he closed the lids, then folded her hands over her chest. Then he stood up straight and turned away, staring off into an empty corner of the chamber.

After a few minutes, Revan went over to stand beside him.

"I'm sorry." His voice sounded strange to him. His hearing was still distorted by the grenade, and he wasn't sure if Canderous had heard him. "I'm sorry," he repeated, this time more loudly.

Canderous turned his head to look at him. "Me, too," he answered before turning to stare back at the wall, his words hollow and flat. "Me, too."

CHAPTER FOURTEEN

CANDEROUS CONTINUED TO STARE at the cavern wall while Revan stood by in respectful silence. Eventually he turned back to Revan and said, "We shouldn't just leave them lying here like this. It's disrespectful."

Revan nodded. The Mandalorians still lay where they had fallen, their bodies crumpled in unnatural positions.

Together the two men gathered them up one by one and lay them down side by side in the center of the room. As he had done with Veela, Canderous closed their eyes and crossed their hands over their chests.

If there had been any way to make a funeral pyre, Revan would have suggested they burn them in the Mandalorian custom. But with no fuel that wasn't going to be possible.

"What am I going to tell the others?" Canderous wondered once they were done arranging the bodies.

Revan understood his dilemma. There would be a lot of questions when they returned alone with Mandalore's Mask, and Canderous didn't want to bring shame onto Veela's name.

"Keep it simple," Revan suggested. "Say we ran into unexpected resistance from guardian droids programmed to protect the crypt. Tell them Veela and the others died in battle, and they fought like true warriors before they fell."

Canderous nodded, then slowly walked over to the sarcophagus. He took out Mandalore's Mask, then, almost as an afterthought, picked up the datacron.

"What's this?" he asked, looking curiously at the small cube.

"It's a chronicle of the Sith Lord who was buried here," Revan said. "I think Malak and I found it hidden in the tomb the last time we were here."

"Do you remember what's on it?"

"Mostly."

"Tell me."

Revan knew Canderous was hoping there would be something in the history that would help him understand why Veela had turned on him. From what Revan remembered of the story, it would offer little solace, but he wasn't about to deny the request.

"His name was Lord Dramath the Second. A thousand years ago his father, the original Lord Dramath, ruled over a planet called Medriaas. He was overthrown by another Sith named Lord Vitiate, who renamed the planet Nathema. With his father's death, the younger Lord Dramath fled. He hid on Rekkiad with a handful of loyal followers, and when he died they buried him here with the datacron."

"So it has nothing to do with Mandalore or his Mask?" Canderous asked, shaking his head. "You just decided to hide it here, too?"

Revan hesitated for a moment. "Actually, it has everything to do with Mandalore," he said finally.

Canderous had a right to know the truth, but first Revan had to put all the pieces back together for himself. Coming to the underground burial chamber had triggered the return of a host of lost memories. They had come to him in disconnected scraps and momentary flashes of insight. He needed time to process the information—to sort it into something that made some kind of sense.

"Can we talk about this later?" was all he said.

Canderous studied Revan's face, seemed about to say something, but then nodded. "Let's get some rest," he suggested. "We can't make it back down the mountain tonight, anyway. We can talk in the morning."

Spending the night exposed on the plateau's surface wasn't an option; not while they could stay underground in a geothermally heated cavern that was sheltered from the elements. They unrolled their sleeping bags near the edge of the chamber, as far away from Veela and the other bodies as possible. Sharing the room with six corpses was unpleasant, but it was better than freezing to death.

Neither man slept well. Revan could hear Canderous tossing and turning. Once Revan thought he heard him whisper Veela's name.

Revan's thoughts wouldn't let him sleep, either. He had hoped finding Mandalore's Mask would be a breakthrough, the key to unlocking all his lost memories. But the more he tried to reassemble the fragmented images swarming in his head, the more he realized how much was still missing. He had taken only a small step forward, and he suspected the journey was far from over.

When sleep finally overcame him, he dreamed about the world of endless storms and perpetual night again. It seemed more vivid than before; more substantial. More *real*.

He couldn't say how long he slept; it was difficult to sense the passage of time in the chamber. When he woke he didn't feel refreshed, but he knew it was pointless to try to go back to sleep.

Canderous was already up, pacing slowly back and

forth from one side of the chamber to the other, staring at the Mask he held in his hands.

Revan stood up and stretched, working the kinks out of his neck and shoulders. "I'm ready to tell you what I remember about Mandalore," he said. "If you still want to know."

"I do."

Taking one last breath to help gather his thoughts, Revan launched into the tale. "About two years before he declared war on the Republic, Mandalore was approached by a man with skin the color of blood—a Sith."

"I thought the Jedi wiped the Sith out."

"So did the Jedi. The Sith species vanished after the Great Hyperspace War. One of their kind hasn't been seen in Republic space in over a thousand years. But this red-skinned being came to Mandalore. He claimed to be the emissary of a powerful Master—a descendant of the Sith Lord who had driven Dramath into exile—and convinced Mandalore to help him search for his enemy's tomb."

Revan was speaking slowly, the words coming out only as fast as the details came into focus. His recollections were still hazy and jumbled. The original time and place of each specific memory was unclear. Mandalore had told him some of this. Other details had come from the datacron in the tomb. Most of it he had learned much later, after he and Malak had journeyed into the Unknown Regions themselves.

It was impossible to sort it all out. Out of necessity, his damaged mind had collapsed his memories into one another, merging them into a semi-coherent whole as he'd slept.

"Mandalore helped the Sith find Dramath's hidden crypt," he continued. "The Sith took the remains to give to his Master, and in exchange he told Mandalore of a vision his Master had had of the Mandalorians rising up against the Republic. He told him they would conquer world after world, crushing their enemies until the Republic collapsed in on itself. He promised the Mandalorians a glorious victory, and Mandalore believed him."

"Mandalore the Ultimate wouldn't lead us into war against the Republic just because some stranger told him we'd win," Canderous protested.

"It's more complicated than that. The Sith used the power of the dark side to manipulate him. Only as Mandalore lay dying at my feet was the spell finally broken and he realized he'd been tricked. That was why he told me about this place. So I could come and see for myself."

"This doesn't make any sense," Canderous said. "You say the Sith tricked Mandalore into attacking the Republic. But why?"

"I don't know," Revan admitted. "Maybe it was a test of your strength. Or ours. Maybe the Sith are planning another invasion, and they sought to weaken the Republic."

"But you don't know for sure?"

"I'm remembering more and more, but there's still so much missing." Revan paused before adding, "Maybe I'll find the answers on Nathema."

"Nathema?"

"The hyperspace coordinates are on the datacron. I think Malak and I went there to try to learn more."

"Is Nathema the world you keep dreaming about? The one covered in storms and darkness?" Canderous asked.

Revan closed his eyes and concentrated, summoning the image that had haunted him for so many nights. He tried to associate the vision with the name, but somehow he knew it didn't fit.

"No. The planet in my dreams isn't Nathema."

"You're sure?"

"I can't really be sure of anything," Revan confessed. "But it just doesn't feel right. I think . . . I think we went there after Nathema."

"And when you returned, you tried to conquer the Republic. Just like Mandalore."

Revan shook his head. "It's not the same. Mandalore was a warrior, and he had no loyalty to the Republic. Convincing him to attack was more persuasion than domination. The Sith was only telling him what he wanted to hear; he was playing off Mandalore's own hidden desires.

"But Malak and I were Jedi. It would take more than some persuasive words and a subtle push from the Force to turn us to the dark side. Something else happened to us out there. We found something that changed us."

"You don't think going to Nathema again is a little risky?" Canderous asked.

"I have to," Revan answered. "It's the only way I'll find out what happened."

"What if the same thing happens again?"

"I'll be more careful this time. My guard will be up."

"Do you think that's going to make a difference?"

"I hope so."

"So when do we leave?"

"You're not coming," Revan said. "You have to stay here with your people." He held up his hand to cut off any protests. "Veela was right about one thing—you should be the leader of the Mandalorians. The Mask is there, just waiting for you to claim it."

"You need my help," Canderous insisted. "I turned my back on Veela when she needed me. I'm not going to make the same mistake with you."

"That's why you have to stay," Revan told him. "The

Mandalorians were tricked into a war that nearly destroyed them. I don't know who the Sith was or what he was after, but he knew you couldn't win. He knew a war against the Republic would leave the Mandalorians devastated."

"If the Sith are planning another invasion of the Republic, they'd have to come through Mandalorian space first," Canderous muttered. "Maybe they were trying to get us out of the way."

"Maybe. Or maybe they wanted to twist your culture and beliefs in the hope you'd join them. Many of the Mandalorians are bitter, and hungry for revenge. Without a new Mandalore, how hard would it be for someone to manipulate them into going to war again?" Revan frowned. "Your people have lost their way, Canderous. You need to help them find it again. The fate of the galaxy could depend on it."

Canderous stared at Revan, and then down at the Mask in his hands. He stood stock-still for a moment. Then, slowly, he raised the Mask and slipped it over his head.

"Mandalore has returned," he declared. "I am Mandalore the Preserver, and I will restore the honor and glory of my people!"

T3-M4 GREETED REVAN'S RETURN to the *Ebon Hawk* with a shrill stream of beeps and whistles. The astromech was spinning in place so rapidly that Revan feared he might burn out a circuit.

"Settle down, little fella," he said, reaching out to pat the droid. "I'm glad to see you, too."

T3 stopped spinning and responded with an inquisitive chirp.

"Canderous is staying here," Revan explained. "These are his people. This is where he belongs."

T3 beeped twice.

"No, we're not going home yet," Revan said, settling into the pilot's chair and punching in their hyperspace coordinates.

"We're headed into the Unknown Regions, to a planet called Nathema."

CHAPTER FIFTEEN

SCOURGE KNEW THAT Nyriss was watching him carefully. For the past week, ever since she had told him the truth about Xedrix, he had felt her presence constantly. He had promised not to act on his knowledge until he saw Nathema for himself, and he intended to keep that promise. He knew she didn't trust him, and he knew she'd try to kill him if she felt threatened—and also that she was powerful enough to have a good chance of succeeding. But he had his own reasons for obeying. He was curious about what she had told him. He wanted to know more about the Emperor's mysterious past. And if it turned out that Nyriss was telling the truth—if the Emperor really was mad enough to start another war with the Republic—then maybe Scourge should consider taking her side.

Now the day of reckoning was here. Nyriss had come for him early, waking him with a subtle whisper in his ear.

"It's time."

He'd dressed quickly, then followed her out to the spaceport, where a private shuttle was waiting for them. Unlike the rest of her fleet, this one bore neither her colors nor her crest. This journey would be conducted in utter secrecy.

The shuttle was clearly built for speed; there was no armor to speak of, and at first glance it was easy to miss the single blaster turret mounted under the cockpit. Scourge was no expert on starship weaponry, but he guessed it would only be effective at close range.

The interior was more functional than luxurious, with room to seat six. On this trip, he and Nyriss would be the only passengers.

She settled into the pilot's chair, her fingers moving rapidly over the controls with a dexterity that belied their gnarled, wrinkled appearance. Neither of them spoke as the shuttle took to the sky, climbing rapidly through the clouds and lightning until it broke free of the atmosphere.

Nyriss made a few more adjustments and punched in their route, and the ship jumped into hyperspace, leaving Dromund Kaas—and Nyriss's loyal followers—behind.

"Nothing I tell you can prepare you for what you will see on Nathema," Nyriss warned him. "But I will tell you the history of the Emperor and his homeworld."

"How can I know you're telling the truth?"

She shrugged. "Believe it or not as you see fit. If nothing else, it will help pass the time."

She settled herself more comfortably, and as she spoke, her voice took on the singsong tone of children's storyteller. "The Emperor's name was Tenebrae," she began. "They say he was born with eyes as black as the void of empty space, and that he never cried, even as an infant. No animal would come near him, and when he began to talk, his voice carried a weight and power that should not come from a child.

"At the age of six he began to manifest signs of the Force, marking him as one of the ruling elite. But his parents were simple farmers, and the Force was not strong in them. Suspicious about the boy's power, his father confronted his mother, who admitted to having an affair with the Sith Lord who ruled over them.

"The father flew into a rage, attacking the boy's mother. Tenebrae stopped him, feeding on his father's anger and hate to call upon the dark side. He snapped his father's neck with a mere thought, killing him instantly. His mother died more slowly. Tenebrae made her suffer for months as punishment for betraying the family, torturing her with the Force as he honed his powers.

"Now orphaned by his own hand, he made the others in his village bow down to him. Those who refused, he tortured and killed through the Force.

"Over the next few years his reputation and influence spread to nearby villages, and he amassed legions of both fanatical and terrified followers. He killed thousands during his rise to power. Many died just to feed his insatiable appetite for suffering, tortured for days in public executions so he could savor their agonizing ends."

"This sounds more like a legend than a history," Scourge remarked.

"I cannot guarantee the truth of this story," Nyriss admitted. "Those who witnessed the events no longer live to verify them. But if you had ever met the Emperor in person, you would not be so hesitant to accept the tale as fact."

"What about Nathema's ruler? The boy's father? You claimed he was a Sith Lord. Surely he didn't sit back doing nothing while a child conquered his people village by village?"

"Tenebrae's father was named Lord Dramath. He heard rumors, but they came from a remote and insignificant territory. He had long forgotten the simple commoner who had borne him a son, and he considered the plight of a few small villages beneath his notice. Had

Dramath acted more swiftly, the Emperor might have been stopped. But it took almost four years before he decided to go see Tenebrae for himself.

"Lord Dramath intended to judge the child's power to determine if he was worthy of serving the Sith Lord, or if he should simply be executed. But Tenebrae had no intention of serving—or of dying. When they met face-to-face, Tenebrae proved the stronger. Only ten years old, he stripped his father of his power and his mind. Lord Dramath spent his last moments weeping in terror, gazing up into the black eyes of his son.

"It took Tenebrae three more years to gain control of the rest of Nathema. Dramath's firstborn son fled rather than face his formidable half brother, but other powerful Sith sought to seize the empty throne. All fell before the dark prodigy, and with each victory he grew more powerful and more ruthless.

"At thirteen he presented himself to Marka Ragnos, the Lord of all Sith and the ruler of the Sith Council. Impressed by the teenager's ambition and power, Marka Ragnos granted him the title of Lord Vitiate. His position as ruler of Nathema officially recognized, Lord Vitiate returned to his home to conduct his research into the depths of the dark side's power.

"He stayed there for a hundred years. When Marka Ragnos fell, Lord Vitiate did not join in the mad rush to claim his position. He was not part of the Great Hyperspace War against the Republic. When Naga Sadow and Ludo Kressh fought for leadership of the Sith, he took no side. But in the aftermath of the war—after our defeat at the hands of the Republic and our flight to escape the massacre of our people by the Jedi—he emerged from his solitude to call a great council of all the Sith Lords who remained. He invited them to his palace on Nathema, built on the site of his childhood home, the place where he had killed his adopted father and tortured his mother to death. He invited them to participate in a ritual to unlock the full potential of the dark side; he promised they would unleash power beyond anything they had ever witnessed or imagined."

"Didn't they suspect a trap?"

"Perhaps." Nyriss shrugged. "Some refused to answer his call. But many more came. After all, what could one man do against a hundred Sith Lords? Remember, he was not the Emperor back then. He was merely Lord Vitiate, ruler of a single planet of no particular importance. He hadn't fought in any battles of note or achieved any great victories or conquests beyond his homeworld. He had the reputation of a scholar, not a warrior.

"And the Sith Lords were driven by fear. Many thought the Jedi would soon wipe them all out. They were desperate for anything they could use as a weapon against the servants of the light side. Lord Vitiate played upon these fears, convincing those who answered his call to set aside their suspicions of him and of one another to join in a single glorious cause.

"Once they arrived on Nathema, they quickly fell under Lord Vitiate's control. He dominated their minds, crushed their resistance. He turned them into slaves to his will, forcing them to participate in the most complex ritual of Sith sorcery ever attempted. Calling on the dark side, Lord Vitiate devoured them. He fed on their power, absorbing it into himself, utterly obliterating all traces of his victims.

"But the ritual was not confined to the doomed Sith Lords. They were but the eye of the storm; the center of a vortex that spread across the entire planet. Every man, woman, and child on Nathema died that day. Every beast, bird, and fish; all the insects and plants; every living being touched by the Force was consumed. When the ritual ended, Nathema was no longer a world. It was a husk sucked dry. Lord Vitiate sacrificed millions, stealing their life force to make himself immortal. Their deaths also made him stronger than any Sith who had come before, and he ceased to be known as Lord Vitiate. On that day, the Emperor was truly born."

Scourge wondered if Nyriss expected him to be horrified by the tale. If so, she was about to be disappointed.

"The Emperor seized what was his by right," he said. "The strong take from the weak. That is our way. Doing it on a scale of millions doesn't change anything—it just proves he deserves to be our Emperor."

"So I used to think," Nyriss said, smiling ghoulishly. "And then I saw Nathema for myself."

She didn't say anything else for the remainder of the trip, leaving Scourge to wonder in silence why she was so confident he would come around to her side.

He felt the first hints of what was waiting for him when the shuttle dropped out of hyperspace. Through the windows of the cockpit he saw a gray-and-brown planet looming large before them. Gazing at it, he felt something strange and unsettling. Something unnatural.

It took him several moments to realize what was wrong, and even when he did, he didn't fully grasp the implications. He wasn't feeling the Force.

The sensation was completely alien. The Force was omnipresent. It radiated stronger in certain places and at certain times, and the balance of the dark side and the light constantly shifted. But it was always there in some way, shape, or form.

Now, however, he felt nothing. He had become so accustomed to the presence of the Force in the background that its complete absence was almost overwhelming, leaving him unable to speak.

"Prepare yourself," Nyriss said. "We're going down to the surface."

The absence grew steadily more pronounced as the shuttle approached and then landed on Nathema.

"Come with me," Nyriss commanded, rising up from her seat.

Still mute, Scourge followed her down the shuttle's boarding ramp and out onto the world itself.

They had touched down at a spaceport in a city. Or what used to be a city. The spaceport was surrounded by the buildings, speeder pads, and streets one would expect to see in a planet's major metropolitan center. But it was eerily quiet; the incessant murmur of the crowds and the constant hum of traffic whizzing past on busy streets were missing.

There wasn't even any wind, and the air tasted stale in Scourge's mouth. The temperature was neither cold nor hot, but he felt himself starting to shiver.

"You feel the chill of the Void," Nyriss told him. "The Force is energy; it gives heat to our emotions and our minds. But here it has been stripped away."

She led him along the deserted streets as Scourge stared in fascinated horror, trying to grasp the magnitude of what he was witnessing. The buildings seemed to be almost fully intact; there was none of the damage and destruction normally associated with millions of simultaneous deaths. However, there were other signs of what had happened here.

Mangled speeders and shuttles were strewn about, the remains of vehicles in motion that had crashed to a halt when their pilots were taken by the ritual. And everywhere Scourge looked there were small piles of clothes: jackets, slacks, and boots that had survived what their owners had not. Normally these remains would have been picked over by scavengers, but on Nathema even the vermin and insects were extinct.

"Where are the droids?" Scourge asked.

He was shocked at the sound of his own voice. It was flat and dull, as if even sound waves had been distorted by the ritual.

"The ritual overloaded their circuits," Nyriss explained, her voice as hollow and washed out as his. "The damage was irreparable; even their memory cores were completely wiped out."

Scourge glanced upward and noticed something else unusual. The sun shining down on them from above—a star that had appeared bright orange as they'd approached the planet—was now a pale shade of brown. In fact, everything around them was either brown or gray, as if the colors had been leached out.

Scourge was well acquainted with death. He had no trouble understanding massacres and mass slaughter. Death and destruction unleashed powerful emotions like fear, suffering, and hatred; they fueled the power of the dark side. But what had happened on Nathema was different, and it disturbed him in a deep and profound way.

The Emperor had consumed *everything*. Life, sound, color, even the Force—nothing remained. This wasn't about conquest or domination or destroying an enemy—all concepts Scourge embraced.

Everything on Nathema had simply been snuffed out, extinguished so completely that it ceased to have any meaning or purpose. It was a vacuum of existence; a blight on the natural order.

"I've seen enough," he declared.

Nyriss nodded, and they turned and made their way back to the ship.

Scourge finally understood why Nyriss and the others wanted to take the Emperor down. Destroying your enemies—even destroying a planet—was understandable. But this wasn't simple destruction. It was annihilation; obliteration. The very fabric of the Force had been shredded. Anyone capable of turning an entire planet into a nihilistic abomination had to be completely mad. After seeing the horrors of Nathema, he truly believed the Emperor might declare another war against the Republic, exposing them to the Jedi and leading to the eventual extinction of their species.

By the time they reached the shuttle, Scourge's stomach was churning. He had lived his whole life attuned to the Force; having it stripped away had left him physically ill. The shuttle shook as they took to the air, and he fought against the urge to vomit.

As they broke the atmosphere of the cursed world, some semblance of normalcy returned. Scourge felt the Force rushing in to fill the emptiness inside him; he felt its power invigorating him and restoring his strength. At the same time, he also felt something else: the presence of someone strong in the Force—someone who was neither Nyriss nor him.

Nyriss suddenly began punching away at the shuttle's controls, scanning the system for another vessel, and Scourge knew she felt it, too.

"There," she said, pointing at the readout. "A ship just dropped out of hyperspace in this system."

"Could the Emperor have sent someone to follow us?" Scourge asked.

"I don't think so," she replied, staring at the screens. "Its signature doesn't match any design I've ever seen before."

From her voice it was clear she was as puzzled as he was. If the ship hadn't followed them here, the odds against it showing up at the same time they were here were astronomical. But Scourge understood the ways of the Force too well to believe in coincidence. There had to be some connection between them and the unexpected visitor.

"Looks like a small freighter of some kind," Nyriss muttered. "I don't think they've seen us."

Scourge realized they had two options. The first was to make a quick jump to hyperspace in an effort to escape before being noticed.

Nyriss decided to take the second option. Reaching out a finger, she activated the shuttle's ion cannon, locked onto the unidentified vessel, and fired.

THE INSTANT THE *EBON HAWK* dropped out of hyperspace near Nathema, Revan was overwhelmed by a barrage of mental images. Everything came crashing in on him, the memories he was so desperate to regain fusing with a trauma he had tried so hard to repress. Caught between the two, he cried out and clutched his head in his hands.

For several seconds he didn't move, his conscious will battling with his runaway subconscious. One by one, he was able to take the recollections, process them, and store them away, slowly regaining control.

He knew with absolute certainty that he had been to this world before. He remembered its deserted city and its lifeless surface. He remembered searching the empty buildings with Malak, looking for archives, records, and astrogation charts that would guide them on the next step of the journey. But most of all, he remembered the horror of a dead planet entirely stripped of the Force.

T3 was at his side, beeping with concern. Revan blinked away the last of his fugue state and glanced down at the *Hawk*'s sensors to see what had the little droid so upset.

The sensors had picked up another vessel in the system. It was difficult to draw on the Force so close to the ravaged world, and he struggled to get some sense of the passengers on the other ship. By the time his groggy mind registered the threat they posed, it was too late.

The ion blast hit the *Hawk* full-bore, shorting out its circuits and engines and leaving them at the mercy of the gravitational field from the planet below.

Revan scrambled to steer the ship as it was pulled down into Nathema's atmosphere, wondering at the chances of surviving a second crash landing in a row. The ion blast had damaged the flight controls and stabilizers, and the ship veered wildly as it plummeted toward the surface. He had no idea if the other vessel was following him; his sensors had been knocked out along with everything else. But he knew if he didn't get the engines and repulsors back online, the *Ebon Hawk* would be smashed to pieces by the fall.

"Tee-Three!" he shouted, but the astromech had already sprung into action.

T3 had connected himself to the cockpit's main control panel with a twenty-centimeter-long slicing tool. Lights on the cockpit dashboard began to flicker and flash as T3 rerouted power from damaged circuits. Through the cockpit window, Revan could see the distant outline of a city far below, the skyscrapers seeming to growing rapidly as the *Hawk* rushed toward them at terminal velocity.

Inside the control panel something crackled and popped. Smoke poured into the cockpit. T3 squealed in alarm, but his warning was drowned out by the sound of the *Hawk*'s engines roaring back to life.

Revan pulled back hard on the stick, and the nose of the *Hawk* grudgingly angled upward, emergency repulsors screaming.

"Brace for impact!" he shouted an instant before they slammed into the edge of one of the massive skyscrapers, sending a shower of permacrete and plasteel tumbling to the empty street below.

The *Hawk* ricocheted off the building and began to spin wildly. Then it slammed into the ground at an awkward angle, skipping along the street like a stone cast across water before finally coming to rest.

CHAPTER SIXTEEN

SCOURGE HAD NO DESIRE to return to Nathema, but he didn't raise any objection when Nyriss redirected their shuttle back toward the planet's surface in pursuit of the damaged freighter. They had to find out who was on that vessel, why they were here, and if they were still alive.

It had crashed down in one of the handful of cities that dotted the world, leaving a path of damaged buildings and mangled speeders in its wake. The ship itself still seemed to be relatively intact; it lay wedged against the base of a skyscraper at the end of a main thoroughfare.

Nyriss brought the shuttle in cautiously, wary of return fire as she scanned the enemy vessel.

"Anybody alive in there?" Scourge asked.

Anywhere else in the galaxy he would have been able to sense the survivors through the Force. Here on Nathema, however, the aftermath of the Emperor's grim ritual blinded his abilities.

"I'm picking up readings of an organic life-form on board," Nyriss confirmed.

They brought the shuttle in for a landing roughly fifty meters from the other vessel. There had been no reaction of any kind from the enemy craft as they approached.

"Search the interior," Nyriss ordered. "I'll wait here."

Disembarking, Scourge got his first good look at the ship. It was an unusual shape—flat and circular, like a disk. He approached it cautiously, his heart pounding. Normally he relied on the Force to warn him of potential danger; without it he felt vulnerable and almost helpless. It was a feeling he most definitely did *not* like.

He was halfway to the vessel when another thought struck him. What if Nyriss simply decided to take off in her shuttle and leave him here? The thought froze him for a moment, until he realized how ridiculous the idea was. If Nyriss had wanted to get rid of him, she could have done so a dozen different ways already. There was no reason to abandon him on Nathema—not after risking her own life to bring him here in the first place.

Scourge steeled himself and continued his advance until he reached the strange ship's underbelly. He pushed the access panel on the hull, and the boarding ramp slowly descended. He wasn't surprised to find it unlocked; most ships had emergency overrides on their security systems in case of a crash, in order to allow rescue workers to get inside and help the injured.

Scourge activated his lightsaber. The familiar hum and hiss of the blade springing to life sounded weak and distant, and the crimson blade appeared faded—even his weapon was not immune to the effects of the dead planet. But he suspected it would still get the job done if he encountered any resistance.

He climbed up the boarding ramp and into the hull of the ship. He followed the circular layout, briefly glancing into storage rooms and passenger bunks in his search for whoever might be on board. He found nothing until he reached the cockpit.

Strapped into the chair was an unconscious—or dead—human male clad in simple brown robes. He appeared to be about forty standard years old. He was thin and wiry, with dark, shoulder-length hair and rough black stubble on his cheeks and chin. Blood poured from a deep gash on his forehead and covered his face; during the crash something that wasn't strapped down must have struck him.

Coming closer, Scourge put two fingers on the side of the man's neck, checking for a pulse. He had barely registered the faint flutter of life when his gaze fell on the hilt hooked to the man's belt: a lightsaber. Instinctively he tried to reach out with the Force to get some sense of the man's power, but he felt only the emptiness of Nathema.

Grabbing the lightsaber and clipping it onto his own belt, he unbuckled the man, slung him over his shoulder, and carried him off the vessel.

The weight of the unconscious man made it difficult to move any faster than a brisk walk, but Scourge pressed the pace. He was eager to leave Nathema behind him for good this time. Nyriss was waiting for him back at the shuttle, standing just inside the boarding ramp. Scourge strode past her and onto the ship, where he tossed the unconscious man roughly onto the floor. He was about to mention the lightsaber, but Nyriss spoke before he had a chance.

"I know this man," she said, her voice grim. "His name is Revan. He's a Jedi and a Republic spy."

"A Republic spy?" Scourge's brain took the news and jumped to the next logical conclusion. "If the Jedi know we exist, they will come for us. They will try to finish the extermination of our species that they began in the Great Hyperspace War!"

"Our existence is still hidden," she assured him. "Revan and another Jedi—a man named Malak—discovered Dromund Kaas by accident. They were captured before they could return and report their findings to the Republic."

"When did all this happen?"

"Five years ago. The Emperor sentenced Revan to death."

"Then what's he doing here?"

"I don't know," Nyriss admitted. "But he couldn't have escaped the citadel's dungeons unless the Emperor allowed it. It stands to reason that he wouldn't still be alive unless he was working for the Emperor."

"How is that possible?" Scourge countered. "The Jedi are our sworn enemies."

Nyriss didn't answer. "Watch him closely," she said, returning to the pilot's seat. "He is powerful and extremely dangerous."

"Why don't we just kill him?"

"Not yet. Not until we know why he is here. We'll take him back to my stronghold for questioning."

"I've never interrogated a Jedi," Scourge said after a moment. He smiled. "I'm looking forward to it."

REVAN HAD NO IDEA where he was when he awoke, though it was obviously some kind of prison cell. He was propped up in a cold metal chair. His hands were bound to the arms, his ankles tied to the legs. For the moment, he was alone.

His mind felt slow and dull, and he knew he'd been drugged. It was difficult to concentrate; impossible to focus his thoughts enough to use the Force. It took all his willpower just to recall the last moments of the *Ebon Hawk* crashing on Nathema.

He struggled to take stock of his situation, but he couldn't pierce the haze of the drugs.

The door to his cell slid open and two figures entered, one male and one female. The sight of their red skin tweaked something in his addled brain, but it took several seconds before he could make the connection.

"Sith," he whispered, his throat dry and his voice hoarse.

"Welcome back, Revan," the female said in Basic.

He stared at her withered, wrinkled face, trying and failing to dredge up her name. "Do I know you?"

The tall male Sith beside her reached out with a hand and casually delivered a backhanded slap across Revan's cheek. "We don't have time to play games," he said. His voice wasn't angry or threatening; it was calm and completely matter-of-fact.

Revan tasted blood; the smack had cut the inside of his mouth. He could feel the sting of the wound and the swelling of his lip. Apparently the drugs used to dull his mind had been carefully selected so they would not interfere with the sensation of physical pain.

"I don't think this is a game," the female said, raising an eyebrow. "I think he's actually forgotten me."

She leaned in close beside him and whispered in his ear: "What happened to you, Revan? Where did you go? Why did you return?"

When he didn't answer, she stepped back and nodded. Then she waved a hand and an interrogator droid—Revan hadn't even noticed it hovering behind the two Sith—floated over and extended a long, thin needle into his neck.

He grimaced in pain as the needle punctured his skin, then screamed as it discharged a powerful electrical burst, setting his nerves on fire.

The Sith male waved a hand and the interrogator droid retreated.

"What happened to your partner?" he asked. "Malak?"

"I killed him," Revan said.

"Why?"

"It's complicated."

The male's expression didn't change, but the female smiled in amusement, the expression transforming her wrinkled features into those of a grinning skull.

"Eventually you'll tell us everything we want to know," the male assured him.

"Maybe so," Revan conceded. "But I'm going to make you work for it."

AFTER FOUR HOURS of questioning the prisoner, Nyriss ordered Scourge to take a break. They left him in his cell, tied to his chair, neither of them speaking until they were outside in the hall and the door to his cell had closed behind them.

"How much longer will it take to break him?" Nyriss asked.

Scourge considered the question carefully before answering. Early in his training, he had shown a knack for torture and interrogation, skills the instructors had encouraged during his years at the Academy. He was an expert in the field; he knew that wringing information out of an unwilling source was about far more than just inflicting pain.

Apply enough punishment and everyone would talk, but most of what they said would be desperately babbled lies, evasions, and half truths. Without any way to verify accuracy, information gathered through torture was often unreliable and even worthless.

Effective interrogation was an art, and Scourge had an innate ability to parse fact from fiction. He knew what questions to ask and in what order; he understood when to ratchet up the intensity and when to pull back. He knew how to use the threat of pain and the reward of mercy to control his subjects.

His advanced techniques, combined with his ability to draw upon the dark side, allowed him to quickly dominate weak minds. Strong-willed subjects were more of a challenge, yet in the end he always got results. Until now.

Interrogating the Jedi had resulted in nothing but frustration and dead ends. His will was strong, as was his command of the Force. Even drugged to the edge of unconsciousness he was able to draw on it to help him endure the pain and the relentless barrage of questions. But there was something else, as well.

Nyriss wanted to know how he had escaped the dungeons of the citadel. She wanted to know about his relationship with the Emperor. She wanted to know why he had come to Nathema. On all those counts, Scourge had come up empty. Revan was resisting him, true, but at some times it almost seemed as if Revan himself didn't know—as if the information had been wiped from his mind.

"We might be wasting our time," he finally admitted. "His pain threshold is high, but we're already at the limits of what a human can endure. If I press any harder, we risk killing him." Scourge had seen it happen many times. Unskilled or overeager interrogators could easily push their subjects too far. In his mind this was the ultimate failure: you couldn't get answers from a corpse.

With difficult subjects you had to be patient. It might take multiple sessions over several days to get anything useful. But even knowing this, Scourge didn't hold out much hope for his chances with Revan.

"I could question him for months, but the information you want just isn't there."

"That is unfortunate." Nyriss sighed. "I was hoping to verify my theory."

"What theory?"

"The Emperor has the ability to dominate and enslave the minds of those who serve him," she explained. "It's one of the reasons he has ruled for so long. Those that are transformed become fanatical zealots who live to serve; they are not capable of betraying him." She glanced back at the door behind which they had left the Jedi. "I suspect that instead of executing Revan as he publicly proclaimed, the Emperor turned him into a puppet of his will and sent him back to the Republic to gather information."

"If he's been gathering intel on the Republic for five years, the Emperor must be closer to launching his invasion than we thought," Scourge noted, alarmed at how close their mad ruler had already come to exposing them to the Jedi.

Nyriss shook her head. "The Emperor is more patient and careful than any being in the galaxy. He has lived for nearly a thousand years; he might live for ten thousand more. He leaves nothing to chance. If necessary, he will spend decades, maybe even centuries, preparing. No, we still have time. And Revan may still be of use to us."

"How so?"

"You said it yourself: something happened to his mind. His memories are lost, but so is his knowledge of and loyalty to the Emperor. Whatever was done to him, it freed him from the Emperor's domination. If we can learn how this happened, we might be able to use it to bring the Emperor down. Remember that all those who have direct access to the Emperor—the Emperor's Voice, the Emperor's Hand, the soldiers in the Imperial Guard—are under his spell. Breaking that spell, turning his most loyal followers against him, is our best chance of defeating him and saving the Empire from his mad plan to attack the Republic.

"We need Revan alive so we can study him," she concluded. "He is too valuable a resource to throw away."

What she said made sense, but Scourge knew it would

be far more difficult and complicated than she made it sound. "It might take years before you understand what happened to him," he warned her.

"The Emperor is not the only one who can be patient," she replied.

PART TWO

CHAPTER SEVENTEEN

BASTILA TUCKED HER SON into bed and leaned down to kiss him on the cheek. At the door of his room she turned and looked back at him, marveling at how much the three-year-old boy already looked like his father. He had the same dark, shoulder-length hair and the thin, angular face. His eyes were closed now, but she knew they were dark and brooding . . . just like Revan's. And though he was already drifting off to sleep, his expression was still unusually serious and intense for a child his age.

She sighed and turned away. Bastila often worried about the effect her son's turbulent childhood would have on him. Growing up without a father was difficult enough, but the first few years of his life had been scarred by war and terror.

After Malak had been defeated, Bastila, like most other citizens of the Republic, had hoped to enjoy many decades of peace. Instead, a group of rogue Jedi had broken away from the Order, plunging the galaxy once more into civil war.

Led by a woman named Kreia, the rogue Jedi turned to the dark side teachings uncovered by Malak and Revan. Kreia took the name Darth Traya, and her followers called themselves the Sith after the long-lost species that had invaded the Republic a millennium before. They began a systemic purge of the galaxy, hunting down those who still held fast to the Jedi Code, killing them by the tens of thousands. Their relentless pursuit virtually wiped out the Order, and only those few who managed to flee or hide survived.

Had Revan returned to face this new threat, Bastila would have eagerly fought by his side. Together they might have been able to quell the uprising, ending it before the horrors of war enveloped the Republic and millions lost their lives. But she had heard nothing of her husband since he had set off with Canderous four years earlier.

Alone, she dared not challenge Darth Traya and her followers. Instead, she had focused on keeping her son alive. It had been the Exile—Meetra Surik—who had taken up the fight against the rogue Jedi. Three years after Revan's unsuccessful attempt to locate her, she had emerged on her own to oppose and eventually defeat Darth Traya. Like Revan before her, she became the savior of the galaxy. And also as with Revan, there were many who felt her recent actions could not atone for the sins of her past.

And now this woman—hero to some, villain to so many others—was sitting in the living room of Bastila's apartment, patiently waiting for her to finish putting her son to bed.

"He's asleep," Bastila said as she returned, speaking softly.

"He's beautiful," Meetra answered, adding, "He looks like his father."

Bastila nodded at the compliment. She wasn't sure what to make of the woman before her. Meetra had short brown hair, pale white skin, and piercing blue eyes. She was taller than Bastila, and almost a decade older, though she would still be considered beautiful by any empirical measure. She possessed a presence and confidence, along with an enviable natural grace. She was clad in the simple robes of a Jedi Master, but somehow she managed to make even the drab brown cloth seem stylish.

Foolish as it was, Bastila couldn't help but feel some hint of jealousy. Meetra had known Revan long before Bastila; she had answered his call to go to war against the Mandalorians, and in doing so she became one of his most trusted advisers and closest friends. Bastila knew they had shared a special bond not unlike that of Padawan and Master. Worst of all, Meetra was an integral part of Revan's lost past—a past he had felt compelled to go in search of, even though it meant leaving his pregnant wife behind.

There is no emotion, there is peace, she thought. The familiar words of the Jedi mantra were easy to recite, but much more difficult to follow.

"You said we needed to speak," Bastila said.

"I wasn't sure if we should come," Meetra admitted. "I understand this might be difficult for you. But Tee-Three insisted." She reached out and patted the little astromech accompanying her on the head.

The last time Bastila had seen T3-M4 he had been boarding the *Ebon Hawk* with Revan and Canderous. Her husband was still missing, but the droid had returned. Clearly he had latched on to Meetra, following at her heel as he had once followed Revan . . . one more small detail to feed Bastila's irrational jealousy.

"As much as I tried, I couldn't get him to tell me anything," Meetra added.

Bastila smiled faintly. "I gave him special instructions the night before he left with Revan. I told Tee-Three if they ever became separated, he had to come find me. I programmed him so he wouldn't tell anyone else what had happened until I heard it first."

Meetra nodded. "A wise move. We've both experienced enough betrayal to understand you never know whom to trust."

"I never imagined I'd be in hiding when he returned," Bastila continued. "I'm sorry about that, Tee-Three. If I'd known you were back, I would have tried to contact you."

The droid beeped in acceptance of her apology.

"Fortunately he found me," Meetra said. "I guess he thought I was the next best thing, given my history with Revan."

Bastila bit her lip to keep from saying anything. She knew her feelings of resentment were neither justified nor fair, but even her Jedi training couldn't quell her emotions.

"Or maybe he just knew I'd need his help," Meetra added quickly, perhaps aware she had in some way offended her host.

"The little guy does have a knack for joining up with galactic saviors," Bastila remarked, trying to keep her voice neutral.

The droid beeped in agitation.

"I'm sorry," Bastila said again. "You're right. You've been very patient so far. I'm just not sure I'm ready to hear what you have to tell me."

She'd often wondered if Revan was still alive. She'd always imagined their love would let her sense him through the Force, even across the breadth of an entire galaxy. Once he left, she learned that wasn't true. Some nights she would dream of him, but she was never sure if these were true visions or merely manifestations of the loneliness she'd felt since he'd gone.

Still, she believed she would have sensed a disturbance in the Force if he had died. Clinging to that gave her hope. Now, however, her belief might be exposed as a mere illusion if T3 told her that Revan was dead. She wanted to hear the truth, of course, but she was determined to hang on to the fantasy for just a few seconds longer.

"Take your time," Meetra said. "I know this is difficult. Tee-Three's waited three years for this; he can wait a little while longer."

Her words were meant as comfort, but they had the opposite effect. "Maybe this would be easier if Tee-Three and I spoke in private," Bastila said.

It was clear the request had caught Meetra off guard, but she quickly regained her composure. "I understand you want to be cautious," she said sympathetically, "but Canderous told me all about Revan and his search for the storm-covered world."

Bastila grimaced. She'd heard rumors that a Mandalorian had aided the Exile in her battle against Darth Traya.

"Is it true?" Bastila asked. "Is Canderous the new Mandalore?"

Meetra nodded. "Revan helped him find Mandalore's Mask before continuing on alone."

"What else do you know that I don't?" Bastila asked, trying to keep the bitterness out of her voice.

"I would never intentionally keep any knowledge of Revan from you," Meetra assured her earnestly. "You are his wife; you have more right to the truth than anyone."

Bastila swallowed hard, suddenly ashamed. "You have the same right," she said. "You stood by Revan's side at the beginning; he had no truer friend. Whatever Tee-Three has to say, we should hear it together."

Meetra nodded her appreciation, but didn't speak. Taking a deep breath, Bastila sat down on the living room chair, facing her guests. She folded her hands in her lap, mentally bracing herself for what was to come.

"I'm ready," she said.

In a series of beeps, chimes, and holorecordings T3 relayed his story. He began with Revan returning to the *Ebon Hawk* on Rekkiad. He told them how he and Revan had left Canderous behind and journeyed to Nathema alone. He described the unexpected attack on the *Ebon Hawk* and the near-fatal crash landing on Nathema's surface.

He explained how he had checked on the unconscious Revan to make sure he was still alive, then been forced to hide when someone else boarded the ship.

When he played the holorecording he'd made of the red-skinned man who'd taken Revan off the ship, Bastila gasped.

"I guess the Sith aren't as extinct as the Jedi thought," Meetra said.

"The Order is wrong again," Bastila muttered. "Big surprise."

T3 let out a low whistle, apologizing for his cowardice, but Bastila shook her head.

"That wasn't cowardice," she told the little droid. "If you hadn't hid, they'd have captured you, too. Or turned you into scrap."

"The only way you could help Revan was by making it back in one piece," Meetra added.

Mollified, T3 continued his story. He told them how Revan was taken onto a waiting shuttle and whisked away. With his master gone, returning to Bastila became the astromech's primary purpose, as per her last-minute instructions before they'd left Coruscant.

The first step involved getting the *Ebon Hawk* airborne again. The droid described in detail his arduous efforts to repair the damage done by the crash. For months he scoured the streets of the deserted city, gathering scrap, salvage, and other necessary parts.

"And you never saw anyone during that time?" Meetra asked. "No refugees? No looters?"

T3 chirped out a confirmation.

Bastila blinked in surprise. "No animals? No insects? Not even any plants? How could the entire population of an entire world just be wiped out?"

Meetra shifted uncomfortably in her seat, and Bastila knew she was thinking back to her role in the massacre of Malachor V. She felt a sudden burst of empathy for the other woman. Bastila didn't condone what she had done, but she understood what it was like to be ashamed of acts in your past. She herself had let Malak turn her to the dark side; only the power of Revan's love had redeemed her.

Bastila sensed that despite all Meetra had done to stop Darth Traya, she was haunted by guilt and remorse. She was still looking for redemption.

Unaware of the awkward tension in the room, the droid continued his tale. After nearly a year he was finally able to get the *Ebon Hawk* airborne again, though its hyperdrive core was only operating at minimal efficiency. The *Hawk* limped back to Republic space; by the time it arrived, Traya and her followers had all but wiped out the Jedi. Bastila was gone; T3 didn't know where to search for her, or whether she was even alive.

It was during this time that the little astromech droid stumbled across the disassembled pieces of HK-47, abandoned on a remote and nameless world. Recognizing his old companion, the little droid gathered up the pieces and stored them on the *Ebon Hawk*.

The chance encounter was the kind of coincidence that Bastila would have chalked up to the influence of the Force had T3 been an organic being.

"Do you have any idea how he got there?" she asked.

"I always wondered what happened to him after he disappeared."

Meetra shook her head, answering on behalf of the droid. "His memory core was damaged. Even after I repaired him, he was unable to recall anything. Actually," she admitted, "I had hoped you might be able to tell me what had happened to him."

Bastila shrugged. "When he found out Revan had left, HK decided to go after him. But I refused to tell him where my husband had gone."

"A wise move," Meetra said. "The last thing Revan needed while helping Canderous and the Mandalorians was a homicidal droid following him around."

"HK stormed off, swearing he would track Revan down on his own," Bastila continued. "That was the last I heard of him until he showed up again with you."

"There must be some part of his programming that compels him to seek Revan out," Meetra muttered. "If I had known that, I would have been more careful."

"What do you mean?"

"I left HK under the supervision of the new Jedi Council. I didn't think it was safe to have him roaming the galaxy, and I assumed he would be content to stay with the Jedi, awaiting further orders. But he disappeared soon after I left. Now I realize he's probably gone in search of Revan again."

Suddenly worried, Bastila asked, "Is there any chance he'll find him?" She directed her question to T3. "Did you tell him anything about what happened to Revan?"

T3 responded with a negative buzz that sounded almost offended. Clearly the astromech felt the same reservations about involving the hunter-killer droid as his human counterparts.

Relieved, Bastila muttered, "Someone should try to track him down. Find and disable him before he hurts anyone else."

There was little conviction behind her words; as dangerous as HK was, he was only one droid. She had more important things on her mind. Her husband was still missing, and for the first time in years, she was on the verge of being able to do something about it.

"The Jedi are already searching for HK," Meetra assured her. "Don't worry about him."

Bastila nodded. "Tee-Three," she said. "Tell us the rest of your story. What happened next?"

The astromech continued his tale.

After finding the disassembled bits of HK-47, he fell in with Meetra, joining her as he had joined Revan many years before. By the time he learned Bastila was alive, he was once again caught up in a battle for the Republic's survival. Despite his instructions, he knew he couldn't abandon Meetra until the safety of the Republic was secured.

His confession caused Bastila to feel another surge of bitterness. T3 had chosen to help Meetra instead of following Bastila's instructions. He'd put the Exile's mission above his loyalty to Revan.

The emotion passed quickly, replaced by guilt and shame. Bastila's love for Revan had once again momentarily blinded her to logic and reason. Her husband was one man; it was foolish to value his life against the fate of millions. If Revan had been standing in the room, he would have congratulated the droid for putting the greater good above personal wants and desires.

"Revan would be proud of you," she told the little droid. "I'm proud of you, too."

"I think our path is clear," Meetra declared. "I will go to Nathema and see if I can learn Revan's fate."

"You?" Bastila said, her voice showing more anger and surprise than she intended. "What about me? You expect me to just sit here and wait, not even knowing if he's alive or dead?"

"What has changed since Revan left?" Meetra asked softly. "You stayed behind to care for your son. Are you prepared to leave him behind now?"

"Of course not!" Bastila spat. She almost added, *I'll bring him with me,* but at the last second she realized how reckless and ridiculous that would be.

Revan had left because he believed there was something in the Unknown Regions that was a far greater threat than any the Republic had ever faced. Guided by his visions of a storm-covered world, he thought his journey was the only way to protect the future of his family. Following in his footsteps might expose their son to the very threat Revan was trying to stop; it would be a betrayal of the very principles that had sent him on his journey in the first place, and it would endanger their child.

"I'm sorry," Bastila whispered. "I didn't mean to . . . I just . . . I miss him. I feel so helpless. So useless. All I do is wait. You don't understand how hard it's been."

"I can only imagine how you've suffered," Meetra replied gently. "I wish I could say it will get easier. But I fear that may not be the case. We all have burdens to bear, and this is yours."

Her words offered little comfort, but Bastila appreciated her honesty.

"I will do everything in my power to find Revan," Meetra promised. "If he is still alive, I will do whatever it takes to bring him back to you."

T3 beeped twice.

"I would be honored if you came," Meetra told him, "as long as Bastila doesn't object."

Bastila wanted T3 to stay with her; his holorecordings and data banks were all she had left of her husband. But she was thinking rationally now.

"You're going to need his help," she said. "He spent

months exploring Nathema while searching for parts to repair the *Hawk*."

"Then we must leave as soon as possible," Meetra declared, rising to her feet.

"Please, wait just a moment longer," Bastila said.

Leaving Meetra and T3 in the living room, she rushed into the bedchamber and opened the wooden chest tucked away in the back of her closet. She grabbed two items, then returned to her waiting guests.

"Give these to Revan," she said, placing the items in Meetra's hands.

The first was a holorecording she had made of their son's last birthday celebration. The second was a heavy object wrapped in a swath of black cloth.

Meetra glanced at her, silently asking permission to unwrap it. Bastila answered with a subtle nod. Meetra unwound the cloth carefully, revealing a worn and scarred metal helmet with a red-and-gray faceplate.

"Revan's mask!" Meetra gasped. "I thought it was lost when he was captured by the Jedi strike team."

"I led that strike team," Bastila reminded her. "I don't know why, but I took it when Revan fell. Perhaps even then I sensed our fates were intertwined. I never told anyone. Not the Council. Not even him."

"Why not?"

Bastila hesitated, then decided Meetra deserved to know the truth. "Revan wore the mask during the Mandalorian Wars, and during his time as Darth Revan. To me, it symbolizes his dark past—a relic from a time before he became the man I loved. I was afraid that if I showed it to him, it might trigger something inside his mind. It might awaken some dormant evil, rekindle the spark of the dark side."

"Then why give it to me now?"

"I tried to keep Revan's past at bay, but now I understand that was wrong. I was being selfish. His past is a part of him, whether I like it or not." She looked away from the mask. "When you find him, give him the mask. It might mean nothing to him now, but there's a chance it will bring back some of what he has lost. Seeing it might restore crucial memories that will help you return safely."

"What if your fears are right?" Meetra asked, her voice grim. "The mask could bring back his memories. But what if it does more? What if it unleashes the power of the dark side in him?"

"I don't care," Bastila said defiantly. "Not if that power helps bring him back to me."

As a Jedi, her words were blasphemy. She half expected Meetra to throw the mask to the ground in disgust. Instead the other woman rewrapped it in the cloth and tucked it safely away beneath her robes without saying a word.

CHAPTER EIGHTEEN

MEETRA DIDN'T KNOW what to expect as the *Ebon Hawk* dropped out of hyperspace and began the approach toward Nathema. T3-M4 had told her that the planet was deserted, but the little droid had found no apparent cause of the mass extinction. While exploring the surface on his last visit, he'd run tests that confirmed the environment was free of toxins and radiation; beyond that everything else was speculation.

As the ship drew closer to the dingy brown world she felt a growing sense of unease and discomfort. In some ways it reminded her of Malachor V—the massive and instantaneous loss of life on that doomed world had created a wound in the Force. The activation of the mass-shadow generator had obliterated two armies, shredding apart the bonds of the Force that linked all living things.

Meetra had been close enough to feel the shock wave; to survive it she had cut herself off from the Force, shielding her psyche against the horrors of what she had unleashed. Many years had passed before she regained her connection to the Force, but in the end, surviving the trauma of Malachor V had given her the strength to defeat Darth Traya and her followers.

At first she assumed some similar tragedy had occurred

on Nathema; a superweapon capable of snuffing out an entire planet would leave a blanketing echo of death and darkness. As the *Ebon Hawk* descended through the atmosphere, however, she realized this sensation was markedly different.

It took her a few seconds to put her finger on it, her mind analyzing the problem even as her hands automatically made the necessary adjustments to bring the ship in for a landing near the coordinates T3 had given her.

The events of Malachor had left a mark on the Force; a wound that would not heal. Here, however, the Force was simply . . . gone. It was as if someone had ripped it away, leaving only an empty void behind.

Her discomfort grew as the ship drew closer to the surface. This world was unnatural, and her body's instinctive reaction was one of illness and revulsion. She glanced over at T3 hovering anxiously near her in the cockpit, but the droid seemed unaffected. His lack of reaction merely reinforced the nature of her own suffering; as a droid, T3 could not sense the Force, and he wouldn't notice if it was suddenly missing.

Through the cockpit window Meetra saw a path of destruction winding its way through the city below: the remnants of Revan's crash landing. A massive chunk of permacrete had been smashed loose from a skyscraper passing by on the ship's starboard side. The pavement of the street and sidewalk below had been torn up when the vessel had skipped and skidded down the thoroughfare. The mangled remnants of hovercars and speeders traced an irregular line down the street, the smaller vehicles crushed by the passage of the far more massive starship.

Meetra selected her landing spot and set the ship down carefully. The oppressiveness of the Void was bearing down on her, but she did her best to ignore it.

"Come on, Tee-Three," she said, unbuckling herself

from the pilot's chair. "Let's take a look around and see what we can find."

As she stepped off the shuttle she felt like she had been punched in the gut; she doubled over, and T3 beeped in concern.

"I'm okay," she gasped, slowly straightening up.

She had visited Malachor V years after the cataclysm of the mass-shadow generator. Traversing its surface had been agony. Mentally, she had still sensed the anguish of all who had lost their lives there. Physically, the intense gravity of the world had held her in its crushing grip, leaving her gasping for breath. It had been the most awful and horrific experience of her life . . . until now.

On Malachor she'd felt the echoes of unimaginable pain and suffering—but at least she'd felt *something*. Here on Nathema, there was only a cold emptiness. It was unnatural; abhorrent. On Malachor she had felt the echo of great destruction; here there was only the unbearable void of annihilation.

Her body reacted with a revulsion so strong she felt physically ill. Her mind briefly tried to imagine what had happened to cause such an abomination, then recoiled from the answers. Her mind went blank and her body numb.

She stood motionless for several minutes, or maybe it was several hours; time had no meaning here. But the incessant squawking of T3 eventually roused her from her stupor.

Drawing on the mental focusing techniques she had learned as a Padawan, she forced herself to concentrate on something—anything—besides the inescapable nonpresence of the Force.

You've come here to find Revan, she thought. *There has to be some clue as to where the Sith might have taken him.*

"We need to find some kind of archive," she said out loud. "Something that can tell us more about this world."

Her voice sounded hollow and washed out, but it was just one more unsettling detail of Nathema that she refused to dwell on.

The lights on T3 blinked rapidly as the astromech quickly scanned his memory circuits. A few seconds later he beeped excitedly and took off down the street.

Meetra followed him, her long legs allowing her to quickly catch up to and keep pace with the droid. The brisk walk made her feel more normal; physical activity seemed to help keep Nathema's oppressive emptiness at bay.

The droid led her to the entrance of what appeared to be some kind of official government building. On the outside were characters she couldn't read. In the Republic all government business was conducted in Basic. And while it was likely the inhabitants of Nathema had been familiar with Basic—the lingua franca of interstellar trade was known to virtually every spacefaring species in the galaxy—they had obviously marked their building in a native tongue.

The building was three stories high, with only a handful of windows looking out to the street and a pair of uninviting doors that seemed to be the common fashion of bureaucratic strongholds across every culture of the galaxy.

The doors were locked, but she carved through the security bolt with her lightsaber, trying to ignore the dim and washed-out appearance of the glowing blade.

Focus on the task at hand, she reminded herself. *Just find the information you're looking for as quickly as possible and you can get off this blasted world.*

She stepped through, T3 following at her heel. It was dark inside; whatever source had once powered the building had long since fallen into disrepair. Meetra pulled a glow rod from one of the many pockets sewn into the wide fabric belt on her waist and ignited it, illuminating their surroundings with its eerie green glow.

The first things she noticed were the piles of clothes scattered haphazardly about. She realized they must have fallen to the ground when the wearers vanished. It took all her mental discipline to keep her mind from speculating on what kind of event could have caused the bizarre phenomenon.

Exploring the ground floor revealed it to be some type of reception area or lobby. There was a large desk set up to face the door, perfectly positioned for the person behind it to greet visitors. Apart from several uncomfortable-looking chairs arranged in what was probably a central waiting room, there didn't seem to be much else of interest on the lower level.

There was a lift in the corner leading to the upper floors, but with no power it was of little use. Fortunately, a quick search located a staircase behind an unmarked door near the back of the building.

"Let's check out the upper floors," she said, and T3 beeped in agreement.

For some astromech droids stairs could be a problem, but T3 was remarkably versatile. By locking his wheels to keep from rolling backward, he was able to use his front legs to lever himself up the steps one at a time. It took him a little longer to reach the top of the flight than his human companion, but at least Meetra didn't have to try to carry him.

The second floor was filled with data terminals and cubicles—workstations for the government drones who had once wandered the offices and halls. Unfortunately, without power the computer network had ceased to function, rendering the terminals useless.

"Let's see if we can find the main data bank on the next floor up," Meetra suggested.

A few minutes later they were on the third floor. Like the level below, it seemed to consist primarily of offices, cubicles, and workstations. Near the back of the building they found a single durasteel door. On the wall beside it was what appeared to be a security keypad.

"Show me what you've got," Meetra said, pointing to the pad.

T3 rolled up to the wall. A panel on his body slid open to reveal a long, thin electrical probe, which he extended so that it pierced the security pad. There was a brief pause, then the unmistakable *zap* of a powerful electrical discharge. The keypad lit up and the door slid open.

As Meetra had hoped, the room beyond housed the primary computer data banks.

"Grab anything that looks useful so we can get out of here," she said.

T3 hustled to oblige, inserting his versatile probe into an interface port so he could slice into the defunct network. As he had done with the door panel, T3 gave the data bank a powerful electric jolt to temporarily reactivate it so he could download the relevant files.

The entire process took less than five minutes, but for Meetra it might as well have been an eternity. She had managed to keep busy up until this point, but while waiting idly by for T3 to finish she began to notice the absence of the Force once more.

She could feel the Void pressing in on her from all sides. At the same time it was pulling on her, trying to rip away the very essence of her existence. Nature abhors a vacuum; the emptiness was trying to fill itself with her energy. For an instant she felt as if she were going to become undone, her physical body discorporating into trillions of subatomic particles that would scatter across the entire surface of Nathema.

No! she screamed in her mind. *The Void will not take*

me! I am more than just a collection of random matter and particles! I am a living being. I am Meetra Surik!

The affirmation of her own existence seemed to push the Void back, at least for the moment. But Meetra knew she couldn't hold out against it much longer. As much as she tried to ignore what she felt—or, more precisely, didn't feel—all around her, she knew it was only a matter of time until the horrors of Nathema stripped away her sanity.

She was just about to tell T3 it was time to go when he beeped triumphantly and retracted the probe.

"I need to get back to the ship," she told him. "You can tell me what you found when we're off this world."

Once she was in motion she felt better, but she could still sense the Void hovering on the fringes of her awareness. It was like being stalked by some nameless, faceless, invisible creature. She felt it lurking around every corner, just waiting for her to let her guard down so it could take her.

She quickened her pace, trusting her droid companion to keep up, too intent on keeping a grip on herself to reply to his indignant chirps.

By the time she reached the *Ebon Hawk* she was running, though she wasn't even aware of it. One single thought dominated her conscious mind: *Escape!*

She strapped herself into the pilot's chair and fired up the engines just as T3, who had fallen behind, came racing up the boarding ramp.

"Hold on," she warned as she closed the hatch and punched the engines.

The *Ebon Hawk* took flight, hurtling itself up toward the sky and beyond. They broke atmosphere, but Meetra didn't slow the ship down. She kept the engines on full until they were on the very edge of the solar system. Only then, with several million kilometers between her and Nathema, did she feel safe enough to throttle back.

T3 rolled up beside her and let out a worried whistle.

"You wouldn't understand," she told him. "But I'm okay now. Just give me a few minutes and we'll take a look at what you pulled from those data banks."

IT TOOK LONGER than Meetra expected for T3 to decipher and translate the files from Nathema into something she could scan with the ship's computer. It was nearly two days before she could begin looking through the files. However, she reminded herself, considering he was processing millions of terabytes of data originally compiled on computers using fundamentally alien technology, the fact that he accomplished anything at all was a small miracle.

During her initial investigations several things quickly became clear. The building they had raided had been some type of archival storage office, a mundane but vital component of any complex government. It contained government documents, historical accounts and transcripts, and, most promising of all, detailed census records collected from numerous worlds.

From the census data it became clear that Nathema had once been part of the Sith Empire. Oddly, all the records seemed to predate the Great Hyperspace War. Whatever event had stripped Nathema of all life and left it devoid of the Force must have happened almost a thousand years before.

Because of that, it was impossible to tell if the Sith Empire as described in the records still existed. But given T3's holorecording of the red-skinned being taking Revan, Meetra was willing to bet it still survived in some form.

Revan had left Bastila behind because he feared the greatest threat to the Republic's survival was lurking in the Unknown Regions. The reemergence of the Sith Empire certainly qualified.

The theory also fit with what Canderous had told her. The Mandalorian had claimed that Revan asked him to restore the glory and strength of his people so they could stand against the Sith should they ever try to invade the Republic again.

According to the census records, the Sith Empire comprised several dozen planets. The Sith who had taken Revan might have come from any one of those worlds; if she could figure out which was his home, she might be able to narrow her search.

However, as she cross-checked the names and galactic coordinates of the listed worlds, Meetra quickly realized that they were all planets already known to the Republic. Over the last thousand years, the Jedi had systematically purged every planet mentioned in the census of their Sith influence: these were the records of a Sith Empire that was no more.

Refusing to give up, she dug deeper into the datafiles they had gathered, examining records pertaining to Nathema itself. For several days she pored through the archives, stopping neither to eat nor to sleep. Every few hours she refreshed herself with a quick meditation break, drawing on the Force to replenish her fading stores of energy and mental focus so she could continue her work.

There were tens of thousands of government documents and reports collected from over fifty different agencies, but Meetra refused to be daunted by the monumental task. She continued to pore through the archives, and slowly a picture began to emerge.

The people of Nathema had spent their last days in a terrified and desperate state. They had known it was only a matter of time until the Jedi found them, and the ruler of Nathema—a Sith named Lord Vitiate— had preyed upon his people's fear. Transcripts of Vitiate's public speeches were filled with graphic warnings of what the Jedi would do once they arrived. Records confirmed that his speeches had been broadcast and transmitted across the whole of the Empire, sowing the seeds of terror among all the Sith worlds. Vitiate had consciously and carefully driven the people into a state of panic, knowing they would blindly follow anyone who offered hope.

Vitiate was quick to fulfill that role, and he put out a call for all the other surviving Dark Lords to join him on Nathema in a ritual that he promised would lead the Sith to salvation.

At the same time he was doing this, Vitiate also had top historians and scientists secretly trying to determine the location of a planet called Dromund Kaas—the long-lost homeworld of the original Sith species.

Meetra discovered this only because of T3's exceptional slicing skills. The astromech had not only copied and translated all the data from the archives, but also decrypted the pass codes to unlock classified government files, which he had then marked as having top priority to help simplify Meetra's investigations.

The team Vitiate assigned to search out Dromund Kaas had operated in total secrecy, sequestered day and night in a research lab as they studied the ancient star maps and astrogation charts. Fortunately the leader of the team had been a meticulous record keeper, and every step of the process had been carefully documented—including the moment of triumph when they were finally able to theorize a hyperspace route that would lead them safely back to Dromund Kaas, where the Jedi could never follow.

The final entry in the team leader's project log detailed her efforts to prepare her findings so they could be presented to Vitiate in person. Lord Vitiate publicly proclaimed the commencement of his great ritual just three days later.

Chronologically, there were no records after the proclamation. Nothing from the research team; nothing from any of the other departments. It was as if every member of Nathema's sprawling government had simultaneously vanished from existence. Even without any official account of what had happened next, however, it wasn't hard for Meetra to put the missing pieces together.

The ritual had obviously destroyed Nathema, snuffing out all life on the world. Lord Vitiate had offered his people hope, and instead had brought them a fate worse than death—utter eradication of life, existence, and even the Force.

Meetra was no expert on dark side sorcery, but it was safe to assume Vitiate not only survived the ritual, but emerged more powerful than ever. And with the destruction of everyone on Nathema—including his research team—he alone would have known the location of Dromund Kaas.

The plan was both horrifying and brilliant. In addition to becoming more powerful than Meetra could imagine, Vitiate could blame the extinction of his homeworld on the Jedi, further panicking the remaining Sith worlds. Then he could have offered them a glimmer of hope, promising to lead all those who swore loyalty to him to a place where the Jedi would never find them.

If Vitiate had been as cunning as Meetra imagined him to be, he wouldn't have led his followers directly to Dromund Kaas. Instead, he would have taken them on a long and trying exodus—during which the Sith would have been forced to turn to him time and again for support and guidance, their dependence on him growing until he went from leader to hero to savior. By the time they finally reached Dromund Kaas, they would likely have worshiped Vitiate as a god—all-powerful and all-knowing.

Fascinating history, to be sure, but Meetra didn't

know how it could help her find Revan. Vitiate's grand plan had taken place over a thousand years earlier. Surely Vitiate himself was long dead, and even if he had led the Sith to Dromund Kaas, there was no guarantee they were still there.

There were other possibilities to consider, as well. The Sith were an aggressive and war-like species; it was possible that Dromund Kaas was just one of many worlds in the Unknown Regions that had fallen under their control over the last thousand years. It was possible— and even likely—that the red-skinned being who had captured Revan had taken him to an entirely different planet, one she had never even heard of. But at least she had a lead. And no matter how slim the odds of finding her mentor, Meetra wasn't about to give up. She trusted in the Force; eventually it would lead her to him.

From the census records, it was clear that humans were—or had been—part of the Sith Empire. If Vitiate's followers had settled on Dromund Kaas, she should be able to pass among them by posing as a mercenary, a role she knew well from the years she had spent living as the Exile in the Outer Rim.

As she punched the hyperspace coordinates from the research team leader's logbook into the nav computer, T3 came over and chirped inquisitively.

"We're going to a world called Dromund Kaas," Meetra said as the *Ebon Hawk* made the jump to lightspeed. "If Revan's there, we'll find him."

CHAPTER NINETEEN

SCOURGE TYPED IN the access code to unlock the door leading to the underground holding cells built beneath Nyriss's stronghold. He didn't acknowledge the guards standing watch as he stepped through, and they made no move to stop him. He had passed the checkpoint hundreds of times, and they had stopped bothering with Murtog's official security protocols long ago.

He descended the stairs to the dimly lit, dead-end hall at the bottom. There were four doors, two on either side. Beside each door was a monitor, showing a holovid of what was happening inside each cell. Three of the cells were empty; the fourth had been occupied by the same prisoner for the past three years.

The image showed Revan seated in a familiar position, his legs crossed and his hands resting palms-up on his thighs. His eyes were closed, his face calm . . . though Scourge knew that had as much to do with the medication as the meditation.

The prisoner had not left his cell for even a single moment since his capture. There was a refresher in the corner, a small sink and a bed against one wall. In the beginning they had brought in a chair to strap him to for his interrogation sessions, but after the first few months

Scourge convinced Nyriss that torturing Revan was an unproductive waste of both time and resources.

By that time Revan had already told them everything—as much as he could remember, at least. He had revealed that the Jedi had wiped away most of his early memories, including all traces of what had happened to him in the Emperor's dungeons. He had confessed that he had come to Nathema in the hopes of reclaiming his lost past, following the same trail he had embarked on years before.

He couldn't tell Nyriss anything about what she really asked. And though she still suspected he had been dominated by and then broken free of the Emperor's will, the scientists she had brought in to study him had been unable to find anything useful with all their testing and research.

After six months Nyriss had lost interest in her Jedi prisoner. Her attention moved on to other plots and intrigues, though she kept him alive just in case. But while Nyriss ignored Revan, Scourge had become obsessed with him.

The Jedi's command of and connection to the Force was unlike anything Scourge had sensed in anyone else. Even though Revan was constantly drugged, it was impossible not to sense his strength. After years of studying him, Scourge had come to understand why the Jedi had such a fearsome reputation among the Sith. With men and women like Revan in their ranks, it was easy to see how they had beaten back the Sith invasion a thousand years earlier. And it confirmed what he already suspected: the Emperor's plan to launch another invasion against the Republic at this point in time was tantamount to suicide.

However, it was more than the Jedi's raw power that interested Scourge. Unlike all the instructors at the Academy, or even Nyriss herself, Revan had experienced both the light and dark sides of the Force. He had a unique perspective on its strengths and weaknesses, and Scourge was eager to learn from his experience.

It hadn't been easy, of course. Revan had regarded him as an enemy at first: Scourge was the being who tortured him for information. But over time that had slowly changed. Revan was held in almost total seclusion. The guards were forbidden to speak with him, and once Nyriss all but forgot about him, the weekly visits from Scourge were his only source of conversation or contact.

Scourge understood that long periods of solitary confinement could be even harder to endure than the brutal physical suffering of the interrogations. Loneliness and isolation would eat away at the mind and the spirit; it was inevitable that Revan would forge a relationship with the only person he ever had any contact with.

It was a slow and subtle process, and even now they still regarded each other with suspicion and mistrust. But eventually the instinctive need for interaction had caused Revan to open up. He would give carefully guarded answers to Scourge's questions about his beliefs and philosophies, or let slip bits and pieces of his knowledge of the Force.

No matter how long they spoke, Revan was careful to say very little, but over the years the tiny drops of wisdom had accumulated into a great reservoir for Scourge to draw on. Nyriss may have had no further use for Revan, but Scourge was going to exploit this invaluable resource for all it was worth.

Scourge unlocked the door to Revan's cell. The Jedi was still wearing the same brown robes he had been captured in; the clothes—like the prisoner himself—had not been properly cleaned in three years. Scourge winced at the stale, pungent scent wafting off the human, but it was a small price to pay, considering how much he had already gained from their regular visits.

"Revan," he said, noting that the prisoner's eyes were still closed. "I wish to speak with you."

REVAN OPENED HIS EYES as if responding to the Sith's voice, though in truth he had sensed his approach from the moment he began to descend the staircase. It was difficult to draw upon the Force through the veil of mind-altering chemicals in his system, but over the years he had learned a handful of tricks.

Though they had spoken hundreds of times, the Sith had never told Revan his name. Not that it mattered. To Revan he was nothing more than a tool—his one hope of ever getting out of the cell alive.

In the first few months he had hoped that someone would come for him: Canderous, or T3-M4, or maybe even Bastila, drawn to him by the Force. But as time passed, his drug-addled brain finally realized he was truly alone.

He had tried reaching out to Bastila with the Force, but the drugs and the vast distance of an entire galaxy must have stopped her from sensing his need. He had almost given up once he realized there would be no rescue; his situation seemed hopeless. And then his muddled mind seized on the Sith interrogator.

It was clear the red-skinned being was subservient to the withered hag who had been present during the early interrogations. It was also obvious that he was more than just a thug hired to torture information out of prisoners. Revan had sensed the Force in him; he had incredible potential. Fortunately for Revan, he was also arrogant, overconfident, and ambitious.

Over the course of many months, Revan fed that ambition with tiny crumbs meant to draw the Sith Lord in. He spoke of his past, knowing his triumphs over Malak and other powerful individuals would feed the young Sith's desire to rise above his current station.

Revan also made a point of bringing up the Force regularly. He had once served the dark side, and he understood its insatiable lust for power. The chance to learn something—anything—new about the Force was a temptation the Sith could not resist.

He was willing to give the Sith glimpses of his wisdom because with each conversation he learned a little bit more about his captors. The interrogator was careful; he tried to reveal as little of himself and the world outside the cell as possible. But over many months and hundreds of conversations it was inevitable some things would slip.

To facilitate the process, Revan had carefully forged a relationship with the anonymous Sith, establishing a familiar rapport that made it easier for the Sith to unknowingly open up about himself even as he thought he was using Revan.

His efforts had been well rewarded. Over the past three years he had learned much about the Sith society the Republic believed to be extinct. He knew they were ruled by an Emperor; he knew they controlled hundreds of worlds.

About a year earlier, he had learned the name of the female who had overseen the first few interrogations. Her name was Nyriss, and she was one of the Emperor's handpicked advisers.

At one point his captor had let slip that the Emperor was secretly planning an invasion against the Republic. More important, he had revealed that he and Nyriss—along with many other Sith—were determined to stop him.

Revan had seized on that shared goal, and for the past few months he had been playing on it at every opportunity.

It all might be futile. All his efforts might amount to nothing more than a game he was playing merely to help

pass the endless hours of his incarceration. But if there
was a chance, however small, that he could somehow
use this knowledge to break free of his prison, he intended to take it.

THE JEDI HAD OPENED his eyes, but he still seemed to
be lost in thought. Scourge wondered if they had altered
his medication recently. Every few months they had to
switch him to a new formula as his body became more
resistant to the daily dose of drugs meant to keep him
docile and helpless. For the first few days after each
switch, Revan seemed even more out of it than usual.

"Revan," he repeated, speaking more loudly. He
clapped his hands sharply, the sound echoing off the
walls of the cell.

"I'm sorry, my lord," Revan said in response, slurring
his words slightly. "I'm having trouble . . . focusing. It's
good to see you again," he added with a faint smile. "I
always enjoy your visits."

Scourge would never admit it to anyone, of course,
but he also enjoyed them. He had developed a great respect and even admiration for Revan; ironic, given how
much his opinion of Nyriss had gone down in the last
few months.

"You seem troubled, my lord."

"Nyriss still refuses to take any real action against the
Emperor," he grumbled.

It felt good to say the words out loud. That was an
unexpected benefit of being the only person who ever
spoke to the prisoner. Anything he said in the cell would
never leave these walls; here he could vent his frustrations aloud without fear of reprisal.

"She tells me we must be patient, but her energies and
resources are focused on besting her rivals on the Dark
Council."

"Nyriss is driven by fear," Revan explained, speaking

in the slow, monotonous cadence Scourge had never really gotten used to. "Openly striking against the Emperor puts her life at risk. Her own immediate survival is more important to her than the fate of your Empire."

"There are powerful allies who could be persuaded to help her," Scourge replied. "All they need is someone to step up and take charge. All they need is a leader to spur them to action."

"I was betrayed by Malak," Revan reminded him. "Nyriss is afraid the same thing could happen to her. If she steps forward as leader, she can no longer hide in the shadows with the others. She will be exposed, and it would only take one ambitious rival to betray her to the Emperor and bring everything crashing down."

Scourge nodded, remembering how Nyriss had done the same thing to eliminate Darth Xedrix. At the time he had believed her when she said it was for the good of the cause, but now he suspected it had just been an excuse to remove a rival from the Dark Council.

"If all the conspirators are too afraid to step forward, the Emperor will never be stopped," Scourge muttered. "Eventually he will lead us into a war we cannot win, and the Jedi will wipe us out in retaliation. Ultimately doing nothing is the most dangerous choice of all."

"Nyriss blinds herself to that truth. That is the way of the dark side," Revan said. "Those who follow it are driven by fear and ambition. They are too selfish to see that great victories often require sacrifice."

Scourge grimaced. Sometimes he grew tired of Revan's preaching against the dark side. In this case, however, the Jedi was at least partially correct. Nyriss wouldn't think twice about sacrificing an ally or a follower, but she would never consider sacrificing herself.

Revan, on the other hand, had journeyed across the galaxy in the face of unknown dangers because he thought there might be something that threatened his beloved Republic. He had put himself in harm's way for something he believed in.

A year earlier Scourge would have laughed at his foolishness; after all, what had Revan accomplished besides becoming a prisoner? Now, however, he understood that though the Jedi had failed, at least he had made the effort. At least he'd had a chance to succeed. Nyriss, it seemed, wasn't even going to make the attempt. She had failed to stop the Emperor before she had even begun.

"You need to find another ally to your cause," Revan said. "Someone powerful, but who is not caught up in the politics of the Dark Council."

Scourge laughed out loud at what Revan was clearly implying.

"You must be growing desperate if you think you can talk me into helping you escape."

MENTALLY, REVAN WINCED. He had pushed too far too fast. Instead of subtle manipulation, he had stumbled into revealing a clumsy and obvious ploy. He never would have made such a foolish mistake if his mind was clear.

But he thought it might still be possible to salvage the situation. He had to give the Sith something else to focus on, something he cared about above everything else.

"We share a common goal," Revan admitted. "We both want to stop the Emperor from invading the Republic. But I am not proposing an alliance." He paused. "I do not need your help to escape. The Force has shown me that my freedom is drawing near."

"The Force has shown you? What do you mean? Have you had a vision?"

As Revan suspected, his jailer had never experienced a vision through the Force. It wasn't unusual: the phenomenon was much rarer in those who followed the dark side. Their focus was internal—they used the Force as a tool, rather than seeing themselves as instruments of the Force's will. They were not accustomed to opening themselves up to the Force for guidance and direction.

"The Force has shown me that my future lies beyond these walls," Revan lied.

"I don't put much faith in visions and prophecy," the Sith said.

"Have you ever felt a premonition of danger through the Force?" Revan asked, trying to help him understand. "Sensed a threat before it was revealed?"

"Of course."

"The visions are merely an extrapolation of this. The Force flows across both space and time; it links the past, present, and future."

"It is said that Naga Sadow had visions of the Sith crushing the Republic during the Great Hyperspace War," Scourge countered. "We both know that never came to pass."

"The future is always in motion. The Force grants us visions that show us only one of many possible outcomes."

"Then what use are they?"

"They can guide our actions, give us direction. They can show us a path we wish to follow, or one we can try to avoid."

"Like the vision that brought you here," Scourge asked. "The dream of Dromund Kaas and its storm-covered sky?"

"That was a memory, not a vision," Revan reminded him. "But the Force does sometimes speak to us through our dreams."

"And what does your vision show you? How do you make your great escape from this dungeon?"

Revan chose his next words carefully, his dulled wits sensing an opportunity. He knew his best chance—perhaps his only chance—of escape was with the Sith's help. But he could not be the one to suggest the alliance; the Sith Lord had to think it was his idea.

That was why he had fabricated the lie about the vision: to draw attention away from his clumsy efforts to convince the Sith to help him. Now, however, he had an opportunity to plant a seed.

"You will understand in time," he said cryptically, knowing the other would dwell on the hidden meaning behind his words.

The Sith was already obsessed with him. He hungered to tap into Revan's understanding of the Force, and the Jedi knew he dominated the red-skinned being's conscious and unconscious thoughts. It would only be natural for Revan to sometimes be the subject of the Sith Lord's dreams.

Hopefully, the Sith would come to believe that his ordinary dreams were actually visions granted by the Force. If all went well, he would come to believe there was a greater power trying to draw them together. He might decide of his own accord that Revan was the key to defeating the Emperor, spurring him to help the Jedi escape.

It was a long shot, but Revan had nothing else to hope for.

"I have no wish to play your games," the Sith snapped, annoyed by the enigmatic response. He turned on the heel of his boot without saying a word and marched out of the cell, sealing the door behind him. Revan knew from experience it would be at least a week before he returned. The abrupt ending to their conversation and the impending prolonged absence were intended as punishment; his interrogator had long ago replaced physical torture with the supposed mental anguish of isolation.

For most prisoners this would have been an effective tool, but Revan was able to endure the long periods alone by meditating on the Force. At times like these he would try to reach out to Bastila, hoping at least to let her know he was still alive.

He opened himself up to the Force. As it flowed through him, images of the woman he loved danced through his head. And then suddenly they were gone, replaced by the amorphous face of another.

"Meetra," Revan gasped as the features shifted sharply into focus. They held for an instant, and then vanished.

Revan knew this was more than some mere recollection of a lost friend. It had been too intense and powerful to be a memory. It was almost as if in describing the nature of Force visions to the Sith, he had triggered one of his own.

Though it had lasted only a second, the meaning was abundantly clear. Meetra was coming to rescue him.

CHAPTER TWENTY

MEETRA FOUGHT TO KEEP the *Ebon Hawk* steady on its descent through the fierce storms raging in the skies above Kaas City spaceport.

She knew the storm-ravaged world had to be the world Canderous had spoken of; the one Revan had seen in his dreams. The dark side was powerful here. It was strong enough to send a shiver down her spine, but the sensation was infinitely better than the awful nothingness of Nathema.

As she brought the ship in to land, she knew with a sudden and unshakable certainty that Revan was somewhere on this world.

"He's here, Tee-Three," she informed her companion, trying to contain her excitement. "I can feel it."

The droid beeped eagerly.

"It won't be that easy," she replied. "I'll need to scout around a bit, get a feel for this world."

The droid whistled apprehensively.

"Just stay close and follow my lead," she told him. "We'll be fine."

A few minutes later she had successfully settled the *Hawk* on one of the spaceport's many landing pads.

"Nobody here knows I'm a Jedi," she reminded her

astromech companion just before they descended the boarding ramp. "Let's try to keep it that way."

Her lightsaber was tucked safely out of sight, and she had changed from her brown robes into black pants and a sleeveless red top. It was unlikely anyone here would recognize the traditional outfit of the Jedi Order, but she wasn't taking any chances.

A customs official was waiting for them outside the ship—a middle-aged human female. The fact that humans could hold official government positions was a good sign: they were obviously common enough on Dromund Kaas that she wouldn't automatically draw attention here because of her species.

"Your vessel is unregistered," the woman told her in Basic, her voice simultaneously accusing and bored. "You'll have to come with me."

Meetra wasn't surprised to be greeted in the familiar language. The Sith had once been an Empire controlling multiple worlds, cultures, and societies; naturally they would fall back on a common language, and Basic was by far the simplest and most widespread choice.

"I like to keep my comings and goings off the record," she replied.

"That can be arranged," the woman said with a quick glance to make sure there was nobody within earshot. "Naturally we charge a fee for that kind of premium service."

Meetra had no idea what kind of currency was used on Dromund Kaas, but she highly doubted they'd take Republic credits. "I converted my funds into something a little easier to carry," she explained, holding up a small but perfectly cut diamond.

The customs official's eyes lit up as she stared at the valuable gemstone.

"If you keep my arrival off the record I'll make sure

you're rewarded once I turn these into something a little easier to spend," Meetra promised.

The woman's eyes narrowed suspiciously. "I have a strict payment-up-front policy," she said.

"Maybe you could make an exception this one time, seeing as how we're both human," Meetra suggested, reaching out with the Force to give the woman's psyche a gentle nudge.

"I guess I could make an exception this one time," the woman said with an affable shrug. "Seeing as how we're both human."

"I knew we could work something out," Meetra replied with a smile. "Now, I don't suppose you'd know the name of someone in the city who'd give me a fair price for my stones?"

"Larvit's your best bet," the other woman told her. "He drives a hard bargain, but he won't try to cheat you. Let me give you the directions."

Meetra decided to walk to Larvit's store, rather than hire a speeder. Wandering the streets of Kaas City on foot would give her a better feel for the planet and its people, making it easier to fit in.

The population seemed to be primarily made up of the red-skinned Sith and humans, all dressed in standardized uniforms or military garb. She noticed a handful of Zabrak and Twi'leks; unlike the Sith and humans they did not wear uniforms, and without exception they were all fitted with shock collars. With a start Meetra realized that the unfortunate slaves were likely descended from prisoners who'd been taken by the Sith a thousand years earlier during the Great Hyperspace War.

The directions the customs official had given her were simple, and she found her destination without any trouble. From the outside, Larvit's shop didn't look like the kind of place one would chose to conduct illegal business. It was situated in the middle of the street, and its window boasted the same official government seal she had noticed on virtually every building she'd passed along the way.

She stepped into Larvit's store and made a quick evaluation of her surroundings. It looked like a cross between a pawnshop and a supply post. The tall, gray-haired man behind the counter was wearing a red shirt and black pants, both freshly pressed. On his left shoulder were several bars that probably represented some kind of military rank, and the left breast pocket was emblazoned with the same symbol that adorned his window.

Meetra had expected to find herself in a shady black-market operation, but clearly she was in some kind of official government-controlled business. Still, she had nowhere else to go, so she marched straight up to the gray-haired man and dumped a handful of gems on the counter.

"Please present your Imperial identification card—" he started to say, but the routine greeting died in his mouth when he saw the small fortune scattered across his countertop.

His eyes went wide, first with greed and then with fear. Leaping from behind the counter, he rushed to the front of the shop and quickly closed and locked the door.

"What do you think you're doing?" he demanded in a low voice, peering through the window to see if anyone had noticed his sudden dash across the store.

Meetra slowly brought her right hand up to the lightsaber hidden at her belt. "I was told you're the man to see about business I want to keep off the record."

"I am, I am," Larvit assured her, regaining some of his composure. "But you can't just toss your stuff out on the counter for anyone to see. What if an Imperial inspector happened to wander in?"

"Sorry," Meetra said. "I didn't realize it was a big deal."

Larvit snorted derisively. "Great. A Subjugate. Here's a tip, offworlder. Next time you visit Dromund Kaas, learn the customs first."

Meetra nodded and let her hand drop, but she remained vigilant.

"How did you find out about me?" Larvit asked. "Who sent you?"

"Does it matter?" Meetra replied.

Larvit shook his head and made his way back over to inspect the stones still sitting atop the counter.

"Is this the full extent of your collection?" he asked, picking up one of the gems and bringing it up to his aging eye for closer inspection.

"It's as much as I'm willing to sell right now."

"I understand," he said with a smile. "Do you need the credits immediately, or can you wait a few weeks?"

"What's the difference?"

"I can offer more if you give me time to find the right buyer," he explained.

Meetra shook her head. "I don't have that kind of time."

"That is unfortunate," he said sympathetically. "That will have to be reflected in the price, of course."

"Of course."

"I'm willing to offer seven thousand Imperial credits for the lot," he said, leaning back and crossing his arms to signify the price was non-negotiable.

Meetra wasn't about to fall for such an obvious ploy. Even though she had no concept of what an Imperial credit was actually worth, she had done enough haggling in her day to know that his opening offer was merely a baseline.

"Twenty thousand," she countered, knowing it was a ridiculously high number.

"Even if you could wait to find a buyer I could never go higher than eighteen," he answered. "I'll give you ten."

"Make it fifteen and I promise I'll come to you first the next time I'm looking to deal."

"I'll give you twelve," he said, wagging a finger in her face. "You won't find anybody else who'll go higher than eleven!"

"I'll sell them for thirteen and some information," she answered.

"What kind of information?"

"I'm looking for someone. A friend. I need the name of a contact who knows how to find people."

"People that don't want to be found?"

"I'd rather not say."

The storekeeper crossed his arms again and stroked his chin thoughtfully. "Make it twelve-five and we have a deal. I'll even set up the meeting."

Ten minutes later Meetra walked out of his establishment with twelve thousand, five hundred Imperial credits and an appointment to meet someone called Sechel in two days.

MEETRA WAS SURPRISED by the high-class atmosphere of the Nexus Room.

Over the past two days she'd come to learn that Imperial society was all about status, caste, and class. Clearly her contact was a being of significant rank.

She was greeted at the door by a young human male wearing expensive clothes and a prominently displayed slave collar. Larvit must have provided a description of her, because he seemed to know who she was.

"Welcome to the Nexus Room," the young man said, casting his gaze respectfully to the ground. "Master Sechel is expecting you."

In Meetra's eyes, slavery was one of the most vile and despicable practices in the galaxy. The Republic had officially condemned slavery, though she knew it still existed under euphemisms like *indentured service* or *lifelong personal attendant*. And on Hutt-controlled planets, which were outside Republic jurisdiction, individuals were openly bought and sold like chattel. But somehow what she had encountered on Dromund Kaas seemed much worse.

In the Sith Empire slavery was a societal institution, governed by laws and regulations and seemingly accepted without question by the citizens. Slaves were symbols of rank; the wealthy and powerful used them as status symbols to be paraded out in front of their peers.

There was an abject hopelessness in the eyes of the slaves; they were condemned to a lifetime of servitude with no chance of freedom. Even on Hutt worlds slaves could at least dream of one day escaping to the Republic and starting a new life. But in the Sith Empire, slaves had nowhere to run. Every planet would condemn them; at best an escaped slave would be returned to a wrathful owner, or claimed by a new one. Multiple escape attempts were met with public execution—a slow and agonizing death according to what Meetra had seen in the official records from Nathema.

"Forgive me, mistress," the young man said, bowing low and folding his hands together in a universal gesture of supplication, "but droids are not allowed inside the club."

"Wait here, Tee-Three," Meetra said. Her voice was sharp as she fought to contain her outrage at the young man's circumstances. Unfortunately, the slave thought her barely contained anger was directed at him, and he began to tremble.

She could see the terror in his eyes, and she could only imagine what punishments he would be subjected to if he offended a guest of the club. But he no doubt faced even worse consequences if he were to violate the rules and let T3 accompany her inside.

She didn't dare offer him any words of comfort. She

couldn't do anything that might draw attention to herself. So she simply had to let the young man suffer, silently hoping his mental anguish would quickly pass once she went inside.

"P-please follow me," he stammered.

Still trembling, he led her to a table in the back where a Sith in expensive courtier's clothes was already seated. She could tell by his appearance—and even by the way that he sat—that he was more diplomat than warrior. There was something soft and supple about his appearance; his muscles were not well defined, and he didn't seem to possess the physical self-awareness common among those who relied on their martial skills to survive. He was clearly part of the aristocracy.

Meetra made a mental note not to underestimate him; what he lacked in physical prowess he probably more than made up for with intellect and cunning.

Sechel dismissed the young slave with a disparaging flick of his wrist, then motioned for her to sit down at the table in the chair across from him.

As she did, he flashed a well-practiced smile and she noticed something odd about his face. In addition to their red skin, the Sith were marked by fleshy tendrils that dangled from cheeks and chin. On Sechel, two of the tendrils were disfigured stumps; it appeared as if they might have been cut off.

She pulled her focus away from his cheeks and up to his eyes, lest he catch her staring at his deformity.

"Larvit tells me you are looking for someone," Sechel said, jumping right to the matter at hand.

"He said you could help me find him," Meetra replied.

"For the right price I can find almost anyone," Sechel assured her. "And I happen to know you have more than ample funds to cover my costs."

"I see Larvit does not believe in discretion when it comes to discussing business matters," Meetra grumbled.

"If you didn't want him to discuss the terms of your deal, you should have negotiated that into the price," Sechel replied. "Shall I assume you want our discussions to remain private?"

Meetra nodded, wondering how much of a premium that would be.

"Tell me about the person you are looking for."

"I'm looking for a Sith."

Meetra wasn't foolish enough to admit she was looking for Revan. Without knowing who had taken him or why, even bringing him up would be too great a risk. Thanks to T3's holorecording, however, she knew what the Sith who had captured him looked like. Hopefully, if she could find his abductor, he might lead her to Revan.

"Does this Sith have a name?"

"He probably does, but I don't know what it is."

"Ah, progress," Sechel said, clapping his hands together and rubbing them in anticipation. "Now we know he is male. Can you provide me a description?"

"I can do better than that," she answered, pulling a personal holoprojector from one of her pockets.

She flicked a switch and it displayed a still image she had copied from T3's holorecording. The image was carefully cropped to remove all traces of Revan or the *Ebon Hawk*, leaving only a close-up of the Sith who had taken him.

Sechel's reaction to the image was so subtle that Meetra almost didn't notice it. His eyes widened slightly in recognition; an instinctive, unconscious reaction. It lasted only a fraction of a second, and Meetra was impressed with how well he was able to hide his surprise.

"Interesting," the Sith said, pretending to study the picture. "He appears to be a Sith Lord. That means I will have to charge extra."

There was no doubt in Meetra's mind that Sechel knew exactly who the Sith Lord was, but she thought there was more benefit to playing along than calling him on his lie.

"I need to speak with him on an urgent matter."

"Perhaps if you tell me the nature of your business, it will help me track him down. Is he a friend? An enemy?"

"Not a friend, exactly," Meetra said evasively. "But certainly not an enemy. He has information about a private matter that I wish to discuss."

"Keeping information from me will make my job more difficult," Sechel warned her. "It will drive up the price substantially."

"You already know I can pay," she reminded him. "My business will remain private."

"If I do locate this being, what should I tell him?"

Meetra hesitated. She didn't know the exact nature of the relationship between Sechel and the mysterious Sith. If they were friends, he wouldn't simply tell her where to find him. Not without warning him first.

"I would like you to set up a meeting between us," she said finally, hoping her answer was vague enough that Sechel might still suspect she didn't mean the other Sith any harm.

"A private meeting, yes?" he asked with a smile.

Meetra nodded.

"Very well," he said. "I will try to locate him and offer to set up a meeting. Of course, I can make no promise that he'll agree to see you."

"It's in his best interest," Meetra said. "I'm sure you can be very convincing."

"Certainly. But that also costs extra."

Meetra sighed wearily. "How much?"

"Five thousand credits."

Sechel proved to be a much shrewder negotiator than Larvit; he knew he had all the leverage. In the end they settled on four thousand credits, much closer to his opening offer than Meetra had originally intended.

She rose to leave the table, then was hit by a sudden inspiration. "How much to purchase the slave at the door?" she asked.

If she could buy the young man, she could give him his freedom.

"If you are interested in purchasing slaves, you'll find a much better selection in the city's central market," he assured her.

"I'm interested in him specifically," she said.

"Why?"

There was no mistaking the sudden suspicion in Sechel's voice, and Meetra knew she had misplayed her hand.

"I like his look," she said with a coy smile.

"You can hire his services by speaking with the concierge of the club," he said.

"That's something I'll have to look into," she said, her heart sinking as she realized she could do nothing for the young man now.

Sechel wouldn't just forget about her unusual interest in an otherwise anonymous slave. If she did anything to help him win his freedom, it would certainly get back to Sechel, and she couldn't risk blowing her cover.

"Would you like me to have him escort you out?" Sechel offered.

"Thank you," she said, grinning lasciviously.

The young man was summoned to the table, and she could feel his fear at being singled out by the woman he thought he had offended earlier. He didn't speak as he led her to the door, where T3 was waiting for them.

"It was our pleasure to serve you, mistress," he said, his voice cracking.

"Everything was satisfactory," she said, her voice dripping with disdain and contempt.

The slave bowed and backed away, obviously relieved at what he perceived to be a more normal reaction from a patron of the club. Once he vanished back inside, Meetra spun on her heel and walked away quickly, anxious to put the club behind her.

T3 scurried to keep up, beeping out a question.

"We're getting closer," she promised him. Then she added, "The sooner we're off this accursed world the better."

CHAPTER TWENTY-ONE

YOU WILL UNDERSTAND IN TIME.

Back in his private quarters, Scourge tried to push the last words of his most recent conversation with Revan from his mind, but they kept returning.

It had been almost a week since he'd walked out on Revan, abandoning him to suffer the torments of his solitary confinement. They had been talking about visions: how the Force could speak to you if you listened; how it could show you visions of your possible future.

The Jedi had implied that he had witnessed something to do with his eventual release from Nyriss's prison, but Scourge knew better than to take anything the captive said at face value.

Revan was smart. Even as Scourge used him to learn about the Force, the Jedi was trying to manipulate Scourge into helping him escape. It was possible everything he'd said had been nothing but lies. It was also possible he had been telling the truth. Maybe he really had seen something that gave him hope of escape.

Scourge knew he should tell Nyriss about this latest development, but so far he had kept silent on the matter. If she knew, there was a strong chance she would simply decide to execute Revan rather than allow him any opportunity to escape.

And that was the real problem. If Revan died, did any real chance of stopping the Emperor die with him? When the Jedi said Nyriss would never step forward to lead the others against the Emperor, the words rang true. Revan, on the other hand, had already proved he was both eager and willing to stop the Sith from invading the Republic. He had hinted at an alliance between them, and as ridiculous as it might have seemed at first, Scourge couldn't help but see some merit in the idea.

They shared a strong commitment to a common goal; alliances had been forged on far less. But agreeing to work with the Jedi wouldn't just mean freeing him from his cell. It would mean a betrayal of Nyriss, and Scourge wasn't ready to take on both her and the Emperor quite yet.

Especially when all of this was predicated on an alleged Force vision of Revan's that might not actually have existed.

The sharp knock on his door came as a relief. His mind was running in circles; it would be good to have something to distract him.

When he opened the door, he was surprised to see Sechel standing on the other side. For the most part, the sycophantic Sith had avoided him for the last three years, partly out of fear and partly because Nyriss had forbidden him from seeking vengeance for the brutal interrogation that had left him scarred for life.

There had been occasions where they had been forced to work together on some task or mission for Nyriss, but the innate mistrust all Sith had of one another had escalated between them to the point that it actually impacted their ability to work effectively together. It hadn't taken long for Nyriss to realize their talents were put to better use independently.

"Why are you here?" Scourge asked.

"I have news you will be interested in," Sechel replied, smiling in a way that made Scourge want to strangle him.

"Did Nyriss send you?"

"I am here of my own volition."

"What is this about?" Scourge demanded.

"Aren't you going to invite me in?"

"No."

Sechel shrugged. "I was only trying to show some discretion. For your sake."

"Get to the point," Scourge said through gritted teeth.

"A woman came to me today. Human. She's looking for you."

"A human? Why?"

"She didn't say. She didn't offer her name, and given her reluctance to discuss the matter I didn't ask."

"If she found you, then she already knows where to find me," Scourge said.

Sechel shook his head. "We crossed paths quite by accident. She has no idea you and I know each other at all. She simply hired me to find you."

"Maybe you'd better come in and tell me the whole story," Scourge said, relenting and stepping aside.

"On second thought, I think I'll stay out here," the other Sith replied. "I get the feeling you don't like the answers I'm giving you."

"Do you think I need to get you alone to inflict pain?" Scourge asked, casually reaching out with the Force to give Sechel's windpipe a quick squeeze.

Sechel gasped and threw his hands up to his throat, his eyes wide with fear. "Nyriss will have your head if you harm me again!" he blustered.

"That won't bring you back if you're dead," Scourge pointed out. "Now stop playing games and tell me exactly what happened."

"This woman was referred to me by a business associate," Sechel explained. "She offered me a substantial sum to track down the man in her holoimage."

"A holoimage?"

"Apparently she doesn't even know your name. But she has an excellent image of your face, and she's willing to pay a substantial sum to meet with you."

"And you have no idea why?"

"I can speculate."

"Please do," Scourge said grimly.

"Think of how many lives you have ended. How many assassinations you've performed. Isn't it possible that on one of these missions your face was captured by a security cam?"

Scourge was always careful on his missions, but nobody was perfect. "It's possible," he admitted grudgingly.

"Now imagine someone who knew the victim finds the footage. Maybe a wife, or a daughter. Driven by her lust for revenge, she could search the whole Empire for the one who wronged her."

"You think she wants to kill me?"

"Probably. Most people do. But she insisted on meeting you in person."

"Why are you telling me this?" Scourge asked abruptly.

"I have a reputation to protect. She paid me to do a job; I don't want rumors to spread that I cheated a client. It's bad for business."

"Does Nyriss know about your so-called business?"

"She allows me to freelance as long as it doesn't interfere with my work on her behalf. And in this case, it may actually benefit her. And you," he added. "If this woman intends you harm, she must be dealt with appropriately. That is why I think you should meet with her."

"And there's always a chance she might actually succeed, isn't there?"

"Doubtful," Sechel said. "Just to be on the safe side, though, I wouldn't suggest you go to meet her alone."

"You want to come with me?"

"Not in the least," Sechel assured him. "This seems more like a job for Murtog and his crew."

Scourge didn't speak right away. He ran over everything Sechel had told him, trying to determine if he was being set up. The mere fact that Sechel hadn't simply turned the woman away was enough to make Scourge wary of the meeting.

If someone really was looking to do him harm, it was doubtful that Sechel would warn him simply because they both served Nyriss. But if he suspected the woman was tied to something in Scourge's past—some dark secret or inconvenient truth—bringing it to light was an effective way to make Scourge look bad.

If she turned out to be someone looking for revenge, it would prove that Scourge had been sloppy in the past, planting seeds of doubt about him in Nyriss's mind. And even if she wasn't, the situation was still likely to create some kind of mess for Scourge to clean up. That alone might be enough to convince Sechel to help her.

Simply refusing the meeting wasn't an option, however. Now that he knew she was out there, Scourge had to take action. Whatever the motive behind her search for him, he had to face her. It was the only way to unravel the mystery.

Sechel knew all this, of course. That was why he'd suggested sending Murtog along. On the surface it appeared the best way to deal with a possible enemy, but Scourge knew what he really wanted was to have somebody else there who would report back on the meeting if the truth turned out to be embarrassing.

On the other hand, if he decided to meet her alone he was putting himself at greater risk. It might also look like he had something to hide, and he had no doubt

Sechel would twist that fact to suit his own needs somewhere down the road.

"Congratulations," he said to the smaller Sith. "You've backed me into a corner. Set up the meeting, and tell Murtog and his men to be there."

"Of course, Lord Scourge," Sechel said with a mocking bow. "I'm always happy to be of service."

MEETRA WAS WARY of a trap even before she felt the warning premonitions through the Force.

Sechel had given her a time and location for the meeting; he'd even told her the name of the man from the holovid—Lord Scourge. But she still didn't trust him.

Arriving at the location only confirmed her suspicions. Sechel's instructions had led her to an isolated cave on the outskirts of the city—the perfect place for an ambush. A single speeder was parked in a clearing about fifty meters away from the entrance, evidence that somebody else was already there. It was possible the Sith had come alone, but Meetra estimated the vehicle could hold as many as six adult humanoids. There was also the possibility that other speeders had been hidden nearby, meaning she had no idea how many might be waiting for her inside the cave.

T3-M4 obviously shared her concerns. The droid twittered nervously as she brought the speeder in for a landing on a patch of bare dirt near the other speeder.

"I know, I know," she muttered. "But this is the only lead we've got."

She climbed out of the speeder and extended a small cargo ramp so T3 could exit as well. The mouth of the cave loomed before them, black and forbidding.

Earlier, she had discussed several dozen strategies with T3, laying out contingency plans for the most common conceivable scenarios. Fortunately their planning had included a potential ambush by enemies hiding under the cover of darkness.

"Operation supernova is a go," she whispered.

T3 beeped uncertainly.

"We'll give them every chance to surrender," she assured him. "But be ready for this to get ugly. Hopefully it won't come to that," she added. "Maybe Lord Scourge is curious enough about why I'm here to hear me out before he tries anything."

T3 didn't reply; she took it as a bad sign that he was suddenly speechless.

Walking slowly, she entered the cave. It was too dark to see more than a meter in front of her, but she could sense several other beings inside, watching her approach. She assumed they were using night-vision goggles; it was the only way for anyone's sight to pierce the darkness of the cave.

She tried to act timid and unsure, a clueless victim walking heedlessly into the waiting trap. The more vulnerable she appeared, the closer they'd let her advance before taking any action.

"Stay close, Tee-Three," she whispered, keeping her voice low so only he could hear her.

"Is anybody here?" she called out, making her voice tremble slightly.

She took another seemingly cautious step forward.

"Hello? Is anyone here?"

"Don't move!" a voice shouted from the darkness. "We have you surrounded."

"Lord Scourge," she called out. "Is that you? I only want to talk."

"Lie flat on the ground and put your hands behind your head," the voice ordered. "If not, we open fire."

"Now, Tee-Three!"

The little droid turned his headlamp to full power. In the tight confines it had the intensity of a small sun, easily illuminating the entire cave. The sudden flash of brightness also overloaded the night-vision goggles of her adversaries, temporarily blinding them.

It took Meetra less than a second to see and process the odds she was up against. Four soldiers—two male and two female, each wearing heavy armor and carrying a blaster carbine—had taken up positions around the cave, forming a loose semicircle around their intended victim. A tall Sith stood in an alcove near the back corner of the cave.

The four soldiers opened fire. Even blinded by the flash of T3's lamp, they were disciplined enough to react by unleashing a volley of blaster bolts at the last known location of their target. Unfortunately for them, Meetra's reactions were quicker than theirs.

By the time the bolts hit home, Meetra was already on the move. She snapped off a quick back handspring to dodge the blasterfire, then reversed her direction with a flying leap toward the nearest assailant.

Her lightsaber was already in her hand when she landed, and she plunged her blade through the vulnerable joint between the chest plate and right shoulder guard of the soldier's combat suit. Unlike his cortosis-laced armor, the man's flesh and bone provided almost no resistance to the lightsaber as it drove straight through his heart.

As he fell to the ground, Meetra thrust her free hand out toward the next closest soldier, palm open. The woman flew backward, lifted off her feet and hurtled across the cave by the Force until she slammed into the rock face of the far wall. She slid to the ground, dead.

The other two soldiers had ripped off their night-vision goggles and opened fire again. Meetra deflected the bolts with her lightsaber.

With their attention focused on the Jedi wreaking havoc in their ranks, the soldiers forgot about T3-M4.

The droid took full advantage of the situation, rolling forward until he was close enough to unleash a jet of flame from the short nozzle jutting out from the center of his torso.

The flames engulfed the nearest soldier; as his dying shrieks momentarily distracted his companion, Meetra charged forward with a burst of speed to deliver a vicious two-handed slash of her blade that cleaved through the plates of the woman's armor and bit deep into her chest.

At last, Meetra turned to face the Sith. Now that she had a chance to focus her attention more closely, she recognized him from T3's holovid. Apparently Lord Scourge had decided to show up after all.

Curiously, he hadn't done anything to help the soldiers during the short and violent encounter. He hadn't tried to flee, either. In fact, he hadn't seemed to have moved at all, other than to draw and ignite the crimson blade of his lightsaber.

He held his weapon in front of him in a standard defensive posture, staring at Meetra with a look of utter disbelief on his face.

Wary of a trap, Meetra took a single step toward him.

"You're a Jedi," he said, his words causing her to freeze in her tracks. "What he said was true. He saw you. He knew."

Meetra wasn't about to attack someone who didn't seem to want to do her any harm; that went against everything she believed in. But she wasn't going to let her guard down, either.

"What are you talking about?" she demanded.

"You're here because of Revan," he said, his voice filled with wonder. "You've come to rescue him."

"I'm impressed you figured it out so quickly," she admitted.

"I didn't figure it out," he said. "Revan told me."

* * *

THE INSTANT THE BLUE-BLADED lightsaber had materialized in the human female's hand, Scourge realized she was a Jedi. And he could only think of one reason a Jedi would come to Dromund Kaas in search of him—she was here to rescue Revan.

He was impressed with how easily she had dismantled Murtog and his handpicked team. He could feel her channeling the Force, yet it was somehow different from what he had felt when he battled other Sith.

She wasn't afraid to kill, but he sensed she took no real pleasure in it. Instead of feeding off her anger and hate, it was as if she kept her emotions at arm's length so the Force could flow through her unhindered.

Part of him wanted to leap into the fray: battling this Jedi would be a true test of his skills. He didn't know which of them would prove the stronger, but he was intrigued by the challenge. Yet another part of him knew she represented something far more significant than a worthy foe.

"What do you mean Revan told you?" she demanded.

"When I last spoke with him he said something I didn't believe. I thought he was lying to manipulate me. I didn't understand what he was trying to tell me."

Actually, Scourge still wasn't sure he understood. Not fully. The female Jedi's presence was proof that Revan was telling the truth about his Force vision. He had hinted to Scourge that his freedom was close at hand; he must have had a premonition of her arrival.

The revelation was what had stayed Scourge's blade. He wasn't willing to do battle with her until he had carefully considered all the implications and alternatives.

"If you spoke to Revan, then you know where he is," the woman said.

She was still poised in a combat-ready stance, as was

Scourge—neither willing to make the first move, but each ready to respond to an attack by the other.

"Revan is a prisoner," Scourge told her.

"Then I order you to set him free!" she demanded.

"It's not that simple."

Nothing about this situation was simple. As he spoke to the Jedi, Scourge was still trying to understand why Revan had mentioned his vision to him at all.

At the time he'd thought the prisoner was simply trying to manipulate him, to trick him into helping him escape. Now, however, it seemed as if Revan's words had been a warning—almost as if he knew Scourge would find himself in this situation.

It made no sense to give any kind of warning to an enemy. However, if Revan believed that he and Scourge were destined to become allies, then his words did make sense. Was it possible he had seen a vision of Scourge working with him?

It seemed to be the only answer that fit. He had sometimes sensed that Revan was trying to recruit him to his side; the feeling had been even stronger in their last conversation. He'd dismissed it as desperation to escape, but what if Revan knew the events he had foreseen were drawing near? What if he had witnessed this confrontation in the cave, and he had been trying to make Scourge understand that they had to become allies to stop the Emperor?

"Tell me where Revan is," the woman said. "Tell me where he's being held and I will let you walk away."

He realized his adversary was misinterpreting his reluctance to fight as fear. She was as confused about this as he was. Yet the more Scourge thought about it, the clearer it became.

Nyriss would never move against the Emperor; he knew that now. He had come to accept that neither she nor any of the other Dark Council members who had plotted with her would ever actually dare to strike.

If anyone was going to stop the Emperor from his mad invasion of the Republic, it would have to be Scourge. But he couldn't do it alone.

"Come with me and I will take you and your droid to see Revan," he said, deactivating his blade. "He will tell you the truth."

The Jedi wasn't so quick to lower her weapon.

Her astromech droid rolled up to stand beside her, squawking loudly.

"Tee-Three's right. I've already walked into one trap today," the Jedi answered. "I think I've hit my quota."

Scourge understood her reluctance. Under normal circumstances she would be a fool to accompany him. But this situation was as far from normal as he could imagine.

"Revan told me you were coming," he tried to explain. "I think the Force gave him a vision of us working together."

"Then why did you set an ambush?"

"I didn't know who you were," Scourge pointed out. "You wouldn't tell Sechel any of the details of who you were or why you were looking for me."

"You're lying," she said with a disbelieving shake of her head. "You're afraid to face me. You'll say anything to avoid a fight."

"Do I seem afraid to you?"

"No," she admitted. "You seem strangely calm."

"That is because I finally understand what Revan meant. He wants us to unite against a common foe."

"What common foe?"

"Our Emperor is planning an invasion of the Republic. Revan wants to stop him. So do I."

"Why would you want to stop an invasion of the Republic?"

"The Emperor is mad. He wants to repeat the mistakes of the Great Hyperspace War; he wants to plunge us into a conflict that will end with our extinction."

The Jedi lowered her lightsaber, but didn't deactivate it. "Then why did you take Revan prisoner on Nathema?"

"That was before I knew his purpose here."

He could tell she was still suspicious, and rightfully so. But he thought of something that might convince her. "You spoke of Nathema. Have you been to that world? Have you walked upon its surface?"

"I have," she said quietly, and he could tell from the haunted expression on her face that she spoke the truth.

"That was the Emperor's homeworld. To give himself greater power, he unleashed a ritual that devoured everything. When I saw what happened there, I understood the true depths of his insanity. I realized his mind was so twisted and disturbed that he was not fit to rule, and I swore to find a way to stop him."

He paused and looked steadily at Meetra. "You walk the path of the light; I have chosen to follow the dark side. But we both know the horrors of Nathema are a blight upon the galaxy. Revan knows this, as well. That is why he wants us to work together."

The Jedi considered his words carefully, then deactivated her blade. But Scourge could tell she still wasn't wholly convinced.

"Before I go anywhere with you, I'm going to need more to go on than just your word," she said.

Scourge nodded. Her caution was a good thing; if she'd believed him too easily he would have had to question her judgment.

"I can bring you proof," he told her. "Wait here and I will return tomorrow."

"How do I know you won't just come back with more reinforcements?"

"You will sense me through the Force before I actually arrive. If I'm not alone, you will have plenty of time to make your escape."

"What about Revan?" the Jedi asked.

"He is safe for the moment," Scourge assured her. "But I cannot free him without help."

"You have until tomorrow," the Jedi told him. "Return with proof and we can work together to free Revan."

Scourge tucked the hilt of his lightsaber back into his belt and walked slowly past the Jedi and her droid toward the entrance of the cave. They stepped aside at his approach, keeping a safe distance between them.

Just before he left the cave, the Jedi called out a final warning.

"If you betray me in any way—if you come back with reinforcements, or even if you don't come back at all—I will hunt you down."

"Save your anger for the Emperor," Scourge called back over his shoulder. "He is the real enemy."

CHAPTER TWENTY-TWO

SCOURGE KNEW HE HAD TO ACT QUICKLY. With long, rapid strides he marched from the cave to the waiting speeder and took to the air, heading back to Kaas City.

He'd promised the Jedi he would return to the cave within one day, but that wasn't his biggest concern. Sechel had set up the meeting and maneuvered Scourge into taking Murtog with him; no doubt he was eagerly waiting for the security chief's report on what happened. He had to find Sechel and deal with him before the adviser became suspicious.

Sechel would most likely be at the Nexus Room, enjoying a selection of fine wines while waiting for Murtog to call in. As a Sith Lord, Scourge had access to the facility, but he didn't want to confront Sechel in a public setting.

He brought his speeder in for a landing a block away from the club, jumped out, and walked to the building. The slave on duty greeted him as he entered the lobby.

"Welcome, my lord," the young human said, bowing low.

"I have a message for Sechel," Scourge told him.

"Of course, my lord. Follow me."

As the slave turned to enter the club, Scourge reached

out a hand and grabbed him by the shoulder. "I did not say I wish to speak with him," he hissed, "I said I had a message."

"F-forgive me, master," the slave stammered, obviously terrified. "P-please tell me what you wish me to do."

"Wait until I leave," Scourge explained slowly, as if he were talking to a simpleton. "Then tell Sechel that Murtog needs to meet him. He'll know where." He stared down at the slave. "Do you understand?"

The slave nodded, his eyes wide with fear.

"Do not tell him I was here," Scourge instructed. "Do not mention me at all. Simply deliver the message. If you fail me, I will have them flay the flesh from your bones."

They both knew it was not an idle threat; by right Scourge could inflict any punishment he chose on a disobedient slave. Of course, the young man would also be punished if anyone discovered he had lied to a member of the club, but Scourge had far more important things to worry about than the fate of an insignificant slave.

The young man stood, still and silent, knowing anything he said could only make things worse.

Scourge turned and left the club. Once outside, he ducked around a nearby corner where he could watch the door.

Sechel emerged a few minutes later and made his way quickly down the street. He didn't appear to be particularly worried or cautious; he had been expecting to hear from Murtog, so he had no reason to be suspicious.

Scourge followed him at a safe distance, careful not to draw attention to himself. Sechel didn't head back to Nyriss's stronghold; as Scourge expected he had a private location where he could conduct business he didn't want others to know about.

He continued for several blocks, then stopped at a small two-story apartment building in one of Kaas City's residential districts. He punched in the security code to unlock the door and slipped inside. Scourge waited a few seconds, then approached the building.

Glancing around to make sure there were no witnesses, he pulled out his lightsaber and ignited the blade, jamming it into the security panel. The lock sparked and sizzled, the circuits frying in an instant. A second later the door slid open; as he'd suspected, the panel had been programmed to open the door if it malfunctioned so the residents wouldn't be locked in or out of the apartment complex.

The interior was little more than a hall giving access to the various apartments. There were four doors on the lower level, but Scourge ignored them—Sechel would never lower himself to rent a ground-floor unit. There was no turbolift, but in the back of the building there was a staircase leading up to the second level.

Scourge made his way up. The suites on the top floor were obviously larger: instead of four doors there were only two. Scourge picked one of the doors at random and pressed the buzzer. He waited for nearly a minute, but there was no reply. Either the unit wasn't occupied, or the resident was not at home.

He tried the buzzer on the other door. A few seconds later he heard footsteps approaching, then the door slid open. From Sechel's expression it was clear he was caught off guard at finding Scourge instead of Murtog waiting for him on the other side.

Before he could react, Scourge jabbed out with his hand, driving his fingers into Sechel's throat.

The other Sith dropped to his knees, gasping for air. Scourge stepped inside the apartment and closed the door behind him.

Sechel struggled to speak, but all that came out was a rasping cough.

"Make any sound louder than a whisper and your life will end in unbearable agony," Scourge warned him.

The adviser held up his hand and nodded to show he understood. Scourge waited patiently for him to catch his breath.

After a few minutes Sechel had the strength to stand up. He brushed his clothes off, trying to compose himself.

"Where is Murtog?" he eventually asked, keeping his voice low.

"Dead," Scourge replied.

Sechel's eyes flickered wide for an instant, but otherwise he showed no reaction. "It seems I underestimated this woman," he said, his tone not in the least bit apologetic. "I assume since you survived that she now shares Murtog's fate?"

"How much did Nyriss know about the meeting?" Scourge demanded, ignoring Sechel's question.

"Nothing."

"You didn't mention it to her?"

Sechel sniffed indignantly. "You have an overly high opinion of yourself if you think Nyriss cares about some anonymous female from your past. This is beneath her notice."

Scourge nodded. Sechel guarded his cards closely; he wouldn't mention anything to Nyriss until he had decided how best to turn the situation to his advantage.

"What about Murtog?" Scourge asked. "Would he say anything? Would he tell Nyriss where he was going?"

"She doesn't keep tabs on us like children," Sechel sneered.

"How long until she begins to miss him?" Scourge asked.

"You mean how long until she finds out you got him killed?" Sechel mocked. "I'd say you have another three days before she begins to wonder about his absence."

"Three days," Scourge muttered. "We'll have to move fast."

"What are you talking about?"

Sechel had obviously sensed Scourge's urgency; he must have assumed something had gone very, very wrong at the meeting. He thought Scourge was in trouble. He wrongly believed the Sith Lord had come here looking for help, and it was making him arrogant.

Scourge decided it was time to clarify the situation. "I want your files."

"What files?"

"The ones implicating Nyriss and the other Dark Council members. I want everything you've gathered that could be used to expose them as traitors."

To his credit, Sechel didn't deny the files existed. It would have been a pointless endeavor; Scourge knew him too well. The adviser was loyal to Nyriss, but his primary concern would always be for himself. If things ever went bad, he would need something to bargain with, and what better bargaining chip than detailed records of everything Nyriss and her co-conspirators had been involved in ever since they'd started plotting against the Emperor?

"You're crossing a dangerous line," Sechel warned. "Nyriss has turned a blind eye to my collection; I'm too valuable for her to cast me aside. You, however, are expendable. If she finds out about this, she'll have your head."

"Nyriss is not your concern. I am. Give me the files. I won't ask again."

Sechel knew the lengths Scourge was willing to go in pursuit of information; the scars on his cheek reminded him every time he looked in a mirror. And this time he couldn't count on a timely interruption to put an end to the torture.

"Wait here," he said, turning and heading into the apartment.

Scourge, who had no intention of letting Sechel out of his sight, followed right behind him.

Sechel glanced back and sighed in resignation. He made his way to a small closet in the back of the apartment and slid the door open. At first glance the closet appeared empty. Sechel dropped to one knee and slid back a small hidden panel on the floor, revealing a security keypad. With Scourge watching closely over his shoulder, he punched in the access code. A panel in the back wall of the closet slid aside, revealing a hidden safe. Sechel punched another code into the keypad, and the door opened with an audible click.

"Slowly," Scourge warned.

"There's a blaster inside," Sechel confessed. "But I have no intention of trying to use it against you."

"A wise decision."

Sechel pulled gently on the corner of the safe's door, allowing it to swing wide and reveal the contents. As he had said, there was a small hold-out blaster inside. There were also several data disks, each labeled with a date and arranged in chronological order.

"Is this everything?" Scourge demanded.

"It's all here," Sechel assured him. "But it's encrypted. If anything happens to me, the data is useless. I'm the only one who can decode it."

Scourge had no way to tell if Sechel was bluffing. But he was willing to take the risk.

"I'm sure I can find a slicer somewhere who's up to the challenge," he said, stepping in close behind him.

He brought his left arm up and under Sechel's chin, the forearm pressing hard on his windpipe. At the same time his right hand reached around and gripped the top of Sechel's head.

Sechel had become a liability. Scourge couldn't leave him behind, and taking him with him was far more trouble than it was worth.

The smaller Sith struggled to break the hold as Scourge began to apply pressure to the vertebrae in his neck. There were literally hundreds of ways he could have killed Sechel, but given their history he wanted their final moments to be up close and personal.

Sechel tried to kick him, but Scourge had positioned himself so that the flailing foot of the other Sith only struck feebly against his thigh. He took a deep breath, braced his left arm, and yanked hard with his right hand. There was a surprisingly loud *pop,* and Sechel's body spasmed once before going completely limp.

Releasing his grip to let the body slump to the floor, Scourge gathered up the data disks and left the apartment, the door automatically sliding shut behind him.

MEETRA SAT STILL and silent on the floor of the cave, her legs crossed and her hands held at chest height, palms facing each other. She had opened herself up to the Force, looking for guidance and wisdom, but here on Dromund Kaas, where the dark side prevailed, it was difficult to find the inner tranquillity necessary for enlightenment.

Having T3 running long, nervous circles around her certainly didn't help, but she was afraid if she told him to stay still he might have a meltdown. And she understood the droid's anxiety.

She still wasn't sure what to make of Lord Scourge. She had sensed that his offer to work together was sincere, though she wondered how much of that was Revan's doing. It was easy to understand how Scourge could be drawn to him; Revan's command of the Force was greater than that of anyone else she had ever met. And she knew how charismatic he could be. Even though he was a prisoner it wasn't hard to imagine him being in total control of the situation.

But if he had recruited Scourge as an ally, it had been

out of necessity rather than choice. The Sith was wholly consumed by the dark side. He had no respect for life, no desire to serve any needs but his own. Even if what he said about wanting to stop the Emperor was true, his motivations were survival and self-preservation.

She didn't trust him, but if he could prove that he and Revan were on the same side she would work with him. The risk of betrayal was one she was willing to take if it gave her a chance to rescue her friend.

The little droid was passing by her on one of his many, many laps when she heard the sound of a speeder approaching. T3 stopped and dimmed his light, casting the cave in shadow once more.

"I told you he'd come back," Meetra said. "He's alone," she added before T3 could ask the obvious question.

She scrambled to her feet as Lord Scourge marched confidently into the cave, ready to respond at the first hint of aggression.

"I have what you need," he said, holding up several data disks. "This will prove what I said about trying to stop the Emperor. You will see that we are on the same side."

Scourge stepped forward and extended his hand, offering her the disks. She hesitated for only a moment before coming close enough to take them from his grasp. She returned to T3, carefully retracing her steps so as not to turn her back on the red-skinned Sith.

"We'll need time to look these over," she said.

"They might be encrypted," Scourge told her.

"I've never come across a code my friend here couldn't crack," she said, and T3 beeped his agreement.

"I suspected as much. How long do you think it will take?"

"Why? Are you in a rush?"

"Events have been set in motion," he explained. "We

have two, maybe three days before the window of opportunity closes."

"Work fast, T3," she said. She looked up at Scourge. "We'd be more comfortable if you weren't hovering over us.

"I will return in three hours," he said. "Alone, of course."

It only took half that time for T3 to decrypt and verify the authenticity of the data. As promised, it confirmed what the Sith had said—he really was plotting to overthrow the Emperor. However, it wasn't just Scourge. Several members of the Dark Council, the Emperor's circle of handpicked advisers, had joined together in a conspiracy to remove him from the throne.

Yet after more than a decade, they had made no real progress. Instead, the disks cataloged a litany of power plays and double crosses among the various leaders of the conspiracy. They spent so much time plotting against one another that the idea of them actually working together to defeat the Emperor seemed ludicrous.

"No wonder he's willing to work with Revan," Meetra muttered. "He's just sick of waiting."

By the time Scourge returned, she had made her decision.

"I believe you," she said. "I'm ready to work together."

"Does this mean you'll tell me your name?" the Sith asked.

"I'm Meetra. And this is Tee-Three-Em-Four."

The droid let out a shrill chirp.

"What's he saying?" Scourge asked.

"He says it's time for you to take us to see Revan."

"The situation has changed. That isn't an option any longer."

"Why not?"

"He is being held by a Sith Lord called Nyriss."

"She's on the Dark Council," Meetra said, recalling the name from the data disks. "She's the one who brought you into the conspiracy."

Scourge nodded.

"If she's holding Revan, why can't you take us to him?"

"When I first made the offer, I was hoping Revan could convince you that we should work together," Scourge explained. "Going to see him now would only be an unnecessary risk."

"I don't understand."

"I could probably get you in to see him, but that won't help get him out of his cell. And it might raise suspicion."

"Just take me to him," Meetra insisted. "Leave the escape to me."

"You can't fight your way through Nyriss's entire army of followers," Scourge said. "Even with my help. She has hundreds of guards and dozens of acolytes trained in the dark side. If we're going to break Revan out, we need a distraction. Something to draw the attention of the guards away while we sneak in."

"I assume you have a plan?"

"I do," Scourge said, smiling. "I'm going to get the Emperor to help us."

CHAPTER TWENTY-THREE

THOUGH HE APPEARED CALM on the outside, Scourge's heart was pounding as he mounted the steps to the Emperor's citadel. He was playing a dangerous game, but there were no other options. Time was the enemy; if they had any hope of getting Revan out of her dungeon alive, they had to act before Nyriss realized Scourge had betrayed her.

Soon—maybe tomorrow, maybe even today—Nyriss would begin to wonder about Sechel and Murtog's absence. It wouldn't take her long to learn that they had been working with Scourge, and from there she would easily fill in the blanks.

He'd briefly considered approaching one of the other members of the Dark Council, hoping to convince him or her to help him get rid of Nyriss the same way she had used him to eliminate Darth Xedrix. But even if they agreed to help him, it would be weeks before they put a plan into place. Like Nyriss, they were too cautious—too afraid—to take any action that might put them at risk.

The Emperor was the only Sith on all of Dromund Kaas with the will to take the kind of quick and decisive action required. Convincing him that Nyriss was a traitor would be simple enough with the files he'd acquired from Sechel. The trick was making the Emperor believe Scourge had been an unknowing pawn in her plans.

T3 had doctored the data disks, removing all evidence of Scourge's part in the conspiracy. Scourge would claim that he came forward as soon as he learned of the plot . . . but there was no guarantee the Emperor would believe him.

Scourge was going to present the evidence in person. If the Emperor suspected he was lying—or if he was simply powerful enough to see the truth—escape would be impossible. He was putting himself at great risk for the sake of the cause—something he never would have considered before he met Revan.

At the top of the stairs he was stopped by a pair of Sith soldiers clad in red armor—two of the famed Imperial Guard. An army of elite warriors, the Imperial Guard underwent months of brutal training to transform them into the most disciplined and deadly troops in the Empire. Many didn't survive, but those who did emerged as fanatically loyal zealots willing to sacrifice their lives to defend the Emperor.

"State your business," one of the guards said, barring his way with a heavy electrostaff.

"I must see the Emperor immediately."

He hadn't known what kind of reaction his bold statement would produce—mocking laughter or flat refusal were the most likely options.

"Only those on the Dark Council can speak with the Emperor," the second soldier told him, her tone curt and official.

"My name is Lord Scourge; I serve Darth Nyriss. I am here on her behalf."

The soldiers looked at each other, and he sensed their uncertainty.

"The Emperor is in danger," Scourge insisted. "I must speak with him."

"Wait here," the male guard told him.

He disappeared inside the Citadel and didn't return for several minutes. The entire time passed in silence; the remaining guard saw no reason to speak to Scourge, and he knew better than to say anything more to her. Simple lies were the most effective, and Scourge had no intention of saying anything more than was absolutely necessary.

When the first soldier emerged, he was accompanied by four more of his comrades. All were Sith, and three wore uniforms identical to those of the guards stationed at the door. The fourth was also clad in red armor, but her outfit was more elaborate.

"I am Captain Yarri," she told him. "Come with me."

They left the original two guards behind as she led him into the citadel. She walked in front of him, while two of the newcomers flanked him. The fourth fell into line directly behind him so that he was completely surrounded.

The design of the citadel reminded Scourge of Nyriss's stronghold; not surprising, given that she had built her edifice in the same style to honor the Emperor. The interior was a virtual maze of corridors with gray and forbidding stone walls, punctuated by heavy wooden doors leading off to antechambers and side rooms.

However, where Nyriss lined the halls with statues, busts, and wall hangings glorifying her reputation and achievements, the decor of the citadel was far more utilitarian. Statues were few and far between, and the few splashes of color in the scattered wall hangings were muted by the dim lighting that cast everything in shadow.

"You are taking me to the Emperor?" Scourge asked.

"You may speak with one of the Emperor's advisers."

"Unacceptable. I did not come to meet with a servant."

"The choice is not yours to make," Captain Yarri replied brusquely.

Scourge stopped in his tracks, causing the soldier walking behind to stumble into him. The Sith Lord angrily shoved him back. In response, the two guards who had been at his side whipped out their electrostaffs.

"Stop!" Captain Yarri shouted, and they froze in their tracks.

"I am a Lord of the Sith," Scourge reminded him. "And an agent of Darth Nyriss. I order you to take me to the Emperor."

"That is not permitted."

"These are exceptional circumstances."

"How so?"

"That is for the Emperor's ears alone. I must speak to him in person."

"The Emperor does not like to be disturbed."

"He will want to hear what I have to say."

"If he feels you've wasted his time, you will be punished," the captain warned.

The calm, almost casual way she spoke the simple threat was far more effective than providing gruesome details. But Scourge wasn't about to back down now.

"It will not be a waste of his time."

The captain considered the request, then nodded. "As you wish."

As she led him down the twisting corridors of the citadel, Scourge made a mental note of their path. When he and Revan finally struck at the Emperor, they would need to know as much of the layout of the citadel as possible.

Eventually they turned down a hall that terminated at a pair of large durasteel doors.

"The throne room lies beyond," Captain Yarri told

him. "There you will find the Emperor." She turned to face him. "I will give you one last chance to reconsider."

"I've made my decision."

"Then you must proceed alone. I will not violate the sanctity of the throne room."

She motioned with her hand, and two of the soldiers stepped forward, one by each of the massive doors. Grunting with exertion, they pushed the doors inward; then they stepped to the side, standing at attention with their backs against the wall just outside the throne room's now-open entrance.

Scourge expected them to search him, or at least instruct him to turn over his weapons. But Yarri and the others simply stood at attention, waiting for him to enter. The fact that they showed no concern over letting an armed Sith Lord speak to the Emperor face-to-face without any kind of preparation was a testament to the Emperor's unfathomable power.

Thinking about that power gave Scourge pause. Like Revan, the Emperor understood the Force in ways Scourge never would. It was possible he experienced the same kinds of visions as the Jedi; it was also possible he could peer into Scourge's mind and instantly know the truth of everything he was saying. Meeting him face-to-face could be tantamount to suicide.

No, Scourge thought. *If that were the case, he would have sensed Nyriss's betrayal long ago.*

As powerful as the Emperor might be, he was not omniscient. He was, however, intelligent and cunning enough to have held on to his throne for over a thousand years—an unprecedented reign among the conniving and cutthroat politics of the Sith. Which meant Scourge would have to be very careful not to say anything that might give him away.

Captain Yarri and the other guards were still patiently waiting. No doubt they were used to seeing this kind of hesitation in those who were about to meet with the Emperor.

Steeling himself, Scourge stepped inside.

The throne room was enormous: twenty meters wide and at least forty meters long, with an arched ceiling that rose fifteen meters above. Apart from the throne at the far end, it was virtually empty.

The throne sat on an elevated circular pedestal, several meters in diameter. As Scourge walked forward, he noticed that the throne was facing away from him, its high back effectively blocking any view of its occupant.

After a few more steps, the pedestal swiveled around, turning the throne so that it faced him. And for the first time in his life, Scourge set eyes upon the Emperor.

The figure before him appeared unremarkable. The Emperor was clad in unadorned black robes, the raised hood effectively hiding his face. Yet Scourge could feel the power of the dark side emanating from him with such intensity that it caused a faint rippling of the air.

The Emperor rose to his feet, and the durasteel doors swung shut behind Scourge with a booming crash. Scourge's step faltered briefly at the sound, but he continued forward.

As he reached the foot of the pedestal he dropped to one knee, bowing low, his eyes focused on a spot on the ground in front of him.

"Rise, Lord Scourge," the Emperor told him, "and speak your piece."

Scourge stood up to address the Sith looming above him. The Emperor had thrown back his hood to reveal his face; his eyes were as black as the Void itself.

Staring into the hollow darkness of the Emperor's gaze, Scourge's mind flashed back to Nathema, and he shivered at the memory.

He tried to speak, but the words stuck in his throat. His mouth was suddenly so dry he felt as if he might choke. He swallowed hard and coughed, finally bringing up enough saliva to talk.

"Three years ago I went to serve Darth Nyriss at your request," Scourge began. "I discovered that Darth Xedrix was a traitor. He had allied himself with separatists to kill Nyriss, and I executed him for his crimes."

"Your service has been noted," the Emperor assured him.

There was something strange about the Emperor's voice. It didn't sound like the voice of a single being. It had an unusual echo and resonance, almost as if a great multitude were speaking his words in perfect symphony.

A grim theory passed unbidden through Scourge's mind: was it possible all those that had been consumed by the ritual on Nathema still existed in some form within the Emperor himself? Nyriss said he'd devoured them, but what if she was only partially correct? What if he had imprisoned their spirits inside his own corporeal form, slowly feeding on their life energy over a thousand years to keep himself young and strong?

Scourge pushed such thoughts away; he needed to focus. One wrong word and the Emperor might see through his lies.

"I continued to serve Darth Nyriss after Xedrix's death," Scourge explained. "And I continued to investigate the separatists."

He paused, waiting for the Emperor to ask what he'd found. After a few seconds he realized the inquiry was not coming.

"I became suspicious of one of Nyriss's advisers, a man named Sechel. I turned the focus of my investigation to him. But Sechel was careful; he covered his tracks well. It took me until yesterday before I was certain of his guilt. He was also secretly working with the separatists, and he suffered the same fate as Xedrix."

"You should speak to Darth Nyriss if you seek to be

rewarded for your actions," the Emperor said. There was no change in his tone, but the implied threat was clear: *This is beneath me and you are wasting my time.*

Scourge swallowed hard, his mouth dry once more. "That is not why I have come before you. Among Sechel's effects I found these datafiles."

He held up the disks.

"They show that Darth Xedrix was not the only member of the Dark Council to betray you. He was merely sacrificed to keep the involvement of the others secret. Darth Nyriss was also involved in the plot, along with several others."

The Emperor had no physical reaction to the revelation; he stayed as still and calm as death itself. But the air around Scourge seemed to grow colder.

"Are you certain of these accusations?"

"I would stake my life on them, my lord Emperor."

"You already have."

Scourge felt a shiver trace its way down his spine, and he knew that far more than his life was at risk. The Emperor was no longer a member of the Sith species; his power and immortality had transformed him into a being unique in the galaxy. When he spoke of life and death, it had far deeper meaning than the mere physical existence of the lesser beings that served him.

"Does Nyriss know you are here?"

"No. I came to you as soon as I deciphered the data on Sechel's disks."

There was a long silence, and Scourge had the distinct impression that the Emperor was somehow communicating with someone outside the room.

A few seconds later the doors to the throne room opened and Captain Yarri strode in, accompanied by a Sith wearing the same dark robes as the Emperor.

They approached Scourge, and the robed Sith held out his hand expectantly. Scourge handed him the disks.

"Keep Lord Scourge in custody until this matter is settled," the Emperor intoned.

"Forgive me, Lord Emperor," Scourge said, speaking quickly but trying to keep his tone humble. "But Nyriss is expecting my return. If I am absent, she will grow suspicious."

The Emperor's dark eyes seemed to flicker with annoyance, and Scourge feared he had gone too far. The best he could hope for as punishment for his insolence would be a quick and relatively painless death.

However, when the Emperor spoke again it was not to pass judgment on him.

"You are bold to speak to me in this way," he stated. "And because you are right, I will reward your initiative . . . this time. When Nyriss falls, you will be first in line for her seat on the Dark Council."

"Thank you, Lord Emperor," Scourge said with a bow.

"If your information proves false, however," the Emperor added, "you will suffer a fate more terrible than anything you can imagine."

As he spoke, the dark circles of his eyes seemed to fill with a swirling red mist, and for a brief instant the Emperor gave Scourge a glimpse of his true self.

Scourge cried out in anguish as the Emperor's mind brushed against his, then he collapsed to the floor, shaking like a child. The touch lasted less than a second, but in that time he witnessed indescribable horrors that dwarfed anything the dark side could conjure even in his worst nightmares. And beneath the formless terrors lurked the unbearable Void, the pure emptiness of total annihilation.

It was over as quickly as it had begun, the awful vision retreating into his subconscious like a repressed memory as Scourge picked himself up off the floor. Neither Captain Yarri nor the robed Sith made any move to help him.

"Come with me," the captain said once he was on his feet.

Only then did Scourge notice that the Emperor had retaken his seat on the throne, and that the pedestal had spun around to face away from him.

The dark-robed Sith stayed behind as Yarri led Scourge out of the throne room and into the hall beyond.

"I see why you tried to talk me out of this," Scourge muttered as they made their way back toward the citadel's main entrance.

"You took a great risk," Yarri said, though it was hard to tell if she thought him admirable or foolish. "But if your information is good, it sounds like you'll be on the Dark Council the next time we meet."

"What about Nyriss?" Scourge asked. "What will the Emperor do to her?"

"She will be purged by the Imperial Guard," Yarri said. "Along with her entire staff of followers."

"I'd rather not be there when it happens," Scourge said. "When will you make your move?"

"Soon," the captain said. "For now, return to Nyriss so she doesn't grow suspicious."

They had reached the top of the staircase leading down from the citadel's entrance to the street below.

"I will tell my people not to harm you," Captain Yarri promised before turning away.

Just before she disappeared into the citadel she added, "But when the battle starts, try to stay out of the way just in case."

CHAPTER TWENTY-FOUR

MEETRA DIDN'T LIKE THE IDEA of pretending to be Scourge's newly purchased slave, but the Sith had assured her it was the best way for her to infiltrate Nyriss's stronghold without drawing unwanted attention.

To complete the ruse, she had changed her functional pants and top for a revealing purple outfit more suited to a dancer in one of the low-rent clubs she'd frequented during her days as a mercenary. The tight-fitting clothes left her arms and midriff bare, but an excess of exposed skin wasn't the worst part of the disguise.

Scourge had also insisted she wear a slave's shock collar around her neck. It was nonfunctional, of course—she'd had T3 carefully inspect it to make sure—but she still rankled at the idea of adorning herself with a symbol so closely linked to the galaxy's most vile practice.

However, as distasteful as it was, she knew Scourge was right. Every slave on Dromund Kaas was forced to wear the collar; without it, no one would believe their story. T3 was accompanying them, as well, similarly equipped with a nonfunctioning restraining bolt.

"Welcome back, Lord Scourge," a guard stationed just inside the main entrance said as the trio passed by. "Darth Nyriss was just asking about you."

"In what regard?" the Sith asked, as Meetra struggled to hide her interest.

"Sechel and Murtog both left two days ago; she wondered if you knew where they had gone."

"They didn't include me in their plans," Scourge said with a shrug. "I've been scouring the slave markets for the past few days, looking for a worthy purchase."

"Of course, my lord," the guard said with a slight bow. He snuck a quick peek at Meetra, a knowing glint in his eye and a faint smile on his lips, before turning his attention back to Lord Scourge. "I will inform Darth Nyriss that you have not seen the others," he said.

"Good. Once I am settled, I will go speak with her myself to see if she wants me to inquire after them."

He turned on his heel, dismissing the underling as he continued down the hall with long, quick strides. Meetra and T3 scrambled to keep pace, staying a respectful two steps behind their supposed owner.

Once they were out of sight and earshot of the guards, Scourge stopped and turned to address them. "This could complicate things," he said. "Nyriss wouldn't have asked after the others if she wasn't growing concerned. I had hoped to avoid her until the Emperor made his move, but if I put off seeing her now it will look suspicious."

Scourge had spoken to the Emperor just that morning; Meetra imagined it would take at least another day or two before he assembled his forces to strike at Nyriss.

"I'm not letting you out of my sight," she warned him. "If you meet with her, Tee-Three and I had better go with you."

"Ridiculous!" Scourge spat. "I would never be so insulting as to bring one of my personal slaves into a meeting with someone of Nyriss's rank."

"Then you'd better think of something fast," Meetra

said. "Because if this all goes sour, I'm going to whip out my lightsaber and start chopping off heads."

"I could bring you if I was presenting you to Nyriss as a gift," Scourge said. "But then there would be no reason for me to keep you close by."

"Forget it," Meetra snarled.

T3 echoed her sentiment with a shrill squawk.

"Then what do you suggest?" Scourge demanded.

"Take me to Revan now," Meetra said. "I'll take my chances on fighting our way out."

"I didn't bring you here so you could throw your life away. And I have no intention of becoming a martyr."

Meetra was about to fire back another angry retort when the stronghold was rocked to its foundations by a very loud explosion coming from somewhere off to the east.

"The Imperial Guard," Scourge gasped. "They're here!"

Alarms began to ring through the corridor, mingling with the sounds of shouts and running feet as Nyriss's people responded to the sudden attack.

Meetra reached up and yanked the slave collar from her neck, hurling it across the floor. T3 mimicked her by popping off his restraining bolt.

"The dungeon is this way," Scourge said, quickly putting their now-pointless argument behind them. "Follow me."

The explosions continued as he led them through the twisting passages. They were coming from all sides; obviously the Imperial Guard had the entire stronghold surrounded. Based on the frequency and size of the distant explosions, Meetra guessed they were using an artillery assault to try to breach the walls at multiple locations. Males and females ran past them in both directions, some rushing to join the fray and others scrambling to safety. The unexpected attack had caught

Nyriss's people completely off guard. They were in disarray, their efforts to defend the stronghold uncoordinated and disorganized.

"I would have expected someone on the Dark Council to put up better resistance," Meetra said as they turned a corner and raced down another hall.

"The security chief and three of his top lieutenants aren't here to rally them, thanks to you," he reminded her.

They rounded another corner and confronted the first real sign of any kind of counterattack. Eight soldiers led by a lightsaber-wielding Sith acolyte had taken up positions in the corridor roughly ten meters away from a large, smoking hole in the wall.

As the smoke cleared, dozens of red-uniformed soldiers poured through the breach, armed with blaster pistols and electrostaffs.

Nyriss's people opened fire, mowing down the first wave. Those in the ranks behind never even slowed. Driven forward by their furious devotion to the Emperor, they charged the enemy line with a reckless disregard for their own safety.

Had the defenders held their ground and continued to fire, they might have survived several more waves. But their morale was shaken by the berserker mentality of their attackers, so instead they broke ranks and tried to flee. None of them succeeded.

Three were taken down by blasterfire, shot in the back as they turned to run. The other five, including the acolyte with the lightsaber, were swallowed up by a sea of red-uniformed guards and smashed down with electrostaffs.

The entire incident took less than ten seconds; plenty of time for Scourge to lead Meetra and T3 in another direction. But instead of trying to avoid the melee, the Sith had simply held his ground and watched.

As the last defender fell, the invaders broke into two teams and set off in opposite directions down the hall. The chance to hide until they passed was lost; as the red-robed butchers approached, Meetra started to reach for the lightsaber hidden inside her black, knee-high leather boot.

Scourge grabbed her wrist and shook his head. He stepped back against the wall, dragging her with him. Recognizing Scourge as a friendly target, the Imperial Guards ran past without even a second glance.

"The dungeons are close," Scourge told her once they were alone again.

They were fortunate enough not to encounter any more battles for the rest of the journey, though they came across the aftermath of several violent skirmishes. Some of the bodies wore the red uniforms of the invaders, but for every one of them there were at least five of Nyriss's people.

Security guards, acolytes, and even civilian staff lay strewn about the halls and corridors; the Emperor's Guard had spared no one. Meetra understood there had been no other way to free Revan, but she still felt revulsion at the wholesale slaughter. When she noticed the body of a young Twi'lek slave lying on the floor with her throat cut, she forced herself to look away.

"Nyriss's personal attendant," Scourge noted. "But I don't see Nyriss among the dead."

T3 beeped and Meetra shook her head.

"I don't think she escaped," she said, remembering the ruthless efficiency and organization of the attacking troops.

"Her fate is irrelevant," Scourge declared.

"Right. Take us to Revan."

They rounded a final corner, bringing them face-to-face with a massive durasteel door. Scourge stepped up and punched in a security code, but the door didn't open. He tried again, and the pad responded with a sharp buzz.

"The whole place is in emergency lockdown," he said. "My security codes won't work."

"Don't worry," Meetra said confidently. "Tee-Three can slice through any security system."

"He'd better hurry," Scourge said. "I don't sense guards on the other side of the door."

"You think they fled?"

He shook his head. "I think when the alarms went off Nyriss told them to execute the prisoner."

AT FIRST REVAN THOUGHT the distant explosions were an unusual side effect of some new drug combination his captors were trying on him. But when the alarms started blaring, his addled mind realized the facility was under attack.

"Meetra," he mumbled.

He struggled to his feet, battling the mind-numbing effects of the chemicals coursing through his veins. Had his mind been able to focus, he could have purged them from his system. But of course, the entire point of the drugs was to keep him from drawing on the Force.

A few seconds later he heard someone outside the door of his cell. When the door opened he expected to see Scourge, but instead he found himself faced with an unfamiliar guard.

The young man was a dark-skinned human. He was holding a blaster out at arm's length, pointing it at Revan. His hand was visibly trembling.

From outside another voice shouted, "Hurry. Do it!"

Even in Revan's clouded state, the situation was obvious. In the wake of the attack, someone had ordered them to kill the prisoner.

"Squeeze the trigger and it will be the last action you ever take," Revan warned.

"Come on," the other voice said. "Just do it! What's the problem?"

"Shut up!" the young man shouted to his hidden companion. "You were too scared to even open the cell!"

Their fear was completely understandable. Since his incarceration, Revan had been held under strict quarantine. Nobody had been given access to his cell without Scourge being present, and even then the Sith had mostly come to see him alone. No doubt it had been drilled into the guards' heads over and over how powerful and dangerous the prisoner was. They'd been warned against having any dealings with him whatsoever; his mysterious reputation built up over years of speculation and rumors among his jailers.

"Set the weapon down if you want to live," Revan told the young man. Through the veil of drugs, he strained to reach out with the Force, amplifying the other's fear and confusion.

"No!" his friend shouted above the piercing alarms, still staying hidden around the corner. "He'll kill us!"

"I promise to spare you," Revan said. "I give you my word as a Jedi."

"See? See?" the man with the gun squealed. "I told you he was a Jedi!"

"Nyriss has sent you on a suicide mission," Revan told them.

"How do you know who we work for?" the man barked, the pitch of his voice rising.

"The Force shows me many things."

Another explosion from above, this one much closer, caused the guard to nearly drop his weapon. He fumbled it briefly before seizing it with both hands and quickly bringing it up again to point at Revan.

Revan briefly contemplated making a grab for the blaster, but the drugs slowed him physically as much as mentally. Instead he remained still and calm.

"This is bad," the young man said, squeezing the blaster's handle so hard that his knuckles were becoming discolored. "This is bad."

"Just walk away from all this," Revan told them. "It's your only real chance of survival."

"We can't walk away," the guard moaned. "The door upstairs won't open. We're locked in!"

"Just shoot him!" his friend shouted. "He can't hurt you. If he was going to stop you, he would've done it by now."

There were several seconds of silence, punctuated by the alarms and another series of explosions in rapid succession.

"Nyriss will kill us if she finds us down here with you still alive," the man with the blaster said, his voice almost apologetic.

"Nyriss is already dead," Revan said, trying a different tactic as he tried to apply even more pressure through the Force. "Do you hear the explosions? The alarms? My friends are coming to liberate me.

"You say you're trapped in here. What do you think my friends will do if they find you standing over my corpse?"

"He's got a point," the unseen speaker said reluctantly. "Listen to all those bombs going off. This isn't just some quick hit-and-run attack."

"Surrender to me and I will guarantee your safety," Revan said. "I give you my word as a Jedi."

The young man's head turned quickly back and forth, from Revan to his friend outside the cell and then back to Revan again. Then he dropped the blaster as if it were on fire.

Revan calmly stepped out of the cell and got his first look at the other guard: another human male, perhaps a few years older than the first. Both guards were frozen with fear, watching his every move intently. Each time the alarm whooped overhead, they flinched.

"I will not harm you," Revan assured them.

Both men seemed to relax a little, and Revan tried to project calm, soothing waves through the Force to further ease their minds.

"Sit down over there against the wall until my friends arrive," he suggested. "You don't want them to mistake you for a threat."

Seeing the wisdom of his words, both men scrambled to follow his instructions.

Several minutes later they heard a loud crash from above, followed by the sound of footsteps racing down the steep stairs.

And then Meetra descended into view, dressed in some type of dancer's outfit. Seeing Revan, her face broke into a wide grin.

"I knew I'd find you," she said, rushing over to embrace him fiercely.

"It's been a long time," Revan whispered, wrapping his arms around her.

After a moment she broke the embrace, and Revan noticed her nose had crinkled up against the powerful odor wafting off him.

"A real long time," he said with an apologetic shrug, eliciting a soft laugh from Meetra.

"A touching reunion," a familiar voice said.

"Lord Scourge!" one of the guards shrieked in terror.

Revan spun Meetra to the side and stepped in front of her, an instinctive but foolish move. Meetra was a Jedi; she knew how to handle herself. And unarmed he was no match for the Sith.

"It's okay," Meetra said, placing a hand on Revan's shoulder. "Scourge is here to help us."

It took Revan's foggy mind a moment to process what

she was saying. Once he figured it out, he couldn't help but laugh out loud.

"So I finally get to learn your name," he said. "Scourge. No wonder you didn't want to tell me."

"Make jokes once we're safely away from here," Scourge said.

"He's right," Meetra told him. "Tee-Three's keeping watch at the top of the stairs. Come on."

"Go ahead," the Sith told them, drawing his lightsaber and approaching the guards cowering on the floor. "I'll take care of the witnesses."

"No," Revan said. "I promised to protect them."

Scourge gave him a look of utter disbelief. "It's going to be hard enough to get out of here without escorting these pathetic excuses for soldiers."

"I gave them my word," Revan said. A rush of dizziness swept over him, and he reeled.

"What's wrong?" Meetra asked, reaching out to catch him before he fell.

"They keep me drugged," Revan said. "I just need a minute."

With Meetra's help he lowered himself to the floor. His heart was pounding and his head was spinning. During the confrontation with the guard, he must have instinctively used the Force to keep the worst of the drug's effects at bay. But he wasn't strong enough to keep it up any longer, and now his body was responding with an acute overreaction.

Scourge stepped over to a medkit on the wall and yanked it open. He grabbed a hypodermic filled with a green luminescent fluid.

"This will help," he said, injecting it into Revan's arm. "But it will take a few minutes."

"I have something else," Meetra told him. "Bastila asked me to give it to you."

She nodded at Scourge, who pulled a package from

the large pouch on his hip. He tossed it to Revan, who didn't even try to catch it, but just picked it up off the floor.

The object was wrapped in cloth. It was clearly metal, and there was something oddly familiar about it.

"You spoke with Bastila?" he asked. "You saw her?"

Meetra nodded. "And your son. They're both well."

Revan smiled. His mind felt like it was floating blissfully away, but he wasn't sure if the euphoria was triggered by thoughts of his family or the drugs still working their way out of his system.

He unwrapped the cloth to reveal the masked helmet he had worn during his campaigns against the Mandalorians and the Republic. In an instant, all his lost memories came flooding back to him.

A million images—years upon years of forgotten people, places, and events—flooded his consciousness simultaneously. In his weakened state it was too much to take. As his brain went into sensory overload, his body went limp.

"WHAT'S HAPPENING?" Scourge demanded as Revan collapsed on the floor.

"I—I don't know," Meetra said, her hands fumbling to check Revan's pulse as he lay motionless on the ground.

His eyes were closed, but the lids were fluttering madly. Otherwise he was completely still.

From the stairs, T3 let out a piercing wail, several octaves higher than the incessant alarms.

"Someone's coming!" Meetra said.

Scourge turned to the guards still sitting on the floor.

"Ready your blasters, you fools!" he shouted.

As they scrambled to their feet, T3 let out what could only be described as a shriek of terror. An instant later, the little astromech came tumbling down the stairs and bounced across the floor as if he'd been shot from a cannon. He landed in the corner on his back, his wheels still spinning.

"Get Revan out of the way," Scourge said to Meetra.

As she dragged the Jedi's unconscious body into the nearby cell, one of the guards drew his weapon, while the other rushed over and picked his discarded blaster up from where Revan had kicked it aside.

Scourge nodded at the guards. In response to his silent command they crept to the foot of the stairs and peered up toward the door above.

A burst of purple lightning arced down the steps, catching both men in the chest. They barely had time to scream before they were turned into charred and smoking husks.

Scourge took a step back, knowing exactly who had been responsible for unleashing the fury of the dark side against the hapless guards.

Nyriss made her way slowly down the stairs, the outspread fingers of her left hand still crackling with electricity. In her right hand she held her lightsaber, the blade humming softly. By the time she reached the bottom, Meetra had emerged from the nearby cell.

She ignited her lightsaber and came to stand beside Scourge.

"What's this?" Nyriss asked, her voice mocking. "Another Jedi?"

When neither of them answered, she turned her head to the side and laughed bitterly. "The Imperial Guard will make sure I never leave my stronghold alive," she told them. "But neither will any of you."

She raised her free hand above her head and fired off another burst of lightning. Both Scourge and Meetra threw themselves clear of the deadly electrical bolt, but in doing so they gave Nyriss the early advantage.

Before they could recover, she leapt at them. Despite her withered appearance, she moved with all the speed and ferocity of a dark side warrior in her prime. She landed right between her two adversaries, her blade flashing back and forth in a series of slashes and cuts that immediately threw her two opponents on the defensive.

Scourge barely managed to parry the first wave of her assault, unable to even think about countering with an attack of his own. Another quick thrust forced him off balance and he staggered backward.

Nyriss seized on the opportunity to focus all her efforts on breaking through Meetra's defenses. The Jedi was clearly overmatched; though she managed to hold her ground, she was forced down to one knee.

In the awkward position her right flank was exposed, and Nyriss brought her blade in to deliver a crippling cut. At the same time, Scourge lashed out with the Force, catching Nyriss flush in the center of her chest.

An ordinary foe would have been thrown clear across the room, but Nyriss instinctively threw up a Force barrier to protect herself, absorbing and redirecting the brunt of the impact. Even so, Scourge's attack knocked her off balance just enough to send her lightsaber wide of the mark, giving Meetra the opportunity she needed to scramble away to safety.

Scourge rushed forward, hoping to drive Nyriss back into a corner, but she met his charge with an invisible wave of rippling energy. It picked Scourge up and tossed him head-over-heels, sending him crashing to the wall.

Dazed, he looked up just in time to see another bolt of violet lightning catch Meetra in the chest. Like Nyriss, she threw up a barrier to save herself from the worst of it, but she was still knocked from her feet.

"Did you think I would be as easy to defeat as Xedrix?" Nyriss shouted, raising her lightsaber triumphantly above her head.

The air around her began to crackle and grow hot as

she gathered herself for the killing blow. Scourge felt the energy building inside her, and he knew he would be powerless to stop it. Nyriss was too powerful; her command of the dark side was too strong.

"Gaze upon me and see your doom!" she declared. "I am Darth Nyriss, Lord of the Sith. I am the conqueror of Drezzi, the destroyer of Melldia, and a member of the Dark Council!"

Scourge braced himself for the end.

Just then, Revan emerged from the cell. He had pulled the hood of his Jedi robe up to cover his head, and he wore the red-and-gray mask, hiding his face.

A dozen bolts of lightning sprang from Nyriss's hand, arcing across the room to incinerate her enemies. Instead of leaping back into the cell to avoid the deadly attack, Revan stepped forward to intercept it.

Both hands were held in front of him, his arms fully extended at shoulder height, his thumbs touching and his fingers splayed wide. He drew the bolts of lightning into his waiting grasp, channeling them away from their intended targets and absorbing their power.

"I am Revan reborn," he said to Nyriss. "And before me you are nothing."

Nyriss's eyes went wide as Revan unleashed the power of her own attack against her. She tried to throw up another Force shield, but the bolts ripped it apart and continued on unabated. The lightning engulfed her, the intense heat consuming her instantly, leaving only a pile of charred ash.

Scourge slowly clambered to his feet as Revan helped Meetra up. In the corner, the upended astromech let out a plaintive whistle and awkwardly managed to rock himself back into an upright position.

Revan walked over and knelt beside the closer of the two dead soldiers. He placed a hand on the man's chest, but didn't speak.

"We have to go," Meetra said softly, coming over and gently touching Revan on the shoulder to interrupt his thoughts. "We don't want the Imperial Guard to know you were here."

He stood up and slowly turned to Scourge.

There was something unnerving about staring into the faceless mask; it made Revan seem more intimidating, more powerful. Or maybe Scourge just felt that way because he'd watched him destroy Nyriss.

Whatever the reason, he was more confident than ever that he'd made the right choice. If anyone had the strength to stop the Emperor, it was this man.

"This is yours," the Sith said, taking the hilt of Revan's lightsaber from his belt.

Revan accepted the gift with a brief nod, then simply said, "Get us out of here."

CHAPTER TWENTY-FIVE

SCOURGE LED THEM UP the stairs and back to the breach in the wall where the Emperor's Guard had first burst in. Though they could hear the distant sounds of battle echoing faintly through the halls, they didn't encounter combatants from either side.

Once they were outside Meetra allowed herself to breathe a sigh of relief.

Night had fallen, but several fires burning inside Nyriss's stronghold illuminated the grounds, giving them a clear view of the destruction. The thick stone wall surrounding the courtyard and the building had been reduced to rubble, and judging by the number of bodies strewn about the courtyard, this had been the location of the fiercest fighting.

They picked their way through the carnage to where Scourge's speeder stood unharmed near the landing pad. Every vehicle around it had been destroyed by artillery fire.

"It's a miracle this thing's still in one piece," Revan remarked.

"The Guard must have been watching our arrival," Scourge said. "They knew which speeder was mine."

The four of them climbed in, Revan and Meetra

helping T3, then headed for the cave where Meetra and Scourge had first met.

During the journey, Meetra tried to study Revan without being too obvious. He was still wearing the red-and-gray mask; for her this was his true face. She knew what he looked like beneath his helmet, but he had almost never removed it during their campaign against the Mandalorians.

Seeing him in the cell without it had struck her as odd. The passage of the years and the suffering he had endured as a prisoner were clearly etched on his features. When he wore the mask, however, all that was hidden. It made him look indomitable, invincible—a legend come to life.

Meetra remembered what Bastila had said to her when she had given her the mask. She said she had hidden it from Revan for all those years because she feared what it represented. She feared it would change him. Now Meetra understood what she meant.

Without the mask he looked more human. It was easier to remember he was just a man, with all the weaknesses and vulnerabilities that implied. With the mask, however, Revan was an icon, a symbol. He was the shaper of history, an individual defined by his actions rather than his thoughts, feelings, and beliefs.

Maybe Bastila was right; maybe Revan needed to become what he once had been to survive this. He had easily bested Darth Nyriss, but the Emperor was a much greater opponent. And yet she couldn't help but feel some small tinge of regret knowing the man Bastila loved might have been swallowed up by the weight of Revan's own past.

Scourge brought the speeder in to land, and the three passengers disembarked.

"You're not coming?" Meetra asked when the Sith made no move to join them.

"I'm going back to Kaas City," he said. "I'll see if I can learn any more details about the attack. If we're lucky, the Emperor has spread his resources too thin, leaving him vulnerable. Now might be the time to strike."

"Bring back some supplies," Revan said. "Food. Water. Soap so I can wash the filth of that prison off me."

Scourge nodded. "I'll be back in a few hours."

The three of them went into the cave, T3 using his lamp to illuminate the dark interior.

The cave was empty now. While waiting for Scourge to return from his meeting with the Emperor, Meetra and T3 had buried the bodies of the fallen security chief and his soldiers in a bare patch of ground a short hike away from the cave's entrance.

"I'm sure you're eager to change out of those clothes," Revan said.

What about you? Meetra thought. *Why haven't you taken off that mask yet?*

"We have something to show you first," she said. "Tee-Three, play the holovid."

The droid rolled up beside them, projecting a thirty-centimeter-tall image of Bastila cooing over Revan's three-year-old son.

"I don't know if you'll ever see this," Bastila said, adjusting a lock of hair on the boy's head as she spoke to the holorecorder. "But I have to believe you'll return someday. And when you do, I thought you'd want to share your son's birthday."

Revan didn't say anything. As if in a daze, he slowly sat down on the floor so the projection was at eye level.

"Wave to Daddy," Bastila said, pointing in the direction of the recorder. "Say, 'We miss you!'"

The boy did as instructed, waving his tiny arm vigorously as he repeated Bastila's words.

To Meetra's relief, Revan reached up and removed his

mask as the holovid continued to play, setting it down on the ground beside him.

"I know we didn't discuss names before you left," Bastila said. "But I called him Vaner."

Revan smiled, realizing it was an anagram of his own name.

"I want him to know who his father is," the holo continued. "I want him to understand you are a part of him."

A tear rolled down Revan's cheek as he watched the vid, and Meetra quietly retreated into a dark corner of the cave to let him watch in private. She'd stashed her clothes here before she and Scourge had left for Nyriss's stronghold, and the shadows gave her the privacy she needed to change out of her slave's outfit.

Instead of the black pants and sleeveless red shirt she'd worn on her first arrival, however, she once again donned her Jedi robes. She didn't consciously think about her choice, and it was only as she was clipping the lightsaber to her belt that she realized what she'd done.

You're following Revan's lead, she thought. *If he's wearing Jedi robes, then so are you. Just like old times.*

As the holovid continued to play, she lingered near the back of the cave. She couldn't help but overhear Bastila say, "I love you, Revan," as the recording came to an end.

"I love you, too," Revan responded, the acoustics of the cave making his voice unnaturally loud.

Meetra shifted her feet uncomfortably at the exchange. She wasn't jealous of Bastila; Meetra loved Revan, but not in that way. She'd never had romantic feelings for her mentor. Rather, she regarded him with deep admiration and intense devotion.

At this moment, however, she was acutely aware that Bastila and Revan shared a relationship that went far deeper than what Meetra shared with him. She knew she shouldn't begrudge them that, but some small part of her couldn't help but feel her reunion with Revan had been preempted by a holovid.

T3 beeped inquisitively as the video came to an end.

"Of course," Revan said. "I'll watch it a hundred times over if I can. But give me a minute."

He stood up and went to join Meetra in the back of the cave.

"Thank you for this," he said. "And for saving me."

"It was nothing."

"No," Revan said, shaking his head. "Do not underestimate all you have accomplished. Nobody else could have found me across an entire galaxy. Nobody else could have saved me from my imprisonment." He studied her for a moment. "I was told you had been cut off from the Force, but I can sense its power in you. I always knew you had great potential, but you have become far greater than I could ever have imagined."

"I'm just following in your footsteps."

"Not anymore," Revan replied. "You have blazed your own trail. I can sense you have walked a path even I would not dare to tread. I owe you everything, Meetra. It is a debt I will never be able to repay."

"No," Meetra said with a wan smile. "Without your teaching, I could never have become what I am today. I am the one who owes a debt she can never repay."

"Then why don't we call it even?" Revan said.

"A wise and just solution," she replied. "As always."

"Would you like to see the holovid of Bastila and my son?" he asked, offering her his hand. "It would mean more to watch it with a friend at my side."

"Of course," she said, a lump forming in her throat. "It would be my honor."

WHEN SCOURGE ARRIVED BACK at the cave he found Meetra and Revan huddled side by side on the floor, staring at a holovid projected by T3. He caught a glimpse of a young human female and what Scourge assumed was her child, but as he approached the droid quickly cut the recording off.

"What was that?" he asked.

"My wife and son," Revan said.

He stood up stiffly and stretched, and Scourge wondered how long he had been sitting on the floor of the cave watching the holovid. He also noticed that Revan had removed his mask; it was sitting on the ground beside him, seemingly forgotten.

"I didn't know you were married," he said.

When Revan didn't answer, it was clear he had no intention of discussing his personal life with a Sith. They might be allies, Scourge realized, but they were far from friends. Which was as it should be—for a Sith Lord, friends were a liability.

"What did you find out?" Meetra asked as Revan extended a hand to help her up.

"It wasn't just Nyriss who was attacked. The Emperor killed them all."

"The files you showed me listed five current members of the Dark Council plotting against him," Meetra said, looking to clarify. "Are you saying the Emperor's Guard wiped out all five in the space of a single day?"

"I said he killed them all," Scourge replied. "All twelve members of the Dark Council—even those who weren't part of the conspiracy. He wanted to send a message no one would ever forget."

"How is that possible?" Revan asked. "He attacked a dozen of the most powerful Sith Lords in their seats of power simultaneously? How many troops does he have?"

"The Imperial Guard were only unleashed on Nyriss and two others. The Emperor must have assumed they were the ones least likely to answer his summons. The other nine were called together in the hours before the attack to meet with the Emperor at his citadel. None of them left alive."

"So what's happening now?" Meetra asked.

"News of the massacre spread quickly," Scourge said. "As you would expect, the result was chaos. Thousands are fleeing for their lives, fearing we are on the brink of civil war. Others see an opportunity to strike at rivals weakened by the sudden loss of political allies, and armed platoons are roaming the streets."

"How did the Emperor react?" Revan asked.

"He's declared martial law and imposed a curfew over the entire city. The Guard are enforcing his orders with their typical ruthless efficiency. He also forbade any ship or shuttle to land or leave before he launched his attack, and he shut down all offworld communications."

"He's quarantined the entire planet," Revan said. "He wants to get everything here back under control before any other worlds hear that he slaughtered the entire Dark Council."

"You told me he was mad," Meetra muttered, "but this is outrageous. There had to be a better way for him to handle this. Thousands of his people are going to die before order is restored."

"The last time I was here on Dromund Kaas, I peered into the depths of the Emperor's mind," Revan told them. "A thousand lives mean nothing to him."

"The last time you were here?" Scourge said, pouncing on the phrase. "Have some of your memories returned?"

"Seeing my old mask triggered something. I remember everything now," Revan admitted. "Malak and I learned the Sith still survived. We came here to Dromund Kaas to investigate. Posing as mercenaries, we spent months learning everything we could about the Emperor and his people. Even back then he was already planning his invasion of the Republic. When Malak and I learned of his preparations, we tried to stop him. We found a member of the Imperial Guard who was willing to sneak us inside the citadel."

"Impossible," Scourge declared. "The Guard are bound to the Emperor's will at the end of their training by a powerful ritual. They would never betray him!"

"True, but we didn't know that at the time," Revan explained. "We were being led into a trap; the Emperor wanted us to come to him. When we got to his throne room, he was ready and waiting." His voice dropped low. "We underestimated his power. When we confronted him, he didn't even have to fight us. Instead, he broke our wills. He dominated our minds, turning us into puppets to do his bidding. He sent us back to the Republic as the vanguard of his invasion, with instructions to report back when all resistance was crushed.

"But though we had underestimated the Emperor's power, he underestimated us, as well. Our wills were stronger than he thought; our minds twisted and perverted his instructions until we thought we were acting of our own accord. Malak and I were turned to the dark side, but in doing so we found the strength to block out all memory of the Sith and the Emperor, partially freeing us from his control."

"But you still called yourself Sith," Meetra said, puzzled. "You still attacked the Republic and brought it to the verge of collapse before the Jedi captured you. And even after you stopped Malak, the Republic was still as vulnerable as it's ever been. Why didn't the Emperor just invade then?"

"He didn't know what had happened," Revan explained. "He was waiting for us to report back. When he heard nothing, he assumed we had failed. He returned to his original plans, slowly and carefully building up his strength so that when he finally did invade there would be no chance of defeat."

Meetra glanced over at Scourge, and the Sith could guess what she was thinking. He'd originally allied with them because he feared invading the Republic would be a disaster. With Revan implying the Emperor could actually succeed, she feared he would turn on them.

Two days earlier she would have been right. However, everything had changed when Scourge met the Emperor in person.

"I won't betray you," he assured her. "When I spoke with the Emperor, I briefly touched his mind. What he did on Nathema only hints at the horrors he is capable of unleashing on the galaxy. I truly understand what he has become, and I know that unchecked he will lead us to annihilation. It is inevitable."

"A good speech," Meetra said. "But why should we believe you?"

"It's true," Revan assured her. "When the Emperor broke my will, he looked into my mind, and I was able to see the reflection of his own evil. Invading the Republic is only the first step of his plan. He has become obsessed with power and immortality. The dark side is like a cancer inside him; it grows faster than he can feed it. He has consumed an entire world, but he still hungers. And with his hunger comes an all-consuming fear. He has lived a thousand years; he knows he could live many thousands more. He is terrified of death."

"Everyone is scared of dying," Meetra said.

"Not like this. For him death is not merely the end of his physical existence. The Emperor has spent a millennium gathering his strength; if he dies he will lose everything. The thought of near-infinite power slipping from his grasp has driven him mad. In his twisted mind, the only way to preserve what he has accomplished is to annihilate every potential threat in the galaxy."

"Nathema was just the beginning," Scourge agreed. "He will destroy world after world, his power and madness growing in concert until he alone is left, Emperor over an empty and lifeless galaxy."

Meetra stared at the two in horror.

"You've been to Nathema," Scourge said. "You felt the Void. You know what the Emperor is capable of."

"She understands," Revan said, reading her expression more accurately than Scourge. "That's not it."

"He's quarantined Dromund Kaas," Meetra said, trying to lead them to the same conclusion. "What if he's preparing to do the same thing here that he did on Nathema?"

Scourge hadn't considered that possibility, and it chilled him to his core.

"Is that possible?" he asked. "Nyriss told me the ritual on Nathema took days, if not weeks. And the Emperor had to trick hundreds of other powerful Sith into working with him so he could draw on their power."

"He's stronger now," Revan said. "But even if it's possible, I don't think he'll go that far. At least not yet. He is too patient, too careful. Dromund Kaas is the heart of his Empire and the seat of his power. He has too many valuable resources here to throw it all away. But once he is ready, there will be nothing left to stop him from launching his invasion of the Republic."

"What do you mean?" Meetra asked.

Scourge answered on Revan's behalf. "The Emperor had to keep his plans secret because he knew the Dark Council would oppose him. Now they are wiped out. And whoever he picks to replace them will remember what happened to their predecessors, and be too terrified to speak out against him."

"He can also use this to rally the will of the people," Revan added. "He can claim the Dark Council was working with agents of the Republic, and that is why he destroyed them. He will claim the Sith Empire has been rediscovered by its old enemy. He will convince his subjects that the only hope of survival is to strike first."

"He won't make his proclamation until order is restored on Dromund Kaas," Scourge noted.

"That doesn't give us much time," Meetra remarked, remembering how efficiently the Guard had overrun Nyriss's stronghold.

"The Guard are patrolling the streets, enforcing the curfew," Scourge said. "Only a handful remain stationed at the citadel. Now is our best chance to strike at the Emperor."

"This time I know his tricks and tactics," Revan assured them. "I can shield my mind from being dominated by his will, and I can show you how to do the same."

"We should wait until dawn," Scourge said. "There will be fewer people out in the light of day. And most of the Guard will be recovering at the barracks after patrolling the streets all night."

"Good," Revan said. "That gives us a few hours to try to get some rest."

Both Meetra and Scourge nodded in agreement, though the Sith doubted any of them would get much sleep.

CHAPTER TWENTY-SIX

SCOURGE HOVERED ON THE EDGE OF SLEEP. His body was exhausted, but his mind was churning. Unable to still his thoughts and let sleep wash over him, he tossed and turned.

Unlike his Jedi companions, he had never learned to sit and meditate in order to draw sustenance from the Force. The dark side was about action and activity, not restful contemplation. But he knew that if he didn't try something, he would have to endure a long and restless night.

He propped himself into a sitting position and closed his eyes, trying to open himself up to the Force. Taking slow, deep breaths, he focused on letting his mind open itself to the infinite possibilities swirling through time and space. After several minutes he managed to drift into a state of semiconsciousness.

Revan lay motionless on the floor of the Citadel's throne room. Meetra and Scourge lay beside him, their bodies twisted and broken, clinging to the last moments of life.

The Emperor approached the trio, regarding them with a cold and casual contempt as he loomed above his fallen adversaries. Scourge tried to stand and flee, but his crippled limbs wouldn't support his weight. All he could do was crawl on his belly like a worm.

His efforts drew the attention of the Emperor, who didn't speak but came over and lowered himself to one knee. He grabbed Scourge by the shoulder and rolled him over so he was staring up into the twin voids of the Emperor's eyes.

As he reached out a hand and placed it on Scourge's forehead, the Sith began to scream.

Scourge's eyes popped open as his mind snapped to a fully alert state of consciousness. His heart was pounding, and he could still hear the sound of his own scream ringing in his ears.

Glancing around the cave he realized the scream must have been confined to his mind; neither Meetra nor Revan had reacted in any way. She was sitting in the same cross-legged pose Revan had often assumed during his time in Nyriss's prison. Revan was kneeling in front of T3-M4, hunched forward as he rewatched the holovid of his wife and son.

Scourge shook his head, trying to push away the remnants of his dream. But the memory stayed with him, and he began to realize that what he had seen was something more than a mere nightmare.

The experience lacked the hazy, surreal feel of a dream. It had been too vivid, the details too sharp and precise to be a figment manifested by his subconscious. There was only one possible explanation for what had happened: the Force had given Scourge a vision.

Scourge's hands began to tremble slightly as he realized he had witnessed his own destruction at the Emperor's hand. Even worse, the vision made it clear that both Meetra and Revan would suffer the same fate. He had opened himself up to the Force, and it had shown him that their coming mission would end in failure.

He glanced over at the Jedi, wondering if he should warn them. Even if he did, would they believe what he said? Could *he* believe it?

His training at the Academy had taught him little about the prophetic abilities of the Force. Was what he had seen inevitable, or was it a fate he could somehow avoid? Maybe his strong connection to the dark side would somehow color his visions, distorting them so they showed the worst of all possible futures.

The simplest course would be to tell Revan what he had seen and hear his opinion of it. But Scourge knew his allies' trust in him was already fragile. If he admitted he thought their mission was doomed, it could convince them he couldn't be trusted. They might even decide it was his presence that caused their failure; after all, he was the one who had seen the vision.

Scourge continued to struggle with what he had seen, trying to understand what it meant and what he should do about it. But after several more minutes of silently talking himself in circles, he realized he simply wouldn't find the answers on his own.

He pushed himself to his feet and went over to where Revan was sitting. T3 paused the playback of the holovid as he approached, but left the still image of Revan's wife and son hovering in the air.

"May I speak with you?" Scourge asked, taking a seat beside the Jedi without waiting for a reply.

"You may," Revan said, not bothering to tear his gaze away from the projection of his family.

"I want to know more about the Force," Scourge said. "I want to understand it as you do."

Revan turned to give him a quizzical look. "You want to know this now?"

"This might be our last chance," Scourge said. "I've been thinking about something you said to me the last time we spoke in your cell."

"What is that?"

"You knew Meetra was coming to rescue you because the Force had given you a vision."

Revan smiled. "Actually, I was bluffing. I was trying to trick you. I was hoping you might dream of me escaping, and think the Force was guiding you to help me."

"Is that how it happens?" Scourge asked, slightly miffed at Revan's confession. "They come to you in your dreams?"

"No. A Force vision is more powerful than any dream. There is an intensity that jumps out at you, and the details do not fade. But I figured you wouldn't know the difference."

I do now, Scourge thought.

"I won't apologize for lying to you," Revan said, mistaking the reason for his companion's silence. "And if it makes you feel any better, I actually did have a vision of Meetra after we spoke."

"That seems a highly unlikely coincidence," Scourge noted.

"That is the way of the Force," Revan said. "Cause and effect are not a simple linear relationship. The Force transcends space and time; it flows through us and around us; it influences our past, present, and future. Maybe I spoke to you of visions because I knew the Force was trying to reach out to me. Or maybe Meetra came to Dromund Kaas because I told you someone was coming to rescue me."

"But she started looking for you long before we had our conversation," Scourge protested.

"It's complicated," Revan answered with a cryptic smile. "Jedi scholars have devoted centuries to understanding the ways of the Force, and we have only scratched the surface."

Scourge silently tried to digest what he was being told. At the same time, he tried to form the questions that would give him the answers he wanted without revealing what he had seen.

"Once you had the vision of Meetra, were you certain she was coming? Did you know for sure that she would help free you?"

Revan shook his head. "We can never be certain about anything. The future is always in motion, and a vision shows you only one of many possible outcomes."

"Then what purpose do visions serve?"

"They guide us," Revan explained. "They give us focus. They show us a goal to strive for, or something we can work to prevent."

"So the visions are not absolute?"

"As I said, the future is always in motion."

There was another long period of silence before Scourge asked another question. "Have you had any visions of what will happen when we face the Emperor?"

"No," Revan said. "The dark side obscures my sight. We are walking into a time and place of shadows, and I cannot promise you that we will ever come out."

"Doesn't that terrify you?"

"Fear is only an emotion; a trick the mind plays on us. You must learn to set your fear aside."

"We Sith are taught to embrace our fear," Scourge told him. "We transform it into anger and use it to fuel the power of the dark side."

"But then your actions will always be driven by that fear," Revan said.

"And what are your actions driven by?" Scourge asked. "Logic? Reason?"

"No," Revan admitted. "If I were reasonable, I would never have left my family behind to face the Emperor."

"Then why did you do it?"

Revan nodded in the direction of the holoprojection. "For them. I want my son to live a long and healthy life.

I want him to know peace, not war. I've come to stop the Emperor for him."

"And what if we don't stop him?" Scourge said, treading perilously close to the heart of what he really wanted to say. "What if he's too strong?"

"That is a possibility," Revan admitted. "But even if we fail to defeat the Emperor, there is still hope. My return will give him pause. He will wonder how I threw off the chains of his will. He will wonder why I have returned, and how much the Republic now knows of his plan. He will even wonder about Malak. For all the Emperor knows, Malak is still out there, plotting to take the Emperor down if I fail."

"You're just trying to buy time," Scourge gasped. "You don't care if the Emperor kills us all—you just want to delay him!"

"No," Revan said. "I want to live. Even more, I want to purge the galaxy of his evil once and for all. But I understand that there can be victory even in defeat. Even if we fall, we will buy time. Maybe a few years. More likely a few decades."

"Time for your son to become a man," Scourge noted bitterly. "Are you hoping he will finish what you might not?"

"Him or someone else," Revan admitted. "The Force always strives for balance. The Emperor is an agent of darkness and destruction. It is inevitable that a champion of the light will one day rise to oppose him. I may be that champion." He spoke with no hint of hubris. "I've played the role before. At the very least, I will make the Emperor step back and reconsider his plan. If that is my fate—if my role is to sacrifice myself for the one who will come next—then I embrace it."

Scourge shook his head. "I'm beginning to think you are as mad as the Emperor. I have no intention of dying tomorrow."

"Neither do I. But if death comes, I will face it without fear. You will find our task easier if you can convince yourself to do the same," he said, before turning his attention back to the holoprojection.

"Start over from the beginning," Revan told T3, and the astromech obediently restarted the recording.

Scourge got to his feet and walked back to the section of the cave he had been sitting in earlier. He briefly considered talking to Meetra, then realized that would be a waste of time. She would only echo what Revan had said.

The Sith sat down and crossed his legs again, closing his eyes. But he wasn't able to clear his mind this time. Instead, he kept running over Revan's words, playing them against the enduring images of his vision, trying to understand what it all meant.

CHAPTER TWENTY-SEVEN

AS PLANNED, Revan, Meetra, Scourge, and T3-M4 left the cave at dawn, though *dawn* on Dromund Kaas was a term with little meaning. The black storm clouds completely blocked out the sun, and the sky was only marginally lighter than it had been during the night.

A steady drizzle fell on them as they climbed into the speeder. They rode in silence, all of them preparing in their own way for what they knew lay ahead. Meetra had gone into what Revan called her warrior's trance; she sat still and straight, her eyes focused on nothing as she stared straight ahead.

He had seen it many times during the war against the Mandalorians. Before each major battle she would try to center her emotions, cleansing herself of all fear and hatred lest the imminent violence draw her toward the dark side. She believed she could transform herself into a perfect conduit for the Force, an incorruptible weapon of light.

Revan was no longer sure such a thing was possible, but he didn't say anything to Meetra for fear of disrupting her routine.

With his memories restored, Revan recalled that he, too, had once clung to a set of rituals before each battle.

He would stare at his reflection in the mirror, his face covered by his mask as he recited the Jedi Code over and over until the words seemed to blend together, their meaning lost in the rhythmic repetition of a mantra.

In those days, he had believed this would protect him from the dark side, but he no longer had any such illusions. He was older and wiser. He understood that the two sides of the Force were more closely intertwined with each other than either the Jedi or the Sith would ever admit. He had learned to balance on the knife-edge between them, drawing on both the light and dark sides for strength.

As much as things had changed, however, he still felt the old stirrings of glory as they set off—a faint echo from the impetuousness of youth that had caused him to defy the Council and lead his fellow Jedi into war so many years before.

Even T3 was strangely subdued, the gravity of their situation weighing as heavily on the astromech as it did on his organic companions.

Revan knew he didn't have to worry about Meetra or the faithful droid. Scourge was another matter, however. The conversation they'd had during the night left little doubt that the Sith was troubled.

Unlike the Jedi, he had not spent a lifetime preparing for this. The concept of self-sacrifice came easily to those who walked the path of the light. Even though he occasionally strayed into the dark side, Revan still embraced the nobility of the idea.

For the Sith, however, there was no such thing as a noble death. Scourge understood the concept of sacrifice, but only when it came to sacrificing others. He had been taught to value survival above all else. Even his willingness to join with Revan and Meetra was driven by his desire for self-preservation; ultimately he wanted victory only for his sake, and not for the sake of others.

Perhaps there was no greater illustration of the difference between the light side and the dark, and Revan knew it would make their mission more difficult for Scourge. He had tried to make him understand during their brief conversation, but it was hard to undo years of teaching in a single night.

Still, the Sith seemed to be holding himself together well enough this morning.

"I can't bring the speeder in too close," Scourge said now, taking them in for a landing on the farthest outskirts of Kaas City. "They might have set up ion cannons to shoot down any unauthorized vehicles."

They continued on foot, making their way through the empty streets heading toward the citadel. They didn't encounter a single living soul on their journey; apart from the Emperor's Guard, nobody dared to violate the curfew. And three Force-sensitive individuals and an astromech equipped with top-of-the-line optical and audio sensors had no trouble avoiding the handful of patrols still wandering the streets.

As they drew closer to the city's center, the signs of the previous night's mayhem became more frequent and more striking. Most of the windows were shattered, and many of the buildings were blackened by smoke or completely gutted by fire. The street was pockmarked with craters and covered with the burned-out husks of speeders lying on their sides. Most of the dead had been carted away, either by friends or Imperial cleaning crews, but there was still the odd body slumped in a doorway or half hidden under a refuse pile down a side alley.

When they finally reached the citadel, there were no sentries standing by the entrance at the top of the stairs.

"If we run into anyone, let me do the talking," Scourge whispered as they mounted the steps.

They were only a few meters away from the entrance when the door flew open and half a dozen of the red-uniformed soldiers spilled out, armed with blasters and electrostaffs.

"You are in violation of the Imperial curfew," one of the soldiers informed them. "Surrender your weapons and you will be escorted to a nearby prison facility."

"You fool!" Lord Scourge spat at the Guard, his voice rising with arrogant indignation. "Do you know who I am?"

"Only those explicitly authorized by the Emperor are permitted on the streets," the soldier replied, his voice wavering only slightly.

"I need no authorization! My name is Lord Scourge, and I demand a meeting with the Emperor."

From the reaction of the soldiers it was clear they recognized the name. No doubt every member of the Emperor's Guard was aware by now that Scourge had been the catalyst for the Emperor's sudden purging of the entire Dark Council.

"We will escort you to him," the leader replied, lowering his weapon. "But the others must wait here."

"No," Scourge said. "They will come with me to speak with the Emperor in person."

The soldier seemed on the verge of denying the request, and Revan mentally prepared himself to unleash his fury, but at the last minute the man relented . . . at least partially.

"Follow me," he said. "I'll ask the captain to meet us outside the throne room. She will decide whether to allow this."

Revan was impressed by Scourge's performance, not to mention relieved. On his last visit to Dromund Kaas, he and Malak had learned everything they could about the Imperial Guard. Though not attuned to the Force in the classical sense, the elite soldiers had a connection with the Emperor, allowing them to draw strength from the dark side. They were formidable opponents, even for a Jedi.

He'd feared they'd have to fight through dozens of the Guard before reaching the throne room, giving the Emperor ample time to prepare his counterattack. Now, however, they had a chance to take their adversary by surprise.

They were led down a twisting maze of corridors, a long and winding journey that Revan remembered from his last visit to the citadel. He and Malak had followed the same route, led by a Guard they had bribed for access, completely unaware that they were being led into a trap.

It was possible the same thing was being done to them this time, as well, but Revan didn't think that was the case. The guard who had betrayed him and Malak had met with them numerous times before leading them into the citadel, no doubt reporting back to the Emperor after each visit. This time, however, events had moved too quickly and too spontaneously for the Emperor's patient hand to be behind them.

As they drew closer to the throne room, Revan's thoughts drifted back to his last confrontation with the Emperor. In all his battles, he had never faced an enemy with that kind of power. The dark side had radiated from him in palpable waves, his physical shell barely able to contain the crackling energy.

In their last meeting he had overwhelmed Revan completely; it wasn't even fair to call it a battle. Revan had grown since then. He was far more powerful now, but was he a match for the Emperor?

Alone, probably not. With the combined strength of Meetra, Scourge, and even T3, however, he believed they stood a real chance of victory.

Despite this, he still felt a chill in his gut when he saw

again the enormous durasteel doors of the throne room. They were shut, of course, but he knew all too well what lay beyond.

"Where is your captain?" Scourge demanded, and Revan realized there was nobody there to meet them.

"She is coming," the Guard assured him.

"I will not be kept waiting," Scourge snarled, continuing to play his part. "I demand you open these doors immediately!"

The soldier hesitated, then motioned for two of his men to do as Scourge had commanded.

Revan braced himself for what was to come. They had discussed this part of their plan before leaving the cave. The instant the doors were pushed opened, all four would charge inside. While Revan rushed the Emperor, Meetra and Scourge would hang back and hold off the guards long enough for T3 to close and seal the doors.

Their timing had to be almost perfect; Revan knew he couldn't go toe-to-toe with the Emperor by himself for very long. He sensed Meetra tensing beside him, and his own hand drifted to the hilt of his lightsaber beneath his belt in anticipation.

"What is going on here?" a female voice called out from behind him.

The two soldiers who had been about to push open the heavy durasteel doors froze in place.

"Captain Yarri," said the man who escorted them in, snapping off a sharp salute. "Lord Scourge demands another meeting with the Emperor."

Revan was standing with his back to the captain, but he didn't need to see her face to recognize the name: Yarri—the Guard who had led him and Malak into the Emperor's trap.

"This is not acceptable, Lord Scourge," she said, the heels of her boots clacking as she approached. "If you wish to speak with the Emperor, you must do so alone."

"I do not take orders from you, Captain," Scourge said.

"In the citadel you do," she answered. "You other two and the droid, step away from there."

Revan had been carefully facing away from the speakers during the entire conversation, his eyes fixed on the massive doors. Suddenly he felt a hand on his shoulder as one of the soldiers tried to pull him clear of the entrance.

He slapped the hand away and turned to face them. Yarri was standing beside Scourge, a few meters away from the rest of the group. She had come alone to meet them, bringing their escort up to a total of seven.

The captain's eyes went wide with shock as she saw his unmistakable red-and-gray mask.

She gasped, then shouted out, "Assassins! Kill them all!"

Revan lashed out with his foot, delivering a side kick to the chest of the guard who had grabbed his shoulder, sending the man stumbling back. T3-M4, his electrical circuits instantly processing the situation, reacted by firing off his built-in blaster; the beam struck the soldier square in the chest. At the same time, Meetra threw herself at the two guards standing in front of the doors to the throne room, her lightsaber materializing in her hand.

Ordinary soldiers would have been chopped down before they could even draw their weapons, but the Imperial Guard were not so easily felled. The first soldier met her charge and parried the first strike with his electrostaff, the resilient metal of his weapon deflecting the energy blade of the Jedi off to the side so that it carved a deep scar in the wall.

The second soldier leapt into the fray, forcing Meetra to fall back a step to absorb their coordinated attack.

Slightly farther away, Scourge and Captain Yarri were also already engaged in close-quarters combat, his light-saber clashing against her electrostaff as they battled in the narrow confines of the entrance hall.

An alarm began to ring out in the hall, triggered by one of the other three soldiers. Before they could join in the fight, Revan thrust his hand, palm up, in the direction of the sealed durasteel doors, blasting them wide open with the power of the Force.

"Into the throne room!" he shouted, rushing forward.

One of the guards battling Meetra broke off and tried to cut Revan off. The Jedi gathered himself and leapt high in the air, tucking his knees in tight to somersault over his opponent. The guard reacted to the unexpected move a fraction too slowly, his electrostaff slicing through the air above his head and missing Revan by only a few centimeters.

Revan landed on the ground and wheeled around to face the other man. He thrust out with the Force, the impact hitting the soldier square in the chest. Instead of sending him flying, it only staggered him back half a step—this close to the Emperor they were sworn to protect, the guards were able to draw on his power to protect themselves.

Still, the slight stumble gave Revan enough time to draw his lightsaber and go on the offensive. He came in with a high, overhand chop—an obvious feint meant to draw the defenses of his opponent upward, leaving his legs exposed to a quick follow-up strike.

The guard recognized the familiar ploy, countering it by parrying the overhand chop then quickly dropping his blade low to intercept the inevitable slash at his legs. Only Revan didn't go for his legs. Anticipating that his opponent's defenses would go low, he kept his blade up high, allowing him to end the battle with a horizontal cut across the man's suddenly exposed throat.

T3 had followed him into the throne room, but Meetra and Scourge were still locked in battle with the guards in the hall outside. They were waging a fighting retreat; they had maneuvered themselves so they could back into the throne room while keeping the guards at bay.

At the far end of the hall, another half a dozen of the Imperial Guard rounded the corner. Revan reached out with the Force and ripped the vaulted stone archway in the ceiling above them free from its setting. A shower of dust and debris rained down on the reinforcements, sending them into temporary retreat.

It wasn't enough to block the passage, but it did buy Scourge and Meetra a few precious seconds to complete their retreat into the chamber. They crossed the threshold, still engaged with Captain Yarri and the three surviving Imperial Guard that had escorted them to the throne room.

Revan reached out with the Force and slammed the durasteel doors shut, the clang echoing loudly in the throne room.

"Seal the doors!" he shouted at T3. Then he turned his attention to the other end of the throne room.

The Emperor was seated on his throne, watching the proceedings with cold detachment. Revan felt the same chill he had experienced the last time he had come into the Emperor's presence, the physical manifestation of his enemy's malevolent power.

"I did not expect you to return," the Emperor said, rising to his feet.

Revan didn't bother to reply as he charged forward.

SCOURGE WAS AN EXPERT SWORDSMAN; at the Academy even the instructors had been reluctant to face him in the training ring. When the dark side flowed through him, his blade was more than a weapon. It became an extension of his will.

Captain Yarri's skill with her electrostaff was impressive, but ultimately she was no match for a Sith Lord. Knowing this, she had wisely adopted a defensive style to hold off the first few flurries of Scourge's attack, her focus on stalling him long enough for one of her companions to join the fray before switching to a more aggressive form.

Now Scourge was forced to defend himself on two fronts as he backed into the throne room. In his peripheral vision he saw that Meetra was in a similar situation, retreating while battling a pair of enemies.

The fact that Revan hadn't come to their aid told Scourge that the Jedi had gone to confront the Emperor, conjuring up images from Scourge's vision of him lying broken and beaten on the floor at the Emperor's feet.

Yarri's staff slipped through his defenses and clipped him on his right shoulder. Scourge's armor absorbed the worst of the blow, though he felt a painful jolt from the electrostaff's charge that made his hand and arm tingle.

Even as Scourge cursed himself for allowing thoughts of his vision to distract him, he deftly switched his blade from his temporarily numb right hand to his left. The move was dangerous; it left him momentarily vulnerable as he made the switch. Fortunately his opponents were unprepared for the unorthodox tactic, and neither was able to take advantage.

While he and Meetra fought the quartet of guards, T3-M4 was busy sealing the doors. The droid was spraying black foam along the edge where the double doors came together. Scourge recognized the foam as a powerful contact adhesive commonly used to repair starships; seconds after being exposed to air it would harden into a substance that could be cut only with a plasma torch.

Yarri's blade nearly caught him again, narrowly missing his cheek, and Scourge swore out loud. If he didn't stay focused on the fight, his vision of the Emperor killing him wouldn't even have a chance to come true.

"Go help Revan!" Meetra shouted to T3 as the astromech finished his task.

Scourge pressed his attack, calling on the dark side to transform his uncertainty and fear into white-hot rage. He felt the power coursing through him, the spark of fury deep inside him igniting into a firestorm of death and destruction.

Left-handed, Scourge unleashed a pair of savage chops at Yarri's partner, using raw brute strength to overpower his physically weaker opponent. The guard parried the blows, but the first knocked him off balance and the second sent him stumbling backward.

While the guard struggled to recover, Scourge focused his assault on the captain. Yarri sensed the shift in her opponent too late to switch back to a more defensive form, and the Sith Lord was quick to exploit the tactical flaw.

A four-move sequence overwhelmed Yarri, causing her to leave her right flank unprotected. Scourge seized the opportunity, his blade biting deep into her hip. Yarri screamed, dropped her blade, and fell to the ground. The other guard leapt to her defense, recklessly throwing himself between his fallen captain and Scourge. The only reward for his effort was a quick death, delivered by a diagonal lightsaber slash across his chest.

At Scourge's feet, Yarri fumbled to reclaim her weapon. The agony of her wound made her desperate and clumsy, giving Scourge time to relish her suffering. As her fingers wrapped around the hilt of her electrostaff, he brought his boot down on top of her hand, crushing the bones.

He stared into the captain's eyes one last time, savoring her terror before decapitating her with a single stroke.

"We have to help Revan!" Meetra shouted, and Scourge turned to see that she, too, had just finished off her opponents. "He needs us!"

CHAPTER TWENTY-EIGHT

AS MEETRA AND SCOURGE BATTLED the Guard, Revan charged toward the Emperor.

His opponent stood perfectly still, focusing and channeling his power. At the last possible instant, the Emperor unleashed a wave of energy that swept Revan off his feet and sent him flying backward.

Revan twisted in midair so that he was able to roll with the impact when he landed. He quickly sprang back to his feet and advanced again, moving more slowly this time.

The Emperor stood in the exact same position as before; it was as if he hadn't even moved. Revan began to sense the oppressive presence of the dark side weighing down on him. The Emperor was trying to crush his will: to dominate and enslave his mind as he had before. This time, however, Revan was ready.

Instead of charging forward, he opened himself up to the Force, letting both the light and the dark side flow through him like twin rushing rivers. But instead of focusing or channeling the Force, he released it in its purest form.

There was brilliant flash as the air between the two combatants lit up. The energy unleashed was powerful enough to send Revan staggering. The Emperor, unprepared and with much of his strength diverted to his effort to dominate Revan's mind, was sent flying backward.

He landed in a heap on the floor and Revan raced toward him. The Emperor rolled over, lifted himself up on one knee, and his hands flew forward as he hurtled a bolt of dark side lightning at his enemy.

Revan intercepted the bolt with the blade of his lightsaber, though the impact stopped his charge dead in its tracks.

The Emperor unleashed three more bolts in quick succession. Revan batted the first aside with his lightsaber, ducked the second, then deflected the third back in the direction of its source.

It struck the Emperor in the chest, sending him sliding several meters back on the floor. For the first time the Sith's emotionless veneer cracked as he let out a primal hiss of hate. The sound sent shivers down Revan's spine.

The Emperor rose to his feet, his robes smoking and singed where the lighting had struck him. His black eyes flashed red, and he raised both hands high above his head.

Revan knew he was gathering his power to unleash a swirling storm of pure dark side energy, just as Nyriss had done. The Jedi quickly calculated his options. Realizing he couldn't close the gap between them quickly enough to stop the assault, he gathered his own energy and spread his hands before him, ready to catch and absorb the Emperor's attack.

A dozen bolts of purple lightning arced from the Emperor toward him. Revan tried to draw them in and contain them, but the Emperor was infinitely more powerful than Darth Nyriss had ever been.

Revan's body was engulfed in agony as the electricity coursed through his body. His skin began to boil and blister, the flesh of his face melting and sticking to the superheated metal of his mask as the Emperor poured more and more power into him.

Through the haze of indescribable pain, he saw T3-M4 rushing in to help him. The droid let loose with his flamethrower, bathing the Emperor in fire. At the last instant the Emperor cocooned himself in the Force to save himself from being incinerated, breaking his focus on Revan.

The Jedi collapsed to the ground, burned but still alive, the hilt of his extinguished lightsaber lying on the floor less than a meter beyond his grasp.

Almost too weak to move, Revan managed to raise his head just in time to see the Emperor turn on the brave little astromech. A tremor rippled through the air as the Emperor unleashed the full power of the Force against the defenseless droid.

T3 never stood a chance. The little droid exploded into a million pieces, internal circuits and external casing obliterated in a single instant.

"No!" Revan screamed from the ground as bits of his friend rained down on him in the form of unrecognizable shrapnel.

He tried to rise, but his injured body refused to respond. Instinctively, he called on the Force to give him strength and heal his wounds.

The Emperor was approaching him with calm, purposeful steps. Once he reached Revan's side he calmly bent down and picked up the Jedi's fallen weapon, igniting the blade.

The healing properties of the Force were powerful, but Revan's wounds were severe and he needed more time to restore his strength. Helpless, he could only stare up at the Emperor as he raised the lightsaber to deliver the killing blow.

* * *

EVEN AS SHE CALLED to Scourge to help, Meetra was already sprinting toward the far end of the throne room. Scourge hesitated before joining her, taking a moment to survey the situation, memories of his vision of their failure still fresh in his mind.

What he saw was not good. Revan was being electrocuted, his body spasming uncontrollably as the Emperor blasted him with dark purple lightning.

Revan's astromech launched a jet of flame at the Emperor, freeing Revan, who collapsed to the ground. In retaliation, the Emperor disintegrated the offending droid, strode over to where Revan lay, and picked the vanquished Jedi's lightsaber up off the floor.

It all happened in the space of only a few seconds. Meetra was moving fast, but she was too far away to stop the Emperor from eviscerating the prone Jedi at his feet.

In desperation, she hurled her lightsaber with a wild sidearm throw, guiding it with the Force so that it spiraled end-over-end to intercept the descending blade, knocking it from the Emperor's grasp and sending it skittering across the floor.

Suddenly empty-handed, the Emperor took a quick step back. His attention had been focused solely on Revan; Meetra's trick had caught him by surprise. Scourge realized that if she had aimed at the Emperor instead of the blade, she could have ended his life even as he ended Revan's. But her instincts to save her friend overrode her desire to kill her enemy, and Scourge could only lament the lost opportunity.

Meetra was still rushing forward, using the Force to return her lightsaber to her waiting hand.

Sensing hesitation and uncertainty in the Emperor as he tried to evaluate the strength and weaknesses of his new foe, Scourge rushed forward to join Meetra and Revan.

Meetra had placed herself between the Emperor and Revan, valiantly protecting her wounded friend. As Scourge reached them, Revan managed to stand up again. He reached out with an open palm and his lightsaber sprang from the floor and into his waiting grasp.

The three of them stood side by side, two Jedi and a Sith Lord against the Emperor.

"I expected better from you, Lord Scourge," the Emperor said.

Scourge wondered if he was stalling for time so his Guard could break through the sealed door. There wasn't much chance of that, however; by the time they broke into the throne room the battle would already be decided, one way or the other.

"He has seen the depths of your evil," Revan declared. "He stands with us now."

"Then he will die with you, as well."

"You can't defeat all three of us," Revan said. "United, we are stronger than even you."

"That remains to be seen," the Emperor replied.

For Scourge, the universe suddenly seemed frozen in place, as if time itself had stopped. He realized he was at a crux in history; fate and destiny would be forever altered in the next few moments.

The Force washed over him in a wave, and a million possible futures flickered through his mind simultaneously. In some the Emperor was no more; in others he had transformed the entire galaxy into an empty wasteland. He saw both Revan's triumph and defeat in the throne room; he saw variations of his own life and death played out over and over in every conceivable way, shape, and form.

He had to choose, but there was no way to know which was the most likely outcome, or what actions of his would lead to which results. Revan had said visions could guide the Jedi, but for Scourge they brought nothing but confusion.

The moment passed and the universe began to move again, though everything seemed to be happening in slow motion. Revan and Meetra stepped forward, ready to initiate the final confrontation. Scourge knew he had to act now; he had to make his choice.

In a sudden moment of clarity he saw the Emperor lying defeated at the feet of a powerful Jedi . . . but that Jedi was neither Revan nor Meetra. And the Sith Lord knew what he had to do.

Instead of advancing with his two companions, Scourge stepped to the side so that he was standing directly behind Meetra. There was a flicker in his consciousness as the universe snapped back to full speed, and he slid the blade of his lightsaber between her shoulders.

Meetra gasped and toppled forward, dead before she hit the floor. Revan's head snapped to the side, shock and horror emanating from him even though his mask hid his expression. The distraction gave the Emperor the opportunity he needed, and he unleashed another blast of lightning into the Jedi's chest.

Scourge could smell burning flesh as Revan screamed once then collapsed to the ground, unconscious.

The Emperor turned to face Scourge, and the Sith Lord dropped to one knee, head bowed in supplication.

"Explain yourself," the Emperor said, and Scourge knew if he chose his words poorly they would be the last he ever spoke.

"The Jedi was working with Nyriss," he said, speaking quickly. "He claimed he had once been your servant, but that he had returned to destroy you. I knew I was not strong enough to defeat him myself, so I lured him here to face you."

"Why didn't you mention this when you told me about Nyriss's betrayal?"

"I didn't know," Scourge lied. "I only found out after the Guard razed her stronghold. The Jedi sought me out. They knew I worked for Nyriss; they never suspected that I was the one who had betrayed her."

"So you led them to me."

"I knew they could never defeat you," Scourge said. "So I played along, waiting for my chance to turn on them and prove my loyalty to you once more."

"If this is true," the Emperor said. "Then you must finish it."

Scourge nodded, and rose to his feet. He walked over to Revan, bent down, and ripped off his helmet. The Jedi's face was badly burned, the outline of his mask indelibly seared into his cheeks and forehead. He was still unconscious, his body in shock from his wounds; without medical attention he would die soon anyway.

The Sith Lord raised his lightsaber to deliver the coup de grâce. He brought his arm down, but it suddenly stopped as if an invisible and impossibly strong hand had seized his wrist. He glanced back at the Emperor in surprise.

"Put away your blade. You have passed the test," the Emperor said. "But Revan can still be of use to me."

Despite his curiosity, Scourge knew better than to ask how. He couldn't risk anything that might make it appear he was concerned about the Jedi's fate. To sell his lie, he had to make it seem as if everything he had done had been for the most obvious and selfish of reasons.

"Twice I have stopped those who sought to defeat you," he said, extinguishing his blade and bowing before the Emperor. "I trust you will remember this when you select the members of the new Dark Council."

The Emperor smiled, and Scourge's entire body went cold.

"I promise you will be given your just reward."

CHAPTER TWENTY-NINE

"THE RITUAL IS ABOUT TO BEGIN," the Emperor intoned.

Scourge nodded, though even if he had wanted to refuse it was far too late now.

He was standing in the center of a cylindrical metal platform roughly two meters across. Dozens of wires and IV tubes had been hooked to his body. The wires were connected to several generators arranged in a circle around the platform, the IV tubes ran to clear vats filled with a strange green bubbling liquid.

They were still inside the citadel, but this private chamber was much smaller than the throne room. It was unfurnished and, apart from the Emperor, Scourge, and the infernal machinery he was hooked up to, completely empty.

In the wake of Revan's defeat, the Emperor hadn't made him a member of the Dark Council after all. Instead, he had created a new position for Scourge: the Emperor's Wrath.

The Emperor had believed his explanation about Revan. As a reward Scourge was to become his personal enforcer and executioner, taking his orders directly from the Emperor and answering to no one but him.

That wasn't the full extent of his reward, however. For his role in exposing Xedrix, Nyriss, and Revan, the Emperor had promised to grant Scourge the gift of eternal life. He would forever serve at the Emperor's side, an honor far greater than even that of being selected for the Dark Council.

Scourge had eagerly accepted, knowing his new position would give him both time and opportunity to find another way to stop the Emperor before his madness and hunger consumed the galaxy.

"Open yourself to the dark side," the Emperor said, and Scourge felt the air around him begin to swirl with power.

Betraying his allies had not altered the inevitable outcome; the Emperor would have won regardless. At least this way Scourge was still alive to carry on their cause.

Revan was still alive, too, but he was as good as dead to Scourge. The Emperor was holding him prisoner in a secret facility, and Scourge knew he could never risk trying to find its location. He couldn't do anything that might suggest an ongoing connection between him and Revan. Doing so would expose the truth to the Emperor, making his sacrifice of the Jedi pointless.

"Let the spark of eternal life ignite within you!" the Emperor called out.

Scourge felt a sharp burst of heat in his chest. He gritted his teeth in pain as the heat grew more intense.

He felt no guilt or remorse over what he had done. He knew the Jedi would never have chosen this path, of course. They would have felt the price of betrayal was too high.

Scourge knew they were wrong. There was no sense in throwing his life away with theirs. Betrayal was the cost of stopping the Emperor, and he alone had been willing to pay it.

Revan had been right about one thing, however: the

attack had made the Emperor step back from his plans to invade the Republic. Instead of looking beyond the borders of the Sith Empire, he had turned his attention inward, focusing on restoring stability and control over Dromund Kaas and the other worlds he ruled.

The Dark Council would have to be rebuilt. It was inevitable there would be infighting and high turnover in the first few years as the new members vied with one another to curry favor with the Emperor. And he, in turn, would keep a close eye on the actions of the Council until the plots and schemes returned to a more normal and expected level.

It would be several decades, maybe longer, before the Emperor revisited the idea of invading the Republic. In that time, much could happen. Revan had spoken of another champion who would rise; Scourge had seen that champion in his final vision. Blessed with eternal life, Scourge would serve faithfully at the Emperor's side, biding his time as he waited for that champion to emerge from the mists of time.

While serving, he would study the Emperor. He would learn everything about him. He would come to understand his strengths and weaknesses so that when the time came, he could help Revan's prophesied champion destroy the Emperor once and for all.

"Feel your mortality as it is stripped away."

Scourge screamed as invisible claws tore at his insides, seemingly shredding his vital organs.

The heat in his chest had spread to the rest of his body; it felt as if his blood were made of fire. The agony became unbearable, and he shrieked and collapsed to the floor.

"The ritual cannot be undone," the Emperor said as Scourge writhed and wept at his feet.

Through his torment, Scourge realized with dawning

horror what the Emperor was saying. The ritual was over, but the searing heat and the rending of his insides continued unabated.

Focusing his will, he managed to still the convulsions racking his body. He forced himself to his knees, though every movement seemed to amplify the pain. Trembling, he rose to his feet and addressed the Emperor.

"How long will this anguish last?" he asked, his jaw clenched.

"As time passes you will learn to accept and endure your suffering," the Emperor answered. "Your mind and body will find ways to deal with the pain. After many months you will become accustomed enough to it to function in your role as the Emperor's Wrath. Eventually you will simply become numb, unable to feel anything at all."

"Why?" Scourge asked, his voice something between a sob and a moan.

"Everything has a cost," the Emperor explained. "This is the price of immortality."

REVAN'S CELL WAS AS MUCH LABORATORY AS PRISON. Trapped in a suspended cage of shimmering power, he hovered somewhere between life and death.

His paralyzed body was in some kind of stasis, preserved and protected so that even time itself could not touch him. But his consciousness was fully aware.

Meetra could sense his suffering. When she had died, she had not become one with the Force. Loyal to the end, her spirit had remained with Revan, an invisible presence hovering just outside his cell.

She couldn't speak with him; whatever arcane Sith sorcery the Emperor had used to bind Revan in his cell made that impossible. She doubted Revan was even aware she was there. Yet even though she couldn't communicate with him, she was able to offer aid and support, her power trickling through the energy barrier that surrounded him, a lifeline he could cling to in the dark ocean of his imprisonment.

As the Emperor fed off him, Meetra was allowing Revan to feed off her. Her sustenance strengthened his resolve whenever he grew weak, refreshing and restoring him so he could continue his never-ending mental war.

Because of her, Revan was able to do more than just fight to keep the Emperor at bay.

REVAN COULD FEEL THE EMPEROR FEEDING ON HIM, drawing on his power to sate his endless hunger. Though the two were physically separated by a dozen parsecs, there was still an unbreakable mental link, fashioned by the Emperor and sustained by the infernal machines powering the cell.

Yet the Emperor wanted more than to leach off his fallen adversary's power to sustain his own twisted existence. Revan could feel the enemy inside his head. He could sense the unmistakable darkness of the Emperor sifting through his thoughts and memories, seeking, probing, digging for answers.

He wanted information on the Republic and the Jedi. How strong were they? Where were they vulnerable? How much did they know about the Sith and the Emperor himself? He wanted information on Revan. What had happened during his own invasion of the Republic? Why had it failed? How had he freed himself from the Emperor's control?

The answers were all there, but Revan would not surrender them easily. Though he was physically helpless, mentally he was strong enough to wage war against the Emperor, guarding and protecting his secrets for however long it might take.

And Revan knew something the Emperor did not. The

connection between them went both ways. There were brief moments—times when the Emperor was intently focused on something else—when he could subvert their relationship by planting seeds in the Emperor's thoughts.

He had to be careful, lest his enemy discover what he was doing. But he was able to push and nudge the Emperor's own thoughts and beliefs, subtly manipulating them in ways that could have profound effects. Revan played on the Emperor's caution and patience, constantly pushing them to the forefront of his enemy's mind. He augmented his irrational fear of death. At every opportunity he reinforced the idea that invading the Republic was reckless and dangerous.

It was impossible to know what would have happened if Scourge had not betrayed them in the throne room. They might have lost anyway, but they also might have defeated the Emperor, forever freeing the galaxy from the threat of annihilation at the hands of a madman. There was no way to be sure, and no point in dwelling on the past.

Revan was certain of one thing, though: for however many centuries his body survived in stasis, he would fight to stop the Emperor from invading the Republic.

He clung to this certainty; it gave him hope. He knew there was no chance of escape from his prison. He knew it was inevitable that one day the Emperor would win their endless battle of wills.

But if he managed to delay him for fifty years, Bastila might never have to experience the horrors of another galactic war. A hundred and his son could live his whole life in an era of peace, never knowing the fear of facing utter annihilation.

Whenever his thoughts turned to his wife and son, he tried to reach out to them through the Force, offering comfort and strength from the other side of the galaxy.

He didn't know if they ever felt him, but he liked to imagine that they did.

Even if they couldn't, just thinking of them gave him strength. Revan was fighting for the future of his wife and child, and it was a fight he did not intend to lose.

EPILOGUE

"WHY IS YOUR HAIR ALL GRAY?" Reesa, the youngest of Bastila's grandchildren, asked.

"Because I'm an old, old woman," Bastila replied.

"Is that why you're all wrinkly, too?" her brother Bress asked.

"Come on, you two," their mother said, scooping them up in her arms. "I think it's time for bed."

She hustled the kids out of the living room, leaving Bastila alone with her son.

"I'm glad you came today," Bastila said. "It means a lot to me."

Vaner reached out to wrap his hand around his mother's fingers and gave her a reassuring squeeze. "I know this is a tough time for you," he said. "You always get down when your anniversary comes around. Have you been thinking about him?"

"I think about him a lot," she answered.

"So do I," her son admitted. "I wonder what he'd say to me if we ever meet."

"He'd tell you he was proud of you," Bastila assured him.

"You don't think he'd be disappointed that I never joined the Jedi Order?"

Bastila shook her head. "You've done too much in your life to have those kinds of regrets," she told him. "The Jedi are guardians and protectors of the galaxy, but these past fifty years we've needed so much more. The Republic had to rebuild. We needed leaders to unite us, to help us work together. You saw that need, and you filled it."

Her son laughed. "You sound like my campaign manager. Vote Vaner Shan for Supreme Chancellor!"

Bastila shook her head. "You joke, but if you wanted that post you could have it."

"I'll get back to you on that."

"Besides," she added after a moment's thought, "if you were a Jedi you never could have married Emess."

"When we first met, you said she was too young for me," he reminded her.

"I'm older and wiser now," she said.

"Aren't we all?"

They were quiet for a few more minutes before Vaner asked another question. "Do you think he's still alive?"

"I don't know," Bastila admitted. "If he is, why didn't he come back? On the other hand, there are times when I think I can still sense his presence, like he's reaching out to me from somewhere far away."

Vaner smiled, but didn't say anything.

"You think your old mother's going senile, don't you?"

"Sometimes the Force is a little hard to understand."

"You'd better get used to it," she told him. "It's in your blood. I can already sense it in those kids of yours."

"I guess it skips a generation," Vaner said with a soft laugh.

After a few more minutes of silence he spoke again; it was a question Bastila had expected to hear for many years.

"Do you ever wish he had stayed with you instead?"

"I miss your father every day of my life," she said, "but I never once thought that."

"Why not?"

"Revan knew there was something out there—something that threatened the Republic. Maybe something that threatened the entire galaxy. He went to stop it, and I know he succeeded."

"How can you know that?"

"Because you and I are here talking about this," she said. "We haven't been wiped out by war, or turned into refugees. The galaxy hasn't come to some kind of horrific end. Whatever Revan did, he made it possible for you and me to live our lives without fear and hardship. And for that, I will always be grateful."

She reached out and placed a wrinkled hand on each of her son's cheeks, pulling him in close and kissing him softly on the head.

"I better go check on Emess and the kids," he said, standing up.

"Of course," she said, waving her hand. "Go, go. I'll just stay here on the couch and have a little nap."

Her son headed off to the guest room in the back, and Bastila closed her eyes, quickly drifting into sleep. As always, she dreamed of Revan.

Read on for an excerpt from
Star Wars: The Old Republic: Annihilation
by Drew Karpyshyn
Published by Del Rey Books

THERON SHAN walked quickly through the packed streets of Nar Shaddaa's Promenade. His unassuming features—pale skin, brown hair, brown eyes, average build—allowed him to blend easily into the crowd. The cybernetic implants visible around his left eye and right ear were his most distinguishing features, but he wasn't the only one sporting them on Nar Shaddaa, and they typically didn't draw unwanted attention.

The Hutt-controlled moon was a landscape of unfettered urban sprawl, marked by towering skyscrapers crammed too close together and gaudy, glowing billboards that dominated the horizon as far as the eye could see in every direction. Sometimes called Little Coruscant, it was hard to accept Nar Shaddaa as a true homage to the Republic capital world; in Theron's eyes it was more akin to a grotesque parody.

Coruscant had been designed with an eye to aesthetics: There was a pleasing flow to the cityscape and a consistent and complementary style to the architecture. The city was carefully divided into various districts, making it easy to navigate. The pedestrian walks were crowded but clean; the endless stream of air speeders overhead stayed within the designated traffic lanes. On Coruscant, there was an unmistakable sense of order and purpose. At times, Theron found it positively stifling.

Here on the Smuggler's Moon, however, it was a glorious free-for-all. Rundown residential buildings were scattered haphazardly among seedy-looking commercial structures; factories abutted restaurants and clubs, with no regard for the toxic clouds of filth spilling out over the patrons. With no traffic rules in force, air speeders and swoop bikes darted and dove in seemingly random directions, sometimes flying so low the pedestrians would duck and cover their heads.

As Theron turned a corner, he realized someone was following him. He hadn't actually seen anyone on his tail, but he could sense it. He could feel eyes watching him, scoping him out, measuring him as a target.

Master Ngani Zho, the man who'd raised him, would probably have claimed Theron's awareness came through the Force. But despite coming from a long line of famous Jedi, Theron wasn't one of the Order. In fact, he had no special connection to the Force at all.

What he did have was a decade's worth of experience working for Republic Strategic Information Services. He'd been trained to notice minute details; to be hyperaware of his surroundings at all times. And even though his conscious mind was distracted by the details of his coming mission, his subconscious had instinctively picked up on something that had set the warning bells off in his head. He knew better than to ignore them.

Careful not to break stride, turn his head, or do anything else that might tip off whoever was following him, Theron used his peripheral vision to scan the area around him, looking for his tail.

At street level, everything was a chaotic mishmash of bright, flashing colors: a constant assault from an army of pink, purple, green, and blue signs and billboards—perfect camouflage for whoever might be following him. Fortunately the intensity of the inescapable neon was muted by the layer of grime that clung to every surface; a reminder of the unchecked pollution in the atmosphere that would eventually transform Nar Shaddaa into an uninhabitable wasteland.

It wasn't easy to pick someone who looked suspicious out from the crowd. The population of the Smuggler's Moon was as varied, unpredictable, and seedy as the surroundings. In the seventeen years since the signing of the Treaty of Coruscant, the Hutts had remained staunchly neutral in the ongoing cold war between the Republic and the Sith Empire, making Nar Shaddaa a common gathering place for criminal elements from all corners of the galaxy: Black Sun slavers, Rodian pickpockets, Twi'lek hustlers, Chevin stim dealers. Any and all illicit activities were tolerated on Nar Shaddaa, provided the Hutts got their cut.

Still, there were those too greedy or stupid to cut the Hutts in on their action. When that happened there were consequences. Things got messy.

Is that what this is about? Theron wondered. *Is Morbo onto me? Did he send someone to take me out?*

He passed by the statue of Karragga the Unyielding that dominated the Promenade. Though he'd been to Nar Shaddaa many times, he couldn't help but pause for a second and shake his head in disbelief: a thirty-meter-tall Hutt made of solid gold was too impossibly ostentatious to ignore. Shaking his head also gave him a chance to quickly glance from side to side, expanding his field of vision just enough to catch a glimpse of someone darting into a doorway off to his left. He didn't get a good look at whoever it was, but the sudden movement was unnatural enough to stand out.

Someone working alone. Could be a mugger. Or a trained assassin.

Theron was on a tight schedule; it was time to force the action. He turned down a narrow side street, leaving the worst of the crowds—and the relative safety they provided—behind. Off the main thoroughfare there were fewer neon lights and more shadowy corners. If his tail was going to try something, this was the perfect place to make a move.

A slight buzzing of the cybernetic implant in his right ear alerted him to an incoming transmission. There was only one person who knew his private frequency, and Theron knew he had to take the call.

"Accept incoming," he whispered. Louder, he said, "Director."

"Theron." The head of Strategic Information Services, as he so often did, sounded annoyed. "Where are you?"

"I'm on vacation," Theron replied. "I put in for some R and R. Remember?"

Theron realized the director's call could work to his advantage. Whoever was following him would think he was distracted, vulnerable. All he had to do was pretend to be oblivious while listening for his stalker to creep up close, then suddenly turn the tables.

"Vacation, huh?" the director grumbled in his ear, as Theron continued farther into the deserted alley. "That's funny, because I have a report that one of our field agents has been spotted snooping around on Nar Shaddaa."

"Are you keeping tabs on me?"

"What are you doing on Nar Shaddaa?" the director demanded, not bothering to answer Theron's question.

"Maybe I just like the climate."

"Smog clouds and acid rain? Not likely. You're up to something."

I'm about to be ambushed in a dark alley, then I'm going to go save someone's life, Theron thought.

Out loud, he said, "I'm taking care of some personal business."

"What's Teff'ith mixed up in now?" the director asked with a sigh.

Even though he couldn't see the man on the other end

of the call, Theron could picture his boss rubbing his temples in exasperation.

"Teff'ith's not a bad kid," Theron insisted. "She just tends to fall in with the wrong crowd."

"Guess that explains how she ended up working with you," the director grumbled.

Theron had stopped walking and was standing with one hand up to the cyber-link in his ear, pointedly staring straight ahead.

Might as well be wearing a sign that says, "Come and get me!" Time to make your move.

"Ngani Zho saw something special in her," Theron said to the director.

"I know Master Zho raised you, but by the time he met Teff'ith he was . . . troubled."

You almost said crazy, didn't you?

"She has key underworld contacts," he explained, "and she knows how to handle herself in a tough spot. We might need a favor from her someday. I'm just looking out for a potential asset."

"What makes you think she'd ever help us? Didn't Teff'ith say she'd kill you if she ever saw you again?"

"Then I'll make sure she doesn't see me."

"I hate to do this, Theron," the director said. "But I'm ordering you to pull out of Nar Shaddaa. It's for your own good."

Theron felt the unmistakable shape of a vibroblade's tip pressing up against his back, and a deep voice growled, "Move and you're dead!" in his other ear.

"You worry too much," Theron told the director, keeping his voice light. "Everything's under control." In a whisper he added, "Disconnect," and the comlink in his ear shut down.

"Get your hands up!" his unseen assailant snarled.

Theron slowly raised his arms in the air, silently cursing himself for letting his assailant get so close.

Never even heard him coming. Was I really that sloppy, or is he that good?

"Lose the piece."

The words were in Basic, but the voice was definitely not human—too deep, too rumbling. The speaker was large, but without turning around there was no way for Theron to pin down what kind of alien he was dealing with.

The comlink in his ear buzzed again, but this time Theron ignored the director's call. He clicked his teeth together twice, temporarily shutting the cybernetics off so he could focus on getting out of the alley alive.

"I said lose the piece!"

The order was accentuated by an increase in the pressure of the blade against Theron's back. Reaching down slowly, he slid his blaster pistol from the holster on his hip and let it drop to the ground. He briefly considered making a move; there were a dozen ways he could try to surprise and disarm his opponent. But without knowing exactly who or what he was facing it was too risky.

Patience. Analyze the situation. Wait for your chance.

"Those are some fancy wrist guards you got. Maybe have a poison dart or a pinpoint blaster built in, right? Lose 'em."

Any hope Theron had of catching his assailant by surprise with the weapons in his customized bracers vanished as he unclipped the metal bands from his forearms and let them fall at his feet.

The fact that his assailant had marked the bracers as potential weapons also meant this wasn't some run-of-the-mill mugger. An Imperial operative would probably recognize the bracers, but it didn't make sense for any of them to be targeting Theron on a Hutt-controlled world . . . especially now that Imperial Intelligence had been officially disbanded. That left only one other likely—and unsettling—option: a bounty hunter or assassin working for Morbo the Hutt.

"Now turn around, real slow."

The pressure of the blade eased as the ambusher took a step back. Theron turned to see a violet-skinned Houk towering over him, his heavyset torso and thick, muscular limbs seeming to fill the entire width of the narrow alley. His froglike features were set in a grim scowl, his eyes fixed intently on his victim.

He was pretty sure the Houk didn't have any backup—he would have noticed if there was more than one person following him. But even if he was acting alone, Theron was no match for the massive brute's raw muscle. Under normal conditions he could make up what he lacked in strength with speed, but in the tight confines of the narrow alley avoiding the deadly vibroblade might be difficult . . . especially if the Houk was trained in close-quarters fighting. Given his choice of weapon, Theron had to assume he was facing a capable and deadly opponent.

"What's your interest in Morbo?" the Houk demanded.

"I have no idea what you're talking about," Theron said, his earlier hypothesis about his ambusher working for the Hutt confirmed.

"I've seen you scoping out Morbo's place for the past three days," the Houk snarled. "Lie to me again, and I won't ask nicely next time," he added, waving the vibroblade back and forth for emphasis.

The implied threat didn't bother Theron nearly as much as the realization that he'd been made during his recon trips to Morbo's club.

"Never saw you at Morbo's," Theron admitted. "Didn't think anybody saw me, either."

"I've been trained to know what to look for," the Houk answered.

Trained? Theron wondered. *By who? Imperial intelligence?*

As if echoing his own thoughts, the Houk asked, "Who are you working for?"

Theron wasn't about to reveal his connection to SIS, and he suspected another evasive answer would be met with violence.

"Take the shot!" Theron shouted, as if calling out to an unseen accomplice.

The Houk's head turned just a fraction as he reacted to Theron's bluff, his survival instincts forcing him to sneak a quick look for a hidden sniper in the alley.

Seizing on the distraction, Theron lashed out with a quick kick to the Houk's midsection. The impact caused no real damage, but it momentarily knocked the big alien off balance, giving Theron more room to operate.

He was already backpedaling in anticipation of the counterattack; even so he barely avoided the expected lunge of his opponent. As he feared, the Houk wasn't just some clumsy brawler—he was quicker than he seemed.

As the Houk moved in, Theron tried to disarm him with a wrist lock, reaching out for the hand that held the blade. The Houk countered by twisting his body and throwing his opposite shoulder into Theron, sending him stumbling back.

Unable to set his feet, Theron was forced on the defensive. The alley was too narrow to dodge from side to side, so his only option was full-scale retreat, backpedalling rapidly as the Houk charged forward, the blade slicing and stabbing the empty air mere centimeters from Theron's chest.

With all his opponent's momentum moving forward in his pursuit, Theron suddenly stopped short and dropped to the ground, rolling into the thick legs of his advancing foe. The move caught the Houk by surprise; he tripped over Theron and tumbled to the ground, the fall knocking the vibroblade from his grasp.

One of the Houk's knobby knees caught Theron in the chin as he fell over him, splitting his lip and making him see stars. Woozy, Theron ignored the pain and leaped to his feet, and with his first step he staggered sideways into the side of the alley before crashing back down to the ground.

A massive hand closed around his ankle as the still-prone Houk tried to drag Theron close enough to finish him off. Theron lashed out with his free leg, smashing his foot twice into the Houk's corpulent face. The vise-like grip slipped just enough for Theron to free himself with a twisting roll, and he scrambled on his hands and knees toward where his blaster and bracers lay on the ground.

The Houk struggled back to his feet, but by the time he was upright Theron had seized one of the bracers, slapped it onto his right forearm, and taken aim.

"Toxicity seven," he muttered, squeezing his hand into a tight fist.

A small dart launched from a thin barrel built into the bracer and buried itself in the Houk's chest. The mighty alien went rigid as a powerful electrical charge surged through him, convulsed for several seconds, and then dropped to the ground, twitching slightly from the after-effects.

Theron considered what to do with the immobilized but still conscious Houk as he quickly gathered his gear. It wouldn't take long for the effects of the electrical blast to wear off, but for the next few minutes the Houk was basically helpless. Theron wasn't about to execute a helpless opponent . . . but he wasn't above interrogating him. "Toxicity two," he whispered, firing another dart into the Houk's thigh from point-blank range.

He waited thirty seconds for the mind-clouding drug to take effect before he started asking questions.

"How did you spot me?" he asked. "You said you were trained. By who?"

The Houk shook his head groggily, struggling to resist the effects of the chemicals coursing through his system. In a few minutes it would render him unconscious. Theron needed to get answers before that happened.

"Hey!" Theron snapped, slapping the Houk's meaty cheek. "Who trained you?"

"Republic SIS," the Houk mumbled.

"Republic SIS?" Theron repeated, his mind struggling to accept what he'd just heard.

"Covert surveillance," the groggy Houk confirmed, his tongue loosened by Theron's truth serum. "Watching Morbo. Part of Operation Transom."

SIS has eyes on Morbo. No wonder the director knew I was here.

Theron had never heard of Transom, but that wasn't unusual. SIS had ongoing missions all across the galaxy, and only the director and the agents involved would be aware of the details.

Just my luck to stumble into an active SIS mission.

"What are you going to do with me?" the Houk asked, slurring his words and struggling to keep his eyes open as sleep slowly dragged him down.

"Relax, big guy," Theron said. "We're on the same side."

The director had ordered Theron off of Nar Shaddaa; obviously he was worried about him interfering with Transom, whatever it might be. But Teff'ith's life was at stake, and Theron wasn't about to abandon her . . . even if it meant defying a direct order.

The Houk began to snore loudly, ending any hope Theron had of asking him for more details about Operation Transom.

It has to be in the early stages, Theron reasoned. *They're still just observing the target. If I get in and out quickly, it shouldn't have any significant impact on the mission.*

He knew the director would never buy that argument as justification for what he was about to do. But it was always easier to ask forgiveness than permission.

Grabbing hold of the Houk's arms, he dragged the sleeping alien into a corner of the alley, hiding him behind several trash bins. He'd wake up in a couple hours with a pounding headache but otherwise unharmed. Plenty of time for Theron to meet with Morbo and bargain for Teff'ith's life.

He set off down the alley at a brisk trot, trying not to think about the fact that he was putting his entire career in jeopardy.